Discovery

Raymond M. Crome

PublishAmerica
Baltimore

© 2004 by Raymond M. Crome.
All rights reserved. No part of this book may be reproduced, stored in a retrieval system or transmitted in any form or by any means without the prior written permission of the publishers, except by a reviewer who may quote brief passages in a review to be printed in a newspaper, magazine or journal.

First printing

ISBN: 1-4137-2698-4
PUBLISHED BY PUBLISHAMERICA, LLLP
www.publishamerica.com
Baltimore

Printed in the United States of America

To Ellen Sangster and Beverley Crome

To Peter with
Best Wishes.
Ray Crome

The adventures of the fictional Peter Wright at sea follow circumstances and events as recorded in A Voyage of Discovery to the North Pacific Ocean and Round the World 1791-1795 Captain George Vancouver.

Discovery:
To invent, manifest, declare, disclose, reveal, divulge, uncover. To unmask oneself, or find out what one is made of. To discover ourselves or have others discover us. This is a story of discovery in all its various forms. It is set in the eighteenth century.

Prologue
November 1849

    The goings-on, both on board and about the British full-rigged East-Indiaman, Jane Wright were significant. The normal day-to-day labour of sailing a merchant trading vessel gave way to the circumstance of a shore nearby and an end to an arduous voyage.
    The clatter of the protesting sails, the call of orders to men high in the rigging, the rhythmic heaving on lines and the general organized activity carried on the wind over the agitated, misty waters of the bay. The canvas cracked and thundered in noisy protest at various and sudden changes of course towards the barely visible, heavily forested shore. The vessel displayed the ravages of a hard voyage round the Horn and a heavy beat up the Pacific coast of the Americas.
    It heeled over as the sails responded to the onslaught of the brisk breeze, the blue and white house flag, tattered and forlorn, flew with little regard for pride from the masthead. It appeared the vessel was bent on destruction as it picked up a freshening gust and propelled forward toward the white speckled cliff, home to a myriad of sea birds. Desperately they swooped and dived, in a vain attempt to dissuade the intruder from their domain. The ship straightened as the sails filled to perfection. Miraculously an opening appeared, narrow, churning and anxious, dark with the tide racing in to the east. In perfect safety, the salt-caked merchant vessel propelled by the breeze from the west and urged on by the incoming tidal flow, entered into an inner harbour to drop anchor amid native canoes and log booms, lost against forested shores guarded by the sentinel snowy mountains towering over the northern shore.
    A tall, heavy set, white-haired man stood at the prow, the collar of his great coat tight about his neck to ward off the cold of the west wind, a foretaste of winter to come. Despite his obvious age, he still displayed a straight back

and a latent energy. Mr. Peter Wright Esq. gazed about him. He looked towards the newly snow-clad mountains and saw twin, bare, icy, granite peaks standing guard, over lush forested slopes and the beautifully protected harbour, named so long ago by George Vancouver after Lord of the Admiralty, Sir Harry Burrard-Neale. Apart from a small rustic shed and rafts of logs floating near the northern shore, little sign of any change was obvious. In the distance to the south across the bay barely visible amid the heavily forested shore, the outline of a few buildings was discernable. Peter Wright thought to himself apart from that it has not changed at all.

"It's a great country, sir." The young man stood beside the elder, who appeared startled at the intrusion.

"Yes it is, Captain. Yes it is."

"Come along there men. Watch your work. Mr. Potts get the bow-hatches opened and rig a boom as soon as the anchor is set. Winter is almost on us, I do not want to be on this coast in November. We must get those logs aboard and get out of here as soon as we can."

"I have been here before."

"Your pardon, sir, you spoke." The younger man became attentive to the elder.

"I've been here before. 1791. In all that time it has barely changed."

The old man was pleased. It could be considered of little import in the great scheme of things, that he was again in the Pacific North West, or that he had used this great land for his own employment and financial benefit. He had made no mark on this sublime work of nature to distinguish his passing. He was convinced his impact could not alter this vast country, any more than the resident children of nature had since time immemorial. For many years, he had traded on this coast. His vessels took pelts and logs to China, which he bartered for silk, tea and spices; these items would then be sold on the London market. He could not see any trace or mark from where the logs, floating serenely on the gentle waters, had been taken. He saw the native canoes coming from the river mouth at the entrance to this safe haven as they had in 1791, but now their purpose was different. Even at this distance, he could see furry pelts piled in bundles between the paddlers. Ever had it been since he had commenced his life as a merchant trader. He had learned his lessons well and his mind went back to those early days, to the Captain of *Discovery* and his years before the mast. He thought of the trials and tribulations, which had molded his character. He remembered the names and still he saw the faces, Vancouver, Menzies, Puget, Baker, Johnstone and

Thomas Pitt, officers who had influenced his life in so many ways. He thought of his shipmates in the fo'c'sil and the comradeship born in adversity and danger. He was pleased, he had traded honestly and had not disturbed the way of the land and its people to any notable extent and had treated all with dignity and fairness. Yes, he was pleased with his life of adventure and discovery.

1

Captain Henry West
London, 1789

"Sir, I understand your situation. The financial distress that plagues you can be held at bay for little more than a year. As your financial advisor, I have made repeated efforts to satisfy your creditors, but I fear that to a man they now refuse my overtures on your behalf."

"A year you say. What then?"

"I am afraid those same creditors will demand all that is yours. Believe me, sir, there's not enough to satisfy them."

"It is intolerable for a man of my military and social stature to be in a situation such as this, I must keep up appearances. My father purchased my commission in the guards from Captain Light. Now I am well in line to be raised to Colonel. You know I am to be promoted to that rank. I must have money. It is expensive to keep up the style I have come to be renowned for and on half pay tis well nigh impossible. I have considered selling my commission, but what then. I am a military man and it gives me the stature I need."

"Well my dear sir. I suggest you arrange a patron, some sponsor to cover your debts, or the court will decide your destiny for you. Macclefield Prison and its owner will be your lot. Lord Derby's pleasure will be your destiny. Mark my words, young sir, there is no doubt about it, debtors prison, sir. Surely not to be contemplated."

"There's no one left, I fear. All used up, perhaps you yourself could you see your way clear to assist me. There must be some one that will see me through this lean point in time."

"No Captain West, that is out of the question. It is only due to your father that I have become involved at all. In fact, he has intimated to me that if you do not mend your ways, he will seriously consider cutting you from his will. He will not see you. His words to me, I will look on Henry no more until he shows some responsibility. Perhaps you may wish to consider marriage, some lady of your own class with a suitable dowry and financial settlement from a devoted father. This may be a solution to all your problems."

"Umm? Perish the thought, completely repugnant to me. For these many years I have escaped the chains of matrimony, but then, as you say, desperation calls for desperate measures."

"Surely there's a suitable young lady of good lineage replete with a good dowry and cash as a marriage settlement, some family of means that would appreciate the prestige of pedigree and connections, a lady that you could feel some affection for."

"Perhaps I could suffer a temporary arrangement till I see better times. A year you say. I shudder at the thought of marriage, but then the alternative gives me no comfort. Perhaps I will give this prospect some consideration. I have been managing to avoid service in India, only though the good auspices of my uncle, but he will not support me much longer. He has intimated that if I do not get my finances in order India will be my lot, not something I would anticipate with joy. I cannot give up my present way of life. You have likely suggested the most pleasant alternative, even if it is against my principals. Yes, perhaps that is the answer."

Captain Henry West was an aristocrat by birth, by nature he was of a lower ilk. Even at the early age of five, he had begun to display a degree of vanity and narcissism, which seemed out of place for one so young. Perhaps it was the excessive attention of a mother, who at thirty-nine years found she could have but one child. She doted on young Henry. In an age when so many children died at birth, or barely managed to survive five years, when maturity or old age was generally considered to be thirty-seven or so years, an indulgent mother with but one infant might be forgiven for lavishing every attention on her child. Whatever Henry wanted Henry received. She loved him to distraction, she considered him brilliant and above average in all he did. She told him so until he believed he was extraordinarily special, gifted and far above those even in his own circle, the aristocratic wealthy. Therefore, it is little wonder as he advanced in years he became more and more demanding and riotous, with little regard for those around him and no regard at all for those below him.

The angel of death visited all classes randomly. The privileged received no special treatment. Fevers, typhus, dysentery, measles, and influenza all struck in frightful epidemics. Mercifully, by the mid 1700s the plague seemed to have left the shores of England. It was considered, the rats, harbingers of this dreadful scourge, which infested the whole country, had become immune to the disease. Still, in an age when many women died in childbirth and large families were accepted as normal, Lady Cornelia de Lacey-West thought of herself as fortunate. Her only beautiful, male child was alive and well. Perhaps it could be considered a sign from God, she could have no more children, but her Henry was so special in every way.

Cornelia had always been thought of as beautiful, although a little flighty. As she attained womanhood she changed from a witless, flirtatious, beautiful girl, to what could only be described as a ravishing and conniving woman. It was little wonder she was pursued by the gentry. Single gay blades in search of a suitable dowry and a family connection preyed on the daughters of the wealthy and the nouveaux riche. Older well-established men, who had lost their wives, usually in childbirth and now wished to re-establish a life of wedded bliss, elder fellows who usually came comfortably off with perhaps a title, a good name and a fortune. In addition, to be contended with were the rakes and the roué, those steeped in infamy, gamblers, drinkers, frequenters of the lower life of London of the 1700s, ever on the lookout for eligible wealthy widows or spinsters to relive of their good name and fortune. It should be remembered the 18th century was the age of invention and change. It was a period when England was rapidly moving from an agrarian society to one of business and commerce. The cities were growing and the country was being daily denuded of the farm workers who came to the cities looking for an easier life and a fortune.

Cornelia avoided marriage for many years until she eventually married Lord Cedric de Lacey. Lord Cedric was well into his sixties when the marriage took place. It was rumored Cornelia married Lord Cedric to ward off the failing fortune of her family. He was an aristocrat, well connected and related to highest in the land and a Member of the House of Lords. His title, inherited on the death of his father, William, discovered dead, in suspicious circumstances, after an orgiastic night at the notorious *Hell Fire Club*. Cedric, besides becoming heir to a seat in the Lords, inherited all the baggage of his notorious father, from an uncontrollable temper, to a mad desire for women and a penchant for unnatural devilish practices. Cornelia found herself wealthy again and mostly alone. When her husband did present himself, he was ever inebriated and inflicted himself on her with all the vigor and debauchery of a

Discovery

Pan in heat.

At the birth of Henry, Lord Cedric was beside himself with joy. He looked on the arrival of this beautiful, perfect cherub, as fitting perfectly well with the mystical rites of the *Hell Fire Club*. He saw the child as a gift from the gods, an omen, which foretold of great events. He took to calling Cornelia, Marcia the nymph and in turn, his son received the name Latinas. He insisted all call him Faunas. Lord Cedric was riddled with the *French Disease* or pox and he was in fact quite mad.

As the years past, Henry grew more handsome. By the time he entered his teen years he became increasingly self centered and selfish. His youthful years were spent under the complete domination and tutelage of his mother, who denied him nothing. Young Henry learnt the art of the tantrum as a means of attaining his own way. He was cruel and he delighted in tormenting the two spaniels his father had bought for him just weeks after his birth. Some years later when Henry was five, an unfortunate animal was found hanged in a storeroom. The servants knew instinctively it was Henry who had carried out this execution, but young Henry blamed the son of the groom who was subsequently whipped. He treated the servants abominably, delighting in rearranging and sometimes breaking items, casting the blame on a maid or a butler, his rapture in the subsequent punishment was beyond all, which was normal. Once he had entered his teenage years, no serving girl or maid, in any way attractive, was safe from his predatory advances. At the age of sixteen, Henry raped and assaulted a chambermaid. For this action, the girl's brother beat Henry. Henry shot him dead with the excuse that he had caught the fellow poaching. His father doted on him and on occasion allowed him to accompany him to dark and unnatural ceremonies at the *Hell Fire Club*. It was not until Henry's debts became of concern that a rift occurred between Lord Cedric and his son, for nothing aroused the ire of his Lordship more than the wasteful use of his money.

As the years passed, both his mother and father finally despaired of him. His debts were overwhelming, as was his lack of control where women were concerned. This of course caused little disquiet to Lord Cedric, who saw his son as a living image of himself in his relations with the fair sex. In fact, Lord de Lacy became quite jealous of Henry's conquests. In desperation, Henry's father bought him a commission in the army. £3500 bought a Captaincy in the Life Guards. It was hoped this would give some direction and purpose to Henry's life. The army in peacetime placed officers on half pay, Lord Cedric made up the balance to allow Henry to live in the style to which he was accustomed. It was, of course, not enough. The cost of nightly gambling and wenching far exceeded Henry's income and his debts mounted. The protests and threats of Lord Cedric and Cornelia had no effect at all. The years of indulgence had created a monster with no thought for anything or anyone but himself.

By 1791, Lord Cedric de Lacey no longer caroused at the *Hell Fire Club*. He was stooped and bent and walking was difficult. He was a senile old man, rife with the disease, which had rendered him almost blind, taken all of his teeth and part of his nose. His mind was almost gone, but he still maintained a firm grasp on money matters. Despite desperate pleas from Cornelia, he cut his son off from all financial support. He also saw to it that other members of the family would not come to Henry's financial aid.

From time to time Henry would see his mother, she would fawn on him, quietly give him money and marvel at how stalwart and handsome he was. In her eyes, he was an archangel. She would beam and glow when he told her of some occurrence, a duel, a fight, a gambling win or a conquest of the heart. She loved to hear his wild plans, which he believed would see him financially solvent again.

Lady Cornelia de Lacey died suddenly. She complained of a cold, a headache and a sore throat. For two days, she was racked with fever and agonizing bouts of coughing. She sucked Dr. Sydenham's Patent Lozenges to no avail. A fever gripped her and she was bled, but on the third day, Cornelia lapsed into a coma. She passed from this life the following morning. Dr. Singer, Family Physician, with great sagacity, informed all she had died of the Kings Evil, scrofula. Lord Cedric was beside himself with grief. He locked himself away and for some strange reason, which seemed quite logical to his demented state of mind, blamed Henry for her death. Lord Cedric despite his disease and lack of mobility, summoned his lawyer, who carried out his wishes to exclude Henry completely from any mention in his will. He pronounced to all, he would never look on his son again.

Now Henry had come to the end of his tether. He had used his friends, there were none left who would risk their wealth with him. He was desperate for cash and this desperation required desperate measures. If it must be marriage, then marriage it would be. He would think of his family, perhaps some cousin would fill the bill. Some country lass, preferably distantly related. One who boasted wealthy parents and little intelligence? A wife he could deposit with her parents while he carried on his usual way of life in London and the flesh pots at which he had become accepted as a man of substance.

2
Peter Wright and Sir Neville Brown KC. Norfolk, 1796

Peter Wright gazed from the coach window and excitement gripped him. At every mile nearer his home, he began to look for and recognize landmarks, a tree here, a field there and a fence still broken as it had been before he had left his birthplace. All the way from London, he had imagined and looked forward to the joyous welcome that awaited him, his mother and sister swooning and crying with joy. He could almost feel his father's embrace. He longed to receive the adulation of Sutton and Clement his setters, canine companions from earliest childhood. His feeling of anticipation grew as the coach swept down the dusty, narrow way between hedges, where pheasants fluttered away and scurried for the shelter of thick brambles. There was the old mill oak, its gnarled branches as they had always been, reaching claw-like and bare to the sky. Around a sweeping bend was the old church of Saint Mary the Virgin, still the same in its checkered Norfolk style of black and white flint and there again the old tall bell tower. Amid the trees, the moss-covered headstones of those departed of the Burnham Towns. He saw the familiar buildings and heard the sound of the trumpet as the coach driver and his assistant alerted their destination of their arrival; it was as though time had ceased its relentless onslaught. He was here at last, home. Round the common and across the market place, the coach proceeded towards an imposing building. With a tortured protest and squeal of brakes; a huffing, a snorting, a jingling of harness amid calls of welcome, a noisy barking of dogs racing beside and nipping the hooves of the sweating horses, the London coach finally drew to a welcome and exhausted halt before the Pitt Inn.

Peter had never before entered the Pitt Inn. For 140 years, it had stood here. At first it was the manor house of Burnham; now it was the last stop before the run down to the coast and the seaside town of Wells. Peter knew a little of the history of this historic place. His father often told him of the heroic sailor Captain Horatio Nelson, who would attend the inn each Saturday to receive his dispatches from London as he languished on half pay during the silly season of peacetime. He knew of its connection to the Pitt family and their vast holdings and political power. He knew the tales of the Burnham Market housewife murderers and the Assizes held at the Inn, where these villains were sentenced to death at Norwich Prison. He also knew of the wild times and drinking bouts, but he had never entered this establishment. His predilection towards the church had steered him in a direction away from the usual pursuits of his fellow young friends; his position as the only son of a respected and established family precluded much association with those lower on the social scale.

Peter stood and looked about him. It was as he had left it. Nothing had changed. All the houses were there, the market, the long green, which divided the town, the island of homes and businesses at the east end. Although he could not see it, he knew the old Sutton Church would be where he had left it. It was a joy to return and find all the same. He was well aware he had changed, but all else would be as it always had been.

Peter entered the inn. He took a seat in a vacant box near the door, well within the sphere of warmth from the fire burning brightly to his left.

"A pint of ale, inn keeper and some food, if you please." For the first time in his life Peter Wright ordered food and drink in a tavern. He considered this moment. He was no longer the innocent lad of years past. "Whatever you have, inn keeper."

"Ah, you be off the London coach. Not much to eat this time o day. I'll get yer something. Yer kin av some game-stew and there's bloaters left over. I'll get yer something."

"Tell me my man, do you know of Mr. Brown Esquire, the lawyer, is he at his residence?"

"No. Yer will not find him there no more. E does not live in these parts now. E's come up in the world. E be living in Lynn. E be Sir Neville Brown now."

Peter pondered inwardly, the town has not changed, but there you are, people change.

"E be here today. E's the magistrate for these parts, newly made. Yer'll find him at Sutton Church, yer will. E be staying here at the Inn tonight."

The innkeeper brought ale and food, Peter still could not believe he was home and eating good Norfolk fare. He ate appreciatively and heartily. The long journey from London had left him dirty, dusty and tired. His clothes were ill fitting and threadbare, with a cut obviously that of a seaman. His features were deep and sun-browned, his strong hands tattooed, the deep scar over his left eye, which reached down onto his upper cheek, singled him out as a man not to be trifled with. Peter attracted the stares of the various local people who began to fill the room. He thought he recognized one or two of these as they walked in the door.

The sun had well set and twilight had begun to cast deepening, long shadows across the countryside. The windy warmth of day slowly gave way to the cool of evening, with the promise of winter not far distant.

The door opened to reveal a figure, well muffled against the cool winds, which had increased in velocity as night fell. The man virtually swept into the warmth of the inn together with a dozen dancing leaves and chilly breezes, which caressed the legs of the patrons and swirled the dust on the floor.

Peter recognized the rotund, black clad figure the moment he removed the three-cornered hat from his head and unwound a woolen scarf from his lower face. Peter felt at last he was home—here was Uncle Neville. He rose, standing silently as the new arrival walked towards him.

"Uncle Neville. Don't you recognize me?"

Neville Brown stopped and stared at the young man standing before him. Perplexed, he considered the tall, heavy-set figure barring his way.

"Why do you call me uncle? Who are you, sir?"

"Your voice is familiar, but I don't know you sir."

Peter grasped the old man by the shoulders.

"Look at me, sir. It is I, Peter. Peter Wright. I have returned."

Neville Brown stared closely at the face before him. He paled, then grasped his chest and staggered back onto a seat, fortunately positioned right behind him. For a moment he gasped, then struggled for sufficient breath to mouth the words, "You're dead. You're dead." The old man clutched at his breast and gulped for air.

"No, dear Uncle Neville, I am alive and I have returned to my friends and family." Peter knelt beside the shocked old man. Various locals, seeing the distress of Neville Brown, crowded about to render him assistance, assuming Peter a vagabond who had perhaps assaulted the old man.

"I recognize you, Tom Parr, and you, Billy Sykes. I am Peter, Peter Wright, I have been at sea through no fault of my own and I have at last returned home to the place of my birth."

Peter saw the look of recognition and surprise dawn on the faces of those around him; he also sensed and noted their confusion and uncertainty. He had left a gangling stripling, pale-faced and bent on the church. Now he stood before these young men, strong, brown of feature, tattooed and clearly able to take care of himself.

"Peter, my boy, it is you. All were sure you were gone forever, where have you been? What happened to you? Oh my heart, it is pounding, I am too old for such a shock. Are you real or an apparition, some ghost of my imagination? Let me touch you." Neville Brown reached out and gingerly pinched Peter's arm. "Yes, you are solid and you are real."

Peter grasped the hand of his old friend. Colour began to flood into the cheeks of the man who had been the confidant and legal advisor to his family, the man who had helped mould his character, his thoughts and actions from his earliest years. It was Neville Brown who had arranged his studies at Jesus College in Cambridge. He remembered well the words of Neville Brown as he left for a stay in London, a stay that promised so much and eventually would have such an effect on his life. Always remember your home with affection; it is where your history resides. Now here he was, home again.

"My parents and Kate, they are well? I am anxious to get to Highfield. I would have walked but for the lateness of the hour and the fact, I heard you were here. I decided to stay until the morrow. What is it? Why are you so crestfallen and sad, is this not a joyous occasion? I have dreamt of this moment and it has helped keep me alive for these last years. In surging seas and boiling maelstroms, in situations where life hung in the balance, it was always thoughts of my home and family, which kept me sane. Tell me of them, are they well?"

Neville Brown sat silent with head bowed he looked at Peter. In the corner of his eye, a glistening tear caught the light of the lamps, which cast a warm yellow glow over the room. Finally he spoke.

"My dear boy, how can I tell you? How can I disclose such sad tidings? I must be the bearer of information, which I would give my life not to have to disclose. Your parents and sister they are no longer with us, they are dead. They lie in the church-yard of Saint Mary's not two hundred yards from where we now are."

It was Peter's turn to be distressed. He sat heavily beside Sir Neville. For a moment, he was speechless. His face paled and an incredulous look of surprise and distress clouded his countenance. Finally, he managed to utter the words, "Dead; how? Why? That cannot be possible." Peter gripped by a dreadful coldness his heart beat almost uncontrollably at these terrible words.

"My dear boy, it is true. I would give anything not to be the one to tell you this. Your dear sister was first to succumb to an illness, which ravaged the whole area. She died peacefully in her sleep. She had not been laid to rest five weeks, when your mother fell to the same malevolent malady. Others, many of our friends fell. It was as though some vile evil had singled out Norfolk for special and horrible attention."

"And my father. What of him?" Peter stammered out the question.

"A year to the day after the death of your mother he died. It was as though he could not face life without the companionship of the two people closest and dearest to him. His added burden was the fact you had vanished from the face of the earth and all presumed you dead. He just did not want to continue in sad loneliness. All three are buried in the Church of Saint Mary's, Westgate."

Peter sat silently. His eyes filled with tears, he could not speak for fear of losing the sobs of anguish, which he managed to retain deep within his person. Eventually, in a subdued trembling voice, in tones barely audible, he murmured, "I must go to them."

The hour was late when the pair returned from the cemetery across the common, once again they sat quietly together, each contemplating private thoughts. It was some time before they spoke. Neville Brown was first to break the silence.

"My boy, why don't we stay here? There is so much to discuss. I will put off my return to Kings Lynn for a few days and I will accompany you to Highfield. All is still there. I must hear your tale and your adventures. There are legalities to attend. Your father has left you well cared for, in fact you are quite the man of substance. Without the figures at hand, I would say you would never be beholding to any man as long as you live. All that remains, is for me is to obtain your signature on the proper documents and your father's estate is yours. You look sad, lad, no need for that, no need at all. You know your father never thought you had left this world. To the very last he would say, *mark my words; he will be back, he is alive somewhere and he will be back.*

Peter pondered his situation. With little money and no clothes except for those in which he stood, he broached the matter of his sustenance to Sir Neville.

"Do not worry, lad. I will advance you whatever you need. We will stay here at the inn and tomorrow we will go to Highfield. It is in fine condition. Harry Best, the retainer, and his wife live there and maintain it in fine manner.

The tenant farmers are gainfully employed and a fellow from this very town manages the farm itself. It is yours now to do with what you will."

"All right, I will repay you for whatever is spent. That is if I am as well fixed as you say."

"Oh you are well fixed, believe me."

Rooms were acquired and the two men retired for the night each with his own thoughts. Neville Brown was both sad and delighted at the return of Peter. Peter retired to his room but his sleep was fitful as the full impact of his situation came home to him. The loss of his family was almost too much to bear. He was sad and completely alone. He recognized feelings of despair as he had in his first confusing weeks at sea. It was in the early hours of the morning that he fell into a disturbed exhausted slumber.

The two men, one well into his seventieth year, the other now nearing twenty-six years and in the prime of life met the next morning in the dining room where already a fire burned brightly in the hearth.

"Peter, you have changed from the lad I once knew. Six years, it must be all of six years. Your dear mother, she never recovered from the shock of your disappearance. She could not cope after the death of your sister, Kate. She went downhill from then on and really had no strength or will to fight the malady, which finally took her."

Peter was forced to consider the fact both his parents and sister was gone. The information now conveyed to him was concise and to the point. It was believed the malady, which took his mother and sister had originated from a Dutch vessel that had entered the port of Kings Lynn. It first made its presence felt along the riverfront in the warehouses, which lined the north side of the River Great Ouse. The malady was influenza, a contagion, which cut a swath across the town, the old and the very young being the first to succumb. For a while, it seemed to cease its onslaught, perhaps the green belt between the city and its ancient defenses acted as a barrier, which for a while halted its progress. A few weeks passed with almost no sign of the illness until it strangely made its appearance outside Lynn. A few of the elderly died in Gaywood. The malady seemed to jump whole villages then to suddenly appear where least expected. Docking and Fakenham recorded a few, even the holiest religious shrine in all England, Walsingham, did not escape the terrible visitor. Eight deaths were recorded in Burnham Market. The Wright women and six others in the Burnham towns succumbed. This was strange since mother and daughter rarely left the confines of Highfield House. It was conjectured that the shock of Peter's disappearance had left his sister, Kate, always constitutionally weak, open to the illness, which she in turn passed on to her mother. Both mother and daughter had always been considered delicate and ready to fall easy prey to any virulent assault. It was twelve months to the day when Peter's father succumbed; it was said from a broken heart. The family home, always a place of joy and laughter now stood silent and still.

Peter Wright sat beside his friend, the man who was his godfather and mentor. He knew Sir Neville Brown as a true dear friend who would assist him to come to terms with his regained existence. In his heart, he searched for some reason and explanation. His anticipation and joy at the thought of presenting himself to his parents, well and alive, were now dashed. He had no family, all had been taken and he was alone.

The younger man sat quietly, his strong, gnarled hands toyed with the tankard before him. From an inner pocket, he withdrew a leather pouch. As he did so, he exposed a deep blue tattooed design, which encircled his wrist like a bracelet. With thumb and forefinger, he extracted a small quantity of tobacco, and placed the golden strands in his mouth. He sucked on the pungent deposit with closed eyes, in silent contemplation of the deep memories he was about to unlock.

Sir Neville Brown, Justice of the Peace and Magistrate, was a small rotund person dressed in black, with an almost white neck-cloth, and powdered wig. His hairpiece, a style popular some years past. His appearance immediately distinguished him as a man of law. His dark and somber dress disguised a hidden personality, which became evident only when he smiled, a personality that bespoke a warmth and brightness, not apparent in his everyday demeanor. He might well be described as one who bustled about, both in manner and speech.

Peter Wright sat before his elder companion. He listened to the words emanating from this dear man who had been so involved in his past life, Sir Neville Brown, friend of his father and mother and his godfather. He had always been Uncle Neville, now it was no longer the same.

"I feel I cannot call you uncle any longer. I am not the boy you once knew. I have changed; circumstances have forced this on me. My mind is in turmoil, I feel most out of place here. Lost, sir, completely lost." Peter's words quietly and earnestly spoken caused Neville Brown to seat himself beside his young companion. "Sir, it is impossible for me to return to my past life, I cannot behave as though the last years never happened. For six long years, I have dreamt of returning to the bosom of my family and friends, but now all that is gone. I am here, but my mind is elsewhere. I do not know how to replace myself into this society. My time in the service of His Majesty's Navy has enabled me to recognize those in a position of authority. It has given me the ability to render to them the deference that is due to those in command. While some deserve this esteem by virtue of their rank only, others deserve it from a loftier position, that of their understanding and good will towards their fellows. I must now address you as Sir Neville with all the affection previously rendered to you when I addressed you as uncle."

Neville Brown saw the distress that gripped his young companion. He was well aware of the turmoil his news had created in the breast of the young man at his side.

"My boy, what you call me is of little consequence, I am so pleased to see you again. It is as though time has stood still for me, while you have progressed to manhood, and returned a different person. I still see the joyful youth who gave us all so much to look forward too. Yes Peter, your father has left you in a fine position. Surely, your past life could not be all that distressing. I see you well, safe and most of all alive. Your dear mother never gave up hope that you would return, right to the day she died. Your father, who left us a short time past, never doubted your return. You have come back to us, hale and hearty, I see no reason for you not to be able to fill your place in the society you left and continue your studies. My dear Peter, you do me the greatest honour. I accept Sir Neville as I did uncle with affection and joy. I await your story, pray you leave out nothing, then I hope I will understand the years that have passed and changed you from a boy to a man you obviously are."

Peter Wright commenced to piece his story together in his mind. He knew that while the years for Sir Neville has remained the same, for himself all had been transformed beyond his wildest imagination.

"Things have changed, Sir Neville, I am not the same person. I have seen things that have no comparison in your society. I was forced into the King's Navy and charged to carry out acts beyond all that was natural to me. It was distressing. For the first year, I was the butt of jokes and the whipping boy of fellows who had no likeness in my previous society. It took every ounce of will power not to throw myself into the sea to escape my loneliness and my tormentors. I have prayed for death as a relief from frigid cold or from muscles that ached from the exertion of constant rowing in the most foul, wet conditions. I have seen men die, one moment alive and full of life, the next gone. I have been the instrument of death for beings not a lot different to us. I have survived and become a stronger person for it. Where this strength of character came from, I do not know. The swine that caused my predicament is still at large. The reason is still unknown. I must tell you here and now, the whole thing had to be a planned situation. Ah my friend, you must forgive me, I find that I have no patience with my circumstances since I have returned. Freedom sits hard with me. I find it difficult to accept my life and now all my hopes have been dashed away. I must come to terms with my new situation. It is like an anti climax. I have changed, but all remains the same despite almost six years passed."

Concern and agitation clouded the face of the older man as he sensed the confusion rampant within his companion. He placed his hand on Peter's shoulder, only to feel him draw away, he sensed his affectionate and intimate touch of concern was welcome, but at the same time, tempered by experiences and trials as of yet not disclosed to him.

"By heavens, what has this navy of ours done to you? I can see you are now your own man. Look at you so tall and strong. Tell me; tell me so I can understand. You speak of freedom; I am forced to believe you were in some way incarcerated. The scar on your face, what terrible accident caused it? I must hear all. The circumstances of your lost years, I promise I will not comment or say one word until you tell me of your turmoil, but I must understand."

Neville Brown gripped the arm of Peter Wright. He gazed deeply into the eyes that had experienced a life and existence he would never experience or understand.

"Sir Neville, I say it with the same affection as when I called you uncle in my youth.

I find it easier to give deference to those in a position to receive it through their just merits. You, sir, have been godfather, loyal friend and confidant for as long as I have lived. I would welcome your advice on my future. My father and mother are gone; I would consider it a privilege, Sir, if you took the place of my father. Advise me and allow me to unburden my thoughts, be my mentor and patron in my struggle to regain my place in polite society."

Neville Brown grasped the hand of his young companion.

"Nothing would give me greater satisfaction than to help fill the void in your heart. I will be a father figure to you. I can never replace the loss you have suffered, but I will be here for you. I promise it as long as I live."

The two shook hands in a moment of camaraderie. They did not speak their silence loud with emotion. It was Peter who first broke their silence.

"Now, Sir, you will hear a story, a tale I must place at the hand of fate, an act of destiny, which has changed my life forever. It remains to be seen if it will be for the betterment or detriment of my future."

Both men moved to the table set by the host of the Pitt Inn, close to the warmth of the fire.

"Let us eat. I will commence my story as we break our fast. Where to start? It is a tale of adventure, of places so beautiful, yet so remote and terrifying. A tale of danger and confrontation with nature in its most violent forms, but most of all I will tell you of the inhumanity of man to man and I will tell you of the King's Navy. It is hard for those who have not experienced it to understand the nature of the sailor. A life made up of the day-to-day work required to operate and maintain the ship, the only refuge and home for those creatures condemned to life on the vast oceans of the world. A life, of complete boredom, which creates a slave to bells, pipes and orders, at times so terrifying, yet so rewarding and gratifying. It is a life where comradeship develops between men, who on shore would not deign to recognize each other. Woe betide the man who errs or makes a mistake, a most trivial incident can be the cause of the most painful, destructive punishment, sometimes the mood of the day of some officer is enough. However, the rules of naval life are just; it is the vagaries of human nature that are at fault. There can be no assistance, no aid. It is only by the efforts of the sea-born society that it is able to survive. No room for error here, do it right or suffer the consequences. For me, at first all was strange and cruel. I knew nothing of anything, which was to be of use to me or to the rest of my companions in those early days at sea. Time and circumstance changed all that and I became a sailor."

3

Henry West Hatches a Plot

"My dear Frederick, it pains me to approach you on a matter so trivial, but I must turn to you. Our past associations give me the confidence that what I am about to propose will go no farther than our selves and this room. We have on many occasions caroused together and if I may be blunt, we have done many things that neither you nor I would want to become the common knowledge of polite society."

"I fear you are about to ask a favour. I trust you are not going to ask me for money, old boy."

"You are correct on the first assumption, though indeed I do need a monetary increase; I have a plan that will lead to our mutual financial benefit. It is a simple matter and I will come directly to the point. A person must be made to disappear.

"Ah? killed and disposed of."

"Perhaps not so drastic a measure as killed. I was contemplating a less permanent state. In my military career, I have terminated many a life without the slightest mind to it, in this matter I thought an ocean voyage of some duration would suffice."

"That should present little problem, my friend. On my vessels the captains regularly press unfortunate devils to make up a crew."

"Perfect, so you can arrange a suitable disappearance. A voyage, the longer the better should suffice."

"My vessels are presently at sea, but I will talk to an acquaintance that has been of service to me. I will see what can be done. Let us meet at the Two Dutch Skippers. Do you know it? It is the tavern, close by Saint Catherine's Stairs at Tower Hill, in two days time, in the evening. We can discuss the matter further over dinner and later perhaps, a spin at the tables."

"I will tell you the full details of my plight at our next meeting. Suffice to say my debts are sinking me. My conscience such as it is, is still manages to keep some semblance of propriety in my actions on this matter. The person is but a young boy who has done nothing to me. A duel is out of the question, so a disappearance seems the most provident way to dispose of the problem he presents. Perhaps he will live and could conceivably return some time later a better man."

"Ah Henry, what is the matter with you? I have never heard you give anyone a consideration before, in fact I know you to be quite ruthless where money is concerned. I have seen you get a fellow tipsy many a time and relive him of his purse, just three weeks ago I watched you extract £2000 from that idiot John Pinkerton and those silly women of his. Your attractive appearance has enabled you to relieve numerous daughters of their inheritance as well as their virginity. How many duels have you been involved in, why, if memory serves me, 'tis four, with two no shows. Yet, here you are letting a fellow off. You may well be sorry in later days. Get rid of him permanently, that is my advice."

"I hear you Frederick, and I will tell you all at our next meeting. I still have some inquiries and arrangements to make. I have a use for the fellow's family that will be of interest to you as well. I know there is a lot of money to be had, which will relieve me of my creditors and increase your coffers as payment for your help."

"Well my friend, I am your man. Think carefully, Henry, I believe it better to get all possible impediments out of the way, permanently. Even without knowing the details of your situation, I tell you this with only your welfare at heart."

Frederick March was a tall sinister man, who favoured dark dress; it accentuated his pale complexion and black straight hair. He spoke with a distinct accent, which could be placed anywhere from Scandinavia to Athens. He was a man who did not make friends in the true sense of the word. His association with Henry West was as close as he had ever arrived at any kind of friendship. He was a hard businessman who used people and would then discard them onto a garbage heap of disillusioned and poorer victims. His family background was a complete mystery, even to Henry West. Rumours and innuendoes surfaced at times. One had March, the son of an illegitimate child of King Charles. Another had him a pirate who had made his fortune preying on vessels as they plied between Europe and the port of Alexandria and still another group were convinced he was a French aristocrat fallen from grace. In Henry West, Frederick March found a person somewhat after his own heart. Both were gamblers, both held women as creatures to be used and then discarded. Frederick and Henry were sexual predators and frequented the secret clubs of London where depravity of every kind was carried on as a normal adjunct to everyday life.

The principal difference between the two was that Henry could not keep or manage money; he parted with it instantly, whereas Frederick was extremely wealthy. Whatever the original source of his wealth, he had maintained his income by astute investments and the profits derived from his vessels, notorious in the slave trade as hell ships of the vilest order. Despite his wealth, he was never invited to the functions where polite society came together. He carried on his business dealings and kept at arm's length by his associates. He was necessary as far as profit was concerned, but not one to be allowed near a wife or a daughter. Frederick March had connections with the highest in all realms of business. He had the ability to cause a profit to appear where it seemed only financial disaster remained. Frederick was well aware of his position and the fact he would never be accepted in social circles. He used these people to his own ends and in the process became a very wealthy though thoroughly disliked person.

"All right Henry my friend, we meet in two days. However, take my advice and finish the fellow once and for all. It is a loose end that will come back to haunt you. Mark my words."

4

How Peter Wright is Taken From His Family and Friends and is Pressed

Peter Wright commenced his story. On the fire close by, a teakettle simmered quietly, ready to refill the mugs both men held.

He told of a second year at Jesus College, Cambridge. A decision to pursue studies in divinity and canon law, greeted with applause by family and friends. He told how his dear mother and Sister Kate were delighted he would consider the church as his chosen life's work.

"I was studious, rather quick at Greek and Latin, of a gentle loving nature, so it was little wonder I set my sights in a holy and liturgical direction. At the same time my father and Edward Sawtell, our dear friend and neighbour, who would, in all probability, eventually become my father-in-law, directed me towards the more earthly occupation of civil law."

Peter was silent for a moment. He lifted his steaming mug and drank before he continued.

"You well know the understanding that had developed between the parents of Jane Sawtell and my parents. Jane and I had grown up together. As the years progressed, we became inseparable. In the minds of our parents, there was never any question that we would eventually wed and inherit adjoining joint family estates. Jane and I certainly did not think this way we always considered ourselves more as brother and sister. It was through Jane's father that arrangements were made for me to go down to London during the period of Whitsuntide. I was to stay as a guest of James Boyd, a gentleman of substance who acted as agent and business manager of the many business ventures pursued by my father and Edward Sawtell. I was to stay in his fine, new dwelling, in a part of London called Hanover Square. I know it was my father's wish to give me an insight into something more than Burnham Market,

Kings Lynn, Cambridge, the church and the county of Norfolk. This was a gentle plot, not without some attraction. At that time, I still had not fully decided on my future. I am sure that while the Church suited my mother and sister, I think my father would rather have seen me in a more business-oriented occupation.

London. What a place to change a young man's dreams and ideas. From the moment I arrived, I was feted in every way. My host, Sir James Boyd, managed the affairs of a number of country squires, who relied on commerce to pursue and increase profits above their agrarian way of life. This was the first time I received an insight into my father's business dealings and the fact that I had never been further than Cambridge and my rustic manners were a source of amusement to the fast crowd in London. In Norfolk, I was considered a fine student and bound to succeed in whatever field I finally chose, but in London, I was a country lad ready to be educated. I remember well the first days in this city, a place not like anything I had seen before. Here everything was new and exciting.

I was to stay for four or five weeks before I would make my way back to Norfolk, and recommence my studies at Cambridge. In that time, I was expected to attend my host and be introduced to the society of both business and pleasure.

The days passed swiftly in the City of London. Every weekday morning I would attend the place of business, a cavernous space, peopled by pale-faced, stooped clerks who would spend their days poring over massive tomes, recording the hundreds of daily transactions. There I would be assigned some task under the supervision of Mr. Edward Black, a nasty fellow, in charge of international accounts. Black was a dour man, he never smiled, in fact never spoke except to give me orders for the day, although when Sir James was present he became a fawning toady. I could not take to Mr. Black and he in turn seemed to have little time for me. I am sure it was only my close relationship with the Boyd family that precluded him from being a complete martinet towards me. Bookkeeping or sorting the invoices representing traders from the four corners of the earth was my lot. I became aware of countries and people of which a short time before I had not the slightest idea existed. The afternoon saw me left to my own devices. The names of the agents, the companies and the exotic goods represented, conjured up in my mind visions of tropical Eden paradises and European cities, Paris, Athens, Berlin, Madrid, places only a young and fertile imagination could imagine. In later life, I would realize by how much this imagination differed from reality. I made it my habit each afternoon to see as much of the great city of London as possible before joining Sir James, Lady Boyd and their three children for dinner. They had two daughters, Melissa, the eldest, Edith and Harold their son who was the same age as me.

I was accepted as family and accompanied the Boyd's on every outing and attended concerts and soirees, where the aristocratic and polite society of London came together. I was acknowledged and accepted as a new member of this prestigious upper class. Most of all I became inseparable from Harry Boyd, a spoilt lad, but with a good and generous heart. I was introduced to the society frequented by the young, wealthy dandies of London.

Harry's favourite amusement was boxing. With him, I attended fights and became a student of this manly art. Two fighters of the day, Jem Belcher and Joe Burke, became my heroes. Harry and I would spar with each other, and it seemed I had a degree of skill in this sport. The fights I attended were bloody affairs and quite illegal. Two men would mercilessly pound each other into insensibility to the cheers and enjoyment of a mixed group of spectators. Wagers would be made and the winner carried bloody, but shoulder high, as bets were settled and money changed hands. Harry and I would drive recklessly, four in hand, with me as passenger, a most popular pastime of young aristocrats. We would terrorize ladies and gentlemen taking the afternoon air in Regent's Park. Sir James excused the wild behaviour of his only son. He would excuse and overlook anything where Harry was concerned. When some report came from an irate neighbour, showered with mud as Harry urged his horses through the park, his father would excuse his bad manners saying, "He has to sow his wild oats."

Harry introduced me to taverns where I tasted liquor for the first time. Until now, my religious bent had ruled out even the slightest sip of the *devil's repast*; a name conjured up and drilled into us young fellows who had decided the church was to be their occupation. Harry also introduced me to the gaming tables. I tried my luck at hazard and the roulette wheel, but the most popular game of chance, E.O, Evens and Odds, where the toss of two coins could relieve a man of his purse almost instantly. I was soon cleaned out of what pocket money my father had given me. Harry constantly came to my financial rescue and I assured him of my intention to repay him at the earliest possible occasion, though he dismissed the subject as of no consequence. The allowance given me by my father, while adequate, did not allow for any great loss through my own fault at the gaming tables.

If one thing came of this London adventure it was my complete confusion as to the direction my future should take. I tried my hardest to keep my interest in the church uppermost in my mind. However, I believe it was a losing battle. The usual afternoon excursion by Harry and me on March 30, 1791 did not occur. What did happen would change my life in a manner that still seems beyond comprehension.

I was asked by Sir James to carry out an errand, which involved my father's affairs. Some documents needed to be delivered, immediately.

"My dear young man, it is so good of you to carry out this charge for us. The gentleman you will see could be of inestimable value to your career no matter what direction it should take. I have enclosed a letter of introduction, I am sure Mr. Richard Etches that is the person to whom you will hand this packet, will be most pleased to meet the son of Philip Wright. Mr. Etches has many friends at parliament; he is also well connected to those great trading companies, the East India Company and the South Seas Company, the two main sources of your father's income. Richard Etches has great influence in parliament, a good man to know, my boy."

James Boyd fumbled with a packet of papers, which he perused individually before tying them in a satchel with pink ribbon.

"So here we are, these must go to Mr. Etches tomorrow afternoon. I have told Mr. Black that you are on my business. Be careful and try not to get lost."

"Sir, it is my pleasure to be of some service to you, but I must have an address and some direction."

"Yes, yes, I have charged Mr. Black to draw a map and provide you with directions. You should have no trouble finding your way to the Temple Buildings; your destination is but a little way from there. This is the address. I must insist that you do not stray from the well-populated thoroughfares. If perchance, dusk should overtake you, this letter charges Mr. Etches to make suitable arrangements for your well-being. There are unsavoury characters at large in London, especially after dark."

Armed with an address and a map of sorts to guide me I went on my way. The map was drawn by the vapid Mr. Black, who was the only person among my new acquaintances that I did not like. With the admonition that I keep to the roads shown, the next afternoon I set out through the labyrinth of streets and alleyways of London.

From the first day of my arrival, I found myself fascinated by the brashness of this amazing city. I watched the antics of the street vendors and performers as I made my way down Drury Lane. The dark narrow side streets had always attracted me since my first days in this wonderful city. The cries and calls emanating from the darkness of these narrow lanes seemed to have a fascination for me. The thought of people living in these smelly, dank places seemed so foreign after my home in Norfolk and my newfound situation here in London. I had never ventured into these foul-smelling, narrow streets where a centre drain acted as a conduit for the contents of chamber-pots thrown from upper window. At any time, an unfortunate could be drenched with the foul effluvia of the night before. There were drunkards both male and female, pickpockets and vendors of all sorts carrying on their nefarious commerce, and ladies whose voluptuous attire both attracted and repelled me. Their calls as I passed left little doubt as to the wares they would have me negotiate.

"There's a pretty young fellow, come on luv, spend a shilling with Betty, take no notice of these whores, I'm the one for you." or "Come with me my pet. I will show you a fine time for a few pennies." For my part, I kept to the newer, grander streets.

The fires of youth, combined with the licentiousness of the city, I must confess, sent the thoughts of the church and my studies at Cambridge into the far recesses of my mind. I was enjoying the attention of my new friends and the excitement of being on the edge of these abhorrent, exciting places. I knew how I would be considered a man of the world among my peers in the country. This thought had an allure, which I found, despite my religious leanings, quite attractive.

I stopped to consult my map, as I had almost come to the end of Drury Lane, where it opened out onto the great curved thoroughfare and buildings of Aldwych, most of which were under construction.

The roadway was packed with people, carriages, mounted riders, sedan chairs, and herds of cattle driven by their Welsh drovers, noisily making for the abattoirs at Smithfield. The animals bellowed and jostled among people strolling in every direction, oblivious of the misty rain, which saturated and conferred gloominess over all. I finally made my way across the Strand and now found myself in an area I had never seen before. I made my way past King's College towards the churches of Saint Mary le Strand and Saint Clement Danes. Here I was at a loss and again consulted my directions. The chief source of my confusion was the two churches standing in the middle of the wide thoroughfare.

"You are in doubt, young sir. Can I be of some assistance?"

I was startled by the voice that interrupted my thoughts. The man who spoke stood well over my height, heavily set and dressed in a fashionable manner, a long black topcoat and white stockings, which encased thick muscular calves and a wide-brimmed hat concealing his countenance from complete observation. He carried a cane with a head heavily fashioned in silver to mirror the image of a lion. His loud, deep voice demanded respect or at least an answer.

"Thank you, sir, yes I am confused. I fear the two churches have caused me some uncertainty as to the direction of the Temple. I would be most grateful for your assistance."

The stranger took the sheet from my hands. In retrospect, I did notice that he seemed to neither read it nor look at it, before he spoke, again in the same loud, rough voice that had startled me.

"Follow me. I am going where you are going, there is the church of Saint Clement Danes and the Temple is but a short distance from there. I will walk with you."

Without waiting for an answer and without returning my map, he began to stride off towards the church, which divided the carriageway a short distance ahead. For my part, I found myself hurrying along after the stranger, perhaps a few steps behind. I was completely taken aback at the speed with which this person sped away; my inexperience and youth did not give me the necessary prestige and stature to do otherwise, so I followed meekly.

"Here is a shorter way to where you would go, we will take this passageway. Come."

I hesitated at the entrance to a narrow thoroughfare barely wide enough for a single horse and rider. It seemed deserted and dark, but without the raucous calls and wild language of Drury Lane. I recalled the admonition from Sir William on my departure not to venture from the open pathway under any circumstances. I began to protest and then my benefactor was off into the gloom. What to do but follow?

"I say, I say," I called out to the man who now disappeared into the alleyway. "I really don't think I should leave the path. Sir, my map and directions, I wish to have them returned

I followed this man into the lane, the end of which was visible some 150 yards ahead. I suppose I felt in little danger, so short was the distance before I would again join the throng ahead. How wrong I was for the stranger quickly vanished into the gloom of the alleyway. I stepped a little way into the lane, berating myself for following this man with whom I had no connection. As I was about to turn back, I heard the same loud voice from an indented doorway to my left.

"Now for you Master Wright." I heard the voice but did not see from where it came.

A sudden explosion of colour and a searing pain sent me to my knees. My hand went to the back of my head. I looked at my hand and even in the gloom of the alley; I could see my palm moist and dripping with my own blood. In a dazed state, I turned to see my erstwhile companion now beside me, the heavy lion's head cane gripped in his hand as a club. I raised my arm to ward off the second stroke descending towards me, but to no avail. The second blow sent me forward to the muddy ground. As I lay there, I heard myself moaning with pain. I rolled onto my back holding my aching head. Through a red mist, I half saw two figures standing over me. I heard words that at one moment came loud and clear then silently mouthed as I began to fall in a state of unconsciousness.

"You didn't ave to it im that hard guv. E won't be much use..." The words thundered at me, as though echoing in a tunnel. Snatches of conversation came to me, interspersed with my own sickening pain

"—whatever you like with him." Now a descending darkness came over me. Before I passed into an unconscious state, I heard words, which plague me to this very day. "Here is your money." In a painful mist as consciousness began to desert me, a final thundering statement seared it self into my mind.

"—away from this country." then. "Aye aye, you won't hear from 'im again" The last words I heard will be forever imprinted on my mind echoing and loud.

"Frederick March is generous, but heaven help you if?"

The words trailed away as colours flashed before my eyes. The scene about me spun in a dizzying circle with ever-increasing speed until in a maelstrom of aching, fearsome nausea, all sensation imploded to blackness and oblivion.

5
A Plot of Seduction and Deceit

"It has all been taken care of, Henry. The gentleman in question is on the high seas as we speak. As I told you before, my vessels are all at sea, but I have arranged an alternative."

"Excellent; excellent. Well done my friend."

"The subject of your plans has joined the navy. It came to my attention that an expedition has been planned, five years in the making. Through a rather ruthless individual, who at times has supplied my vessels with men, I have arranged for your friend to be accosted in a suitable place."

"The navy you say, I find that a little worrying, records are well kept in the military so I assume that the navy will have some attention to detail."

"Have no fear; there will be no connection between your self, myself and this incident. My man waylaid the fellow, no discussion, just a bang on the noggin, enough to put him to sleep. A press gang took him from there."

"He may escape the vessel at some port and return to England before my plans are brought to fruition."

"No chance of that, this voyage goes to the ends of the earth. A Whitbey collier has been acquired by the Navy and fitted out to explore, chart and do business with the Spanish. In any case, I am assured that in navy ships, pressed men are awarded little opportunity to get ashore at any port. After the Cape of Good Hope, there is none. The Pacific, old fellow, the Pacific Ocean is where your man is destined. Now Henry, are you going to tell me what plan you have concocted to improve your estate? I know from what little you have told me it is to do with a lady and her family, who, I am sure, will soon be parted from their fortunes and some other nubile treasure, if I know you, old boy."

"Well, we join forces to better our financial selves. Marriage does not go down well with me, Frederick, but the young lady in question is young, handsome and wealthy. The fellow, you have just sent to sea, was from my understanding, betrothed to the lady in question. He is a lad with a bent towards the church. I could hardly challenge him. It would appear out of order if I killed a fellow who has never fired a pistol in his life and a stripling to boot; this act would not endear me to his betrothed. No this is the only way; he must disappear and be presumed lost. He will be mourned as dead and I will soothe her and make myself indispensable to her. It only remains now to ingratiate my self with the father of the young woman. Here she is, depicted in this miniature. As a military man and not one schooled in the niceties of polite society, I must acquire a gentle, amorous approach that will sweep this untried virgin into my arms along with the fortune that lies ready to be taken. As you and I both know, my amorous liaisons have been of a more temporary and tempestuous nature. I will go to Norfolk tomorrow and make myself known."

"A pretty wench, indeed, and you say there is a substantial family property and business to for our consideration. Bye the bye, here is a trinket I acquired some weeks past; use it in any appropriate way to capture this creature. I pocketed it from our mutual lady, Kate Poole, after the days we three spent together at Bath. She thought she had lost it, I considered it more appropriate to be in my possession than hers. The diamonds are brilliant and it is worth a pile."

"So this young lady is barely seventeen years, aye, an interesting capture, subjugation and tutelage. Now! This is my fee for my assistance in this matter, keep me fully informed on every aspect and I must meet this beauty once you have completed her education. In addition, I will not hold you to repay the money you owe me, but I will want my share of the proceeds to be acquired from this liaison. We will work on our usual percentages. Are we agreed?"

"Done my friend, again we are in business together."

6

An Introduction to Life at Sea

"Come on! Come on! Get those men on deck. Not that one, he'll have a headache for a few days, the poor bugger." A crash; a rattling as of chains; again a crash, again and again the sound of chains. "Leave 'im ere, Arry, but make sure he's well fastened."

The words and sounds registered on some subconscious part of me and alerted my senses to my situation. The pain, which had returned, was now unbearable. Did I imagine it; am I in the midst of a nightmare? I opened my eyes and saw nothing but blackness.

I emerged into a half-conscious state. Unintelligible sounds came from me, though I did not recognize my own voice. I attempted to hold my head, but could move my arm no more than a few inches. As I tried to raise my hand, I felt more than heard another strange sound, a dragging, metallic rattle, trying to move the other arm, the same sensation. In the darkness, an icy hand of fear gripped me.

I heard a groaning, a squeaking, but all along, a crash? crash? crash, which continued in a regular pattern, as though a ram were being propelled against some solid object. Again, I lapsed into a state of painful stupor.

I am aware, but still all is black and I cannot move. My eyes open; I think I can distinguish a light above me. My head aches, such confusion. Could I be in the grip of some phantasm? Why am I moving in such a fashion, I roll, but I do not move of my own volition?

"Ohhh? my head, how it aches." Words agonized and slurred from a voice I did not recognize. "Help, Help. Somebody, what is happening to me?"

My hoarse whispered cries brought no explanation. I tried to move my legs but they could move only a few inches. As my mind cleared, I was assailed by a sickly smell. A rancid, foul odour, which caused my stomach to knot and I vomited into the gloom about me. A violent movement threw me against a hard surface to my left and at times seemed to lift me into the air, till again I fell hard down. A sloshing, splashing sound seemed to be all about me. I called out repeatedly, but no assistance came. I passed in and out of a conscious state, time had no meaning and I was completely alone.

"This man will need some attention." The words shattered a peaceful stupor that had descended on me. "Take the chains off him and get a light in here."

I opened my eyes and for the first time saw what was about me. A lamp hung above swinging in a dizzy fashion and casting a yellow glow in grotesque moving patterns. All around there were crates, casks, bundles, barrels, and iron implements, the use of which was completely beyond my knowledge. At last, my eyes fell on a familiar object; I lay against a great anchor.

"How long has he been in this state? Umm, that is a nasty wound at the back of his head and even worse on his face."

The face, no more than a few inches from mine was thin, almost gaunt. Large, soulful eyes, surmounted by a broad, high brow peered at me. His fair hair was tied back in a tail and his long, thin hands turned my aching head first one way then another. His dress was that of a naval officer. I had seen many jackets such as this in the port of Kings Lynn during my attendance at Grammar School. The River Great Ouse with its preponderance of commercial and naval vessels had given me a ready recognition of seafaring men. Of course, I was always warned by my mother about the perils of a seaport for any young fellow alone and towards night.

"What happened to me? Where am I? For God's sake, what has happened to me? Oh my head, what is this place?" The face so close to mine gave no inkling of me having been understood or even heard. "What are you doing?"

I became aware of a second person at my feet. Then I heard the sound that had confused me as I drifted in and out of consciousness.

"Chains, why am I chained? For God's sake tell me where I am."

"Mr. Hewett, I will have to put stitches in the back of his head, not too bad, but this wound will require close attention for a time. Green, do you have those damn chains off yet? Get a hammock down here for him."

The tall man stood, now in the light of the lantern. The taste in my mouth was sour, a taste followed by a sickness that overwhelmed me. Moaning, I tried to roll on my side realizing that I had vomited over myself.

I was aware of a third person who had not spoke, "Now the poor bugger's seasick, Mr. Cranstoun."

"All right, clean the fellow up and I will stitch his wounds. I hope it is not

Discovery

too late for stitching; it should have been done yesterday. I tell you Hewett, I do not like this way of obtaining men. The press must go. Look what they have done to this fellow, he will be useless for a few days, and look at his hands, he's never done a days work in his life."

"Tell me where I am and what I am doing here; I want to see my father and mother. Oh the pain in my head. I demand some answers." I struggled to rise to my feet but the effort was too much; I fell back to the hard floor and immediately was sick again. When I recovered a little from the nausea that gripped me the two men who appeared in charge had gone.

"Yer better not be demanding anything, matey; won't get you any where here. You're in the Kings Navee now and yer better make the best of it."

The words came to me through my agony, "I don't understand, what King's Navy."

"The Navee of Farmer George, that's the navee yer in. Yer better start now to know yer place. Don't answer back, don't talk until yer talked to, do what you're told and call em all sirs."

Suddenly I was drenched with water; I did not see where it came from. I barely recovered from the shock, when another torrent struck me. From the shadows, I heard coarse laughter and words in a language almost beyond my comprehension.

"Naw. That is enough for the sawbones to stitch im up. Don't want to drown im."

The man who spoke moved into the lantern's light. A short husky man with hair tied back into a tail. He had broad shoulders, with strong, muscular, sinewy arms, grotesquely tattooed from his fingers to the sleeves of the striped, blue shirt, rolled high above his elbows. His tight blue dungaree trousers did little to conceal strong, muscular legs. He was shoeless.

The two men who had left earlier returned. One carried a box, which he set down on a barrel.

"I'll do the back of his head first, lean this way. Come along now young fellow, it's for your own good."

My hair was cut at the back; I winced at the stinging jab of the doctor's needle as he proceeded to stitch my wound.

"Lie on your side, here put your head this way, don't fight me now. Hold him Green."

The wound on my face was finally attended to; the stinging pain of the needle almost unbearable.

The second blue-jacketed man took a vial from the box.

"Tincture of iodine should do the trick, Alexander."
Without hesitation, he poured the contents over the wounds. The agony was instant, as the fluid, pungent and strong found its way into the deepest recesses of my wounds.

"Oh, the pain? OHHH? what is happening to me?"

Sick again. The same sensation, which had gripped me in the lane, came over me until a peaceful oblivion claimed me.

The crashing, regular, now familiar sound that had wakened me from my unconscious state earlier again roused me. It was still dark, but a light from somewhere above gave some illumination. I lay in a hammock of coarse, rough canvas with a cover of similar material thrown over me. My left wrist was shackled to a bolt on the wall of my prison, if a prison it was. Now I was ravenously hungry; I did not feel sick, as before. My head hurt fiercely and in the quarter light I saw the ceiling close over my head was low with interspersed, heavy beams. I realized the smell, which had so assaulted me earlier was in fact partly from me, the odour of urine, feces and vomit, mixed with the foulness of my situation.

"Hey anyone? Hey there? Where am I? Have mercy on me." Repeatedly my calls rang out.

The realization that I was on a boat of some description was now well established in my mind, but what and where and most of all why was well beyond my comprehension. I began to call again.

"Stop yer bloody yellin', won't do yer any good." Two men had again suddenly appeared, one began to undo the chain that held me captive. "Come on, up on deck with yer."

The chain on my wrist was unshackled and I was roughly pulled to my feet. As I stood, a feeling of nausea gripped me. The movement of the space in which I found myself suddenly threw me into the grasp of one of the men.

"Not feelin' too good aye mate. You will be right as rain in a couple of days. You better be, lad."

Both men propelled me into a passageway, at the end of which was a ladder.

"I must protest this treatment, it should not be. Tell me where I am! I want to go to my family. Take me to someone in charge."

"Listen to I'm Salty, blubbering away like an old moll on a pisser. You want to know where you are aye, come on get up that ladder." This man, who seemed in some way in charge, propelled me upward to a platform.

"I'll tell you where you are lad, three days out into the Atlantic Ocean, that's where you be."

"The Atlantic Ocean, how, why, I don't understand, I was at the Temple in London." The sickening motion threw me off balance at every movement.

"Yer can forget all that now, just do what yer told."

The door flew open. I was propelled out into the light of day, dazzled and completely blinded by the unaccustomed glare. I gasped as a salty gale assaulted my senses. I fell and lay on my stomach. As my sight gradually returned, I raised my head to see a pair of black boots, legs in white britches, a blue coat with white piping, gold buttons and trim and a face framed by dark, long hair, swept back by the brisk gusts.

"Welcome to His Majesty's Navy, you are aboard *HMS Discovery*. You have been injured. In two days time you will be expected to do all that is asked of you, without question. Get on your feet and go with this man. Quartermaster Brown, clean him up, and get some clothes on him that do not smell. Put him to work immediately; for the time being keep him in the galley. He will be entered on the ships muster as an idler."

By his diction I immediately recognized an educated man

"Ah, a man of culture, are you the leader of these ruffians? If you are not, sir, I would insist that you take me to someone in charge. I must introduce myself and ask for some protection and a place equal to my station." As my words poured forth, I raised myself to my knees. I looked about me.

Billowing white sails reached high into the sky. Men balanced precariously on booms high above, amid a maze of ropes, pulleys, blocks and other tackle, the use of which I did not have the faintest idea. A line of men on hands and knees scrubbed at the white boards of the deck, with what appeared to be small stones. A tall, blue-jacketed fellow urged them on in the most uncomplimentary terms. Others in similar garb to the man before me, called to men at the ropes and to those high above, orders, which again meant absolutely nothing to me. They could have spoken the language of the Hottentots and would have made as much sense.

"Main topmen! Look alive up there. Brace up the main yard."

Men ran along one behind the other, heaving on lines, urged on by men with a knotted length of rope hitting out indiscriminately. I was to learn this lashing with a length of rope was termed *starting the hands*. As time went on and the hands became more adept and began to work as a team, starting was no longer necessary. The crashing that had so confused me in my previous situation now became obvious. The bow of the ship rose on a wave and then crashed with a shudder into the trough of the next. A blow from behind sent me sprawling forward, again face down on the white boards.

"That's enough of that talk. You won't speak to the officers again, get going you now get along,"

I saw the man who had taken me from my dark place aim a kick at me, a kick, which caught me on the hip and sent me forward. The man who I had hoped would recognize me as an equal was gone. I saw him now on the raised platform behind me in company with a stout, solid man of middle stature, similarly garbed except that he wore a hat trimmed with gold, a man evidently of a higher station.

The violent movement of the vessel threw me first in one direction then in another, the laughter and calls of those on their knees scrubbing the deck was directed at me.

"Here's a pretty fella for us... look ow he dances ...e must be a papist, look at the bald back of is ed"...aye es a long toggie if ever I saw one," then from one who seemed to be in charge of this motley assortment...."get on with it yer lazy bastards,"

I was propelled forward by the man called Quartermaster Brown, towards a raised part of the vessel, into a doorway. I could not see and promptly fell down five stairs. My companion went to a chest, from which he took, a shirt and trousers.

"Get those stinking things off, fill that bucket and clean yourself. There is water in the barrel over there. Jump to it lad. The surgeon said you would not be fit for the deck for a few days. Those press gang-bastards almost did you in."

"Whoever you are, please have compassion, tell me what has happened to me. I must return to my family and studies, what date is it, what day is it?" I was quite disgusted with the smell that emanated from me. It was with some joy that I divested myself of the soiled clothes. I was, of course, quite embarrassed to be standing naked before a complete stranger.

"You can forget studies and family for a bit. The day is April 4th and it is Monday. You were delivered to us in your sorry state on the day we left from Falmouth, we are now well out into the ocean bound towards Cape Town."

His words hit me like a thunderclap.

"Cape Town. In Africa?"

"Yes lad, that's the only Cape Town I know. You are on His Majesty's Ship *Discovery*, the Captn's Vancouver. What name do you go by? Get those clothes on; make your mark in the book, here. The cost will come out of your pay at the end. Come on now, make a mark. You are a landsman and as such, you will be paid eight pence a day, you will pay sixpence to the Royal Hospital, two pence to the surgeon and if you have the pox lad, there is a fine to pay. You were delivered to us by a channel yawl. Strange that is, some one wanted you away from England I'd say."

I took up the quill proffered to me and signed my full name.

"What's this? You can write?"

He looked at the register just signed, my name standing out among the scratches and marks, obviously made by men with little or no literary skill.

"Peter! What's this?" he attempted to decipher my middle name. "Highfield...Wright. Well we are the toff, ain't we? You be Petee now and that's all. Remember that's all you go by."

From somewhere above, a sound resembling the screeching of an injured bird seemed to trigger a thumping. Suddenly the area in which I stood was filled with the most disreputable group of men ever seen. To describe them is well beyond my ability. I must rely on your imagination when I say, they were dressed in a variety of clothes, all were without shoes, most had long hair tied back in a tail, all were clean shaven with just hairy stubble on their face, some of them sported tattoos. One dark-skinned man in particular sported hair in a long plait descending almost to his waist. His appearance was most fearsome, his face grotesquely marked in swirls and designs, which rendered him not unlike a savage of the jungle. I became aware later, how much the tattoo was favoured by men of the sea. In these early days of my initiation, I never considered that I would submit to such a barbaric custom.

I was the centre of the most unwelcome attention. My trousers, far away too large for me, began to fall from my hips. This was the cause of the most uproarious laughter. I was pulled and shoved until my trousers fell to the floor. Two enormously strong young men grabbed me by the arms throwing me over a barrel. I screamed for help, as the dark, tattooed monster made every indication that he would mount me. Quartermaster Brown, who had remained silent through my torment, stepped forward. "Leave the lad alone, you hear me. Anyone who touches him will have to answer to me, let go of him, you hear." He handed me a short length of rope. "Here Petee, pull up your trous and tie them with this. This man has been injured and is sick he has been taken from all that is usual for him. Mark my words I will have no more of this."

The two released me from their grip. I quickly tied my trousers. I stood amid the group of men completely at a loss as to what would come next. They ignored me and went about their business. In a few moments the man

Brown returned, he threw a bundle on the floor.

"Here is a hammock, you will use the bolts here and here, this will be your place. Pack it as it is and stow it in the racks here. Take notice of all you are told, you will only be told once. Do your work well, be cheerful and call all those over you sir. Its light work for you for the next two days, then you will be expected to pull your weight with the rest of the crew."

"I must protest this situation, you must take me to the captain of this vessel and I would be treated as my station...." A roar of laughter greeted my words. Brown, who had shown some compassion, grasped me by my shirt he pulled me forward until his face was an inch from mine.

"There'll be no captain for you sonny Jim, do your work, I'll hear no more about your station. You are nothing to me or this ship, you hear me." He threw me from him, as one would an offending animal. "Betton, I'll tell you now, show him things. He knows nothing, so learn him in the way of the fo'c'sil".

Brown spun on his heel and was gone.

"All right matee, I got to teach yer, aye. Right we are. Stow yer ammock as it is now. Its four turns about it with the tail. Make it ever the same size or the bo's'un will be after yer."

The man Betton, a short bow legged fellow, with no front teeth continued, "If you were on a real ship of the line, it'd be done right and put through a hammock gauge and stowed on deck in the racks, ere it gets stowed ere." He indicated a rack on the wall of the place I found myself.

"When the boson tells yer to shake a leg, get yerself out and about. E might say up or down, if yer don't git up, he might cut the hammock rope and then yer'll be down, on yer ed." My new instructor continued with an almost unintelligible list of dos and don'ts. "The captain won't av profanity, e told us that before we left. I 'eard 'im swearing like a trooper. E'll fine you or you'll get a pump bolt tied into yer mouth. No lying either, you'll get strung up for lying with a broom and shovel tied to yer back and the men will call liar all the while. You will be at it at four in the morning when the middle watch comes in and nine will end yer day after the second dog watch comes in. You do not av to keep watch as the rest of us av to; yer will be working with the cook."

On and on he went. He told me of the food allowance and what to expect, a pound of biscuit bread and an issue of grog each day. On Tuesdays and Saturdays, two pound of beef. Thursdays and Sundays a three pound piece of pork and some peas boiled into soup. I thought the quantity he spoke of to be quite generous, but came to realize this was not to be the case when the length of the voyage varied due to weather or some other condition. He spoke of burgoo, molasses, and other dishes completely strange to me, all of the information I immediately allowed to escape from my mind.

    I was alone, scared, sick and in the company of people, as unfamiliar to me as creatures from another world. In these early days, little did I know the honour, companionship, and trust that would be forthcoming from these fellow travelers whose lives were daily in constant, mortal danger.

7

Henry West Becomes Acquainted with the Sawtell Family

"Fellow, can you tell me of the whereabouts of the master of this property?"

"That I can, sir, but first I would ask the name of the gentleman who seeks him out?"

Henry West remained seated on his horse. He spoke to a roughly dressed character of middle age, vigorous of action and solid of build, energetically shoveling and spreading soil from a large mound of dark, rich loam, obviously a working employee of Edward Sawtell.

"My name is Captain Henry West, run ahead of me and direct me to your master. Come along now."

"Well, sir, I can do better than that, I will stand here and converse with you and I am Edward Sawtell. What business do you have with me, sir?"

Henry West started aback at this disclosure. Here was a fellow, to all intents and purposes a labourer, claiming to be the gentleman he had come to see. On further reflection Henry realized his diction was not of the raw Norfolk idiom, his speech did have a degree of style and education about it.

"I see you are confused, sir. Allow me to persuade you that I am Edward Sawtell, owner of this property. I can understand your bewilderment, but rest assured I am who I say I am. I sometimes work in the fields and garden to preserve my well-being. It seems a useful way to take exercise and inhale copious draughts of fresh Norfolk air, as well as further the welfare of my estate."

"Well, sir, if you are Edward Sawtell I must apologize for my error but I am sure you will understand the reason for my confusion. Allow me to introduce myself. I am sir, Captain Henry West. I have recently acquired the Westgate House, if you are not acquainted with it; let me tell you that it is a pretty place, some few miles from here, near St Mary's Burnham Westgate, off the London Road. I must also inform you that we are related by marriage, sir."

Henry West had ridden from Burnham Market the few miles towards the Wash, where he knew by dint of studious investigation the residence and object of his visit would be found. He was fortunate to find Edward Sawtell immediately.

"Captain West, ah yes, my dear sister living in Bath who had the good fortune to wed Sir William Parkinson. I believe he is the Member of Parliament for that area."

"Yes, sir; I have the honour to be his nephew. I have the privilege to be the son of Lady Cornelia and Lord de Lacey. My dear mother is a kinswoman to the Beckingham family and I am therefore a distant cousin to your good lady. I am come to make myself known to you. As I am new to country life I must throw myself on your good will, I know there are people I should meet. I would meet the polite society of the Burnham towns and become involved in their affairs."

"Captain, a man used to the excitement of military life may find his existence rather dull in the country; I cannot imagine why you would come to a county as remote as Norfolk."

"I feel I need to get away from fields of conflict for a period, to recreate myself so to speak. I need to find myself in the company of gentle people, to commune with nature, to leave the hurry and bustle of London, not to mention the pressure of a military life behind me for a time."

"I understand, Captain, I understand. I sometimes find myself in a similar predicament; my dear wife and daughter constantly change my mind for me. I can appreciate your need for peace and quiet. I tend to lose myself in my books and leave the house to the ladies. So Captain, will we have the pleasure of meeting your family, your good lady and children, perhaps?'

"Ah sir, as yet I have not been granted the privilege of meeting the fair lady with whom I would share my existence. I am sure that somewhere there is a person, kind and good that God almighty has set aside for me, but as yet I have not met her."

"Well Captain, I am sure that a man of your obvious rank and stature will soon be enjoying the benefits of wedded bliss. Perhaps it is here in our little community that you will find the person to fulfill all your desires."

"Perhaps so, sir, perhaps so."

"Sir, perhaps you would care to join me at the house, a cool libation before you make your return journey?"

Although Henry would have readily indulged, he thought better of it. The notion struck him that it seemed more in keeping that he forgo any contact at this early stage. Henry decided to remain distant for the present but he knew that the seeds had been sown.

"I thank you, sir, for your kind invitation but the shadows grow long and I must be away early in the morning to Norwich to complete the transaction of important business, so I will take my leave."

"It has been a pleasure to meet you, sir. Please call on me at any time I may be of assistance to you and I will be at your service."

"You have my thanks, sir. It would be my greatest pleasure to make the acquaintance of your family. With this in mind, perhaps I could send my carriage on Sunday next. I invite you to my humble dwelling and there perhaps, over afternoon tea we could find mutual satisfaction in pursuing a concourse on our respective families. Though we are distantly related I am sure our mutual family ties will be of great satisfaction and interest to all."

"Why Captain, that is remarkably generous of you, I will be delighted to accept your invitation on behalf of my dear wife Mrs. Margaret Sawtell and my daughter, Jane Ann."

"Brilliant. It is agreed then. Until Sunday at, shall we say twelve thirty? Yes, at twelve thirty my carriage will call for you."

Henry West rode off towards Burnham Market quite satisfied with the afternoon's proceedings. Before he was out of sight, Edward Sawtell rushed to tell his wife of the dashing Captain, a distant relative and so well positioned in society. Even at this first meeting, the thought did not escape his attention, that here, despite his daughter's attachment to Peter Wright and his own liking for the lad, was a fine prospect. Thoughts raced pell-mell though his mind. He considered the advantages of an aristocratic relationship and its effects on his business prospects. He knew, though he was extremely wealthy, he was still a common man and could never move in the circles, which were suddenly opened to him by this meeting. These thoughts clouded all other considerations; yes, it would be a fine marriage. By the time, Edward Sawtell had found his wife he had decided he would pursue a course, which would see Jane Ann Sawtell married to Captain Henry West.

8

Peter Commences His Nautical Education and Considers Escape

I will never forget my first days at sea. Everything was new and nothing related in any way to my previous life. The expectation that I would awake and find all was a terrible dream or nightmare was soon expunged from my mind. I longed for the gentle land of Norfolk, the buildings and places with family I knew and loved. Here, all was constantly in movement, nothing was still and everywhere the interminable horizon and sky. My life became structured to a strict and unbending timetable. It was demanded of me that I carry out jobs of the most menial nature. I still had bouts of dizziness and my head ached dreadfully, although the wounds had begun to heal. Thankfully, I was not prone to seasickness; my earlier nausea had been the result of my condition.

"Come along Petee me lad. I got just the job for the likes of you and you better do it right if you don't want to be in trouble. The Captain will not stand for any dirtiness about his ship. Come with me." Quartermaster Brown led me far up onto the bow of the vessel.

The great ocean swells in surging lines raced towards the vessel as though to overwhelm it. The ship would rise up to glide like a Phoenix over the monsters, then plunge down sickeningly into the trough, only to repeat the process again and again.

I was introduced to the seats-of-ease and the pissdales. For the ordinary men these were positioned at the bow of the vessel. A square box was situated on both sides of the bowsprit completely in the open, the resultant effluvia being directed over the side of the vessel. These were not the vilest places. The constant action of the sea and its scouring action took care of most of the cleaning. The officer's heads required all the work, being situated in a closet below deck. No wave action here, I was the engine of cleanliness for these. You can imagine how embarrassed I was to have to perform my toilet functions out in the open before all. I must tell you for months I suffered from the most dreadful constipation, but eventually I came to perform my toilet duty without any thought. The heaving motion of the vessel over the waves made it imperative a firm grip be maintained at all times and often a wave would sweep onto the deck making an uncomfortable process even more distressing. I was amazed to discover that urine was collected in a tub and kept. Salt water was always used to wash clothes with an added scoop of urine, the ammonia there-from having a bleaching effect. When the weather changed, clothing always became damp as the salt absorbed the moisture in the atmosphere.

How my life had changed, from polite society with a bent towards the church, to cleaning these disgusting places where the men relieved themselves and carried out the most basic functions of human nature. I quickly learned the Captain would suffer no slackness when it came to cleanliness. This was the commencement of my new education.

I holystoned the decks, a wet, backbreaking job.

"Listen here Petee, I don't want to see you doin nuthin, on your knees, scrub away if you got nuttin to do. You 'ere me?"

One of the seamen told me they were called holystones because they were about the size and shape of a prayer book. Holystoning the decks was carried out on Sundays and Thursdays, but the deck was washed every day. I was told that the holystoning wore down the deck and left the harder knots standing proud. The carpenter frequently planed down these protuberances.

I worked in the galley where the principal cooking was carried out. I was a slop boy, a washer of utensils. I carried the pots of food, if that is what it could be called, to the various messes, where other lesser cooks would dole it out to the seamen.

I scrubbed and cleaned, I pulled on ropes when I was told, always urged on by the boatswain with his length of knotted rope. After a time I was told to report to the carpenter. But I was still to carry out my usual tasks.

The ship's carpenter was Tom Laithwood, a gentle man. There were two carpenter's mates, Downey, tall and thin and Joe Murgatroyd, a deep, sad man, who would later vanish in the darkness of night. I was never surprised that his death was considered a suicide. These men helped me come to terms with my situation and tutored me in the way of the ship, when to move smartly, and how to look busy without really doing anything. Tom Laithwood managed to keep me for nearly a fortnight. During that time, I worked with these men preparing spare booms and yards, deep in the bowels of the ship. Our task was to cut, smooth and fit the iron implements to the long wooden lengths that had been loaded through ports in the bow of the vessel at Depthford Yard. While I found the work with the carpenters hard, it was not unpleasant.

The ships company was divided into two watches, which meant there was always room enough in the cramped quarters of the fo'c'sil. In a gale or at times when it was necessary to keep a lookout for a shoreline or a rocky reef all hands would be called. I found that certain things aboard ship were always carried out in the same manner and did not vary. The day for me commenced at 4:00 a.m. As an idler, I had to prepare the galley for the cooks and make ready the fire for the days cooking. All this was before the day proper began. The order, "watch below clean the lower deck," started the day at about 6:00 a.m. "Clear decks and up spirits" at 11:30, eventually came to be one of the times I looked forward to most when the first half of the grog issue was passed out. Dinner lasted roughly an hour. The end of the working day was the final meal of the day at 5:00 p.m. and the second issue of rum. Another final order to clean decks again. The last act of the day was the order "down hammocks."

Life in the fo'c'sil was almost unbearable. I was the butt of jokes, pranks and ridicule. It was obvious to these men that I had come from a place of privilege, but as a pressed man and one who was not of the sea, I was considered the lowest of the low.

By the time I left the carpenters, my wounds had healed and my head had stopped aching, although I bear the scars you see today. I was directed to other chores. At any hour, day and night, the shrill scream of the boson's pipe, the cry of "all hands on deck," would summon everyone to haul in, let out or take down sails. In extreme weather, even the topmasts, the highest mast sections, would be lowered to the deck. Some men would leap into the ratlines to scamper high into the rigging, others at the command of an officer would man the lines that controlled the sails, urged on by a boatswain's mate, flicking here and there with his knotted piece of rope. My time with the carpenters had given me the opportunity to learn enough to fit in with the system. Any attempt I made to speak to or converse with an officer as to my situation was instantly repulsed. Not only did I fail to find sympathy with the officers; the men with whom I lived would make my life a misery until they forgot about my attempts to find favour.

"Crawlin bloody bastard. Think yer too good for us eh."

The days passed into weeks then months. I found myself changing physically. I was always a tall fellow but because of my sedentary lifestyle a little overweight in the wrong places. I found the work and constant movement stripped the fat from my body, replacing it with muscle. My hands, once so white and delicate, were now hard and callused. The activity on deck, especially heaving at lines, caused blisters on both my hands. The crevices on my fingers would open and bleed the moment I stretched out my hands.

"Listen Petee, pee on yer ands, that'll fix em."

The donor of this astounding information was the tattooed monster who had first terrorized me. Of course, to do this was completely against my sensibilities, but desperation is all that is left to desperate men. I followed his advice, and amazingly within a few days, the cracks had healed and the blisters turned to calluses. Despite the terrible food, which at first caused me to gag, I began to physically fill out and develop muscles, the like of which I never thought possible. I had become a strong fit young man.

Our fare was plentiful, but of a nature that would not be acceptable in polite society. I learned names for our victuals, food that would never be presented to the two faithful red setters, my boyhood companions. I was soon familiar with sillygolee, lobscouse, burgoo or scotch coffee, watery porridge with pieces of meat floating in it, with perhaps a little sugar and vinegar. Portable soup, a pabulum of vegetables and meat, sauerkraut pickled cabbage. As the time went on the food became progressively worse. Biscuits became infested with weevils, the action of which turned them from iron hard to a useless powder. Our cheese ration, always generous, deteriorated with time into a vile smelling, concoction laced with red worms and maggots. Some of my companions considered these disgusting creatures a delicacy. Salt pork remained always popular in the fo'c'sil, even when it attained a hardness that defied comprehension. I have seen trinkets carved from salt pork and worn as a decoration about the neck of a seaman. Tea, cocoa or chocolate was sometimes given out, but only if the Quartermaster was in a benevolent mood.

I must mention here how the officers ate the same food as the men, with the only exception being, they consumed wine at the evening mess. No sailor would touch wine, the grog issue being the highlight of his daily life.

The most anticipated moment, which occurred twice each day, was the issue of "grog." You cannot imagine the joy in the fo'c'sil at this. Midday and at six in the evening, a gill of rum diluted with three gills of water with lemon and sugar was issued to the various cooks, who in turn would dole it out to the men. I know rum was my salvation in these early days. Imagine the despair and horror of my situation. After the rum, my circumstances became a little more bearable, until the next issue. My life revolved about midday and six in the evening when an alcoholic euphoria seemed to place a gentle mist about the hard constant work and sometimes-cruel supervision. The days slowly wore away to become months and the men became adjusted to the daily grind. Less and less was seen of the short rope length, originally used with abandon on the men. It seemed a team had begun to develop. As the men became aware of what was required of them, coercion became less necessary.

The cry "Land-ho, land to larboard" caused no little excitement in all parts of the vessel. I did not see the land until the next day when we anchored. I was told that it was the Island of Tenerife and we had anchored before the town of Santa Cruz. *HMS Chatham*, our companion vessel, was nearer shore. *Chatham* was an armed tender and a much smaller vessel than *HMS Discovery*. My thoughts returned to escaping from my unhappy situation. The sight of land spurred me on. I thought of nothing else but flight from this floating prison and somehow to return to England. Swimming was out of the question. I had never mastered this accomplishment and the sight of numerous sharks in the vicinity of the vessel put all thought of such a venture out of my mind.

I hoped I might be taken ashore, on some work detail, but alas, this did not occur. I was assigned to a barge tied beside *Chatham* along with most of the hands to shovel tons of gravel into the inside of the vessel. With five others, I was directed into the deepest part of this smaller ship, there to spread and pack the stony cargo as ballast. The heat was unbearable for us in the depths of *Chatham*. For those on deck it was much worse, with no shelter at all from the burning rays of the tropical sun.

The most trying circumstance was the continuing heavy swell rolling into the harbour from the Atlantic. Here I began to appreciate the motion of a vessel under sail, as opposed to lying at anchor in an exposed position. Some of the old hands and officers went ashore. A fracas occurred between our men and the Spanish guard. I saw our Captain, wet and disheveled, return to the vessel in a foul humour. Some of the other officers swam back, preferring to chance the sharks rather than further confrontation with the Spanish soldiers.

I had been at sea for a month and it was May. In that short time, I had begun to consider myself as part of the crew, even if the lowest of the low. I had begun to fit into the daily routine and already I had mastered a new language, the everyday tongue of the sea. I began to recognize and call the various accouterments and ship parts by their correct names and I had taken to keeping some record of the date. On a small piece of wood, which I had got from the carpenters, I was able to scratch off the days and months.

"Aaaaall hands!"

The call brought men from all parts of the vessel. Some sprang into the rigging, some to the halyards, which controlled the sails. The officers congregated on the after deck, spick and span in their best uniforms. I confess that at this time I had no idea of the function that I was expected to carry out.

"Onto the fo'c'sil head with you, get a hand spike."

I followed the others forward to take a wooden pole from a stack that had appeared on the fo'c'sil head. These handspikes at the command of the Quartermaster were inserted into scarlet pigeon holes and for the first time I experienced the long walk'n'heave around the trundlehead. Round and round, eighteen men, urged on by the ever-present mate. His length of rope had appeared again for this new exercise. The pawls clicked as they fell into place to prevent 'walking back.' I noticed that the older hands quickly got to the inside position on the capstan. Such is the manner of the sailor that he will realize where lighter work could be done, the distance covered being much less than those on the outer ends of the capstan bar.

"Come on now yer scurvy sots, who can sing a tune? Who's the nightingale among you?"

A fellow in front of me began to sing a rhyming song; the words were completely unintelligible to me. He began to chant a verse; the men seemed to know the refrain to his words. Eventually I came to know these songs, songs that would be used only for certain exercises that required a continuous chant.

Sally Brown she is a bright mulatter
Way-ay. Roll an go!
She drinks rum and chews terbacker,
Spend my money on Sally Brown.
Seven long years I courted Sally.
But all she did was dilly dally.

On and on these songs would go and when all the verses were exhausted, others were made up most becoming coarse and vulgar in the extreme.

The heavy breathing of the men, the singing chant of those at the capstan, calls to those in the rigging, the heaving on halyards, the vessel moving slowly till a call from the bow, "Up and down."

The weight of the anchor became full on the capstan, sails fell in billowing folds to capture the wind and drive us forward. The anchor hung just above the surface of the sea.

"Anchor awash."

"Cat and fish." The call ordered the anchor brought to the cathead, great oaken timbers protruding out over each side of the vessel. There it was fastened securely until the next use. The roar of the ship's cannons firing a salute to the Spanish dignitaries assembled ashore. The flags, the smoke, the impact of the whole scene made some impression on me. The vessel answered the wind, the Canary Islands rapidly fell astern, and thoughts of escape faded far from my mind. Little did I realize the number of times that I would be called on to heave on the capstan bars over the next five long years.

9

Jane's Future is Discussed

At the arranged time, a carriage had called for the Sawtell family. A most pleasant afternoon was spent in the company of Captain West. The Sawtell ladies were elegant in their most becoming attire and both beamed coquettishly at the dashing Captain, resplendent in his newest undress uniform, recently purchased to aid in the conquest at hand. Edward Sawtell fawned, fluttered and bowed his way through the afternoon. The discussion centered about family and the fact of their relationship. Henry West of course, with his desperate financial plight always in mind, behaved the perfect gentleman. On the return, Edward and Margaret Sawtell discussed the afternoon with all its ramifications.

"Never you mind, me dear, he is an absolute gentleman as well as a military hero and he is our relative and generously has shown a propensity to include us in his sphere of influence. His father, I know has vast holdings in Surrey and Kent, most of all he is kin to the Dukes of Beckingham. Can you imagine me dear, as affluent as we are, we could never move in these elevated circles."

"I do not know. I feel that perhaps he is not the gentleman he seems to be. I cannot tell you why, but there is something about his eyes that disturb me. Of course, he is young and very handsome; indeed he cuts a heroic and dashing figure in his uniform. Any young lady would be easily swept away by him, but he always seemed to be laughing at me."

"Come now. Our daughter appears to look on him with favour and that is all that matters. It is the first time she has been in any way animated since the sad disappearance of Peter. That melancholy event brought a terrible sadness into our lives, but now we must look to the present and the future, no point dwelling on the past. Peter Wright is gone, no doubt dead. He has been taken from us in some foul and mysterious way, but we must carry on."

"Edward, I'm sure you're right. Our Jane has been so unhappy. For months, she has shown no inclination to be part of anything. I must agree that she has shown some interest in the things that amuse her of late."

"Well me love, I think that we should encourage her to think of her future. A union with the Captain would be of inestimable benefit to her, not to mention us. I have often thought of expanding my investments. An alliance between our daughter and the house of Beckingham, I tremble to think of the ramifications."

Not long after this conversation, Edward Sawtell again met with Henry West, perhaps accidentally, perhaps by design. Edward Sawtell had thought long and hard on the benefits of a marriage between his daughter and Henry West. Although he had not discussed the matter in any great depth with his wife, he had decided to make every effort to bring about the union.

The more he thought on it, the more desirable the possibilities became. The most pressing problem was the attachment between Jane and Peter Wright. The two had grown together, side by side. It was a family understanding that they would eventually marry. Now circumstances had changed. He could see a great opportunity to enhance his fortune, as well as his position in society. He liked Peter Wright and considered him the son he would never have, but Peter had vanished from the face of the earth. It was as though fate had played a hand. As sad as he was at the disappearance, he could see no impediment in seizing the opportunity, which had opened for Jane and for the family fortunes.

"My dear Sawtell, how provident it is to see you. Your family is well I trust, and you sir are also in good health?"

Captain West reined in his horse at the sight of Jane's father.

"Captain West, how good to see you. Yes, all is well with my family and with me. Come, sir, will you join me in a draught in the Pitt Inn, what do you say."

"A fortuitous meeting, it would be my pleasure to join you, sir. I have a matter I feel must be spoken of, and what better time than now."

The two men sat in a corner of the inn near a fine fire, which took the chill off the late autumn air. Each had a tankard of ale before him.

"Now, sir, I have a matter of great delicacy of which I must speak. I trust what I am about to say will meet with your approval. It is as though destiny's hand drew us together at this time."

"My dear sir, what is the matter which troubles you so. How can I be of assistance?"

"Pray, sir, let me continue. The fear of a rebuff by you is more that I care to contemplate. I am enamored of your most excellent and beautiful daughter, Jane. My life has been in turmoil since the first day I laid eyes on her. My life changed on the Sunday you, sir and Mrs. Sawtell accompanied by the beautiful Jane came to my humble abode. The moment I saw her, my heart was not my own, in that instant I was captivated completely. She enchants me. Life without Jane by my side seems completely without rhyme or reason. I wish to pay court to her."

"Oh my dear fellow...."

"Let me continue, sir, while my courage is at it greatest. I am speaking to you at this early stage without words having passed between Jane and myself. I seek your blessing to pursue her in a most propitious and gracious manner and I fervently hope she will see the love I have for her and reciprocate in kind. As a man devoted to military pursuits and used to the dangers of shot and shell, I am at a loss to understand the tremors and feelings, which render me helpless in her presence. What do you say to this, sir?"

With great personal control, Edward Sawtell refrained from showing his complete satisfaction at this unexpected conversation. His only outward display of joy was a slight reddening of his features.

"I would only say that I could not wish for a finer man than your good self to call son. You have my blessing and my benediction on your quest. I am delighted. I will speak for my dear Mrs. Sawtell. We both will wait the day when you ask for our Jane's hand in marriage. Marvelous! Absolutely marvelous news."

The two men celebrated the moment with another tankard before leaving the Pitt. Henry West departed to pursue Jane, confident that his reading of Edward Sawtell was correct. Sawtell was a man who prized social status and wealth above all else, even his own daughter. For his part Edward Sawtell left the inn completely satisfied Henry West would become his son-in-law. He was confident this would be the commencement of a rewarding relationship with one of the most influential families in England and in the depths of his heart, he already saw himself raised to a peerage. Straight away, he determined to steer Jane in every way to a rapid marriage with Henry West.

10

Peter Crosses the Equator and Begins to be Transformed into a Sailor

The equator. Here I was at the central meridian of the world. I believe it was Friday the 27th of May, 1791. One of the lieutenants made an announcement. The captain would allow the usual ceremony to appease the great gods and spirits of the sea and an extra issue of grog would be forthcoming. Not having any idea of what this meant, I was ready prey for my tough companions of the fo'c'sil. I was dragged from my hammock and a deep sleep at midnight. Unceremoniously I was manhandled to the main deck with five companions from the fo'c'sil. I did not have the slightest idea what was afoot. We were to receive the full brunt of the ceremony reserved for those neophytes who had never crossed this line. For a moment, I feared for my life until the laughter and banter of my captors dispelled all apprehension.

It seems we were under the command of King Neptune and his minions, members of the crew dressed in a variety of outlandish costumes. My companions and I suffered indignities well beyond our imagination, buckets of slop poured on our head, genitals painted with tar, shaving and ducking. A final indignity, that of running naked between rows of men towards our clothes placed at the other end of the deck, while being whacked with any available object. All the crew participated in this wild night, neophyte midshipmen receiving special attention from King Neptune. Roars of laughter came from the senior officers at their vantage on the quarterdeck, officers and men all enjoying relief from the constant monotony and work of a long ocean voyage. After this night, I felt that I had become part of the crew. I began to feel a comradeship with these young, rough, tough, sailors.

One day ran into the next and always the ocean, a vast, never still place.

I will tell you that for a Norfolk lad, the son of a farmer and merchant, I had no idea of the vastness and quantity of the water, which covered the world. Great white birds called albatross followed the vessel. Mile after mile they soared gracefully behind us, swooping down onto the white foam flecked sea. They flew inches above the water in the blue hollows between the crests of the waves. They skimmed the turbulent surface with their wingtips then soared high into the blue sky only to repeat the performance like children at play. Smaller, sleek white and black divers would plunge and swoop into the sea to gorge on the masses of small silvery fish that sometimes appeared about our vessel. No words from me could do justice to the sight of numberless dolphin, from horizon to horizon, leaping and frolicking across the face of their watery domain. Swarms of flying fish, rising as one into the morning light, only to fall back into their fluid home, before they again repeated the process. No longer did the motion of the vessel cause me discomfort.

Sometimes the surface of the ocean would be as calm as any pond in any village, sails would hang limp, and boards of the deck would begin to open and warp as the heat of day assaulted the vessel and its crew. Then in an instant, the calm would give way to a breeze, then a wind, then a gale, the ocean changing to a roaring demon.

In my short time at Cambridge, I came to know of a fellow student, Sam Taylor, who had written a piece, a poem, which spoke of the trials of a sailor in such conditions as I now found myself. I dismissed it offhand when I first read this poem, but now it spoke eloquently of my present position and the conditions in which I found myself. Men climbing the rigging on masts pitching in dizzying fashion, one moment a great arc, starboard to larboard, then as the ship plunged down the face of a watery mountain, an even greater arc fore and aft.

And the nights! Here the hand of God was brilliantly manifest; stars filled the heavens. On those wonderfully calm nights, it was as though our vessel was suspended in mystical space. A place where it was impossible to tell sea from sky, where stars reflected in the still ocean shone as brilliantly as the stars in the heavens above. A flashing trail left by a fiery meteor plunging to destruction through the atmosphere, reflected itself in the ocean and appeared to hurtle from the depths of the sea to meet its twin from above. The southern seas brought forth a new display. The familiar stars of the north gave way to sights none will experience until the equator is behind them. For one who had contemplated a life in the church, the sight of a wondrous starry cross hanging resplendent in the southern sky, transformed my darkest moments of despair, to feelings of hope and trust that all would be well and God was somehow taking care of me.

I had begun using the terms and language of the fo'c'sil, falling into the routine of the vessel. As an idler or landsman, one who had no previous sea experience, I was used wherever I could be of use. The days dragged on till again the call, "Land ho," brought all to the deck. A line of dark and an accumulation of clouds on the horizon signified Africa, the Dark Continent. It lay but a short distance to the east. I felt an excitement at this my first landfall in such an exotic place. I believe it was July 9th when the anchor again descended into the depths. I did not see any houses or fortifications in this place, I did not know until later why we had anchored in such a desolate spot. I realized that we were waiting for our companion vessel, *Chatham*. I overheard officers discussing the slowness of this vessel in the most uncomplimentary terms. I will forever be amazed at the knowledge, which allowed the officers of our ship to find their way across this watery desert. No landmarks distinguished one day from the other, until suddenly the place at which we were supposed to be appeared as if by magic.

Quite early on the morning of the 11th, orders were given for the boats to be lowered and I was introduced to the cutter, one of a number of small boats carried on the deck of *Discovery* and *Chatham*. It was lifted into the water in company with the yawl and pinnace, words that had no meaning for me at this time, in reality vessels of different size, but of the same basic design.

"Petee boy, get yer doon inter there," Rod Betton, a Glasgow man and the seaman who had instructed me and shown kindness, a man I felt I could call a friend. He directed me over the side of our ship and into the pinnace moving gently on the early morning swell. "Sit yer here, git the oar in there."

"What are we doing where are we going to row?"

The pinnace was in the charge of one of the midshipmen, a tall, strong young man, standing in the rear of the boat.

"Are we going for a row, oh I say how nice, what's your name fellow?

"Peter Wright, sir."

"Well, Peter Wright, you better pull your bloody hardest or I will put you on a report and have you flogged."

I shrank down wishing to vanish from sight. Following the example of my companion seated next to me I managed to get the great oar into position and began to pull in time with the others. As all this was happening, the sails on board *Discovery* were loosed down in the calm air of morning; those still aboard began the walk round the capstan. At the bow of *Discovery,* it suddenly became clear to me that we would be towing the vessel; lines were attached to us as well as the other small boats.

"Pull on there, come along now, I'm watching you, Peter Wright."

I pulled my hardest, once, twice, I missed the water completely, falling back into the boat.

"Ah! Watch what you're doing there, Wright. You're for it now, Wright, its trouble for you."

My companion Betton spoke up for me.

"Ee's a landsman sir, never oared a boat before."

"A landsman ay, get your self up and back into it."

This was my first introduction to Thomas Pitt. He left me alone after this, but later would enter into my life in more ways than I care to disclose at this time. I did not miss the water with the oar again. Occasionally a breeze would spring up but mostly the sea remained mirror calm. After rowing at least ten miles, rounding a headland, we entered Simons Bay, Cape Town. I was in a state of exhaustion when the anchor was let go. *Discovery* anchored in company with seventeen other vessels. My hands, due to the new activity, were back to the same painful condition of blisters and cracks. I again reverted to the sailor's remedy that had cured me before.

Despite my newfound feelings of comradeship, the horrifying news that I was on a three-year voyage of discovery to the western coast of North America, made me determined me to make every effort to run away. Here in Simons Town, I felt my chances of escaping and somehow getting back to England would be at their best. This idea was brought to a speedy conclusion at 11:00 a.m. on a bright and sunny morn. Up to now, punishments had consisted merely of blows with a rope, or cuffs and kicks. On this morning, I was to witness the ceremonial and hideous cruelty of Royal Navy punishment. Not far away from our position lay a vessel, the seventy-six gun, *HMS Gorgon*, My companions and I laboured at the never-ending job of scrubbing the deck with those blasted holystones, a chore which I now detested completely. From the *Gorgon* the call of a boson's pipe clearly echoed across the water, "All hands ahoy to witness punishment."

The men who were my companions suddenly became quiet, the constant banter ceased. Looking across towards the *Gorgon*, I saw her officers had assembled on the quarterdeck. On the fore deck, marines in their red jackets with arms and bayonets fixed lined in ceremony before the crew assembled on the main deck.

It was not easy to observe from my position on my hands and knees.

Later I was to witness other punishments from much closer quarters. My companions did not attempt to watch the proceedings; they remained quiet and diligent at their scrubbing. I was near a gun on the starboard side and could see out of the gun-port. A figure was led up to a grating, normally used to cover access to the ship's hold, now tied vertically to the rigging where it met the main deck. The Captain read from a book, all the officers removed their hats though I could not hear the words. Later I became familiar with the 69th article of war, read prior to punishment for certain crimes, desertion being one of these. The hapless fellow's shirt was stripped from him, a leather apron was fastened about his waist and I was told this was to protect the lower part of his back. Bare to the waist, the unfortunate fellow was secured up to the grating by the wrists and knees. Across the water, the order came loud and clear, "Master-at-arms you will count the strokes. Boatswain's mate. Forty-eight of your best. Carry on."

Until now, I had been on the receiving end of the rope used by our quartermaster and boatswain's mates. I had suffered kicks and punches; this though, was beyond all my comprehension. A heavy-set man stepped forward, carrying what appeared to be a red bag, from which he withdrew an implement. It appeared to be lengths of rope, attached to a handle. Approaching the bound, luckless man, he lay back and swung with all his strength. The rope whistled through the air to cross the shoulders of the helpless fellow. Repeatedly, in a regular rhythm, the arm delivered the dreadful blows; no sound came from the recipient. After each swipe, the wielder of this dreadful implement would wipe the throngs through his fingers and he would flick them. From my distance away, I could clearly see his hand red with blood. The count of twenty-four came, now another man stepped forward, took the dreadful implement and proceeded to continue with the punishment, this man was left handed. This change had the effect of the blows crossing the direction of the previous blows. A most dreadful sound echoed across the blue, tranquil water of Simon's Bay. A horrible cry, not that of a man, more the cry of a wounded animal. Eight times the hideous sound floated across to us and then silence, as the scourging continued to its end. I could not take my eyes from the scene; I was shocked and mesmerized by the cruelty of the procedure.

The marines turned and left the foredeck. Officers moved from the quarterdeck, as did the men on the main deck, except for the few who took the man down from his place of torment. Buckets of seawater hauled aboard were thrown over the unconscious man, before he was carried below. I never did find out what this unfortunate fellow had done, but I had second thoughts on desertion as a way out of my situation. It was two days later that our journey resumed. This occurred much sooner than anticipated and it was with some degree of joy, we again sailed out into the vastness of the Great Southern Ocean.

"My dear Peter, I can barely believe it; you were on the famous, recently completed voyage of Captain Vancouver and his men. There have been many articles in gazettes and other publications, mostly by Dr. Menzies and Sir Joseph Banks on the wonders seen and experienced. It was all the news some years ago; the fleet mobilized, ready to do battle with the Spanish over some place the name escapes me Cooka...Nooka."

"Nootka, Sir Neville, Nootka."

"Ah, yes Nootka. War was averted by the diplomacy of Baron Saint Helens at the court of Madrid. Yes, I remember. Captain Vancouver, a Kings Lynn man, sent out to accept the surrender of the place from the Spaniards. You my boy. On that voyage?" Neville Brown excitedly gestured towards the host. "Bless my soul, I cannot believe it."

"Refill our tankards if you please Mr. Potter. There has been some scandal in connection with Captain Vancouver, I must say that I do not know any of the details of this, it does not make news outside the naval circles and London."

"At the end of next month, it will be six years since I left the shores of old England. In all the years at sea, one thought constantly plagued my days and nights. Why and who was the villain that dispatched me on this voyage, plucked me from family and friends and future. It was the thought of revenge on this scoundrel that kept me from losing my sanity. The words of my original tormentor in the lane near the Temple Buildings. Words that still sound loud and clear in my mind, the name, 'March, and he is generous.' I still wonder who this person is and I will discover him, so help me I will."

Peter Wright thought silently for a moment and then continued

"These thoughts of revenge and hatred, once so foreign to me have become a part of my life, thoughts of the church long since gone from my consideration. I have lived with countrymen of mine that one could only consider a degree above the uncivilized savages we were to meet. The courage of Loyola or the philanthropy of Howard and the eloquence of Saint Paul would prove inadequate to the task of creating Christians of these souls, where constraint, disease, ignorance, insensibility, tyranny, sameness, dirt and foul air exist. In addition, the dangers of ocean, fire, mutiny, pestilence, battle and exile are constant companions. I firmly believe the savages met with on our voyage were, though pagan in nature, more Christian and gentle than our selves."

"You must forgive me, but I am excited by all this. You left a boy now look at you a man, full grown. I must hear more of your tale. Pray continue."

"Some days before leaving Cape Town, a vessel arrived from the East Indies, a Dutch ship. Almost as soon as it arrived, people began to fall ill, on the other vessels in port as well as those on shore. Our captain declared he would leave port as quickly as possible. Numerous fellows from the fo'c'sil as well as officers succumbed to this malady of fever, dysentery and tremors. I did not get sick, even for one moment. This is the reason I say I was delighted to get away from the dreadful pestilence devastating the Cape. Fully half of our crew succumbed to this condition.

Our course took us well south of Africa and the weather became cold. The vessel was propelled at a prodigious speed across the latitudes at the bottom of the southern world by the fierce storms and gales, which circle the globe in these latitudes. As fewer men were available to man the ship, I was called upon to do things far beyond my capabilities. My natural physical abilities and youth, with the gift of being able to absorb, remember and perform, caused me to be placed with the wasters, those older men and those who were not as skilled high in the rigging. Wasters generally were not called on to go aloft, but were deck men, hauling and pulling the lines. The condition of my companions was such that soon I was called upon to climb into the rigging in the most terrible and frightening conditions imaginable, with those amazing men, called the fore-top-men

I will not dwell on a moment-by-moment description of my time at sea, but let me inform you that the first time I was directed to go aloft, I feared that this would be the final moments of my existence. The seas were enormous and our vessel was propelled along at a prodigious speed, diving deep into the troughs of watery mountains, which, from a vantage point high in the rigging completely obscured the vessel below.

"Unbend the top gallant gear. I fear we will lose it if this gale keeps on." Mr. Baker, one of the lieutenants, called out, "Get those men up there, hurry it up now."

"Aye aye Mister Baker, I will have to use the idler there."

"I don't care who you use, if we stay as we are the gallants will go."

"Wright! Get with these men, do what they tell you. Just remember one hand for yourself and one for the ship. Get to it, up you go." With these few words, I was directed to the most fearful experience of my young years.

I grasped the ratlines in a death grip. Gingerly, I hauled myself towards a small platform high in the rigging. I later learned that this was called the top, a grating that rested on the crosstrees and trestle trees, shipboard names that mean so much to me now. At this early stage of my sea life, I was becoming familiar with the parts of the vessel. I finally made the top, sweating with fear despite the cold, wet, tumultuous conditions. I hugged the mast for dear life as it swung sickeningly in wide arcs. The sails all about me taut one moment, then loose and flapping the next, as the vessel plunged into each subsequent trough.

My companions were fearless. Without hesitation they ventured out along the swinging yards, onto the foot-rope to begin the task of furling the sail, a hard and demanding task in calm weather, but for me absolutely terrifying in the present gale. A foot-rope is a rope line, which is suspended beneath the boom and behind the sail. The sea thundered, the wind whistled, shrieked and roared. From my position high atop, the ocean presented a fear-inspiring spectacle in every direction. Giant waves raced past *Discovery*. The crests blew off horizontally to become salty rain, which assailed us even at the height of the topgallants. The violent surface of the sea covered in flying spume and foam, vied with the racing, angry clouds to claim our vessel.

"Come on Petee, git out there onto the foot-rope, stay here near the top, matee."

The men had moved out along the yard, standing on a thin rope strung below in such a manner as to allow one to lean over and grasp the billowing sail in hand. The sail, loosened by those on deck, surged and cracked like a rampaging monster making every effort to escape its fate. The roar and scream of the wind, the thunderous noise of the sails well nigh precluded communication between the men spread out along the gyrating yard. Gripped with fear I knew the slightest mistake would mean the end of my life. I knelt and grasped the mast, frozen in abject terror.

"Out you go Petee. Get yourself onto the foot-rope. We got to do this or the ship is finished and so are we. Get out there; get on with it you sniveling sod."

The man at my side grasped me by the collar, dragging me to the very edge of the terrible abyss below.

"I can't do it, I can't do it." I screamed trying desperately to regain my hold on the mast.

"Yes yer can, yer as safe as houses, lad."

A further pull from my companion almost threw me out into space.

Desperately I found a footing on the rope. I saw the men in the gloom dragging the sail upwards into a bundle along the top of the boom. In a terrified daze, I follow their example. The writhing canvas of the sail tears at me as I drag at the canvas, I battle to keep on the gyrating footrope and get the sail in its proper folded position. The sail is finally captured and tied to the yard. In my ignorance I assumed all was over, we would go down to the deck. How mistaken I was, another set of orders commenced the task of lowering the topgallant gear. Again, I was directed to carry out death-defying feats, which later would become second nature to me.

"Stop the yard rope out, here I'll tie it with a bow line about the foot-rope and send it down the lubber's hole. Ere Petee, grab this, when I say aul, aul it up."

I grasped the line from my desperate position on the top.

"Haul taut the yard rope. Lower away." The yard was sent down to the deck. The more I saw of these men of the sea, the more I admired their expertise. We were not finished yet.

"Clear away the top gallant stays and royal back-stays."

These were loosed with more orders and more heaving and pulling. "Haul taut the mast ropes. Sway away. Lower away." Almost instantly the topmast was lowered to the deck. The procedure was repeated at all three masts. *Discovery* reacted to our work and rode the waves almost effortlessly. At last I was down on the deck again. It was with a feeling of relief but also a sense of accomplishment that I descended to the pitching deck. In a strange way I felt sorry it was all over, a feeling of having met a challenge and come through filled me with a satisfaction I had never before experienced. Observing my fingernails, I found that I had lost three on my left hand. I had not been aware of this in the numbing cold and wet, but now pain had begun to set in.

As I made my way to the fo'c'sil Lieutenant Baker, wet and disheveled came towards me.

"Wright, till you're told otherwise you will be with the top-men, you did well. I will inform the quartermaster of this. What is the matter with your hand? Come man, show me your hand."

"Ummm? go to Dr. Menzies, he will give you a tincture for them." Baker turned on his heel and was gone.

Surgeon Cranston, who had stitched my wounds when first I came on board, was seriously afflicted, as were half the crew with the fever contracted in Cape Town. Dr. Menzies, originally the botanist of the expedition, had now assumed the added role of surgeon. The surgeon lived and worked in a closet at the after end of the vessel, close by Captain Vancouver's great aft cabin. I knocked on the door. Dr. Cranston would leave *Discovery* at a later date on board the store ship *HMS Daedalus* bound for Port Jackson He never recovered from the fever contracted in Cape Town and was declared unserviceable.

"Who is it? Enter."

I entered the dark compartment, which served as his home, office and surgery. Here I was confronted by a graying, tall, dour figure intent on a journal that he held high to the light of the swinging lantern. An untidy mass of papers, books, journals drew my attention.

"What do you want?"

"Sir, Mr. Baker said I should attend you. He suggested that you could furnish me with a tincture for my fingers. I seem to have mislaid three fingernails." I spoke in my normal tone. This seemed to startle the surgeon considering my dress, which was worse than the lowest member of the crew.

"Who are you?" Dr. Menzies barked the question at me.

"Sir, I have had the misfortune to injure my hand, perhaps you would look at it." I proffered my hand to the seated doctor. He looked at me, searched my face somewhat taken aback at the diction emanating from the disreputable character before him.

"Yes, painful I dare say." He rummaged in a chest for some moments. "This will sting, come hold out your hand."

Without ceremony, he poured a yellow, acrid balm over my damaged hand. The stinging pain was instant. I cried out and began to fan my hand.

"Come now, it can't be all that bad. Give me your name for my journal. What is your rating? You can go back to your place now."

The doctor entered some details in his journal as I turned towards the doorway.

"One moment. Your speech is not of the fo'c'sil, you can read and write?"

"Yes, sir, that I can. It is a fact before I found myself in my present miserable situation; I attended Jesus College at Cambridge. I was being schooled in law and divinity."

"Ummm, law and divinity. What an unhappy combination. Your nemesis was a press gang I imagine. Go back to your place; your education will have no bearing on your situation here."

I returned to the fo'c'sil, where I received accolades of a type for my efforts at the masthead.

"Ere's the lad, wasn't too bad aye."

From one, "Gets easier every time, matee."

And from another, "You did alright, just remember keep one hand for yerself."

I felt a pride and fullness in my heart at the compliments of these hard men, all little older than I, but so much more learned in the ways of the sea.

11
Jane Sawtell's Future is Discussed

"I would approach you on a most delicate matter, sir. It has been my privilege to come to know and enjoy the society of your family for some six months. During that time, as I earlier intimated to you, I have pursued our dear Jane with every degree of decorum and propriety. I am sure you have observed the scale of the friendship between Jane and me. I must tell you this is no longer a friendship, it has deepened to affection and blossomed into and dare I say, love.

"Ah Henry, I cannot be accused of being unaware of the feelings building between you."

"Sir, then I can only lay before you with veracity that Jane and I have spoken at length and are of the same mind. I ask for the hand of your daughter in wedlock. I throw myself on your mercy, sir. I await an answer that will ensure the happiness of two souls hopelessly in love."

"Say no more, my boy. She is yours with every blessing possible. My dear wife and I are delighted with this news, delighted I say." Edward Sawtell grasped the hand of Captain Henry West. "I think as men of the world, a nip of fine scotch whiskey is in order to seal this marvelous news."

"Thank you, sir. You have made me the happiest man on the face of God's earth. I must rush to Jane with this information as my first order of business. There will be plenty of time to discuss the terms and arrangements to be made, I must fly to Jane."

Henry West turned and left the room. Edward Sawtell did not see the smile on the face of his son-in-law to be, the satisfied smile of a miscreant who could see his nefarious plans coming to a successful conclusion. Henry West did not see the smile on the face of Edward Sawtell. Edward was not in the slightest way dishonest; he carried out every business transaction with the utmost integrity and aplomb. His was the smile of a man of means, who could see an immediate change in his social standing. Edward Sawtell would do all in his power to make sure his only daughter and this man would marry. He then, would be related by marriage to a noble family with all its attendant benefits

"Mrs. Sawtell, it has happened. It has finally happened."

"What has happened Edward? Calm yourself my dear and tell me what it is that has so aroused you. Is it what I think it is, pray tell me?"

"Our Jane will be married to Captain West, he asked for her hand just these few moments past and of course I gave him my full blessing on it all. He is as we speak, proposing to her. Oh, I am delighted, me dear. Well what do you have to say?"

"My dear little girl to be wed, I just hope it is what she wants. I still have a strange feeling about Captain West. He is a perfect gentleman, but there is something on which I cannot put my finger. It turns me away whenever he converses with me."

"No more of that now me dear, it will happen, of that I'm sure and we will rise in stature in Norfolk and doors will open in London, which till this joyous occasion could never have been contemplated. Perhaps quarters in a fashionable part of London might be of advantage, now that we will be moving in more elevated circles."

Edward Sawtell prattled on, completely overcome at his good fortune and the thought of an exciting future. While he was acquainted with the gentry of Norfolk, he had never been considered part of that class. Now he was sure the doors of those influential local families, the Hogges, Cokes and Turners and others would soon be opened to him.

Mrs. Sawtell remained silent. Her nagging doubts about Henry West spoiled the joy that she would normally have experienced at such an excellent match for her only daughter.

12
Discovery Arrives in New Holland and Peter Fights the Honourable Thomas Pitt

"Land Ho, off the larboard bow."
The call brought all hands to the deck. At first, I could not discern anything though the perpetual sea mist. I shaded my eyes from the sun high in the heavens and could distinguish nothing that would prompt the call. Suddenly there it was a darker blue smudge to the northeast.

The voyage across the southern ocean with most of the men sick had been exhausting. For some reason, known only to God, I remained well throughout the journey. I found that after a time I had no fear high in the rigging and the prestige my newfound accomplishment acquired by me rendered my life rather more satisfying.

The weather on this morning was gentle with a light breeze, and a large oily swell from the south. Such a contrast when compared to perpetual storms and violence of the last two months. The health of the ill deteriorated in the constant dampness and perpetual heaving and rolling of the vessel. Those healthy few rose to the occasion and managed the added work in a manner that could only be described as heroic. All felt the eventual death of a Marine Neil Coil. Those suffering the terrible disorders that assailed them were especially concerned; for perhaps they would be next to depart this tenuous life.

Our Captain, Vancouver, made every effort to curtail and nullify the deteriorating condition of the sick. Fires were ordered set below deck to warm and dry the ship. He was adamant that cleanliness be of prime concern. Ships Surgeon Cranston was in a sad condition and showed every sign of departing this life. It was with some joy that we approached that part of the world called New Holland. I was told that the only inhabited port in this country was Port Jackson. The loss of our American colonies had made it a necessity to find a new depository for felons from the overcrowded goals and prison ships of England. The discoveries of Captain Cook at Botany Bay had opened up a new land. Though still a full month's sail away to the east, the idea of a stay at Port Jackson was looked forward to with anticipation by all.

Our vessel slowly approached the land. The terrain revealed itself as high cliffs devoid of growth assailed by tremendous surf, which sent a spray high into the air to be swept inland as a wispy, blue-grey mantle over the brown of the land. It was a strange feeling for me to be in a place so remote and uninhabited by polite society. The men in the fo'c'sil talked of cannibals and the dreadful consequences of being taken by them.

Eventually the anchor was let go and *Discovery* brought to, in line with our consort *Chatham*, which had led the way into this sheltered bay. Because of her smaller draught, *Chatham* would often lead the way in our entries into strange uncharted places. The sick were taken ashore to recover in the warm sun. Restocking the ships with water and wood, the search for edible plants, fishing and the collection of oysters, crabs and other denizens of the deep became the prime concern of all capable of sustained work. The officers were rowed about the sound by seamen, charts were prepared and anchorages noted. For my part, my companions and I rowed Dr. Menzies on an investigation of this strange, wild, deserted, starkly beautiful land.

One of the most disagreeable tasks was my daily effort to keep clean the seats of ease, toilet facilities for both the officers and men. This had been my lot since coming on board and carried with it the ironic title, "Captain of the Heads." Here in New Holland and I thanked God for it, I was relieved of this odious duty. Dr. Menzies requested that I accompany him on an investigation of the plant life of this most southern of lands. My duty was to act as his servant and scribe. You cannot believe the relief I felt at not, any longer, having to scrub and clean these disgusting places. The man who took my place became my most ardent enemy and did everything he could to discredit me, but I will tell you more of that later.

The land was possessed for King George with ceremony. Flags were raised and shots fired. Our stay here saw an instant change in the health of the sick. Our rations were supplemented with an abundance of seafood and the rest, sunshine and land exercise had an instant effect on the health of all, although it was quite some time before the most ill were back to normal. At no time did we see the slightest sign of the native inhabitants of New Holland, although rude shelters and the residue of fires were evident. I served Dr. Menzies, collecting specimens and recording findings as well as collecting oysters and other seafood for our general larder.

This was a strange land of fearsome craggy cliffs molded by the constant onslaught of the mighty seas, which swept north from the Antarctic. Beyond the influence of the gales and sea, I have never before observed such flowers growing wildly in profusion, yet at the same time a land so arid and harsh. It was as though nature had designed species to suit here alone. Dr. Menzies ran from plant to bush to plant, as excited as any child when presented with a new toy. The trees were scrubby and low but with the most beautiful lemon scent. When fires were lit, the native timber gave off the pleasing odour of eucalyptus. Dr. Menzies demanded excellence in anything done, whether it was service to him personally or writing the many detailed descriptions of the plant specimens collected and stored in the glass compartment assembled for this purpose on the aft quarterdeck.

My thoughts of escape were becoming infrequent. I realized that to set out into the wilderness of New Holland would mean certain death, if not from starvation, then from the wrath of its native inhabitants. With this in mind, I determined to make the best of my situation.

I was amazed at the bird life in this remote land. Parakeets of every colour and size flashed past us in great flocks, their raucous calls drowning out our voices. A strange dead animal was discovered by Mr. Mudge, an officer who seemed to possess a soft heart and was generally well respected by the sailors of the fo'c'sil. It had two short legs high on its chest, two large, muscular hind legs and a long thick tail. Standing, it stood some four feet tall with a small head, and resembled a rat. Dr. Menzies said it was a kangaroo.

Our sick people had commenced their recovery. After about ten days, all were considered well enough and the journey was resumed. I seemed to have become established as a servant to Dr. Menzies, although once at sea, I again reverted to working in the foretop when required, along with the usual day-to-day upkeep required to keep the vessel in good order. In the fo'c'sil, there was an air of excitement. It had always been rumoured that our next port of call would be Port Jackson on the east coast of the land discovered by Captain Cook. It seemed our vessels would visit the penal colony, where, I was informed, rum was the currency and used as barter for anything. This was exciting from the seamen's point of view, for any woman could be had for a nip of rum. To this end, the men began to save their daily ration of rum.

The land in most places resembled the country at Cape Town, wild and desolate, great craggy cliffs assaulted by enormous seas, sweeping up from the icy southern latitudes. Our course was out of sight of land again. In an unusual moment of camaraderie, Dr. Menzies mentioned that enormous reefs and rocky islets were known to exist in this area, which stretched well out into the Great Southern Ocean. Now the sight of land faded from view and it was quite some time before we passed close by the land first seen by Abel Tasman.

In violent weather, we sailed away into the tumultuous ocean in an easterly direction. Great was the disappointment in the fo'c'sil when it was realized that there would be no stay at Port Jackson. In my new position I began to receive requests from the men in the fo'c'sil for news, any information at all as to what was happening. Sailors, I have discovered, are notorious gossips and will enlarge most dreadfully on any snippet of information, no matter how trivial. Now I was in a position to overhear conversation between officers, which would give some indication as to what was about to happen to us.

The weather again became dreadful. Sails were reefed and eventually top-masts were struck. About twenty-one days after leaving New Holland, land was sighted in the east I was told it was Dusky Bay, the southern most extremity of the land of New Zealand, discovered and charted by Captain Cook some years prior.

I feel I must tell you something of the Captain of *Discovery*. Where to begin? I suppose to call him complex would be to do the man an injustice. He was a man molded by naval rules and regulations. Up until now I had not been addressed by the man, it was as though I did not exist. Our vessel was not large, so to a layman it must appear inconceivable when I say I rarely saw him, except from afar on the quarterdeck. He would pace the quarterdeck hour after hour. It was when I began my duties with Dr. Menzies that I first encountered him. I must tell you that for any seaman to go on this deck without reason or permission invited punishment. It was the preserve of the officers and those little buggers, the midshipmen. I had access to this hallowed sanctum, for it was now my duty to tend the various plants and shrubs collected in New Holland.

Captain Vancouver was a portly man, solidly built, but with an unnatural colour. I knew later how sick a man he was; sometimes he would take to his cabin for days at a time. The vessel would be in charge of the junior officers during his absences. On his reappearance, he would look drawn, pale and not long for this world, but would always seem to recover. Vancouver was diligent in the extreme regarding cleanliness. My companions in the fo'c'sil thought him a good captain; they considered our fare the best of any vessel. Extra stores were divided between officers and men, fish, vegetables, waterfowl, shellfish and mussels, even venison, later acquired in New Norfolk. Captain Vancouver was adamant that all share the same. He was cognizant of the health of the men at all times and was sympathetic towards those ill or injured, giving them every chance to recover, though added rations, medical attention and relief from their normal days work.

He was highly intelligent and a navy man through and through. I was to learn the extent the Navy had controlled this man's life. During our voyage, he was no more than 38 years of age. I was told later that he had entered the navy as a midshipman at the age of 14 and had actually spent 22 of his years at sea. He was a Norfolk man, a resident of the town of Kings Lynn and had attended Grammar School in his early years, as did I. When now I compare my forced few years at sea, I can only admire the attention to duty and service, which drove him and ruled his very existence. Men like this keep our nation and its navy the envy of the world.

Do your duty well and cheerfully. Do not do your duty; punishment would soon follow as proscribed in the naval articles of war. Extra duty, chaining, either below deck or above in any weather, hours aloft at the crosstrees and the lash, the fiercest, most dreaded of all. I had witnessed punishment from afar at Cape Town, but I was to see the full force of naval discipline a number of times at close hand and I was to receive my share of it as well. Captain Vancouver, when aroused, had a foul tongue, much to the embarrassment of some of the younger officers. For some trifling misdemeanor he would berate them with the foulest of epitaphs for minutes at a time. The young man at fault would stand first on one leg then the other until the abuse was over. Almost instantly, all thought of what had gone previously was forgotten. Captain Vancouver would again be a jovial, almost good-natured commander, even to the man he had just chastised.

In Dusky Bay, I again acted as servant to Dr. Menzies, as well as assisting in the brewing of a concoction to be used in place of our normal issue of rum. I have since discovered that Captain Cook left a recipe for a type of spruce beer, prepared from the spruce tree with the added benefit of the tea-tree and wort plants. Quite palatable and I must tell you much more effective on the senses than rum. Our vessels were assailed with gales in these southern cold lands, even while at anchor I feared that all would be lost. We would spend our days marooned in this lonely, desolate, dreary place at the end of the world, scrubbing, cleaning, replenishing wood supplies, fishing and the usual rowing expeditions. I learnt that our captain had been to this country before, four times with Captain Cook. This was his fifth visit, but the first in command of a vessel. This gave me some sense of confidence in the man who would have control over my life for the foreseeable future.

Probably the most disruptive group on our vessel was the midshipmen, fifteen young men of privilege. They shared the work of the vessel in every way except that each day they were tutored in navigation and seamanship. They had ready access to the quarterdeck and to all intents and purposes were officers. Most were inoffensive enough, but some were obnoxious in the extreme. All were from well-to-do families; some were related to noble houses. But to a man they were aware of the fact they occupied a favoured class on the vessel. Woe betides any seaman who fell out with these god-like creatures.

The natural leader of the midshipmen was the fellow I spoke of earlier, Tom Pitt. I was a little older then he, but he was a big chap, well over six feet and immensely strong. Thomas Pitt was heir to a vast fortune and a title, as well as a seat in the House of Lords. He was related to the Prime Minister, William Pitt, also the foreign secretary and one of the Lords of the Admiralty and such a complicated fellow. Thomas was a brilliant scholar and above all, a rebel. High jinx, tricks, and constant practical jokes perpetrated on his fellow midshipmen made him feared, looked up to, and their undisputed leader. He had a superior air even with the officers and later on would fall out with the Captain.

Pitt rode roughshod over men in the fo'c'sil, but would display a sympathetic nature to anyone injured, punished, or sick. He liked to fight and displayed a degree of expertise at pugilism. He would often, completely against orders and when the officers were otherwise engaged, arrange a bout with some seaman. The young Pitt usually won with ease. The man beaten was never challenged again and would become attached to Pitt in a somewhat unnatural manner.

Pitt had left me alone since our first contact at Cape Town, but in Dusky Bay, I had the misfortune to be the recipient of Mr. Pitt's attention. All the officers were away on small boat excursions about the waterway in which we had anchored the vessels. I had returned in company with Dr. Menzies. I was left to store and catalogue the various flora gathered, while he joined some officers on another excursion. I completed my assigned tasks and proceeded to go below with the tools used to pot and tend the selected plants. Entering the hold where these implements were stored, I stumbled upon a group of four sailors conversing with Pitt and two midshipmen companions, a Scottish lad John Stewart and Edward Barrie, a high spirited youth who had run away to sea at fourteen.

"Here's a pretty sight. It's old Meany's fellow." (Meany was a nickname for Dr. Menzies.) Tom Pitt broke away from the group and came towards me. "Have you done your gardening, Mary dear? I think this snotty chap needs a lesson in good manners. What do you say; shall I give him a good beating?"

It was too late for me to retreat. I decided to take no notice of them and go about my business as fast as possible. I arranged the tools in their place, as I turned I found my way blocked by the seamen and Pitt's midshipmen companions, leaving Pitt and I face to face.

"Come on now; let's see if you fight as poorly as you row." He adopted the stance of a pugilist, fists raised before him. "You're not going to squirm your way out of this. Now put up your fists and protect yourself."

"I have no argument with you, sir. I would go atop and continue my work. Allow me to pass, sir."

I backed up only to be pushed from behind by the others towards the menacing Pitt. He struck me a good blow on the cheek, spinning my head and making my ears ring. I staggered back only to be shoved forward again. This time he hit me full on the nose. I knew at this point that I would have to defend myself, and at least give a good showing, or for as long as this voyage lasted my situation would be untenable. With a bleeding nose, I was again pushed forward towards Pitt who swung a wide blow at my head. I saw it coming and ducked beneath the blow at the same time driving my fist upwards, catching my adversary at the spot where his rib cage met over his stomach. A great whoop of wind exhaled from his mouth, he doubled over grasping his abdomen. Seizing the opportunity I delivered a second blow to the side of his face, his head spun around and as he staggered back, I hit him again flush on the jaw. His knees sagged and instinctively I pushed rather than hit him again. He fell to the deck, where he lay gasping for breath.

"Leave me alone. I don't want to fight; I don't want to be here, so just leave me alone." I turned to face the people blocking my way. They stood with a look of bewilderment and awe. The fighter Pitt still lay gasping for breath as I pushed past them out onto the deck.

I expected to be challenged, placed on report and tormented at every turn by Thomas Pitt, but this did not happen, in fact, he would nod to me whenever we came abreast of each other. After this incident I seemed to have a better standing in the fo'c'sil. Daily it seemed I was becoming more accepted as part of the crew, but most of all I thanked providence that I had met and caroused with the Honourable Harry Boyd and learnt the rudiments of fisticuffs.

Dusky Bay was a strange conglomeration of bays, channels and waterways. Captain Cook had been confused when he tried to unravel and chart the area, eventually giving up and continuing his voyage of exploration. In frustration, he named this perplexing area, "Nobody Knows What."

To the great credit of our Captain and the efforts of the boat crews, the place became clear and was charted accurately. Captain Vancouver, always devoted to his teacher and mentor, re-named the place "Somebody Knows What."

Our stay at Dusky bay lasted until November 22nd when again, in the first agreeable weather in two weeks, sails were set and our vessels gently eased out to sea. Our course took us south into the most violent weather and seas. We were so remote from civilization, two hundred miles south of the land of New Zealand; we were as remote from our homes in England as it was possible for any man on this earth to be. I wondered if I would ever see the green and pleasant land of Norfolk.

13

Jane is Smitten

Jane was a beautiful girl, warm, generous and openhearted. She was a country girl, but this in no way detracted from her fine style and manner. She had been brought up forthright and honest with a comportment molded by a mother from the upper strata of society and a kind and doting father. She was ripe pickings for a man such as Henry West. Jane was candid, clear thinking and she grasped life with trusting eagerness. Henry had no difficulty sweeping this untried girl off her feet. Henry West was experienced in the ways of the heart; he was older than Jane was by some fifteen years and outwardly an urbane, sophisticated man. His world was far removed from the almost cloistered atmosphere of the Medway Estate and the influence of an adoring mother and father. Jane was accustomed to the boyish banter and charm of the unsophisticated Peter Wright who had been her only companion for so many years. Henry West trifled with her as lightly and as easily as he would a new toy or a pony.

"My dearest Jane, how cruel you are to a person whose heart you have captured. I can see no impediment to an early marriage. I am an inferno, my pet. I can wait no longer to consummate our love. I am a man of passion and the world, not some schoolboy to be held at bay."

"Henry you hold me so tight, your hands wander to places that send blushes to my cheeks and you make me tremble. I fear I will fall to the ground."

"If you should fall, them I will most certainly fall before you so you may fall atop me. Come my dear let us marry within the month, then the fall can be taken in our mutual bedchamber."

"I understand how you feel, dear Henry, but my parents are so desirous of us marrying in the great cathedral at Norwich. You must forgive them for wanting to lavish ceremony on their only daughter and child. Soon I shall be gone from them. It is little to ask that we wait till next June, just seven months away."

"Seven months? Seven months! Never! What do you do to me; I cannot wait seven weeks, not seven minutes, let alone seven months. I have certain commitments both in business and my military calling that demand my presence in other parts. I must have you with me my love, let us go to your father and throw ourselves on his mercy. We could be wed within the month in the dear little church of Saint Mary's Westgate in Burnham Market. Then all bliss would be ours."

"Henry it is beginning to rain, come let us hurry or we will be soaked. It gets heavier. Let us make for the summer house at the bottom of the garden, come my love, over there."

"At last, here we are, my God what a downpour. I fear we are wet. Here my dear, let me put my coat about your shoulders." Henry stood behind Jane, he draped his jacket over her shoulders, his arms embraced her, one hand grasped her silk clad breast, he tilted her face to his, kissing her deeply and long."

"Oh my goodness. Henry you take my breath away, but it is a breathlessness I desire." The two sank to the garden seat without breaking their embrace.

"Beautiful Jane, here we are alone. It is raining and we are away from prying eyes. Let me introduce you to the wonders that await you when we are finally bedded in our own place." Henry West did not hesitate nor did he stop kissing her. His hand found its way beneath her gown. He raised her dress over white clad legs, with a hand that disappeared into the silk folds of her garment and between parting thighs.

"Henry, Henry, what are you doing? I am dying, yes, yes."

Henry West knew they would be married within the month. He knew the young woman writhing in his arms, moaning and sighing into his kisses with each movement of his hand, would arrange it.

14

Port Jackson is Not Visited and the Honorable Thomas Pitt is Punished

With the health of the convalescents re-established there seemed to be a change in the general attitude of the men. We left New Zealand, with all thoughts of a stay in Port Jackson gone from our mind, to plunge into the great swells, storms and dangers of the vast Southern Pacific Ocean. All seemed to have come to terms with the fact that we were entering into a region offering no port or succor, except that provided for by ourselves. The officers seemed more approachable and the ordinary seamen threw themselves into their work with a cheery attitude. For my part, I had resigned myself to my fate. I had through unusual circumstances, attained some stature. I resolved to make the most of it and do my work well; realizing that the only way for me to return to my family and loved ones was through my own efforts.

Storms and ferocious gales again assailed *Discovery*. Our vessel, after days at sea, passed close by some rocky islets over which tremendous waves crashed and thundered. I shuddered to think of the consequences of us hitting these deadly obstacles, when they were invisible during the night. I later learned that these terrible rocks had never been seen before. Captain Vancouver named these deadly obstacles *'The Snares.'* I overheard a conversation between Captain Vancouver and Lieutenant Johnstone. Vancouver remarked that Captain Cook had named a similar group of rocks south of but closer to New Zealand, *'The Traps,'* so he considered it appropriate to call his discovery, *'The Snares.'*

Eventually the weather improved as we began to make our way to the north. The days grew warmer and the seas assumed a more gentle nature as waves reverted to the deep, purple blue of the tropics, crested with vivid, dancing, white foam. The sunsets and sunrises, which defied imagination, were rich with every colour of the rainbow, and brought even the roughest sailor to silent awe. Nights blazed with stars, the iridescent milky haze from horizon to horizon, always graced by the wondrous Crux or Southern Cross. The brightness of these heavenly orbs against the background of the Milky Way with it's wealth of stars, is the most wondrous of sights in the dark tropic night.

An excitement gripped the vessel; some of the old salts knew that we were approaching the Islands of Otaheite. Some of our mates had been to these islands with Cook in 1780 and told marvelous stories. The fo'c'sil thrilled to anecdotes nearly all relating to the feminine charms of the ladies of these islands. At mess, we were regaled with stories, which seemed to describe a place somewhere between the Garden of Eden and the Land of the Lotus-Eaters.

It was about this time that Captain Vancouver issued a most unpopular directive, unpopular both above and below deck. This directive was posted for those with reading skills, but read aloud to the fo'c'sil by the quartermaster. It related to conduct during our visit to the Island of Otaheite. Our Captain laid down rules of behaviour, rules, which seemed quite in order to me, but to some of my companions quite the opposite. It forbade private trade of any kind. Any trade was to be carried on by appointed officers, to retain the value of the goods offered. I was agreeably gratified that all efforts were to be made to encourage friendship between natives and visitors. We were encouraged to treat these children of nature with every degree of kindness and humanity. It also stated that any person working ashore must at all times take care not to lose, mislay or cause to be stolen, arms, tools or implements. All those who broke these orders in any way would be punished in the strictest manner. All were subject to these regulations, officers and men alike.

These orders were issued on Christmas Day, 1791, as *Discovery* approached a tiny smudge on the line of the horizon. All day and night *Discovery* worked up towards her destination. The soft, lush, purple blackness of night faded to reveal a fluffy line of fair weather clouds, bright with the gold of the sun still below the sea. As the deep red arc slowly raised itself above the horizon, the blue grey of the clouds changed to vermilion, then to brilliant pink. The sun, a giant golden orb appeared fastened to a golden sea until suddenly it breaks the thread of night and is almost instantly high in the sky and all is blue and shining. The great cross, Crux in Centaurus was the last heavenly object to pale before the onslaught of day.

It is beyond me to tell you of the beauty of this place. It is mountainous and rises with spires and crags out of the ocean like magic. I saw the coconut tree for the first time, those graceful palms waving their salute in the morning breeze. Beneath palm-fronded huts, we saw the movement of people. Our vessel skirted a reef where the surf broke in fury, but past this was a tranquil, inviting waterway, which served as a highway for commerce and play for the local children. They waved to us as we tacked towards a brush-covered point of land. The palms served as shelter for the rustic dwellings and the flat of the near beach gave way to rising land all the way to the glorious mountains behind.

The entrance to a vast bay opened before the vessels. Canoes began to paddle out to meet us in what I hoped was a welcoming gesture; I did not know what to expect of these people. The canoes gathered about our vessel and accompanied it into the bay. *Discovery* was brought about into the wind and the anchor let loose as the men carried out the task of stowing and furling the sails. As was now usual, I was high aloft but with one eye on the bare-breasted women and stalwart, tall, handsome men, who now piled over the side of *Discovery*. I could not believe that I was seeing, for the first time in my life, the unclad breast of a woman. The smiling, innocent faces, the laughter and congeniality of these natives laid all my fears to rest as to the welcome we would receive.

Here in Otaheite an event occurred that had a bearing on the lives of both Captain Vancouver and me. For me it brought home the unrelenting and savage law of the navy and made Tom Pitt a friend. For Captain Vancouver, it was an incident, which would influence his life until the end of his days.

Our vessels had anchored in the wonderful inlet called Matavai Bay. Canoes of every description surrounded *Discovery* and *Chatham*. A royal canoe, rich in decoration and crowded with the dignitaries of the kingdom, high-prowed war canoes thick with warriors armed with clubs, spears and other implements of war as well as hundreds of smaller, crowded outrigger canoes, all vied for a position near our vessel. The decks of both *Discovery* and *Chatham* answered the spectacle presented by the natives. Officers were resplendent in their best blue jackets rich with gold trim, white breeches and white stockings, black, silver-buckled shoes. All eyes focused on the bare-breasted beauties swimming or canoeing towards the vessels. For young men who had spent so many months confined to the sea, the sight of these beautiful women can only be imagined. The natives literally swarmed aboard, they smiled and chattered with each other in their native tongue and made every effort to talk with the officers and sailors.

From my position, I could see Captain Vancouver who was addressing a major island dignitary. I was amazed how he seemed to have such a grasp of the native language. The dignitary, who was an enormous man, had a smattering of English. Suddenly the Captain stopped his efforts at being understood and glared at a group of midshipmen on the larboard side. I turned in time to observe Tom Pitt throw a piece of hoop iron towards a dusky bare-breasted woman in a canoe below. Her dark smoldering eyes gazed up at the handsome young man. It was obvious the Captain was furious, his face reddened, he turned to Lieutenant Johnstone and spoke to him, pointing at Pitt. Pitt was flogged for this misdemeanor. I later came to know Pitt quite well and I soon realized that he was a person of remarkable ability, but at all times his own worst enemy. I saw Pitt after the punishment. His normally ebullient manner was subdued for some weeks. It was some time later I inadvertently witnessed Pitt receive his second flogging.

Moving ahead in my narrative I will tell you of the second time Pitt was punished. With the permission of Dr. Menzies, I had acquired a small journal in which to record experiences and dates. Sometimes, while Dr. Menzies was out of the cabin and after I had indexed the results of a botanical expedition, I would write impressions of the day's activities. I knew I would be punished and my writing material taken, had I been caught. It was during one of these times I observed from a crack in the bulkhead between the middies cockpit and Dr. Menzies cabin, the second punishment of Tom Pitt. The cockpit was the dark, dank home of the midshipmen, a space separated from the crowded quarters of the men by a canvas hung between. The Sandwich Islands, that beautiful, magical place had been behind us but a day. Our course was set towards the north, the sea gentle and the breeze warm.

"Mr. Johnstone, set the gallants, weather looks settled at last."

"Yes, Captain. Look smart there, set the top-gallants."

Sailors bustled to the positions required to set the highest sails on the ship, a few began the long climb high into the rigging, while others assumed their positions on deck.

"Let go buntlines and clew lines, haul on the sheets and halyards and heave away there."

Time-tested methods soon had the high sails fluttering in the breeze. The halyards and sheets were drawn in. The men on deck heaved on lines to a sailor's chant in time with their efforts. The sails soon drew taunt and billowed out to catch the light southwesterly. The sea, still the marvelous deep blue of the tropics was crossed by high rolling swells.

"Mr. Pitt. That is enough I say. That is enough. Mr. Barrie and you Mr. Stewart stop your skylarking immediately. That will be enough. Lieutenant Baker, you will lecture these young gentlemen on deck behavior. I will not have such a display before the men. We will have some decorum and example. See to it Mr. Baker."

The three midshipmen in their smart blue coats, white breeches and dirks, stood sheepishly before the two officers. Pitt, well over six feet and powerfully built, obviously the leader of the group, turned his head away from the Captain; a grin of disdain distorting his handsome features. He had been in this position before, on the wrong side of the Captain; he knew what was to come."

"To the cockpit, gentlemen, look smart now."

"I say Barrie; I'll owe you one for this."

Thomas Pitt whispered a playful threat to Edward Barrie and at the same time jostled him towards the companionway, leading to the lower deck from the quarterdeck.

"I'll be ready to receive what ever you can muster up Tom, but in the mean time, take this."

Barrie swung a punch, catching Pitt just above the navel. The effect of the blow was completely unnoticed; the years of rigorous heavy work on all the young men, both above and below decks had made bodies of steel. A blow to the stomach was of little consequence.

"You swine ,Bob, take that."

Pitt half-punched and good-naturedly pushed his companion; Stewart was to Barrie's right hand. The blow, though not malicious in any way, caused Barrie to crash into the Honourable Charles Stewart, who in turn crashed into the binnacle. Mr. Stewart's elbow broke the glass covering the compass. The sound of the breaking glass seemed to echo about the deck, all eyes focused on the perpetrator of the incident. Charles Stewart stood completely still. The normal deep brown of his face quickly changed to a sickly yellow.

"What is this? Who is responsible for this, Mr. Stewart, was it you? Answer me now."

"Yes, sir, I broke it, sir."

"No Mr. Baker, it was me, I caused it to happen, not Mr. Stewart."

"Pitt you bloody fool, in trouble again. You know the Captain must hear of this, Stewart and Barrie get below, come with me Mr. Pitt."

It took very little time for the news to travel about the vessel. The Honourable Thomas Pitt was in trouble again. Not five minutes after the incident had occurred, the men in the fo'c'sil, the hard tough young seamen, laughed loudly when Charley Ley left his watch to shout into the crowded deck.

"Barrie punched Pitt in the belly, Pitt pushed Barrie and Barrie knocked Stewart. Broke the bloody compass, they did. Pitt's taking the blame, 'es in for it this time, 'es goin' to get a bloody good cobbing this time, I got to get back or I'll be in for it too."

Thomas Pitt, vibrant, excitable and full of life had again fallen foul of the Captain. Mr. Baker led the way to Captain Vancouver's quarters. It was easy to consider the thoughts passing though the mind of Tom Pitt with his vast fortune and family connections. "Who the hell does this Captain think he is? Why he isn't even a gentleman! I am younger, stronger and heir to a vast fortune. I could have him, all of them, dismissed from the navy if the whim took me."

It would take just word with his cousin, the Prime Minister, or Chatham, first Lord of the Admiralty, or Grenville, the Foreign Secretary, all relatives, all ready to exonerate him and put this Vancouver in his place.

"Captain Sir, I have Mr. Pitt here, a matter of consequence has occurred that needs your immediate attention."

The Captain, who had taken off his heavy coat and jacket, was in the process of attending to his toilet. He did not take kindly to this intrusion and quickly threw on a jacket. With little ceremony, he directed his lieutenant into his quarters.

"Come, Mr. Baker, you too, Mr. Pitt, what have you been up to this time?"

"Sir, this man has broken the glass on the binnacle; it was only by an act of divine providence that the compass itself was not inconvenienced. He was skylarking again and this was the result."

Captain Vancouver closed his eyes and lent against the bulkhead, which formed the wall of his quarters, he was sick and tired of this spoilt aristocrat, his constant play, his constant superiority, but most of all his complete lack of responsibility. He was highly intelligent, even likeable, but here he was again, in trouble without the faintest sign of repentance or concern.

"Well, what have you to say for yourself?"

"Nothing, sir, it was my fault, not the others."

"Nothing to say, young sir? Well, there is only a compass on this vessel, you should know that we require it at all times, it is completely necessary to help us find our way back to England. I am sure you understand this, a young man of your intelligence and quality. This is a serious matter and a lesson must be learnt, Mr. Pitt. Mr. Baker, twenty-four, in private of course. Boatswain's mate will be present to carry out the punishment, immediately. Go to your quarters Mr. Pitt. Stay awhile Mr. Baker."

Pitt said nothing as he left the Captain's cabin. In his mind, he knew what was to come. It was now that a hatred developed within, which would rule his life and indirectly cause his early demise.

"What am I going to do with that fellow? Joseph, he is dangerous to me, such an influential family, each time I punish him I submerge myself deeper into a problem, not now, mind you, later. His father is ageing and eventually he must die. Thomas will inherit a seat in the House of Lords, a title and a fortune. He will most certainly do me a disservice, James."

"I feel that it is necessary to make an example of Pitt, Captain, I understand what you are saying, but in reality our lives depend on discipline, in spite of Pitt's family lineage. Believe me I would not want to be in your position when he is Lord Camelford."

"Well James I have to think of the total picture and let providence take care of the future. Carry out the punishment. You know we cannot have men out of use, we need them all in good health and we especially cannot have them unusable through our own efforts. These are young men full of the exuberance of youth, but I must be strict in discipline, if just to get us all home to England."

"Yes Captain, we must have healthy men, in this I agree, but punishment is laid down by the Admiralty for all occasions, and to render any less would not be lawful, it is expected and received almost as a right. The men in the fo'c'sil carry their marks as a badge of honour. We cannot be lenient; it is neither allowed nor expected. However, as I say, I would not want to be in your position when Pitt is in the House of Lords in a few years time."

Vancouver sighed in resignation as the words of Joseph Baker rang true in his mind. The punishment of Pitt would be carried out, in spite of any repercussions that may come later.

All the seamen not on watch were assembled forward. A line of men, down on their knees, holystones in hand, scrubbed the oaken planks of the deck; another few were filling buckets over the side to slosh about before the swabbers. Below deck, two levels down, small lanterns lit the cramped, smelly, quarters of the midshipmen. This day, light was augmented by an open stowage hatchway; which is normally closed, giving access to the deck, for the mass of bales, stores, odorous tar-impregnated coils of rope, canvas, sails and barrels. From beneath the deck on which the grim group stood all contemplating what was to come, the gurgling sounds and sickening smells of the bilge mingled with the suffocating odour of rancid meat, stale bread and cheese. On a larger vessel, this deck would be termed the orlop deck, devoid of all outside light, receiving whatever fresh air managed to find a way down through the decks, packed tight with all that was needed and essential for a voyage of years into a wilderness beyond all comprehension.

I was in the small area used to store the tools and goods necessary for the botanical work of the voyage. I heard the men come into the area near my position. To leave meant revealing my presence. I had by now become well-schooled by my comrades in the art of doing as little as possible and trying to make myself not obvious. I remained in my position behind bales and casks determined to observe the proceedings.

John Nickolas, John Brown, Charles Mackenzie, Henry Humphries, John Sykes, Edward Barrie, Charles Stewart and Edward Pigot were drawn up on the starboard side of the vessel, against the outer hull of *HMS Discovery*. The oaken planks glistened in the light of the glowing lamps and the intermittent ray of sunlight, which occasionally penetrated through the rarely opened hatchway. Here and there, a running trickle of seawater forced its way between the planks to mix with the foul effluvia of the bilge. A table, which served as dining table for the midshipmen and as operating table for Dr. Menzies, would receive Mr. Pitt, for his punishment.

Thomas Pitt stood between Lieutenant Mudge and the coxswain, Richard Richards, a heavy set, strong man, with muscular, thick arms. Pitt was stripped, the deep tan of his face contrasting with the milky white of his muscular upper body.

"On the table Mr. Pitt, Mr. Barrie and Mr. Stewart, as you had some part in this incident, you will hold an arm on either side, if you please."

Thomas Pitt lay face down on the table, his two companions in the incident with the binnacle, took hold of an arm, one on either side of the table.

"Now coxswain, you will commence your task. Twenty-four of your best, lay on hard."

Richards held a cane in his right hand; it was some three feet long. He drew back and the cane whistled as it descended on the back of Thomas Pitt. Each blow created a series of raised, red welts, which rose above the tender white skin. By twelve blows, Pitt's back was an angry, red mass of welts. Richards now moved to the other side of the table to commence another twelve strokes. Lieutenant Zachary Mudge approached Pitt

"Pitt lad, I will intercede with the Captain, just promise you will not offend again, come on boy it's not worth it." Before Mudge could continue his entreaties, the hapless Pitt, grimacing with pain and mortification snarled at Mudge.

"I will not be begged off by you or anyone else in this matter, much less the Captain. Get it over with. Get it over with for Christ sake, you hear."

Mudge accepted the anger of Pitt; he motioned to the coxswain to continue. He knew he had received the patronage of the Camelford family and was beholden to them. His own status with the crew and Captain could be severely compromised if he was not careful.

"Continue on, Richards."

Thomas Pitt, tears in his eyes, grimaced in agony, biting his lip in anguish. A sigh escaped his lips, by the thirteenth or fourteenth stroke, the pain seemed to have ceased. All that remained was a burning desire to be revenged on that upstart Captain. The young midshipmen looked on, each with his private thoughts. All knew at any time they could be on the receiving end of the Captain's wrath; with each blow a little of the pain and embarrassment of Pitt impressed itself into their young minds. Thomas Pitt had fourteen companions on the voyage, dashing young gentlemen of breeding and family connections. Although they resented Pitt for his good looks, his physical powers and his vast inheritance to come, they felt each blow, and were one in spirit with Pitt in his agony.

Lieutenant Zachary Mudge, deep in thought, watched the punishment. He had tried to soften the Captain's fury in Otaheite at Pitt's previous flogging. Mudge remembered his dressing down for daring to suggest that a flogging was not warranted. He did not intend to become involved again. Pitt was a bloody young fool, always in trouble and always his own fault; a smart young man; in fact brilliant and with his connections, a notable naval career was assured.

As the final blow fell on the hapless Pitt, an almost gentle moan escaped his lips and then it was over.

"Mr. Barrie, Mr. Stewart, you will assist Mr. Pitt."

Pitt swayed and lurched to the side as he was helped to his feet, shaking off the hands that assisted him.

"Leave me alone, leave me alone and get away from me."

Pitt half snarled, half sobbed the words. As he stood, the light from the lamps fell on a back emblazoned with raised, red stripes, on some a trace of blood where the skin had been broken by the cruel cane. If there had been any respect for Captain Vancouver within him, it was gone. Nothing remained except hatred and an all-consuming desire to be revenged. I understood his feelings. My desire to find and revenge myself against the swine that had caused my present predicament was always uppermost in my mind. From my hidden position, I felt every blow. I felt the hatred of Pitt against his captain, as I felt the same against the swine that had consigned me to this earthly purgatory. At this moment, I felt an empathy with Thomas Pitt.

Captain Vancouver had been standing in the gloom of the hold; I had not noticed he was there. I was surprised at the sound of his voice.

"Mr. Baker, lessons for the young gentlemen, Mr. Pitt is excused till the middle watch. Take notice Mr. Pitt, I will not tolerate your actions further."

Captain Vancouver turned and disappeared into the gloom of the lower deck. The midshipmen filed silently towards the open hatchway. The hapless Pitt was left to string his hammock alone and in silence, anger and revenge the only thoughts in his mind.

The young midshipmen, despite their family connections, led lives of privation, as did the seamen. Their punishments were frequent and varied from flogging to mast-heading, an exile aloft in the cross-trees, sometimes for hours and in any weather. Here the offending neophyte would tie himself to the mast to avoid falling. To the seamen they were privileged and officers, entitled to every mark of respect, exactly the same as accorded senior lieutenants, a position often exalted by these upper class young men, to the detriment of many an experienced, old sailor.

Each day from nine until midday and afternoons from two until four, the midshipmen received instruction in the art of seamanship and navigation. They acquired deck instruction in the working of the ship. This, as well as their normal watches was all necessary if they were to pass the exacting exams preceding their promotion to Lieutenant in the Royal Navy.

I waited until all were gone before I emerged from my concealment. I had mixed thoughts and a feeling of sympathy for Pitt, who had left me alone since our bout. I knew what little snots midshipmen could be, each towards the other as well as being completely intolerable to the seamen. I had to pass Pitt who lay in his hammock to leave my position of hiding.

"Who is that?"

"It's Peter Wright, Mr. Pitt."

"What do you want? Get out of here."

I was trapped. I could not pass without some conversation with the hapless Pitt. I decided on a direct and sympathetic approach.

"Sir, you are not well, can I help you?"

"Not well be dammed, I have been beaten into a bloody mess by that miserable man they call the captain of this barge. So now you will gloat to the scum in the fo'c'sil about my predicament."

"No, sir, I will not. If I can do something for you I will, I will say nothing about this."

"All right then, rub that salt into my wounds. Say nothing and I will be grateful to you."

I applied salt to his wounds as gently as I could.

"Ohhhhh? that stings, my God that smarts. Now get out of here and leave me alone."

I was happy to leave Pitt to himself. As I moved away towards the ladder leading to the next deck, I heard Thomas Pitt say quietly, "I will remember you Peter Wright."

Our stay in Otaheite lasted from December 26th, 1791 to February 24th, 1792. During this time went about our business of repairing the vessel, mending sails and restocking our larder with the produce of the island. I made three journeys with Dr. Menzies, journeys which I found most rewarding and informative. I was able to see and understand a little of the culture and habits of this earthly paradise. I saw how children were treated as special beings, almost as gods. I also understood that many children were killed at birth. I assumed this was to control the birth rate on the island. The finite land area could only support a limited number of souls. I was kept busy recording and potting plants for our botanist-surgeon as well as constant work with whoever else required my services.

The sailors were allowed no opportunity to fraternize with the nubile beauties so readily available, much to their anger, frustration and chagrin. However, life was good with plenty of fresh fruit and meat. Those who had been ill soon regained a more substantial appearance than ever and in general, we were a very healthy bunch.

After visits from native dignitaries, we quitted these blessed islands about noon and directed our course northwards. We had been away from England for ten months and it seemed that we were now about to commence the real work and grand object of our voyage.

After an uneventful journey, we again passed into the northern hemisphere and on Thursday March 1st the main Island of the Sandwich Group, Hawaii, was sighted under a mass of stratocumulus clouds. Various native leaders visited our vessel and brought with them offerings of goats, pigs, fruit and vegetables. Nevertheless, we continued past the great main Island and finally anchored well off shore in perfect safety at the island of Oahu.

I cannot begin to describe the feelings rife in *Discovery* over the rules of trade and association with the natives Captain Vancouver had posted. Most of those in the fo'c'sil had not set foot ashore, apart from New Holland in ten months. Here we were in a veritable paradise and again only, the officers had access to the shore. Seamen were only allowed ashore accompanied by an officer and on official business, such as wood gathering, filling water casks or getting the mass of stores purchased from our hosts. There was to be no fraternization. To daily observe beautiful women, naked from the waist up, anxious to bestow their favours for so little and not be able to get at them, left strong healthy men in a state of frustration and anger.

I again accompanied Dr Menzies to collect plants on an interesting but arduous trip. Two native guides and a representative of the chief accompanied our party. Our royal representative was an enormous man, with a name something like Kahowmotoo. Our journey took us to what I must assume was a place of religious observance, the stone walls of which were adorned with the skulls of those executed by the overall king, Kamehameha. This fearsome place of death and ritual was called a morai. Our guides, by gesture and a little English on their part and a word here and there in the native language by the officers intimated that these skulls were revolutionaries against the king's autocratic rule.

On our return to the coast, after having loaded the plants into the pinnace, a great commotion signaled the arrival of the Chief Karkakooa and Captain Vancouver. With this party were four enormous ladies. In all my life, I have never seen such gargantuan women. These women had expressed a wish to go aboard *Discovery*. Eventually all were loaded, together with the various plants collected. I was sure the pinnace would sink, as it rolled in the swell, which swept into the anchorage from the open ocean. I cannot tell you of the efforts required to hoist these ladies aboard *Discovery* and later to get them into the longboats for the return journey. The boat was held close at bow and stern, the noble ladies, probably the wives of the enormous King Kamehameha, commenced the task of clambering up the side of *Discovery*. Captain Vancouver had boarded first, he leant over to present a hand to the ladies, myself and two seamen pushed from behind. The comedy of the situation was not lost on the assembled officers and crew. The Captain tugged and pulled as the men behind used shoulders and hands in the most comprising places to propel these laughing women on deck. This was one of the few times I heard the Captain laugh aloud.

To his credit, I must say that Captain Vancouver refused repeatedly to barter guns for supplies, not only here in Owhyhee, but later in the wild country of America. The native chiefs, wishing to gain an advantage over their neighbours by having firearms, displayed anger. The captain explained that all firearms belonged to King George; consequently, he had no authority to dispose of them at any price. Our stay in the Sandwich Islands, as Captain Cook had named them, or Owhyhee as the natives termed them, lasted from the 15th of February to the 16th of March. On that date in company with our little consort *Chatham*, we departed for America.

The slap of waves against the side of the vessel, the crack of halyards dancing to the light breeze, the creak and groan of the ship's timbers working each against the other, was comforting and peaceful. The cry of seabirds, soaring, swooping, then diving, to feast on a school of tiny, silver fish, churning the sea into a foaming, seething mass about the vessels, seemed to speak of a oneness with nature. It was a tranquil, peaceful scene. Despite the beauty about us, tensions ran rampant between 150 men, far from family and home. Their every thought and action was dictated by naval rules and regulations, by officers who held their lives in their hands, by a distinction of class, which could not be broken. They were all trapped together in the confines of a vessel of 330 tons and barely 100 feet in length.

To our sadness, we departed the beautiful islands and for two days headed northwards before changing course to a northeasterly direction. For four days, the temperature remained pleasant and warm with gentle breezes and sailing conditions. The watch on the fifth day awoke to a gale from the northwest and a sudden and dramatic drop in temperature. The sea rose and propelled us at a fine rate towards the continent of America which lay somewhere in the mist ahead.

15

Jane Changes Her Parent's Plan While Henry Carouses in London

"My dear Papa, please give me the greatest of presents, let it be that Henry and I are not parted a moment longer. The church of Saint Mary has always been our source of joy and comfort, Norwich is so far from here and the cathedral, it is so big and cold."

"My dear Jane, your mother has set her heart on Norwich Cathedral. You know she has a special devotion to that edifice; she is devoted to the Holy and Undivided Trinity."

"But father, Henry and I really do not want the extensive wedding you and mother have planned for us. Let us allow the vicar that baptized and christened me to bind and complete the love Henry and I have for each other. Please, father, please."

"My dear Jane, how can I not give in to you? Of course you know your mother will be broken-hearted."

"I know that, Papa, but surely you will be able to convince mother of our feelings on this matter. You can persuade her that this is really what Henry and I want. We can see no reason to wait. We love each other. Look Papa, Henry gave me this necklace. It is gold with sapphires, a wedding gift to his great-great grandmother and the first of his family to wed a Beckingham.

"How beautiful, Jane. How marvelous. The Beckingham family. I say. You always know when you call me Papa as you did when a child I can deny you nothing. Of course, it will take some persuasion for your mother to relent on this; there will be many things to prepare. Jane, you must remember that you are our only child and both your mother and I deserve the joy of seeing you married in style, as do the friends and relations that love you."

"Of course, Father, since most of our relatives and friends live close by, they will be delighted if my nuptials occur in Burnham Westgate. Just think how much simpler it will be for you and mother."

"Well your betrothed may have something to say about this. How does he feel? Perhaps he desires a more ceremonious ritual. He has guests, friends, and family. Do not forget the prestige of his connections. He would most certainly require a service in keeping with the high station of his family."

"Oh Father, we are in love. Every day apart is a lifetime for me. Henry is marvelous; I can vouch that he feels the same as I. Why on many an occasion he has asked, nay demanded that we elope to Gretna Green. He is so ardent, so impulsive, believe me I have no uncertainty in this. I beg you to arrange our nuptials with all speed. I believe that my dear Captain West would have Mr. Wells, the blacksmith of Burnham Market marry us, if it were legal for him to do so."

"By heavens, Jane, you are obviously completely captivated by your captain."

"My dear Father, I have never known such bliss. Since Henry came into my life I cannot think of, nor can I desire, anything but his company. I love him and I must be with him."

"Oh my dear, then that is what it shall be. I will talk to your mother; nay demand of her, that her plans for Norwich be put aside. Here in Burnham Market, your marriage will be confirmed. Let it be celebrated by the vicar of our parish, the friend who has watched over you all these many years."

"God bless you, dear Papa, you have made me so happy and I know that Henry will be delighted at this news. Father, I am so excited."

Jane threw her arms about her father. She had the rapture of her meetings with Henry constantly in her mind. Her nights were full of dreams and desires, feelings beyond her comprehension. Her gentle upbringing had not prepared her for a man like the dashing Henry West. All that consumed her was a desire to be with this man. A man who had unlocked feelings within her breast, feelings never dreamed of, to love this man and be loved by him.

Henry West and Frederick March sat together deep in conversation. A fire burned bright in the large fireplace, candles glowed yellow. The smoky haze of cigar and pipe smoke hung heavy in the rancid air. Ale flowed copiously, food lay ready for the taking and all were in various stages of inebriation, as the commerce of the Slaughter House Hostelry carried on in full swing. Well-dressed men vied with each other for the affection of women of dubious repute. Some couples made their staggering, inebriated way up a narrow staircase to disappear behind doors, from which the cries and laughter

Discovery

told of liaisons dangerous. Some, no longer caring, carried out their carnal desires in full view of the cheering, raucous room. Men of wealth, men of dubious reputation, lawyers and merchants, here and there a sprinkling of gold piping and blue, or a gold epaulet on red, told of an officer of the crown, all throwing propriety and sobriety to the winds.

"So the wedding will be in a fortnight, how did you manage that?"

"I have been in that boring town now for over six months. It is some little consolation that here is a father and mother who would be most swayed by my family connections. Even if my family themselves will have nothing to do with me. Here is a pretty, foolish girl just waiting to be plucked from the vine, so to speak, not an unpleasant chore I may add.

"Have you established a settlement? Do you know how much this is going to be worth?

"No, not yet fully discussed, but I tell you it will be a pretty penny. My future father-in-law has intimated that he is desirous of becoming involved in some venture with his son-in-law. This of course is where you come into the picture, Frederick. I have no head for business. In the mean time, I have still to play the part of the devoted lover. I tell you my friend this lovely little wench is developing quite well. In fact, she has become quite insatiable. For my part, I am acting the role of the completely infatuated gentleman, though I could have her in a second. I must tell you it is a very difficult piece of work and requires the utmost self-control, a trait for which I am not famous, not to take her at every meeting. What ho Frederick, here comes Fran Beck and her crazy sister."

"Well, well, if it isn't Captain West and Mr. Frederick March."

The tall, voluptuous, red-haired beauty threw herself down on the lap of Henry West; her raven-haired sister clasped Frederick to her ample bosom.

"Where have you been, Henry? You have neglected your Franny, come on now give me a kiss and tell me what games you and this renegade have been up to?"

"Well, Fran me love, I am getting married.

"You? Married? That is the funniest thing I have ever heard and are you also getting married Mr. March, me honey?"

Frederick, gasping for air, extracted himself from the amorous, busty clasp of Maria.

"Who me? No, no, never. Me! Married. Sink me; I think I would die before I would let that happen."

"Now, Henry, tell us of the unfortunate lady who has fallen into your clutches. A wealthy wench no doubt."

Frederick had again submerged himself between the now exposed breasts of the raven-haired Maria, losing all interest in anymore conversation.

"Look at these lovebirds, Henry. What a pretty pair. Is your new love as eager to please as my sister? Come Henry tell me all about her, by how much you can expect to increase your coffers? I know it is only money that would get you to the altar."

Frederick carnally engaged, had forsaken any part in the conversation. Henry had also been busy renewing his acquaintance with his old love, Fran. Kisses were long and ardent, hands busy exploring eager compliant bodies. All the while, the business of the Slaughter House Inn carried on about them. Finally, Fran drew away from Henry.

"Henry, are we going to stay here for the night? Surely, you will get a room and bed where we can continue in more comfort. What do you two say?"

"Oh? Oh! Definitely, let us get out of here Frederick. Pry yourself away from that woman this moment. Get us a room. I have very little money; we all throw ourselves on your benevolence."

"Wonderful idea. Henry, here is enough to buy a few quarts and a bottle of the best whiskey, I will get a room; let us escort these ladies upstairs. Come Maria, away from this noisy place. We will tell you of our designs, both for our financial future as well as our designs on you and your excellent sister."

Silver exchanged hands, ale and a room were procured. The two men, busily exploring the bodies of their voluptuous companions, staggered as they climbed upwards towards a landing, finally to stumble from sight amid gales of laughter along with shrieks of excitement from the ladies.

16

Discovery Arrives in the Pacific Northwest

Peter Wright and Sir Neville Brown sat quietly together in the warmth of the Pitt Inn. Peter reflected in his mind on the previous years, trying to arrange his thoughts in order. After a few moments, he continued with his tale.

"I believe it was April. Yes it was April 18th, 1792 that I first saw the land which would occupy my existence for the next three years. I remember it well, the heavy weather, the gale and then the clear morning when a great monolith stood out on the eastern horizon. The officers seemed to be expecting to see it and some recognized it immediately from their charts as Cape Mendocino. For me it was an accomplishment. I had survived thus far, but little did I know the trials awaiting me in this wilderness of the Pacific Northwest. We had seen logs, branches and flotsam all day and the weather was changing. It was bone-chilling cold. I can still hear the call of Lieutenant Johnstone as he carried out the commands of Captain Vancouver."

"Mr. Johnstone reef the topsails, I don't like the look of this weather. Close reef, mind you, right now."

"Yes, sir. Dillon, Philskirk, Wright, get to it, smartly now, where are those bloody young gentlemen?"

"Come on now lads, heave away there. Ah Mr. Barrie, can you see *Chatham*? Not likely in this weather. Helm, get the compass to the north west, stand in to help there Brown."

There was an excitement in the air. All day we had seen signs of land, logs, branches and birds. Vancouver had not left the deck since dawn; he would constantly peer into the deteriorating weather. A feeling of excitement seemed to flow though the crew. Soon land would be sighted, the great barrier that extended from pole to pole and separated the Atlantic from the Pacific Ocean. The Americas.

Discovery lay well to larboard in the rising gale. The sea, a seething mass of flying spray and spume, crashed and desperately clawed at the vessel. The wind, which had been gentle from the east-southeast, filling the sails to perfection, now tore at the canvas, in wild, ever-increasing gusts. Captain Vancouver strained to observe the men high in the rigging, as they clung to spars, wrestling with the billowing sails, cracking and thundering, in some abstract competition with the noise and confusion of the elements.

"Look alive there, Mr. Johnson, look there."

The captain pointed high in the rigging; he stabbed the air with a pointing finger.

"The main-top-gallant shroud, it's parted, look there."

The rigging had parted under the strain of the gale. Rain and wind swept vessel from stem to stern; the shroud hanging loose placed an unnatural distortion on the top-gallant-mast.

"Mr. Johnstone, get some men onto this now, too much strain there."

"Williams, Matt, get Charlie Bryne and Sam Hall and Petee Wright up there, the top-gallant shroud, get it together, dead eyes on each end, bouse it tight, mind you, tackle to the main end, pull from the mizzen head, get to it now."

Again, I was with my companions high in the rigging, clinging to mast and spars, desperately making every effort to reef the top gallants. Now the added danger of the parted shroud was ours to contend with. A mast head, not fully stayed, moved in opposition to every move of the vessel and our only platform a footrope, below a spar high above the sea.

The Captain watched the shroud slowly come together, the sway in the topmast ceased and the topgallants closed reefed, for now all seemed under control.

The sky darkened even more as swells crossed the set of the waves, to produce a sickening, uncomfortable motion. *Discovery* shuddered as a breaking sea crashed into the side of the labouring vessel.

"That's better Mr. Johnstone, much better. If this increases a tad more we will have to strike the top-gallant masts. The coast must be near, no soundings, can't do much about it in this."

"All right you men, down below, stand ready to strike top-gallant-masts."

The vessel steadied on her course towards the northwest. The gale continued to grow in alarming intensity. *Discovery* sped in a northerly direction approximately parallel to the invisible coastline. With the storm growing stronger and darkness almost on hand, all knew there would be no possibility of seeing New Albion this day.

Zero visibility, rain and sleet, high, confused seas thundered against *Discovery*. The night was almost over; all were showing signs of fatigue. None slept on this night of tension and excitement, with visibility reduced from a score of yards to a few feet. The howling banshee gale in the rigging, the thunder and crack of the close-reefed storm-sails, all but obliterated the cries of the men, high in the rigging. The orders of the officers were lost in the noise and confusion.

Almost as quickly as it had begun, the weather changed. The gale became merely a strong breeze. Captain Vancouver glanced skyward through the scudding clouds, where racing across the heavens a star appeared. Just for an instant, then another, and another. Within an hour, large areas of the heavens blazed with the constellations so familiar in northern latitudes.

"Mr. Puget, make signals for *Chatham*; they can't be too far off, a rocket, fifteen minute intervals should suffice."

Peter Puget, a tall lean man, hunched down into his heavy woolen coat, trying to ward off the intense cold and intermittent icy showers of sleet.

"Clark you hear that order, rocket at fifteen minuets, step lively now. Reeves, come on man, get with him now."

With a crack the rocket rose high in the sky, its baleful red glare tinged the foamy tops of the waves. The sky began to show signs of light towards the east; dawn had begun its march across the heavens. A thick haze lay to the east as rain again began to fall in steady showers.

"By the mark, by the mark."

"What was that mark?"

"Fifty-three fathom, sir. Soft sandy bottom. Look, over there, more driftwood, there's grass as well."

To the west, high in the dawn sky, a rocket, its red glow barely visible in sometimes heavy driving rain-showers, drew the attention of the watch.

"*Chatham*, sir, off to the northwest. Bear down on her and we will press on to the east again."

"I'm going to my quarters, Mr. Puget. I want to know when land is in sight, take care now; we don't want to mess it up, do we?"

Peter Puget looked after the Captain as he went below. He shook his head and said to himself; no, we do not want to mess it up at all.

"Keep your eyes peeled, no slacking off watch. Land is close by now, you hear me, we want to see it, not make love to it, you hear."

"Land, land, away to the northeast, there."

It was America. Here we were on the other side of the world. I cannot tell you the feeling I experienced at this call. I was wet and cold, but a sense of accomplishment filled my whole being. I had survived this assault on my previously safe, mundane life. Exaltation seemed to over-shadow the anger and desire for revenge on the person who had put me in this situation. As the wind dropped to a gentle breeze, waves, confused and steep, threw *Discovery* in every direction. The surface of the still large swells wore an oily, calm face. A low-hanging fog concealed the landmass over which a great, bluff headland stood, placed by the hand of the Maker to guide the seaman and keep him away from treacherous shores.

The clouds began to part, and a misty, watery sun bathed all in cold, silver light. This was the landfall of Sir Francis Drake, the landfall of the great Spanish galleons after their journey from the Spice Islands of the Orient on their way to the Isthmus of Panama. Cape Mendocino. The land, still unseen, was Spanish California.

Discovery rolled with the swell, the weather cold and sunny. The coast lay about three leagues to the east, rugged with islets and rocks both visible and invisible. The rocks beneath the sea lurked in wait for the slightest mistake from us, intruders from another world.

17
Thoughts on a New Son-in-law

Saint Mary's Westgate nestled comfortably in a grove of trees. The gnarled and twisted oaks had witnessed many a new headstone added to the rows marking the last resting-place of the people of Burnham Market. Today it was not a funeral but a wedding, which brought the polite society of the five Burnham Towns together. The heavens had cooperated wonderfully, the sun shone and the few fleecy white clouds low in the western sky posed no threat to the happy occasion.

Jane Sawtell and Henry West had completed their vows and they were now married.

An excited, happy throng gathered outside the old stone church, to await the appearance of the newly wedded couple. It had been said that handsome apparel is a main point, fine feathers make fine birds. The ladies, young and old, friends and relatives of the Sawtell family had used this social occasion to bring out their finest attire. Young wives and their elderly mothers, spinsters and widows, all had spent long hours of difficult contemplation before deciding on their dress. Many a husband or father had been asked to render an opinion on the attire for this brilliant day. They were dressed in their most elegant hats, high and large, or bonnets tight to the head, rich with ribbons, bows and lace, especially created for the occasion. The high bodices and gowns of every hue, flowing from low necklines to the ground were in the height of local fashion, though perhaps a little out of date for the high society of London. Colourful parasols shaded delicate complexions from the warm spring sun and the delicate odour of jasmine from perfumed gloves hung gently on the still calm evening.

Men of all ages accompanied the ladies. All wore coats buttoned at the middle, high white collars and neck cloths, tight breeches, white stockings and sterling buckled shoes. They carried or wore wide brimmed hats or tall round hats, a few sported three-cornered models. Amid the already colourful group, the afternoon sun caught the silver and gold of a ceremonial dress sword, enhancing the dramatic red of the guards or the blue gold-trimmed dress uniform of a dragoon. The dashing military men preened themselves and adopted heroic poses, if for no other reason than to impress the ladies or perhaps their fellow officers. The impressionable young ladies cast many a secret glance at these dashing comrades of Henry West. The hubbub of conversation and laughter bespoke the happy occasion. All were here to celebrate with Jane and her new dashing husband.

"Oh my dear, how marvelous, our dear Jane and the Captain, what a fine couple they make and will they set up house in our little town?"

The well-positioned family of Henry West was not lost on the festive group.

"How wonderful for our little Jane to be married and so well. What a fine turnout you have made my dear, you must be so proud of her, incidentally, who are the relatives of Captain West?"

Mrs. Margaret Sawtell could not answer the myriad questions thrown at her. What is more she did not know which of the guests was a Beckingham or if any of Henry's family were actually in attendance. The days had been bedlam, a flurry of arrangements, a surge of millinery art and a rush of dressmaking, a magnitude of cooking and culinary preparation, all finally culminating in this day. Now it would be back to Medhurst and the reception, which had consumed her every moment these last weeks.

"Oh, Margaret how lovely our dear Jane looks on this her day of days and her young man, how dashing and handsome. Both Mr. Wright and myself are so happy for her."

"Thank you dear Frances, I am so happy that you were able to feel well enough to come today, I know how distressed and ill you have been since the sad disappearance of Peter. Such a loss and so untimely, you know my dear you have our every sympathy."

"Yes, we had such plans for Jane and Peter, but all that is in the past. I find it so hard to come to terms with it all. I do not feel well; it is this malady, which has come to us from Lynn. Kate is also quite ill. Doctor Thorn has informed me many have passed away in Kings Lynn and the surrounding district. He assures me that I have nothing to worry about; all we have is a normal cold. He feels Kate and I will soon be well again. As sad as we are that Peter is gone, all are delighted Jane has found such a fine person and here in the depths of the country so to speak. Such a fine figure of a man you must be so proud and happy for her."

"Thank you so much Frances, my dear friend. Yes, it is indeed a satisfying experience to have an only daughter wed and so well. Ah! The happy couple approaches."

"Jane, how lovely, Captain West, let me introduce you to my very good friend and neighbour. Mrs. Frances Wright, Captain West has today become a son to us."

Henry West, resplendent in the smart red and gold of the Guards, bowed deeply before Frances Wright. At the name Wright he immediately knew to whom he was being introduced, here was the mother of the fellow he had sent to an almost certain death at sea. Jane grasped Mrs. Wright, kissing her cheek.

"Dear Mrs. Wright, it is wonderful you could rise from your sick bed to grace us here on such a day. Henry, let me introduce the mother of the dear friend of whom I told you, Peter Wright, who is no longer with us. Mrs. Wright is my second mother. So many wonderful times we have all spent together."

"Come along me dear; let us be away, I see a person I must present to you. You will forgive us ladies if we beg your leave."

"But Henry, I would talk with Mrs. Wright and my mother awhile. Stay a moment dear, surely your friend will be with us at least till the food is served."

"I do you honour Mrs. Wright, but the chatter of women is not something that I suffer well. Therefore, I will leave you. Join Frederick March and myself as soon as you have finished here, Jane. Good afternoon, ladies."

Henry abruptly turned on his heel and made his way towards Frederick March. Henry had not expected to come face to face with the mother of the man he had consigned to oblivion. He was shocked and did not trust himself to be natural and civil under these circumstances. He thought it best to escape from the possibility of revealing himself in a discomfit he could not explain. He knew he had embarrassed his new mother-in-law as he hurried from the situation. Henry knew he had been terse and quite rude. He reminded himself how he would have to be a picture of propriety in his dealings with Jane, her family and friends, at least till his financial situation had mended itself. He joined Frederick March and both men strolled among the colourful crowd.

The two older women and the young bride were speechless at the tone of Henry West. Nothing was said but thoughts ran deep. Jane made every effort to continue in a lighter vein.

"My dear Henry, he is so used to the military life, I know I will have such a time with him. He is so gruff and to the point, but really such a dear. I'm sure you will all come to love him as I already do."

The festivities continued well into the evening. To all not privy to any social undercurrents, the day passed brilliantly and became the topic of conversation among the polite society of the Burnhams for weeks to come.

Frederick March remarked, "Well Henry, you seem to have fallen on your feet. I see the new and beautiful Mrs. West is wearing the necklace I gave you; she is quite lovely, old man. From the looks of things there is a fine amount to be had if you play your cards right, and not such a terrible prospect with a beauty like Jane to take your mind off your wedded state."

"I must agree with you where Jane is concerned, she is exquisite. However, I must leave you I have fences to mend. I was moments ago rather rude to her mother and her friend. I was taken by surprise; I was introduced to the mother of the fellow we consigned to the sea."

Henry returned to the ladies and in his most charming manner soon had them in a fine state. He finally left with Jane after much bowing, kissing of hands and grand statements of affection and love for his new wife.

Mr. and Mrs. Wright sat in the salon of their fine dwelling. They had left Medhurst to return to Highfield House quite early in the evening. Frances did not feel well. Although Henry West had been dignity and charm itself after his initial introduction, she determined she did not like him. She broached the subject with her husband.

"I do not like Captain West. He is good-looking enough and cuts a fine figure in his splendid uniform. I do not like him, also where were all the aristocratic relatives; they have been so bandied about these last few months. I did not see one person of note, did you Mr. Wright? Why he almost never left the side of his friend Mr. March, except for the time he spent with Margaret and I. Oh, he was gracious enough but I sensed something not correct about him. I do hope dear Jane will be happy and has not made a mistake in her obvious infatuation."

"Now, now dear, he seems quite an astute fellow, although I must say that I received the same attention, or lack of it, when I was presented to him. It was as though he were afraid to speak to me at any length. I put it down to nerves, just married, dozens of strange people all wanting to pry into private matters and the urgency to take a bride away from those that would keep her. As for his distinguished relatives, there was never a mention of them at all. I found this rather strange. No my dear, I can make excuses for him, but I know of what you speak."

"Well, we will see. Nevertheless, I tell you Mr. Wright, if I never see him again it will be too soon for my liking.

18

Exploration Begins and Discovery Has an Encounter With a Lurking Rock

"My dear friend, you cannot imagine the land we now found ourselves about to explore. It was magnificent in every aspect. The gentle Norfolk country with its rolling hills had not prepared me for the grandeur of the scene before me.

Discovery and *Chatham* were in the most tranquil and sublime of all situations. The vessels had anchored at dusk, at the entrance to a vast waterway leading to the east. I believe it was originally charted by a Spaniard, Juan De Fuca and bears his name. The next morning, in the most glorious weather, we left the bay in which we had anchored the night, to sail in gentle and calm conditions. All about us, beauty presented itself at every mile as we progressed into the bosom of this land on a fine wide waterway. We saw superb snow-clad mountains, blue water, and great green forests clothing the shores up to the snowline. Ahead in the distance, a monolithic peak reached for the skies, conspicuous, white and dramatic, rearing its lofty top into the clear blue of the spring sky. Lieutenant Baker saw it first and his name was applied to it. Never was a contrast greater than that which we had been accustomed to. It had more the aspect of enchantment than reality, with each beauty of nature presented, the murmur of delight and admiration was heard on every tongue, from officers to the lowest of menial men. A gentle breeze swelled the canvas above and imperceptibly our vessel skimmed over the glassy surface at about three knots.

The bay in which *Discovery* had anchored the day after sighting the land of California was an anchorage exposed to the ocean. It received most of the swells that reached the shore. It was here that we made our first acquaintance with Indians, so very different from the people of Otaheite and Owhyhee.

The noble savages of the island countries were big, extremely clean and handsome, but here they were generally small in stature, and offensive in odour, having applied some variety of fish oil to their painted bodies. At the entrance to the strait in which we now gently sailed, anchorage was made for the night. Here the natives were of a better stature, but still not of the same beauty as those of the Sandwich Isles.

It now became clear that explorations were to be carried out in the small vessels. I was to curse this before the end of our time in this land, as did my companions. Rowing, I am told is a pleasant enough past time on the gentle waters of the Thames or the Cam, or in the confines of a lake or broad river, but here it was hell for all, both officers and men. Up until now, our small boat excursions had been of a very short duration in the warmer climes of New Holland or Otaheite. Being springtime, sunny days did occur frequently, but most days were cool and most were interspersed with rain or sleet, which seemingly occurred without warning.

What heavenly scenery it was our privilege to behold. Two great volcanic peaks rose out of jagged snow-covered mountain ranges. Tranquil bays and waterways lay peaceful in the midst of forests of the pine and fir, of a size beyond belief. Overhead, flocks of geese in their thousands made their way towards the north. The sea, rich in creatures of all varieties, provided for our every need.

Rowing excursions occupied all our time. All day my companions and I would propel our boats into nooks, crannies and narrow canals as directed by the officers. They, in turn, would take sights with compass and sextant to establish a position for each headland, bay or island. This data would be recorded, later to be inserted into the master charts being prepared in the great cabin of *Discovery*. We rowed south in this vast waterway as far as we could venture, then north back to our anchored vessels, then out again to explore some other passage, always with the purpose of establishing the line of the continental shore.

Discovery and *Chatham* would anchor in a suitable, protected cove. Tents would be set up on shore. Here the blacksmith would work at his forge and the carpenters would carry out repairs to those parts of the vessels in poor repair. The officers not away in the small boats would look to acquiring supplies. Wood for fires was readily available. Other groups would re-supply with water while others scavenged the surrounding forests for edible plants, berries and any game that happened to present itself. The principal source of food was the abundant supply of fish, daily brought up in the seine. The ships would move to some other suitable rendezvous, ever in a northerly direction. Names were applied to conspicuous and important objects and it soon became normal to refer to these names, if ever we became aware of them. The work was exhausting and most of the time all was wet and cold. On occasions, the tide would flow against our boats, in swirling whirlpools and races. During these periods, shore would be made until a more advantageous moment presented itself to continue, but always there was a timetable to be kept.

Indians, on approaching us, spoke in a language which none could interpret. By sign and gesture, trade was carried on using the store of goods brought from England for just that purpose. Copper, knives, blue cloth, axes, beads, mirrors and trinkets were accepted with apparent joy in exchange for spears, arrows, fish and articles of produce. A harmony was established with these primitive souls. Trust was always the first requisite, then speech would be attempted, trade would follow, then finally farewells, as we would move out of the sphere of influence of a particular tribe. I was always surprised at the grasp of language some of our officers had attained; I think Captain Vancouver and Lieutenant Johnstone displayed the most amazing ability at this challenging pastime. Johnstone had spent some years on this coastline with the renowned trader and merchant, Captain Colnett, and of course, our captain had been here with Cook. He also had a remarkable grasp of the language of the Polynesian people.

Our days were filled with rowing, mile after mile, sometimes two separate expeditions would head out in divergent directions hoping to meet up and prove that a land mass was an island, or to enter some channel heading inland towards the east. The hope was to discover a connection with the great lakes of Eastern America, but always our efforts would terminate in a backwater, overwhelmed with gigantic mountains and glaciers, or in some primeval swamp. Even rivers proved to be of no help in this endeavour. They always appeared to rush from distant impenetrable, snowy, mountain ranges.

Initially our voyages were a welcome relief from the constant threat of violent seas and gales of the open ocean, but you must believe me that this feeling of euphoria soon changed to one of abhorrence and boredom. As the years wore on I think this emotion was felt by all on *Discovery* and *Chatham*. Three years later, when it seemed we would be held in the Spanish port of Nootka, waiting for orders from England, I heard Captain Vancouver curse our plight in no uncertain terms, intimating that he felt trapped by the infernal ocean for another winter.

The small boat voyages usually occupied us for a fortnight at a time, this being the limit of supplies that could be comfortably carried. If it were not for the bounty of nature and trading with Indians our plight would have been of some concern. Generally, the food was excellent. The salt pork, biscuits and portable soup of our normal fare would be supplemented with fish, crustaceans, oysters and mussels, waterfowl and venison. Wild strawberries and other fruits of the forest were always available. On occasion, an expedition would return with all supplies completely exhausted and the men tired and hungry. The constant rowing had a fatiguing effect on all. Midshipmen and ordinary seamen each had their turn at the oars. After one fatiguing journey, camp was made for the night on rocky foreshores under densely forested heights. Some slept in the boats, others lay on the seashore to fall instantly asleep such was their exhaustion. During the night the tide rose. Some were in such a state of lassitude they would surely have been carried away by the rapidly swirling current and drowned, had they not been awakened by their companions or the freezing, cold water.

Our captain was very sympathetic to the feelings and customs of the Indians. If a burial place or other native construction were discovered, it would be investigated, recorded and then replaced in the same condition in which it was found. I must say he was scrupulously fair in all his dealings with them. He would countenance no violence, unless we ourselves were threatened. It was strange, the further north we ventured the more belligerent some of the Indians appeared. Those who showed the most animosity towards us seemed to have had more dealings with the various traders from Europe and America. At the top of the great island that was proved to lie off the coast, natives, armed with firearms of an excellent nature, which they used with great expertise, began to make their appearance.

In the south of these inland waterways, the natives seemed to show a more nomadic existence, unless it was their custom to leave their main village on hunting expeditions, building primitive structures for shelter. It was in the wide straits that a village of gargantuan proportions was first seen on a projecting neck of land. The timbers used were enormous and it defied comprehension how they were lifted to their position atop uprights of equally gigantic proportions. I was constantly amazed at the dimensions of the trees of the forest in this magnificent land. This village was completely deserted and had been for some time.

Our officers and young gentlemen went up to the village to investigate. The ordinary men were ordered to remain in the boats. After some time cries were heard from the high bushes that hid the village. We men readied our weapons in anticipation of danger. Suddenly the officers burst from the bushes, running back towards us, led by Dr. Menzies and Midshipman Pitt, followed by Captain Vancouver, the rest some distance behind. All immediately threw themselves into the sea, clothes and all, much to the delight and amusement of the sailors. Apparently, the old village was infested with fleas. Whether this was the reason for its abandonment I do not know, but the sight of our officers who constantly ordered and tormented us, throwing them selves into the water to rid themselves of the pests, was the cause of great mirth and happiness. Captain Vancouver remarked after this incident that he would forever remember Point Roberts, for that is what he had named this point.

Discovery and *Chatham* remained anchored in a protected bay a few miles to the south of the point where this incident occurred. It was pleasant bay with a fine, forested shore rich with a species of black birch trees. It received the name Birch Bay because of these fine trees.

After leaving Point Roberts on this, our longest journey so far, we proceeded north for at least a week then returned down the fine strait. You can imagine our surprise at the sight of two vessels flying the flag of Spain. The vessels proved to be the *Subtil* and *Mexicana* out of San Blas in Mexico, on a voyage of discovery such as ours.

The feelings of us all were beyond comprehension at the pleasant society of fellow Europeans, after so long away from our homes. The language barrier made little difference. Again, I was surprised at the ability of our captain to communicate with the men of the Spanish vessels. The meeting occurred off a bluff headland at the entrance to a vast harbour, which in turn led to a perfectly safe inner sanctum. The inner harbour I later learnt had been named after Sir Harry Burrard-Neil. These Spanish vessels stayed in company with us for some considerable time until we came to what appeared to be an impenetrable barrier raised before us. An enormous tidal current assailed our ships, and with the use of wind, tide and the oars of the small boats towing, the vessels were eventually anchored in a bay protected from the swirling currents and whirlpools emanating from a narrow opening a short distance to the north.

This bay had received the name Menzies Bay, to honour the man who had to all intents and purposes become my mentor and patron. Up until now the tide had risen from the south, but here in this narrow division between the continental shore and the bay in which we anchored, the tide appeared to flow from the north. Captain Vancouver sat on a headland overlooking this narrow opening for two days watching the action of the water and tides. Finally, anchors were hauled, the small vessels were launched fastened to the sides of the larger and hawsers made ready. Sails were let out and we entered this maelstrom of whirlpools and currents at the slack water, with just the right wind, but always the small boats ready to tow us to safety.

A great rock in the centre of the passage rose like a demon just beneath the surface waiting to rend our hull. Tension and fear gripped all at this time, but our captain had read the waters and wind well, for we sped through the narrows with never a hint of danger and not the least need for the boats to tow us from disaster. It now became clear that the land to our left was indeed an island. It was much later on our last visit to the port of Nootka that Captain Vancouver and Senor Bodega y Quadra, the commandant of the Spanish fort, named this vast island after themselves, the Island of Quadra and Vancouver.

Up until now, I had not been aware of the names that the Captain had bestowed on the many points, headlands, bays, straits, mountains or distinguishing objects. Dr. Menzies requested that in my new role as a scribe, I should note a name against each new species classified. A strange tree had attracted his attention in a bay which we had quit earlier. This unusual growth seemed to retain its leaves and lose its bark. It was quite irregularly shaped when compared to the general form and shape of the usual forest trees, and was festooned with large clusters of whitish flowers, evergreen leaves and smooth reddish brown bark. He directed that I record this as having been first seen in *Discovery Bay* and that he had called it the Oriental Strawberry Tree *(Arbutus Menziesii)*. For my own part, I saw a similarity to the eucalyptus trees observed in New Holland. From now on, I had the opportunity to become aware of many of the place names bestowed by Captain Vancouver.

At all times, we were constantly exhorted to keep an eye out and report any unusual movement in a calm sea. At any moment, a reef or some hidden rock could claim us. At the top of the land that we now knew to be a vast island, our vessels progressed north. The sea was calm. Fog combined with light rain concealed all about us, a gentle breeze coupled with the set of the current propelled us into the mist of this grey void. The only sound was the constant call of the men at the lead lines. This was a device attached to a line and thrown forward of the vessel and allowed to drop into the depths of the sea to the bottom. The man with the line would call the depth of water beneath the vessel. Monotonously, again and again the depths would be called. Suddenly without warning, we were aground on a rocky outcrop lying just beneath the surface of the sea. The bow of *Discovery* raised itself high into the air as the vessel struck, a sound resembling that of a wounded animal, a grinding scream of timbers protesting the stress as they were thrust out of their natural element. All forward motion ceased as we fell over on our side, masts and spars adopting an unnatural and dangerous aspect.

My dear Sir Neville, I cannot tell you of the feelings that filled the hearts of all. We were in a wild and primitive part of the world with no salvation except by our own efforts. One redeeming feature was ours; the sea was mirror calm with no swell, not a wave to disturb our plight. Instantly all was bedlam. Orders were shouted. The seriousness of our position was not lost on officers and men alike. All commenced the task of jettisoning cargo, wood, water, and supplies overboard. Masts and spars were lowered and used to shore up the vessel to prevent it falling to a more acute angle as the tide fell. Urgency became the order of the moment.

I had been at the bow, having been charged with others to keep watch for rocks and other obstacles, almost invisible in the foggy conditions. The man at the lead was David Dorman, a Cumberland man. Dorman had come to us from *Chatham*, after an incident for which he had been punished. He had called the wrong depths causing *Chatham* to go aground in the very early stages of our investigation in these inland waterways. He would later return to *Chatham*. This present incident was not caused though any fault of his. He had just called thirty fathoms, plenty of depth for us. He was a rather stupid man with little to recommend him and always in trouble, usually brought about by his own doing. Dorman, Matthew Brown and I were called to account, being the three men at the bow. This was my first face-to-face encounter with Captain Vancouver. The result of the inquiry found that the depth of water changed from thirty fathoms to two fathoms in a space of no more than twenty feet. An audible sigh of relief escaped the lips of David Dorman at this avoidance of certain punishment.

Eventually the tide returned and the vessel with very little effort re-floated itself. There was no apparent damage, but in the re-assembly of the main top gallant, a rope broke under the strain, causing a Lincolnshire man, John Turner, to break his arm. Masts were reassembled, rigging replaced and cargo restored. In a matter of four hours we were again shipshape and on our way.

It was as though the gods of the sea had decided to play with us for sport. No sooner had we overcome the trials of *Discovery*'s grounding, than the next evening *Chatham* found herself in a similar situation on a rocky ledge. This was actually a more dangerous plight, for the brisk swell, which broke on the shore, promised to destroy our smaller consort. Our small boats rushed to *Chatham*'s assistance. As it was half ebb tide, it was not long before *Chatham* was off the rocks without sustaining damage, joining us to continue on our way.

Now it was late August. Leaving the area at the north end of the great island, the vessels made way down the outer coast. It was strange for me to feel gratified by the feeling of movement as the ship rose again to the seas. This gratification was unexpected. I realized that despite all that had happened to me, I was now part of the crew and as such, I had begun to feel a responsibility, a duty to the circumstances that had replaced the love and affection for my family. All relished the respite from the constant rowing, even though the work of sailing was never easy. It had become obvious that the weather was deteriorating and the frequency of storms and colder weather had increased. Now our vessel was directed in a southerly direction along the outside of the great Island, which had been our companion on our larboard side for so many weeks.

Our next stop was Nootka, Friendly Cove. Here was almost civilization. Our anchor fell and we brought up near *Chatham* who had preceded us into the port. A little way from our anchorage, *HMS Daedalus*, our store-ship from London lay in perfect safety awaiting our arrival. Also at anchor were a merchant vessel named *Three Brothers*, out of London, and the Spanish brig *Activa*. Ashore were buildings, the first apart from those of the Indians, which we had seen in what seemed like a lifetime. Today was August 29th, 1792. It was hard to believe that I had been away from my home and family since March 1st, 1791, the day I had received the blows that rendered me senseless and placed me in my present situation.

"Peter, your narrative is consuming me my boy. I look at the time. It is almost one. In a few hours the sun will rise and my old bones will feel the stress that accompanies my age, most especially when I have not slept my usual time."

"Yes, Sir Neville, I must apologies for not having more consideration for you."

"Let me make a suggestion. Perhaps we could impose on Mr. Potter, if we can still find him awake, to give us lodging for another night. We could then continue tomorrow with your history."

"Splendid idea my friend. Stay and I will find him." Peter Wright rose stretched his arms and left the room. "Mr. Potter, where are you sir. Come along now, we need rooms for the night."

Discovery

Sir Neville Brown retired to toss and turn for a time, as those of advanced years are apt to do. For Peter Wright sleep did not come easily, he had been reliving his past years again. He remembered faces; he saw places and incidents clearly in his mind. Before sleep finally came, he again saw the grinning face that had haunted him all these years—the face of the man who had delivered the cruel blows so long ago. The words that had consumed Peter Wright, clearly, repeatedly and distinctly, flashed through his mind, *Frederick March is generous*. Who was Frederick March and what strange set of circumstances had made him prey to this stranger. In due course, a peaceful sleep finally claimed him.

19

A Lonely Jane Befriends Her Housemaid and Henry West Tires of Marriage

Sleep finally came to Mrs. Henry West. The euphoria of her betrothal and subsequent blissful early days of marriage had faded dismally. She had not seen Henry for five weeks. Westgate House, which had promised so much, had now become her prison. Not a word, no letter, no message of any kind broke the monotony of her days.

Each morning, a local girl would come to stay the day, to keep house, clean and prepare meals. Gwen was an attractive young woman who said very little, and was no comfort for a young bride without her husband. Jane's days were spent in pursuits, which occupied her time but not her mind. Henry had taken her from the church, to the cheers and encouragement of the guests. Jane, completely besotted with Henry, resplendent in the scarlet and gold uniform of his regiment, was thrilled and excited as their coach made its way towards what was to be their first home. Kisses that probed long and deep, grasping and feeling that went beyond the bounds of propriety; it was in the rolling, moving coach that Jane made her first most intimate acquaintance with Henry.

"Henry what are you doing? Oh my goodness, the coachman will see and we, we." Henry smothered Jane's words with kisses.

"Here my love, give me your hand, let me introduce you the harbinger of the bliss that soon awaits you. Here is our mutual friend." Henry had loosed his flap. He took Jane's hand and placed it on his exposed self.

"Oh, oh Henry what do you do? My goodness it is huge. Oh my love, my love." Jane caressed Henry as he caressed her until they arrived at Westgate House, excited, breathless and fevered.

There were many nights of passion as Henry introduced Jane to acts of love, which left her drained and exhausted, but always she found herself ready and able to rise to new heights of desire. Henry had captivated the heart of this gentle girl. He had introduced her to mysteries of love of which she had never dreamt. Henry had awakened in her unknown feelings, completely mysterious, but now paramount to her existence. She loved love. She needed love. She craved love.

This day she felt overly depressed, so much so that she approached her housemaid to attempt some conversation. Jane herself had employed Gwen Pratt. Gwen had come with immaculate references from her previous employers. Jane doubted the veracity of these fine recommendations, but she knew Gwen just a short time before she realized she could never have written them herself. Gwen was more than adequate in her work, in her demeanour, always cognizant of her place and completely honest.

"Gwen, would you make some tea and I believe there are some biscuits that I enjoyed so much. Perhaps you will come and sit with me awhile. Join me in morning tea."

"Yes mum, I will make tea and there are some of those biscuits left, but I'll have mine in the kitchen, it wouldn't be proper for me to be with you like that."

"Nonsense Gwen, come, sit and we will talk together.'

"No mum. I will eat in the kitchen if you do not mind. That is my place."

"Then I will come to the kitchen. It is settled."

Jane, desperate for companionship, resolved to make some effort to converse with her housekeeper. Perhaps, she thought, I may be able to establish a better relationship that will help wile away the long lonely days. Her mother had taken to her bed soon after the wedding and daily seemed to deteriorate both physically and mentally, sometimes she seemed to have no memory of the present, but regressed to a time when she was a young girl. Her father, over the last weeks, had become quiet and seemed to be constantly preoccupied. His excitement at the marriage with its possibilities of social betterment had waned. No serious word passed between them. Father and daughter both avoided the topics, which agitated and mortified them. Jane was embarrassed by the loneliness of her existence and the absence of her husband. Her father was uncomfortable with the financial dealings and agreements he had signed with Henry West and Frederick March.

For Jane, the constant thought that she had done something to alienate her husband's affection preoccupied her. The first weeks when all was as it should be were nights and days of passion never before experienced. Henry, so sophisticated in the ways of the bedroom, had excited and thrilled her by both words and action. She longed for the dreamy mornings, as she lay exhausted, reliving their previous night's adventures, breathless in anticipation for some new, exciting facet of lovemaking that would soon be introduced to her.

Four weeks after the day of their marriage, Henry had commenced to ride his horse. Each morning he would be gone before she woke. At first he would return by noon, then later and later, until now it was dusk before he would rage and bluster into the house. At these times, she knew he had been drinking. Henry would fall into a deep sound sleep wherever he settled; only to be gone again before she rose. Jane knew Henry had dealings with her father; it was also at this time her father became silent, withdrawn and preoccupied.

Edward Sawtell felt the tension. His daughter seemed changed. She was no longer the young, happy, excited girl that had left Saint Mary's on that blissful day such a short time ago. He had tried to talk to her to find some cause for her sadness. Always his efforts were greeted with the good nature expected from his daughter, but never anything more than silence on the subject of her relations with her husband. For his part, the marriage had not brought the rewards he had expected. In fact, no connection with the Beckingham family had resulted although Jane had come to Henry West with a fine dowry and a cash settlement, not to mention the business and property, which would one day become hers.

It was a few weeks after the wedding when Henry West had come to him with a proposition. At the time, it seemed financially sound and well thought out. A long and arduous journey to London, meetings with Frederick March, business associate of his son-in-law, resulted in a considerable investment. Edward Sawtell was now principal owner of a vast sugar plantation in the West Indies. His London manager, Sir James Boyd had advised ardently against any large investment, but Edward Sawtell would not be deterred and a very reluctant Sir James had transferred monies to a private account.

"Gwen, is the tea ready? Ah, very good, I see you have made it and marvelous you have set a place for us."

"Yes mum, I feel more at home here in the kitchen. Please don't hold it against me."

"Silly girl, of course I won't, it's just that I feel? I feel lonely here in this house. I would be so happy if we could take tea each morning like this." Jane sat at the scrubbed table, which occupied the centre of the large stone-floored kitchen. It was warm and cozy here before the great stove. Two copper pans rattled and jiggled, spewing forth steam and the comfortable smell of cooking and spices pervaded the air.

"Tell me Gwen, do you live in the village?"

"Yes, mum, I live with my family."

"Do you have brothers and sisters?"

"Yes, Mum, I have four sisters and four brothers."

"Your mother and father, are they alive and well?"

"Yes, mum, they both do very well, thank you mum."

"And where do you live in the village?"

"We live near the mill, mum."

"And what does you father do?"

"My father works in the mill, mum."

Jane realized the conversation was fruitless. The gap between them was wide, the product of a society which placed each in a designated social sphere. Gwen, from a labouring family felt completely uncomfortable and out of place, just as Jane knew in her heart she would feel before aristocracy, embarrassed and out of place. Jane decided she would try to pursue a conversation that related to housekeeping.

"Gwen dear, are you happy here?"

"Oh yes, mum."

"Please don't call me mum, it makes me feel old enough to be your mother and we both know that our ages are within a year of each other. I would like us to become companions. My name is Jane; please call me that when we are alone and Mrs. West when company is present, mum makes me feel so old."

Gwen was silent. Jane could almost sense her thoughts as she struggled with this most unusual and for her, completely unfitting request. Serving girls never called their mistresses by their first name under any conditions. No, it was not right. Haltingly she almost pleaded with Jane.

"Mum...Mrs. West. I could never call you by that name.... It would be wrong, very wrong. What would people think? No, I could never do that."

"All right Gwen, then call me Mrs. West if that makes you feel better, I certainly will be happier. Now let us have our tea." Jane poured and the two girls sat for about an hour. Jane carried on a one-sided conversation, but it broke the monotony of her day and she felt better in herself.

Henry West quickly became bored with his life in the country. It was not the country so much as the complete lack of suitable companions. He enjoyed his role as teacher to his new wife. The mysteries and excitement of love came easy to her and he found her an ardent pupil, so much so, she had begun to make demands on him, which he found hard to fulfill. The last weeks had been a rewarding time. Perhaps it was the new state in which he found himself. As a married man, he found a greater acceptance in society and a new period of luck in his gambling. He had decided to leave Burnham Market after a drunken orgy in the village. He recalled returning home to a very displeased and confused wife. He remembered forcing himself on her, much to her horror and displeasure, but apart from that his next recollection was awakening four days later in a strange bed at the home of Frederick March.

The residence of Frederick March was well concealed amid a fine stand of oaks and adjacent to the town of Morden. He had no recollection at all of how he had arrived there. Henry had been in similar situations many times before, but in all his years, he had never experienced such a result from a drinking bout as this. He opened his eyes to see the room spinning dizzily about him; he retched convulsively, which aggravated his throbbing head; finally, he pulled the cover over his head and passed again into an uneasy stupor.

The weeks passed and Henry made no effort to return to his bride. He spent the days eating and sleeping and the nights gambling.

Captain West rose late. He dressed and descended to the dining room. Breakfast was well under way when he took his place beside Frederick March.

"What ho Henry, sleep well?"

"Perfectly my friend, perfectly. What have we in mind for today?" Henry rose and went to the sideboard laden with silver tureens, dishes and a variety of fruits and condiments. "What of the weather? A perfect day methinks."

"Henry you're here at last. The game last night cost me a pretty penny. Damme, I'll get it back tonight so help me." A tall angular woman seated across from Frederick, who could be taken for a man were if it were not for her enormous bosom, shouted in a coarse, throaty voice. "Shan't let you get away with that. What do you say Willie, shall we get even tonight?"

"Yes, me dear. But it will take more than a night to get back what you have deposited in the pockets of these two plausible rogues."

The man sitting beside Lady Susan Blanchford was not her husband. William Bent, a broker and extremely wealthy and had been Lady Susan's lover for the past ten years. He stuffed his mouth with a large piece of ham. He was a tiny fellow, barely coming to the shoulder of his sturdy companion. Lady Susan was obviously adored this little fellow as she draped herself across him.

"Four thousand is a considerable sum, old dear. But you're worth every penny of it, me love." He lent across and planted a greasy, ham-tainted kiss on her cheek.

The others at the table were a heterogeneous group. Two very rotund men, who could quite easily be mistaken for twins, wore grey, tightly curled wigs, ill applied over their smiling, beaming, polished faces. They ate with great enthusiasm from the variety of food, tureens of vegetables, bowls of Yorkshire pudding, slabs of cheese and a fine porker, which displayed considerable gourmand devastation to various parts of its anatomy.

"Yes, we have let go a goodly sum as well, have we not, James?"

"Indeed we have Edward, indeed we have." The smiling ones beamed at each other as they continued eating while they spoke. "The cards have been very kind to Captain West and Mr. March."

Two ladies, neither young nor old, dressed stylishly in the fashion of the time and displaying their obvious wealth, nestled together like robins in winter, in quiet conversation at the far end of the table. As they whispered to each other, they held hands, occasionally releasing to peck at half-eaten food before them.

"Eleanor and I seem to have fallen before the hand of fate, have we not my dear?" The younger of the two spoke quietly to her companion, but also to the others.

"Yes Betty, we certainly have, but we are together in a society that cares not for propriety." Eleanor looked deeply into the eyes of her partner.

"My dear friends, it is always distressing that luck should be so inconsiderate as to empty the pockets of one to the benefit of another. It will be our greatest delight if the cards set you on a path, which will recover your losses. I speak for my friend Henry on this matter." Frederick looked back at Henry, still heaping his plate from the spread of food on the sideboard.

"Tonight," said Frederick," I feel fortune will be on the side of our friends and guests."

The people seated at the table did not see the smile on the face of Frederick March; neither did they see the eye contact and imperceptible wink that passed between the two.

"Ha, the carriages are ready, let's finish here and proceed to the lake side, the day is warm, the flowers are in full bloom and there are pheasant and quail for the taking."

The ill-assorted group, with noise, gentle argument and banter made their way to the carriages waiting before the wide stone steps. Henry and Frederick followed some distance behind the troupe. They spoke in low, confidential tones.

"We did rather well out of that and I trust that tonight will be even better."

"Yes, my friend, we certainly did. I suppose we should give thanks to your wife and her father. Without that gentleman, a man blinded by a desire for advancement in society, the increase in our good fortune would not be nearly as satisfying"

"Please do not remind me of the distressing reality that I have a wife. I had almost forgotten the fact."

"Henry, you must present yourself to your wife. This marriage has benefitted us greatly; it has been like owning the goose that lays the golden egg. Her father is very wealthy and I am sure he will be the source of a still greater increase in the state of our coffers. After we have divested our guests of as much brass as they are willing to part with, let us contrive a stratagem and return to Westgate house. With all possible contrition, we will re-establish you with your young wife and her family. I, for my part, will convey the problems that have plagued West Winds Sugar Company and the need for more investment till crops are again in fine shape."

"Yes, I know you are right in what you say. Strangely enough, she has grown on me. I never want to experience again the state I was in when I arrived here. It took me nearly a week to regain all my faculties. Perhaps absence does make the heart grow fonder. I was a complete brute to her and have virtually abandoned her, but I do like Jane, she is quite beautiful and an excellent student in the arts of love. In fact, she can be quite insatiable. I almost think I miss her. But now, let us spend the day soothing the ruffled feathers of our guests at their losses of last night."

The two joined their companions in the carriage.

"Let's be off. Walk on, driver. Today, dear friends, is a day of picnic and leisure, but tonight we will see what destiny has in store for those who would again challenge its way with a deck of cards."

Their day was spent lying in the sun, strolling along the banks of the lake. A picnic lunch and the surprising musical ability of Frederick March with the lute gave great pleasure to the oddly sorted group. The warmth of the sun, the effects of copious food and wine and gentle conversation, all added to the enchantment of the day and the satisfaction of those present. All returned to the house at three to rest privately in anticipation of another night devoted to gambling. The state of the deck and the honesty of the proponents were never brought into question, much to the financial shortfall of the guests.

20

Cruel Justice and Surfing the Waves

"Peter, my lad, I slept like one who had been on a long sea voyage, I was quite exhausted, I tossed about for a time, your tale filled my thoughts, but once asleep I knew nothing."

Sir Neville and Peter again sat before the fire.

"I must say I feel in a much better state of mind, it seems that telling my tale has released me from some of the demons that have consumed me for so long. I must still find the villain that sent me on my unwelcome journey and I will not rest till that has been done." Peter raised a steaming mug to his lips before continuing.

"Of course this will not be accomplished here in Norfolk, I must needs be in London and it is there that a man to whom I confided my tale is in a position to help me. I told you of Tom Pitt and my altercation with him. He was a strange fellow, ever in trouble. After our fight, he left me alone. It seemed he had a better opinion of me and would nod whenever he came abreast of me. Since I rendered him assistance after his flogging, he became even friendlier. You know him now as Lord Camelford. It seems that fate destined his life and mine to intertwine in some ways. I had the good fortune to render him another service, which, I suppose saved his life. It is here that I shall continue the tale. Peter Wright poured himself another mug of tea; again, he withdrew the pouch from his inner pocket to extract a portion of the golden leaf as he had done before.

"After a few weeks the vessels left Nootka. During our time here, repairs were carried out and I was again set to work with the carpenters. Our vessel *Discovery* was laid ashore in a pleasing cove, which received the name Friendly Cove. The Captain was in constant contact with the commandant of the Spanish establishment, a pleasant looking fellow as I mentioned earlier, named Bodega y Quadra. Vancouver and Quadra seemed to have become very friendly and there were regular visits one to the other. Eventually, with the wind off shore in our favour and with the aid of the small boats towing the vessels to the entrance to the port, we put to sea. We were confident that all that could be done to make our vessels shipshape had been accomplished. Beating our way out of Nootka, we finally caught a strong nor-westerly and sailed south in company with *Chatham* and the supply ship *Daedalus*."

Peter thought for a moment before continuing.

"Two days south from Nootka, the vessels came into the estuary of a mighty river. Across the whole, the surf broke in a continuous line. With *Chatham* in the lead, we began to make our way into the surf to effect an entry into the river itself. I was informed later that this was the River Columbia, named by a trading master, Captain Gray, to commemorate his vessel. *Chatham* had almost no problem in entering, but we, being a larger vessel, found disturbing depths of water. Twice the Captain attempted to take us across the bar. The impetuous sea rose behind us, great walls of water marching towards a channel, only distinguishable by the fact that the waves did not break. All around us these mountains of water tumbled into roaring tumultuous masses of foam. The stern of *Discovery* would rise to the waves and the vessel would be propelled forward at a tremendous speed, then fall back into the trough as the wave passed beneath us. The tide began to fall and an anchorage was attained in the most dreadful conditions. All night we tossed and rolled from side to side. I can tell you it was a sleepless night for all."

"How did you stay out of the breaking waves? I don't understand."

"We were out far enough beyond the surf. At least a mile and a half from shore, consequently we were at the mercy of an agitated sea, with *Chatham* anchored not half a mile from us."

"You say you trusted a rope to hold you all night. I confess that I have no knowledge of the sea and boats at all."

"Yes, The rope as you call it is very thick and the anchor, iron of some hundreds of pounds. On the next day, our vessels again entered the maelstrom. Again *Chatham* led, the wind from the west, blowing in just the right direction. The waves were if anything taller than the previous day. *Chatham* surged into the almost indistinguishable channel and was soon beyond the point of no return.

As before, the depth of water varied with each toss of the lead, till finally, combined with a sudden change of the brisk wind to a strong gale, Captain Vancouver decided that there was no point in further risking the vessel."

"Where was *Chatham*?"

"*Chatham* was gone; the last we saw of her, she had crossed the bar and had entered the stream."

"The helm of *Discovery* was ordered hard down. All hands were at the sails, gust followed gust, each stronger than that before. The wind clawed at the vessel, heeling us over at a terrifying angle. Lieutenant Johnstone gave an order for three of us, desperately clinging to the rigging on the larboard side to get below. *Discovery* was racing along at right angles to the swells that had grown in size with the onslaught of the gale. I saw a mighty wave just before it broke over the side. Water swept across the deck at least three feet deep, Seaman Richard Jones and my self barely managed to retain our grasp. Tom Pitt was swept away towards the starboard side, where he succeeded in taking hold of the main mast ratlines as he went overboard. Repeatedly the vessel rolled to larboard then back to starboard, each time a mass of swirling water swept across the deck. Pitt was one moment on deck, then as another wave swept across, over the side. I managed to claw my way to him and take hold of his collar and arm, till finally with the aid of another wave from the opposite direction, I dragged him onto the deck and up against the fo'c'sil, a position where the sea could not claim us."

"I won't forget this, Wright, I won't forget this."

The enormous effort required to hold onto the shrouds had drained Pitt of all his strength. We both slumped against the bulkhead. Tom Pitt held my arm in an iron grip and I still had his collar in an equally steely grasp.

"What is this? What are you two men doing lying there?" It was Lieutenant Johnstone, "I believe I ordered all of you below."

"Sir, this man saved my life. I was washed overboard and would have been lost had not this man held me and pulled me back on deck."

"All right then, get below both of you." Johnstone turned and made his way like a drunken sailor across the heaving, rolling deck towards the quarterdeck.

Discovery was now well out of danger; her course was set south and at a more agreeable angle to the still mountainous waves.

A few days later anchorage was attained at the Spanish port of Monterey, such a pleasant place with a wonderful healthy climate. I never went ashore here, but again served with the carpenters for the whole of our stay. The only respite was the unsavoury task of loading cattle and sheep aboard the store ship Daedalus, for the infant colony at Port Jackson, New South Wales.

Eventually all was ready and the anchor hauled. In no time we were out sight of land, our course set towards the Sandwich Islands. It seemed that our Captain had determined it was more practical to spend the winter in the balmy climate of these islands that to stay in the cold and snow of the north. Dr. Menzies called for me and charged me to rewrite journal entries damaged by water during our recent inundation at the Columbia River. I had commenced the work and Dr. Menzies was looking over my shoulder at an entry that was stained and almost completely unintelligible. Both he and I were startled by a voice from the darkness of the companionway.

"Dr. Menzies, what are you about?" Captain Vancouver broke the silence. "I have a matter that I must discuss with you, sir. Walk the deck with me for a while. Who is that with you?"

"It's the man Wright, who has become my assistant of sorts, captain."

"Yes, I know the man." Vancouver's portly frame filled the doorway, "So you are an educated man?"

"Yes, sir," I answered.

"I have had good reports on you. Here against your will, but making the most of it, aye. Mr. Johnstone tells me you saved one of our midshipmen from certain death."

I did not answer the Captain.

"Well, keep him busy Doctor. Do not allow him to get too high of an opinion of himself. Come let us walk to the deck."

This was the first time words were exchanged between the Captain and me.

During our stay at Monterey, two men from *Chatham* deserted and were lost in this great hinterland, one of *Discovery*'s men also made his escape. James Baily, a seaman, said not a word to anyone of his plans. His absence was discovered and search parties were sent out to scour the countryside as well as the Spanish settlements and missions for this man. He was eventually found at a mission, in the sanctuary of the Franciscan priests and brought back in chains. He remained manacled until we were well out to sea. Baily was punished with six dozen lashes at two separate times. I cannot tell you of the anguish I felt for this man. After the second six dozen, he was never the same. Always a quiet man, after this punishment he never spoke and looked towards the quarterdeck with blazing hatred.

Before long, the weather warmed and the influence of tropic latitudes began to be felt. The island of Owhyhee appeared on the horizon on about the 12th of February, 1793. The strange cloud formations signaled land, signifying the still invisible barrier of the big island with its enormous mountains, which prevented the cloud mass from continuing on its westward journey. I was constantly amazed at the heavy rain, mist and dense foliage on the east side of the land, in contrast to the desert on the west side. Most of the land was black lava, which had emanated from fiery volcanoes. The night sky was always red with the glare of these volcanoes and lava flows, which streamed like rivers towards the sea, sending clouds of steam high into the air. It tries the imagination to consider how these islands of paradise began their life in a sea so deep no sounding with our longest lead line was possible.

A canoe appeared out of a small bay. Unlike the last visit here, these people seemed fearful. Dr Menzies told me the priests had put a taboo on trade with any European or American ships. No hogs or other produce of the islands were to be traded, unless for firearms, this under pain of death. Dr. Menzies reflected on the ire of Captain Vancouver at this change in attitude since his first visits here with Captain Cook. Firearms had become gold to these once gentle, generous people. Now they fought with each other, the society with the greater firepower becoming the dominant group.

Captain Vancouver seemed to have a considerable influence in these islands. At another anchorage, a chief named Kahowmotoo came aboard. Though Vancouver spoke in no uncertain terms when he stated trading in firearms was out of the question, the chief supplied our vessels with great quantities of produce and hogs. Again, this same chief and his ladies, who had boarded *Discovery* on our last visit, came on deck. If anything, the ladies seemed larger than barely a year ago. I cannot tell you of the mirth, laughter and screams of delight that accompanied these enormous women to the deck. Their efforts to heave themselves up the side of *Discovery* were aided by sailors who pulled from the deck, as others pushed from behind in complete abandonment of propriety. Hands thrust at buttocks and thighs with no sign of decorum. As before, Captain Vancouver in his dress uniform had difficulty maintaining a straight face, officers turned away to wipe the tears of suppressed laughter from their eyes.

At this time, the Captain directed that all must be well trained in the use of arms, both musket and the cutlass. Captain Vancouver considered that the occasion of hostilities between the various native people and us to be more than a possibility. He therefore instructed the Sergeant of Marines, a nasty, officious fellow, Edward Flynn, along with his corporal, an equally obnoxious person, George Williams, to supervise lessons in this manly art. Each morning we would assemble on deck, to be abused and tormented in the most uncomplimentary terms. It seemed to me our teachers used the premise that the louder voice in which the lessons were delivered, the more readily the lesson sank in. The art of musketry was not all that foreign to me. On many occasions, I had accompanied my father and his friends into the fields and forests, which surrounded my Norfolk home, for grouse and pheasant.

The cutlass, that broad curved sword, which had become the weapon of the navy, was completely unknown to me. Again, as with fisticuffs, it seemed I had some natural affinity to the art. I soon mastered the various positions that were standard teaching procedure. The first and second position, four balance positions, five extension positions, were explained and demonstrated. Soon I was able to display mastery over the teachers, much to their chagrin. The knee-flexing bends, the lunges of a ballet dancer soon made me a deadly force with the cutlass. Tom Pitt, who now spoke to me at any time, conveyed that he considered me a natural and would always choose pistols if ever we were to be involved in an affair of honour. Lieutenant Baker had also become aware of my natural expertise. One day when the captain and most of the other officers were ashore, he called me out.

"I have been watching you, Wright. I see that you have skill with the cutlass. I have a pair of gentleman's weapons. They are French and quite deadly. I am in need of competition and I will show you how to use them. On occasions a bout could be arranged."

"Yes, sir." I was taken aback by this.

The weapons produced were long and light. The blade, if it could be called that, was no more than a pointed rod. The hilt and guard were a handle and cup, with a strap attached. Lieutenant Baker called it a martingale. The strap circled the fingers to prevent disarming. Again, in no time I was more than a match for Lieutenant Baker. These bouts occurred whenever we were at anchor and free time was available. The Captain knew of them and made no move to prevent them.

My companions in the fo'c'sil had by now sensed that I was their superior, if not by experience then by birth and ability. They left me alone and I suffered no more of the nasty banter that had made my life such a misery when first I had arrived on board *Discovery*.

Our stay in the Sandwich Islands lasted from February 12th until the 30th of March, such a pleasant time in sunny, warm, luminous weather. Even the officers seemed gentler to us, as we explored these beautiful islands. The sea displayed a colour without compare when measured against that of the colder climes of the North Sea. With the sun high in the heavens, the blue of the tropical sea defies description, almost black, but at the same time iridescent and bright. Foam, dancing from the bow of our vessel, was a brilliant white contrast against the inky blue-black of the sea. The ocean swarmed with denizens of all descriptions. Whales threw themselves towards the sky in some desperate homage to the warm sun. Dolphins leapt and played in profusion about the bow of *Discovery*.

We were overawed, simple seamen and officers alike, at the sunsets, which stilled voices and bathed all in a golden glow, before giving way to the dark of night and a heaven swarming with infinite stars. We marveled at the enormous moon, rising like Diana, orange and fearsome, only to change her attire as she rose from the sea, her white gown trailing across the purple dark of night.

The people of these islands were blessed beyond that of any other. They lived in perfect harmony of weather and refreshments, both of land and sea.

I must tell you of a spectacle witnessed on the island of Oahu, during one of the many excursions, which I attended as oarsman. A vast bay had opened before us. A great extinct volcano stood sentinel at the eastern headland, sheltering the bay from the enormous seas that crashed ashore at other places, letting only the most perfect waves enter. The gentle people of this land had devised a method of speeding ashore using nothing but a length of wood, carved and pointed. They would kneel on it, paddling furiously until the momentum of the wave would gather them up and then spit them out to rush headlong towards the shore. Some of the more expert would stand upright. On reaching the shore, they would turn and make their way, back out, to again experience this joyous distraction.

In the pinnace, we sailors hovered just beyond the breaking waves. Watching this pastime, the exuberance and cries of joy from the natives filled Midshipmen Pitt and Humphries, who were in command, with a determination to experience this adventure with our longboat. The natives, on seeing that we were about to attempt their exciting pursuit, gathered around us offering what I can only imagine to be advice, for not one of us had the slightest idea of their vocabulary.

"Come on, come on, pull, pull, pull, pull," Pitt and Humphries entered into the spirit of the moment. "Harder, pull."

All now were caught up in the thrill and commotion of the moment, everyone pulled with a will and every ounce of their strength. A wave came up behind us; the stern of the pinnace rose and we were propelled forward at the speed of the wave, until the height of water became more than the shape of the vessel could accommodate. Like lightning, we shot off at right angles to the foamy crest. All became chaos aboard, oars, men, goods were inundated with water, and we laughed and cried out in our exuberance, much to the mirth of our native spectators. Our midshipmen leaders determined to conquer this pastime, and three more attempts were made, each with the same result. It seems a prerequisite for success at this pastime is the design of the instrument used.

However, all was not peace and beauty. Later it came to our notice that the commander of the store ship Daedalus, Lieutenant Hergest, had been murdered on the Island Woahoo. This had a sobering effect on all the people of our vessels and brought home the delicate situation in which we found ourselves. Killed along with him was a seaman of Portuguese extraction and William Gooch, an astronomer, being delivered to *Discovery* at Nootka. From the meager information I gained from Dr. Menzies and others, it seems that against the advice of a native who had accompanied Lieutenant Hergest on a search for water, his party landed in a bay on the north shore of the island. Here a number of bad people reside and while the water was being loaded and again against all advice, Hergest and Gooch went to a village a distance inland. While they were there, an altercation occurred at the beach, resulting in the death of the seaman.

When the news of this event reached the village, the natives thought that to prevent revenge by the Europeans they would kill the chiefs, who were, to their simple minds, Hergest and Gooch. Apparently, Mr. Gooch was killed instantly with a native weapon, a pahooa to the heart. Mr. Hergest attempted to make his way to the boat, but was struck by a stone to the head and then murdered most foully. I was informed how one of the murderers was executed by his chief when he heard of this ghastly deed. The other murderers were living in a village a few miles from our present position.

I cannot tell you of the discussions that were carried on between Vancouver and the chiefs of the island, but suffice to say the culprits were swiftly brought to justice. A double canoe drew up alongside *Discovery*. Aboard the canoe was a former employee of the famous trader, James Kendrik. This man, James Coleman, had entered the employ of the chief, Tennavee, to help regulate visiting ships to these islands. Accompanying him, Tohoobooarto, a lad who had made a voyage to China on a trading vessel and consequently had some grasp of the English language.

All the visitors immediately adjourned to the Captain's cabin. Some time later, three men sitting in the canoe, who had been apprehended by the chief and our marines, were taken below. The face of one of these men was of fearsome aspect, made so, by terrible tattoos, which rendered his visage frightful to see. The other two, though tattooed, did not display the same degree of ferocity as their companion. Two days passed with constant going and coming of both natives and our people. I discovered that Captain Vancouver was determined to make sure of the guilt of these men.

About noon on the 22nd, seamen and marines in their red uniform coats drew up along the starboard side. Gunners manned the great guns, as the three miscreants were taken into a canoe. What followed was a disgusting exhibition by all and a savage disregard for life. The chiefs cut the long hair of one man with little thought for the comfort of the doomed fellow. A ferocious argument followed over who should present the hair to the king of the island. The bound men seemed to have no interest in the proceedings at all and were dispatched by the chief Tennavee. With his own pistol, he blew out the brains of each man with such expertise that I am sure they were dead instantly. No movement or twitch was visible the moment the pistol fired. The canoe carrying the chief and the dead men left our side. Lamentations and wailing could be heard from the shore well into the evening.

I tell you this story of crime and punishment as an illustration of the meanness of man to his fellows, even in this beautiful, natural paradise. If I consider the punishments I have witnessed and suffered at the hands of polite society and compare them with the deeds of these children of nature, I must be ashamed of the whole human race. These people, with no education from us, have perfected their own method of cruel punishments. They have naturally developed engines of war and strive for possession of our more deadly implements. The only purpose of this is to subjugate their neighbours. Ah, Sir Neville, my dear friend, I fear mankind has a long way to go before it can claim a kinship with our Lord and Creator, who I am sure intended a higher purpose for his great work of creation than the oppression of other of his species.

The stay here had a wonderful effect on the general health and demeanour of the crew, both officers and men. It had every aspect of a holiday. Boat voyages were of a short duration, the weather was perfect and warm. The rain of the north seemed a thing of the past. Although all were on constant guard against treachery, none ever became evident. The ladies of these islands were of a beauty and nature that delighted all. The sight of women and men clad only in the vestments of nature was beyond comprehension to those of the colder, more reserved climates. For men who had been out of contact with a gentler life, it is not incomprehensible that talk of women and desertion was uppermost at the various mess times.

These people had Gods in abundance, Gods for all occasions, the most terrifying of all being named Pelee. This was the terrible deity, which resided in the fiery volcanoes spewing forth fire and brimstone on the greatest island, Owyhee. These Gods would on occasion demand the body of a young girl, a maiden, as a sacrifice. This was a people who suffered a slave class. They retained a class purely for sacrifice, whether to appease the fiery wrath of Pelee or to provide a spirit to hold up the corner posts of a temple or dwelling. I tell you these things to demonstrate the fact that we all have the ability to be cruel and oppressive, especially to those of our own nature and race, not to mention those of a different colour or race.

Our stay continued. The time was filled with exploration, charting, shore expeditions and diplomacy. The Captain made numerous excursions to the villages and the chiefs in turn visited *Discovery*, nearly always accompanied by a large retinue of wives, warriors and others of lesser rank. In these islands there seemed to be constant conflict, as one faction vied with another for superiority. British and American sailors now lived in the various villages, having deserted from their trading vessels. These men, it seemed, were in the employ or perhaps under the protection of the various chiefs where they lived. The chiefs, in their struggle for power and supremacy, put the expertise of these expatriates into the manipulation of weapons and training for war.

I must tell you of the presence aboard *Discovery* of two native women from the Sandwich Islands. It appears they were smuggled aboard the vessel *Jenny*, without the knowledge of the commander. Our captain took these women on board in Nootka for return to their native country. These ladies, for I must address them as such, were in every way a credit to their race. The younger, Raheina, was perhaps fourteen, the older, Tymarow, about five years her senior. They were of quite pleasing countenance and nature. They had acquired a wardrobe of sorts from the captain. Both wore a type of riding habit, which, despite the long skirt, so different from their normal scanty clothing, was handled by them with all the aplomb and dignity of any woman of our own society. I must say they were given every respect by all aboard, even the rough seamen. I think the sight of these ladies on deck brought a feeling of nostalgia for family and loved ones, so far removed and still so many years away. The young ladies were restored to their home though the good offices of Captain Vancouver.

I think the Captain had allowed his heart to over rule his good judgment where these ladies were concerned, his usual rather severe features would soften in their presence. Gallant behaviour, smiles and courtly manners, far from that normally evidenced to the crew, became his style when they were present.

We departed from the Sandwich Islands and the sun rose on our right, until on the eighth day out, then the wind changed suddenly and blew from the northwest. The advent of these winds produced the most dreadful fall in temperature I have ever experienced. Immediately this wind struck the warm balmy breezes of Owhyee changed to a bone-chilling gale. What a contrast in temperature from that which we had become used too. The meager clothing which had sufficed during the stay in the Sandwich Islands was changed for the warmer dress that had been ours during the winter past. Now the sun rose out of the sea before us as our new course took us back to the continent of America.

"So now you head back to the east?"

"Yes my friend, we head back to hard, hard work, to gales, rain and rowing. I will tell you that none were happy at this prospect."

"I have remained silent, now I must ask you a question or two. I imagine that you had replenished the ships stores from the produce of the Island."

"Yes we did. All was well until the sudden drop in temperature. Almost immediately all the poultry died. Captain Vancouver ordered double issue of food on this return to the east. Before we sighted land all the refreshments from the islands were exhausted, so again portable soup, beef and biscuits, but of a copious quantity were ours to be enjoyed."

"This was not of a reckless nature considering the wild and difficult land that was to be investigated? Supplies might not be so abundant."

"Ah, Sir Neville, the land of New Albion is without doubt the most generous of all lands. We would again experience its spring and summer. At this time the forest is a riot of berries and fruits, the sea abounds in fish, schools so vast that they extend from horizon to horizon, while above, fowl of every variety await the marksmanship of our hunters. We must also be cognizant of the fact that Daedalus, our store ship would meet us in Nootka at the end of the autumn with supplies from Port Jackson, Manila, China and Owhyee. No, supplies were never of a desperate nature. The life of a seaman on a voyage such as ours was beyond compare when considered against the normal life of the British sailor. At no time were we in want of fine food while we were in the country of the Pacific Northwest."

"I understand. I can see that you were left to your own devices and ingenuity when it came to sustenance."

"The voyage back was as memorable as I had come to expect. A leak in the vessel was discovered a few days out from the Sandwich Islands. This increased so much so that constant pumping was barely enough to keep it under control. The pumps were manned twenty-four hours a day. The coal-hole was the wettest place; water had also found its way to the magazine, which rendered our supply of powder suspect. All our people took turns at the pump, an exercise that barely controlled the flow. We also had the misfortune to have two pieces of rigging carried away in a heavy gale. Aside from these events and adverse winds, the voyage back to New Albion was completed in fine style."

"Eventually we entered Friendly Cove. After the usual salutes to the Spanish masters of this post, the vessel was beached and repaired. As for me, I again became a companion to the carpenters, a past time that I did not at all find objectionable. The carpenters were all good men and excellent companions. It was about the morning of May 23rd in heavy rain and mists that *Discovery* and *Chatham* moved out of Friendly Cove into the ocean. Our goal was to take up our task from where we had left off the previous year, amid the rugged snow-clad mountains and rock strewn waterways to the northeast of the great island."

Peter became again silent. He seemed to ponder his thoughts and arrange his tale in some sort of order. *Discovery* had anchored in a cove, beautifully protected and safe from the gales and seas of the open ocean. From here, the small boat voyages again commenced. The safe anchorage received the name Safety Cove and the sound where the heavy work of exploration again commenced received the name of Rivers Inlet.

21

Henry West Returns to Jane and Renews Their Relationship

"Mrs. West, mum, there is a gentleman to see you and I have shown him into the parlor."

"Is it my father? I worry so much about the condition of my mother. At any time, I expect him to arrive with news that I do not want to hear. Tell me it is not my father."

"No Mum, it is a military gentleman who claims to be your husband."

"Can it be? It must be my husband Captain West. Gwen help me, I must change into something else. The green gown... no, no, the blue, I know blue is my colour. My hair quickly, quickly. Help me. I'm so excited I cannot function as I should."

"Gwen, how does he look? Is he well? Has he changed since the last time you saw him? Oh, I forget, you have never seen him before. I am breathless and aflutter. Help me out of this quickly."

Jane discarded her day dress and rushed to the dresser to sit before the mirror.

"Oh my hair, look at it." Jane removed the pins that restrained her hair high on her head, releasing a flood of deep golden tresses, shimmering to her waist.

"Shoes mum, what shoes will you wear?"

Jane had long ago ceased her efforts to feel comfortable with Gwen. Try as she would, there seemed no way that Gwen could relax in her presence, although things were much more relaxed between them of late. Gwen began to brush her hair in long strokes, taking in the full length at each sweep of the brush.

"I will leave it long, Henry likes it that way and we will just tie it back with a ribbon. Now help me into my dress. Gwen, did you notice any marks or blemishes on his countenance that could foretell of some embattlement or distress? He is a soldier you know. I'm sure his absence must be the result of some official business on behalf of the government." Gwen assisted Jane into a dress of light blue brocade; her excitement was obvious in the rise and fall of her milky breasts, raised by the bodice high beneath. She fixed a cameo, a treasured gift from her grandmother, close to her throat. "Shall I wear a buffon? No, I will leave myself bare."

"Gloves Gwen, I must have my gloves, I know to wear gloves is going out of style, but I will wear them."

"No mum, I saw nothing but a very pleasing face and uniform. Here is a pair of fine lace gloves, mum." Jane almost snatched the gloves from her hand.

"How do I look?" Jane pirouetted before her companion. "Tell me if you see any flaw in my appearance. Oh Gwen, I am so excited I can hardly think." Jane grasped the back of a chair to steady herself. "Shoes, oh heavens shoes, the thin Moroccan pair, quickly Gwen, am I ready? Here I go down to my husband; oh, I am so happy I could cry. No, I will keep him waiting a while; let us wait ten minutes until I recollect myself. Dear Gwen, you will announce me please and make tea in about half an hour."

Jane, after many attempts had finally convinced Gwen Page to become her companion, more than just a maid. To this effect, she had managed to get her out of the black dress and bonnet favoured for the first months of her employment. Jane had given Gwen four gowns from her own wardrobe; she had also rearranged her hair in a more becoming style. Apart from a heavy Norfolk accent, which displayed her lack of formal education and working class upbringing, she had become a very attractive young woman.

Gwen opened the wide doors. Captain West stood with his back to the fire.

"Sir, Mrs. West." Henry gazed at the handsome young lady standing in the entry. He was surprised. He had expected a maid, but this woman was quite beautiful and obviously more than just hired help. Before he could speak, Jane appeared beside her.

"Jane, my love." Henry was taken aback. Here standing before him were two beautiful women. His wife had changed since their last meeting, she seemed older, but barely a year had passed since their marriage. She was stunning in the simplicity of her dress. Her Imperial-style blue gown complemented the golden copper of her hair, cascading across her alabaster shoulders. My God, she is beautiful he thought, but who is this other one?

On his journey up to Norfolk, Henry had rehearsed a story of the past months. He had established in his mind a sequence of events, but strangely, he was speechless; all the lies rehearsed in the carriage from London had abandoned him. Henry struggled to find words for the moment. Here he was returned to a wife he barely knew and did not really want. While he was no longer bankrupt thanks to his marriage, he continued to invent deceptions. He managed to preserve this state by quick wit and a gift of mendacity without equal. Now this woman, his wife, had rendered him speechless and without the wit to speak a word.

"By heaven, Jane, I'm back."

"Oh, Henry, where have you been? I have missed you so and not a word. Tell me my love. Leave us now Gwen." Gwen left the pair and closed the door.

Henry West moved across the room towards his wife. He felt awkward, a new feeling for him. He was eloquent in the art of separating gullible people from their money. He had little conscience and was expert in the skill of cheating at the gaming tables. With no scruples towards the opposite sex, he was aware of his power over women of all classes, who came to him to be separated from their virtue and whatever wealth was theirs.

Here with Jane all was different. He hardly recognized the woman who stood before him. For the first time in his life, he found himself confused and awed by a beautiful woman and it was more than he could come to terms with. Her smoldering, deep, yet gentle eyes gazed into his, innocent of any knowledge of his nefarious existence and deceitful nature. He was faced with a strange circumstance for him. However, he would lie repeatedly to her and in reality had only come to reestablish favour with her family and relieve a doting father of a little more of his wealth. He could not escape the fact she was a beautiful woman, and as much as he detested the thought he found himself almost in love for the first time in his life. Despite this strange sickly feeling, Henry West was confident Jane was his, and he could control her and her family at his will.

"Jane, what can I say? Give me your hand. You look marvelously well." He took her hands holding her away from him, "You have changed. My God, you have become a woman, and in so short a time."

"Henry, tell me everything, what has kept you away so long? I am forced to believe you were employed on a secret venture of some sort. If duty demands it be kept secret then I won't press you."

"You are correct, my dear. I have been on His Majesty's service. Suffice it to say the turmoil that has recently befallen France and Europe in general, has required my presence in fields of endeavour that must remain secret." Henry West breathed a sigh of relief at the opening given him by his wife. He jumped at the opportunity to say no more about his activities over the last months. "Very secret and dangerous work, so much so that I feel fate or a heavenly power has been with me. I will be here for a short time only, then back to the dangerous occupation that my country demands."

"Oh no Henry, you will be leaving again. Tell me, how long I have to bestow my love on you."

Jane threw herself into Henry's arms, completely oblivious to the deception wrought on her and her family.

"My dear, let us use the time allowed us in the pursuit of happiness. Let us renew our love and return to the blissful pursuits of former days. My time here may be of short duration so we must grasp every opportunity to be together."

Henry kissed Jane, a kiss she welcomed, her feelings of abandonment completely forgotten as she nestled into the embrace of the tall, red-jacketed officer of the army of King George. A feeling of anticipation of the night ahead made her almost swoon. In the months she had spent, alone she had realized how much she craved the sexual nature of Henry West and their nights of passion when he would induce her to carry out acts and display feelings she had never known.

"Your father and mother, they are well?"

"Oh, dear Henry. My father is well enough, but the health of my mother is not good. Because of this, he is despondent and sad. I see them quite often and I have a feeling from within that all is not as it should be in his business dealings. However, of course this is not discussed, something that I know nothing about. Now tell me of your family, they are well and no doubt happy to receive you back into their fold."

"Ah, yes, one of the most gratifying experiences for a soldier is to return whole to the loving embrace of family and friends. We will not mention the welcome and promise that you, my dear one, bestow with your kisses and breathless glances."

"I am so desirous of meeting your father and brothers. Tell me, Henry, will we be able to see them? They have a loving daughter and sister they have never met."

Henry did not like the turn of the conversation. His father had again made it quite clear that he would have nothing to do with him while he continued his present way of life. Their last meeting had ended in a battle of words, both hurling insults at the other, until finally Henry strode away from his father, each vowing never to see the other again. As for brothers, he did not have any, but considered it a useful deception to establish his relations as a loving family.

"Yes, Jane, I believe my father will be in Norwich this coming month, perhaps then you will have the pleasure of meeting the sire of the family, which has given you the name you now bear. We must only hope that my military service will not take me away before such a meeting can be arranged."

Jane stood close to her husband. She sensed no deception in his manner, only joy at being again in his company and anticipation at the promise of the night of love ahead. Henry placed his arm about her waist; he drew her towards him. They lost themselves in a kiss, long, deep and passionate, a kiss that did not let them see or hear Gwen as she entered with the tea that Jane had ordered.

"Oh, Gwen, I did not know you were there." Jane, embarrassed, flushed to an even deeper shade than that which already enhanced her cheeks

"Who is this young lady, Jane? I had no knowledge of a companion in the house." Henry did not leave hold of Jane; he gazed at Gwen, his eyes taking in every part of her being.

"Henry, this is Gwen Pratt. I engaged Gwen as a housemaid, now she lives here the week, we have become companions. Gwen this is Captain West, my husband."

"Good afternoon, sir, I have made tea." As Henry West took in Gwen, she also discreetly scrutinized him.

"Tea! Tea! Good God, Jane, I have been traveling all day and you give me tea, I need something a lot stronger than tea, me dear. Miss Pratt, what do we have here, surely there must be more than tea?"

"Sir, there is ale and wine.

"Your mistress will have tea, but bring me ale, me throat feels like parchment." Henry never took his eyes off Gwen; neither did he release Jane from his embrace.

"Gwen it is almost time to prepare dinner, please make this a special occasion, spare no effort to contrive something suitable for the return of your master. My dear husband is back with me and tonight is his. Spare nothing in your efforts to make this as memorable a feast as you are able."

"Yes Mum, I will do all that is necessary." Gwen left the room, she understood immediately the person of Henry West. She knew his glance took in more than her outer appearance. She was well aware that in his mind, Henry West had undressed her. She knew he was a liar and a rake, while she did not have the right words, she also knew here was a man, deeply narcissistic and a sexual predator. She was uneducated, but astute in the ways of the world and men. She also knew that it was only a matter of time before Henry West would cast his glances in her direction.

Gwen could not sleep that night. She heard the sounds, the cries and sighs of her mistress. She left her bed to listen at the door. Whenever sleep would begin to claim her, the sounds of passion would recommence. Every fiber of Gwens being cried out in anguish and desire. Sleep finally came to the exhausted household in the wee small hours of the morning.

22

Native Customs and Mussel Poisoning

"My friend, those balmy sun-filled days in the lush islands of Owhyhee were now well behind us, rain and fog again became our daily lot. Bone-chilling cold winds clawed at our very soul. Our days were filled with a labour so intense that sleep came instantly despite the rock, gravel or forest floor that was our bed. I have never seen such mountains, great towering, ice-clad peaks that were swallowed up into the clouds, passages between stark cliffs, which plunged a thousand feet straight down into the water. Often no land flat enough for a camp could be discovered; in these instances, the boats would be our bed for the night. You cannot imagine how uncomfortable it is to sleep with just an oar for a pillow. It was only the exhaustion brought about by hours of rowing in the vilest conditions, which rendered all so fatigued that sleep came instantly."

"Peter, these were the small vessels and I assume crowded with men and supplies?"

"Yes, you have no idea of the terrible nights experienced in these conditions. Naturally, a watch would be set. This would be necessary to keep a lookout for prowling beasts and natives who might approach us during the night. I am sure that attackers could kill us all in our sleep such was the state of our exhaustion."

It was also necessary in these situations to alter any mooring lines as the tide rose or fell. In these latitudes, tides averaged twenty feet, so constant vigilance was required, lest we become hung up or swamped by the tidal movement. It was of little consequence in fine weather, but in the rain, sleet and cold, a night in these small boats tied to a cliff face, which gave no opportunity to move ashore was beyond comprehension. In canal after canal, granite faces would raise from the depths, only to vanish into the rain-laden clouds and most of the time everything was wet. It was only the warmth generated by constant exertion that kept us in any way warm, but not dry.

"I must say Peter; I would be of no use whatsoever in a situation such as you describe. I have always found it necessary to sleep in complete comfort and now at my age, discomfort is completely out of the question."

"About June 16th, the vessels were visited by a group of ladies. These female visitors behaved in the most dignified and gentle manner. The term lady is loosely used, if a comparison were to be made between these children of nature and our own sweet English lasses. It was noticed that the females of consequence in this group, generally being the elder, were decorated with a most unusual and horrible adornment. A slit had been cut across the lower lip, most likely at an early age, equal in length to the mouth above. By degrees, this slit was stretched to admit a disc of wood. This disc would protrude horizontally. It varied in size, from large, in excess of three inches to the smallest at two inches. These discs, made of fir, about four-tenths of an inch thick, were highly polished. My friend, you cannot imagine the grotesque appearance of these ladies. I was able to come into possession of one of the large discs. I fear the woman who surrendered her ornament had taken a liking to me. As a pressed man, I had nothing to trade. In any case, all trading, by order, had to be carried out under supervision of the officers. She extracted the ornament from her lip and presented it to me, smiling as she did so. Without her lip piece, she appeared to have two mouths, one atop the other. As she smiled at me, I do not think I have ever seen anything so grotesque. While we had all become accustomed to the art of tattooing the body, and the habit in some tribes of cutting the flesh in various patterns, no one had ever seen such a decoration. It struck me that this adornment was a supreme act of absurdity. The women, who were very vocal, presented a sight unrivaled, as the words, which poured from their mouths agitated the lip decoration, this in turn wiggled up and down vigorously with every word."

"I must accept your words as fact; I cannot imagine anything as perverse as what you tell me."

Sir Neville mused aloud on the nature of women.

"Our ladies wear the most disfiguring garments, which give a completely false impression of the shape of the female body, but to mutilate one's principal adornment, the face, seems beyond comprehension."

"I agree completely with that, my friend. Suffice to say that the nature of the primitive ladies with whom I have come in contact follow the same persuasion as our own fair members, the difference being the material used to adorn the body. Our ladies beautify themselves with embellishments of perfume and powder of a delectable nature, but the ladies of the northwest favour oils and greases, distilled, I would imagine, from the whale or seal and of a nature that offends olfactory senses not accustomed to odours of such a high intensity."

"But my friend I seem to remember the anguish you experienced in the fo'c'sil, at the aromas you experienced when first aboard *Discovery*. You came to terms with that."

"Yes I did. In a short time, I did not notice the constant smell from the bilge or the odour of long-unwashed companions, for I suffered the same odorous malady. However, to experience the smell of fishy oil adorning the body of an otherwise attractive person reawakened senses long dormant. I must add that those without the lip adornment were of a very pleasing countenance, especially for men deprived of the comfort of female company for as long as had been our lot. For us, the opportunity of contact with the opposite sex was never a possibility, even in the Sandwich Islands; the ordinary seamen had no real chance of union with the nubile, free beauties of Ohwyhee."

"Then I must ask the question, what did you do in regard to the natural urges of healthy fit men?"

"Among certain of the crew attachments were made, which I am sure resulted in contact of a nature that defies description and cannot be spoken of in a genteel society. For the majority of the men it was a case of gritting one's teeth and trying to ignore the demands of the body for as long as possible, till in the depths of night or in the darkness of the hold, relief would be attained in private and alone."

"My dear Peter, I am at a loss to really grasp the enormity and deprivation of the situation in which you found yourself."

"Sir Neville, I would say that the saving grace for us all was the constant exhaustion, which was generally always upon us. Sleep came instantly in any condition, where and whenever a bed could be found. There was always work to be done, even in the most relaxed of times, exhaustion was always our companion."

"The place where we had met the warriors and the ladies with the lip ornaments, which I have since become aware were named a labret, was the entrance to a phenomenal waterway. A village was built on piles supported by beams, which cantilevered out over the water. Behind, the mountains rose in spectacular grandeur thousands of feet to disappear into the heavy clouds that continually drenched us with rain and concealed all with constant fog.

In my mind I am back there now, a sad and melancholy time."

Peter gazed into the distance as once again he relived memories from the past.

"Look there! The size of the posts supporting the roof, they are immense; how in heavens name would they get them into this position?"

Lieutenant Johnstone mused aloud and then answered himself.

"They surely did not get them from the land on which these places are built; trees of this size were most definitely brought from some other place."

The men pulled on the oars and propelled the boats into the inlet. *Discovery* and *Chatham* were anchored far to the south in a cove at the intersection of two channels. One led to the west, the other extended away to the north. The small boats had gone on their way from this anchorage, to become two ever-decreasing specks in the distance, before being lost from sight amid the mountainous wilderness about them.

"Look, over there, steer us over there Mr. Pitt, towards that great waterfall."

The boats approached the massive tumbling waterfall, supplied by the never-ending rain and melting ice from some glacier, high and lost in the fog overhead. A wind, turbulent and wild, generated by the violence of the cascading, rushing water, blew violently across the otherwise tranquil calm of the inlet. As the vessels drew nearer, the enormity of the falls became clearer. The thunderous roar, the gale of wind propelled out across the mirror-like surface of the inlet, was so strong as to prevent the boats approaching any closer than a quarter of a cable. The pure white of the falling tumult contrasted starkly against inky black of the rocky outcrop, which marked the watery path to the sea.

"Waterfalls everywhere. What great, icy mass is concealed above us in the clouds? The noise from so many cataracts is almost deafening. Take us into the depths of the inlet, pull away men." The boats surged ahead and were enveloped by the profundity of the mountains.

"Never was the hand of the creator was more evident than here. Mr. Barrie, look at that, the cliffs sheer into the water."

"Yes, up there great hollows and chasms, polished I venture, by some ancient glacier receded into the clouds. What a magnificent place."

The seamen rowed quietly, the boats silent of the usual banter and rowing chants. Even rough seamen, were over-awed by the majesty of the surroundings. Eventually the party arrived at the headwater of the inlet, here mountains parted to make way for a flat swampy area and an access into an inner lake through a narrow, rocky entry. The falling tide created a reversing tumult of swirling foamy water as the mass of the inner lake surged out into the inlet. The clouds began to clear, revealing an extent of ice, transparent and blue, high overhead, illuminated and coloured by the deepening yellow rays of a watery, misty, evening sun.

"Petee Wright, I think God 'ad somethin' to do with this place."

John Carter spoke quietly. The majesty of this place had the effect of causing all to whisper. We continued to pull towards the swirling opening of the inner lake, the water of which was at least four feet higher than that outside in the inlet.

"Yes John, I must agree, this country is magnificent. Most surely the hand of God is everywhere evident."

Soon the clouds resumed their dominion over the heavens. Heavy rain began again, drenching the parties; as they left this awesome place steam rose from their bodies generated by the heat of their exertions. Their course took them through a narrow opening, the result of some ancient cataclysmic occurrence that had allowed the face of a mountain to break away and fall into the channel. They all pondered the mighty forces that had caused a three thousand-foot granite cliff to part from its host monolith to lie in perfect symmetry below.

"Ah! We head to the south again. If this channel continues in this direction I feel perhaps we will come upon *Discovery* and *Chatham*."

Lieutenant Barrie, a tall, good looking man and respected by all, stared into the mist. Rain dripped continuously from his three-cornered hat. Water would build in hollows and folds until at a turn or tilt of his head, a small waterfall spilled onto his shoulders, or down before his face.

"Look over there, more Indians. I see mostly women and all wearing their hideous lip ornaments."

The natives had visited them the night before at their camp, but now at first light the boats continued south along the channel without any contact with this group.

"We will continue till we find a suitable place for breakfast and I think I see just the place, over there. Come to larboard, Mr. Pitt. Pull away men, breakfast coming up."

The boats rounded a headland and rowed into a small bay. Here fresh water flowed across a sandy beach, but most rewarding was natures generous offering of mussels and oysters.

"Hurry up there before the rain comes again. By the look of the clouds, our dry spell will be of short duration. Get a fire going Wright, boiled mussels the main course."

The boats pulled ashore and the crews began to collect oysters, not far from the surface of the sandy beach. Mussels that clung to the rocks in abundance were gathered and in no time, a stew was prepared and eaten.

"Pack the equipment, get those utensils washed, McAlpine, don't mess about now. Peter Wright, into the boat with you and get things stowed. Get at it now."

The well-tried procedure, established for these small boat journeys soon had the vessels again heading south in the heavy rain, which seemed to never cease in these latitudes.

"Hey Pete, I don't feel too bloody good, matee."

"Ah! You ate too many mussels, my friend."

Peter Wright answered his companion as they pulled hard at the oars.

"No mate, me face is all pins and needles and I feel tired, real tired. Jesus me toes and fingers are numb. What the bloody 'ell's goin on?"

John Carter began to vomit and fall sideways as though his equilibrium had become askew. His face appeared very flushed and his words slurred incomprehensibly.

"Mr. Baker, sir, John Carter, he's really sick."

Peter Wright called to Lieutenant Baker

"I hear you, Wright, what's the matter Carter?"

"Sir, John McAlpine's crook too." It soon became obvious that something had begun to affect the rowers.

"I don't feel too well either. My God, I think the oysters or mussels may have been contaminated. I feel pretty sick myself. Let's get to shore, row towards that bay over there."

Lieutenant Baker realized instantly the problem and magnitude of food poisoning; years before in northern England, contaminated shellfish had afflicted him.

"Row you buggers, row like hell I tell you, perspiration will help get the poison out of your system. Give me an oar. You Gates, do you feel well? Give me your oar. Any one who feels the least bit dizzy or ill row as though your life depends on it."

The boats pulled into a small bay. The instant the exertion of rowing ceased those most afflicted had to be carried ashore. John Carter was now unconscious and with John McAlpine and John Thomas, were the three most afflicted.

"Peter Wright, get some men with you, get a fire going, any way you can, boil water, now. I feel so sick; it was the oysters or mussels. I know it."

Lieutenant Barrie held onto the side of the boat gripped by nausea. He retched and gagged to no avail.

"I have no doubt what it is James, warm water is all we can do. As soon as the water is warm enough, drink all that you can. Everyone, I mean all of you."

Lieutenant Johnstone knelt beside the unconscious Carter, rubbing his temples.

"Help me massage his body. Get those clothes warm by the fire, as hot as you can, place them on his stomach, we must induce vomiting at all costs."

Water was now warm enough for their purposes, the officers and midshipmen began to drink copious quantities.

"Come on you men, get the water into you."

The seamen, even those violently ill, were obstinate as only seamen can be and refused to drink any water, with the exception of Peter Wright and John Cook the Quartermaster. Those who had drunk hot water began to vomit up their meal to their instant relief.

"Come on; try to get some hot water into Carter. Wright, you seem to have more sense than the others, hold him up and open his mouth."

"Sir, he is beginning to swell about his neck and his lips are almost black."

"Feel for a pulse, my God it's very weak, almost non-existent.

Very quietly and gently, John Carter passed from this earthly life.

"He's dead."

The seamen grouped about the lifeless body of their companion, profound shock written on their faces.

"Well what do you say now, you men? He is dead and you are all going the same way. Your stupid obstinacy will kill you all. I cannot understand how you refuse the only remedy available to us all. One of your own is dead and all that have drunk and vomited are well. So what is it to be? Aye."

"Gimme the bloody water, I'll drink it."

"So will I."

"And I."

The men drank the drink so foreign to their way. With great gagging, heaving and vomiting, all were soon restored to a semblance of well-being, although it was some days before they were back to their normal healthy selves.

"Well James, I think it was not the quantity of mussels that nearly did us in, nor was it the oysters. Those who ate oysters alone had no illness. It seemed that the only ones to suffer were those who ate mussels off the beach."

"Yes, I agree with that surmise. I suppose we must be on our way again. I will get our dead man into the boat, there is no place to bury him here it is all rock. We will have to stop at some suitable inlet on the way. You men, get Carter into the bow of the vessel. You sick men, drink the rest of the tea, we will all take turns at the oars."

The dead man lay trussed up like some parcel in the bow. The other sick lay covered and warm athwart the vessel between the rowers. The boats continued down the channel to a deep round bay where a camp was made for the night. In a glen, no more than 200 feet from the sea shore, John Carter was laid to rest. Lieutenant Johnstone prayed briefly over the shallow grave as the small band of adventurers gathered in silent remembrance and homage to their shipmate. At dawn, the vessels left the bay leaving John Carter to become one with the wilderness forever.

Peter Wright and Neville Brown sat quietly together contemplating the lonely and desolate last resting place of this English sailor, to all intents and purposes lost to the world.

"A lonely and sad demise, forgotten forever."

"Well not really. Captain Vancouver recorded the name of John Carter on his charts. I was always impressed that the Captain remembered the lowly sailor as he did his officers. Of course one had to die to be remembered, especially those from the fo'c'sil. The place of burial became Carter Bay, the place where the mussels were eaten he called Poison Cove and the canal leading to the fatal breakfast, Mussel Canal. I would imagine that as long as sailors frequent these waters this day of sorrow will be remembered."

"So all those ill eventually recovered?"

"Yes, four or five days and all were back to their normal duties and we continued on with the never-ending small boat voyages of rowing, surveying, recording and trading with the natives."

23

Jane's Mother Dies and Henry Finds Gwen Agreeable

Henry had been at Westgate House for three days. These were days of love and passion. For Jane, the early days of their marriage were relived. This time it was better, she had no reservations and answered Henrys every demand, with demands of her own. As for Henry, he realized that he really enjoyed Jane, she had learned to match his ardour and she was quite beautiful, to boot. If his financial position was not in such desperate straits, perhaps he could love this girl purely for herself.

However, for the other resident of Westgate House the last three days had been anything but joyous. Gwen lay awake at nights listening to the sounds, the cries, the moans and the laughter from her mistress's bedroom and during the days, she enviously observed the kisses and the play that continuously went on between the two. She also knew Henry West was not ignorant of her presence. By glance and by touch Henry conveyed to Gwen in subtle ways that he was well aware of her. A lingering contact with Gwen's hand as he took some object from her, eyes that followed her every movement, especially when Jane was not present, and most of all his smile, which he would bestow to great effect. In fact, this girl from the lower strata of English society was enamored of the brash, personable soldier, relative of the ancient and noble family Beckingham, who was also a thief, rake and liar of the lowest order.

"Mrs. West, mum. Here is a message just delivered, it is from your father."

"Thank you Gwen has the messenger waited for an answer?"

"No, Mum. He said no answer was required."

Jane slit the seal on the envelope with a paper knife convenient on a small desk. She read the contents of the short letter. The normal flush of her cheeks paled perceptibly

"Gwen, will you tell Captain West that I need him, please ask him to come to me."

"Yes, Mum."

Within minutes, Henry entered the salon. "Jane what is it? Gwen tells me that you seem distressed by a note just received. What is it?"

"Oh Henry, it's my mother. Here."

Jane passed the note to her husband. Henry read aloud.

My Dear Jane,

I am in great distress; I need your company at this sad time.

If you would again see your dear mother in this earthly life, please come with all dispatch. I fear her time is not long.

Your loving father.

"Jane, what can I say? We will both go immediately. This sounds a serious moment. I think the quickest way will be to ride. I will saddle the horses. Change to suitable attire and we will be away post haste. Gwen, Gwen, where is that girl?"

"Gwen, help your mistress into her riding habit, we will be away as quickly as possible. Send Old Tom to me, in the stable. Quickly now."

Henry West, if nothing else, was an organizer. In no time Jane and Henry were mounted and trotting the horses the few miles towards Brancaster Straithe and Medhurst.

Margaret Sawtell died about three hours after Jane and Henry arrived. She died with her husband and daughter by her side. Margaret Sawtell left this world quietly and with little fuss. It was fully thirty minutes before Jane and her father realized that she had gone. They embraced, drawing comfort one from the other.

"Dear Jane and you sir, what can I say. Rest assured that I will be at your service in every way at this sad time, both as a family member and friend."

"Henry without your assistance I would not have seen my mother before she left us. My dear husband, most surely divine providence has brought you back to me at this sad time."

Henry West found himself in strange territory. He had become a hero in the eyes of his wife and, more disturbing for a man of his nature, he discovered deep within himself, unusual feelings of affection. The young girl whom he had wed in so deceptive a manner had begun to captivate him.

"Now sir, you must allow me to take some of many tasks now required off the shoulders of both you and Jane at this sad time. I will make all the necessary arrangements, in close consultation with the family of course."

"Oh Henry, please, that would be so relieving for father and I. Just to know that you are here with me is marvelous. If you can take some of the arrangements off father's hands it would be such a comfort."

Henry West found this new role to his liking. By nature self-indulgent, in his mind he now saw himself in a new and somewhat disturbing light. He had never considered the possibility that he was capable of such giving of himself without a reward, but now this girl had made him offer assistance with no thought but her well-being. It seemed that the original reason for being here, extracting more money from the family, had deserted him. He was playing the role of a devoted husband and son-in-law. In addition, for the first time in many years he felt quite satisfied with himself.

"I will ride with the doctor and take care of the necessary legalities. Walk with me Jane."

The two left the room to the grieving Edward Sawtell.

"Jane, what of relatives and friends? Who should be informed? Can you discuss with your father how he wishes to handle this? I assume that Saint Mary's will be the venue. I will call there and discuss matters with the Vicar and then at least things will be under way."

"Thank you Henry, I must ask you to call at Westgate House. Gwen must be told of the situation and I would have her come over here to assist me. I need a trunk of clothes; she will know what to pack. I must stay here for a time until father is over the shock of this day. So my darling, bear with me at this time, already you have shown yourself the fine and sympathetic person I know you to be."

As Henry rode back towards Westgate House, he contemplated his situation as it now began to unfold. He saw a wife who had just lost her mother. Mrs. Sawtell was a distant relative, and cousin three times removed and she did not like him. He also knew her family connections and the considerable financial element, which must be involved. As an only child, Jane would most certainly come into an inheritance. He determined to pursue the role of a dutiful husband and use whatever deception necessary to further his financial cause. In the meantime, he would contact Frederick March and have him come to Norfolk. Between them, he was sure they could invent some scheme to part Jane and her father with at least another portion of their wealth.

When Henry West entered Westgate House, at first he could not find Gwen. A scraping sound from the dining room attracted his attention. Gwen knelt before the fireplace cleaning ashes from beneath the grate. Henry stood silently at the door watching the lithe movements of the handsome girl. He noticed the sway of her heavy breasts and the roundness of her body so well displayed by her position. He watched her for a time before pretending that he had just come upon her.

"Gwen! Gwen! Where are you, girl?"

"Here, sir."

"Ha, Gwen, we have had a sad day at Medhurst. Mrs. Sawtell, your mistress's mother, has departed this life. I have some orders for you. Your mistress requires a trunk of clothes, she is confident that you will know what to pack and you will be required there as well, so bring what you need. There will be full mourning. You will bring the best black for your mistress and whatever is required of a black nature for yourself. I will be back in two hours with a carriage."

"Yes, sir, I will be ready."

"Good, in two hours then."

Henry West could not help himself where women were concerned; he had no concept of the value of the great marital relationship that was his for the taking. At present, he had feelings unlike anything before experienced. He had come as close as he had ever been to a state of love for the gentle, passionately demanding Jane Sawtell. Mornings found them both physically exhausted, but it was Jane who always requested more and followed his lead in the subtle nuances of the bedchamber.

The time since his return had been the most rewarding and satisfying of his life. Now he observed Gwen as she walked behind the groom. The groom struggled with a large trunk and cursed the young lad who would ride postillion on the lead horse for having no real interest in his fortunate position in such an excellent household. Henry again allowed his glance and thoughts to wander. He saw Gwen as a beautiful woman waiting to be taken and as a serving girl and an employee, not in a position to resist whatever he demanded. Of course, he knew his natural good looks and social position made any demands of his quite acceptable in any strata of society.

"I will ride in the post chaise, Mr. Clagg; tie my horse behind if you please."

Henry assisted the girl into the cab. He followed after a second smaller trunk had been loaded onto the luggage platform at the rear of the coach. William Clagg, the groom and owner of this hired conveyance climbed onto the dickey high at the back of the cab. The lad mounted the lead horse.

Discovery

"Walk on boys."

With a snort, the grays began to pull; with tossing heads and straining loins and the short journey to Medhurst began. Although not a word had been spoken, the atmosphere in the confines of the coach was fraught with underlying currents of desire and excitement between Henry West and Gwen Pratt.

"Now Gwen you will stay at Medhurst and be of service to your mistress. You will do whatever is necessary for a smooth transition in the Sawtell household. Your mistress will be busy administering to the needs of a father who has lost his wife and companion. You will be expected to assist her in her efforts by releasing her from any involvement in the daily administration of the house."

"Yes, sir, I understand."

The journey from Westgate House to Medhurst occupied little more than an hour and a half. In the cramped confines of the carriage, Henry eyed his companion. Gwen was aware of the tension between them and she waited for his first move, which she knew must soon be forth coming.

"You're a pretty one aren't you Gwen?"

"I wouldn't know, sir."

"Come now, you must be aware of those blue eyes of yours."

"No, sir, I know they're blue, but that's all, sir."

"I'll wager you have all the young fellows of the town a-flutter. I'll wager there's many a broken heart this day in the County of Norfolk."

"No, sir I don't have anyone in town except my parents and brothers and sisters."

"Ah! Then you are free to pursue a young blade if he should come along"

"I suppose so, sir."

Both Gwen and Henry knew where this conversation was leading. Both expected it and both were ready for whatever might happen.

"I am entranced by those ruby lips of yours, Gwen. I'll wager many a lad has tasted them to his gratification and pleasure."

"A few may have, sir."

Gwen felt weak; her hands trembled ever so slightly as the swaying carriage threw her against this handsome man. She thought of the nights when she had agonized to her mistress's delightful sounds of love. She knew how she wished it were she in bed with this man.

"Then come let me kiss them."

Gwen blushed crimson in the afternoon light.

"Good heavens, no, sir. That would be against all that is..."

Henry did not let her complete her sentence; he pulled her to him and began to kiss her with great enthusiasm. To her credit, for a time, she resisted the onslaught, but then her feelings got the better of her and she began to return his kisses with equal ardour.

The sound of hounds barking, the call of the groom to the lad astride the lead mare to rein in the horses signified that the journey was almost complete.

"Please, sir, do give over. It is not proper that this should happen. Please, please how shall I be able to serve my mistress now this has happened? I shall never be able to look at her again."

"Come now my dear, a little kissing is not worth a thought. We will keep this our little secret. I venture your parents are not of substantial means, so let me provide some relief for your family, food stuffs, sweetmeats, something you can take to their home and enjoy."

"Sir I don't know, what if Mrs. West finds out.'

"She will never know anything about it. So don't worry yourself at all."

Medhurst, the beautiful home of the Sawtells came into view through the trees, in a few minutes their destination would be at hand

"Come before we reach the house another kiss. Quickly."

Gwen did not resist at all this time, Henry West also made the most of this opportunity, for now his hands were busy beneath the black, knitted mourning shawl that covered her shoulders.

"You're here at last, Henry. Come, a kiss my love. Dear Gwen, such a sad time for us here, arrange for the groom to take my chest to the bedroom upstairs. This is my father's footman, Edward, he will show you where. I have a room for you upstairs. It is small and at the end of the landing, so you will be close if I need you, my dear. My goodness the journey over must have been trying for you Gwen you look quite flushed. I do hope you are not coming down with some illness. I will send you a tonic that I have found so beneficial, chamomile tea. I swear by its restorative properties."

"Thank you mum, I do feel the heat today."

Gwen almost ran from the elegant stone stairs and landing the moment, she saw Edward, the old footman and retainer who led the way with the trunks.

"Jane darling, you must stop this pampering of the servants. People of that class do not appreciate it and really it is not proper for a lady of your standing to be so friendly with the help."

"Oh come now, Henry, if you could understand the amazing change in the girl since I have had her. At first she would hardly speak and I could barely understand her speech, so broad was her Norfolk accent. These last months she has been a fine companion for me and I have trained her myself. Please Henry, allow me the luxury of her company. Of course, you will, my love. She is the perfect companion for me during your absences."

"How could I refuse you anything, my dear? You have every possible authority where Westgate House is concerned. Come let us go to your father, I have carried out his instructions and have been to the solicitor Neville Brown. I have certain intelligence to impart to your father from Brown."

Henry and Jane passed through the doors to Medhurst, Jane confident in her continuing relations with her husband. For Henry, his thoughts were occupied with the impending funeral of Jane's mother and with the eventual reading of her will and its effects on the financial status of his wife. Most of all he thought of Gwen, the journey over from Westgate House and how he would eventually complete her seduction.

24

The Queen Charlotte Islands and Nootka

"I take it you have kept in touch with Jane, Sir Neville?"

"Yes, I did for a time, but after the death of Edward Sawtell, I never heard from her again and have not done so to this date. As you know, it was about six or seven months after your disappearance she married Captain Henry West. They resided in Westgate House. It was about a year or so after the wedding that Captain West left for places still unknown to this day. Purportedly, he is sent on diplomatic missions of great secrecy. He would be away for months at a time and return to the great joy of Jane Sawtell, only to vanish again in a month or so.

"Strange that Jane would not contact you with at least a letter. After all, you were the mainstay of both our families especially where matters of a legal nature were concerned."

"The very last time I saw her was at the reading of her father's will. You know her mother was very well connected and quite wealthy in her own right. She was related to the Bucks of Norwich, and distantly through her mother's marriage to people of an even higher rank. When she married Edward Sawtell she brought with her a considerable fortune. There was no surprise in her will, she left all her holdings and a sizeable sum of money to Jane, everything.

Jane had no sooner recovered from the death of her mother when her father took ill; it was very quick and he died within a month. I think myself that he did not want to live after the death of Margaret. Jane was forced to go through the whole ritual of another funeral. The usual period of mourning along with the disruption this brings had a big effect on her. Of course, Edward Sawtell left everything to Jane. She had now, at the hand of the angel of death, become an extremely wealthy woman in her own right. It was but a short time later that she moved away and I had no more contact with her."

"Well, Sir Neville, one never knows what the hand of fate will deliver. Had I not gone to London with all the resulting consequences? I most likely would have married Jane Sawtell. It is always strange how destiny arranges our lives for us."

"Jane transferred the stewardship of her holdings to the London Company of Sir James Boyd. You are, I imagine, well acquainted with this excellent family. To this day, I have no knowledge of Jane or her whereabouts. I was always suspicious of her husband. Henry West never became a respected member of local society. He did frequent the two alehouses and I am told he drank to excess and gambled when and wherever he could find a game. There was a rumour that he had a relationship with the girl Gwen Pratt, Jane's housemaid, this of course is hearsay. In my dealings with him, I found him a cold heartless sort of fellow, but then that is my opinion.

Well, my young friend, I ponder the circumstances of the last five years with all its twists and turns, the bizarre way you were taken and now have come back to us. Seems to me the higher order directing our affairs, has no idea of what he is doing to our existence."

"Yes, Sir Neville, I have thought often and long on life over the years. The fact I was spared a watery grave, especially in the first learning months of my time at sea has always caused me some amazement. I was not prepared for the circumstances that befell me, in reality I was but a child, uneducated in the ways of a cruel harsh world. This is especially so when a comparison is made against the tough fellows I found myself incarcerated with, but I managed to survive and draw on inner strengths never imagined and unknown abilities, which existed but undiscovered till this time."

Both men silently pondered on their personal thoughts for a moment. Peter finally broke the silence

"But now let me continue. I believe I was telling you of the death of our shipmate, John Carter."

Those who were ill recovered and we eventually rejoined *Discovery* and *Chatham*. The vessels made their way through the sometimes-narrow canals to re-enter the Pacific Ocean. A few days' sail to the north found us in waters horribly dangerous and rock strewn. In this wild deserted area, you cannot imagine the surprise of all at the sight of a longboat, rowing out towards us. To see a sight such as this attracted all hands to the rail. It proved to be a Captain Brown who had found a passage through the innumerable rocks and islets. Captain Vancouver had a name for hidden obstacles, which lay just under the surface of the sea; he called these deadly impediments *"Lurking*

Rocks," as apt a name as ever I could imagine. Captain Brown was commander of a trading group, which comprised three vessels, *Prince le Boo, Jackal* and *Butterworth*. We anchored behind an island, in perfect safety, in company with these vessels.

The next day, with the sloop *Prince le Boo* to lead the way, our little flotilla of vessels headed north and into a canal leading to the east. Lieutenant Whitbey was dispatched in one of our small boats to follow the inner coastline. I was delighted not to be included in this venture. Mr. Menzies required my services to re-pot and arrange some floral specimens in their glass home on the aft quarterdeck.

"So there were other vessels on this desolate coastline."

"There most definitely were. This magnificent country is ripe with potential opportunities for commerce. To my complete surprise, it was already well established there. Why, Nootka is a Spanish settlement and there are houses, a hospital, and a fort complete with cannon. On our last visit to Nootka, we were in company with seven vessels, from Spain, England and the new United States of America. Yes, there is a great potential for trade here in this country and I would advise you to invest whatever of your finances you can in this new opportunity, I will most certainly be well involved if I am the man of substance you assure me I am."

"Ah! My friend let us talk of business later, please continue with your story."

"Now where to start or should I say continue." Peter recollected his thoughts for a moment before continuing.

"Again the infernal small boats and the never-ending rowing; if I never see an oar for the rest of my life it will be too often. From an anchorage, deep in a narrow canal, we set forth on what must be the most eventful small boat adventure undertaken. All was normal at first, with the usual meetings with the Indians, magnificent scenery in breathtaking inlets that demonstrated the hand of the creator at every turn."

Rounding a bend we came upon a strange rock pinnacle, which, from a distance resembled the lighthouse at Eddystone; this most strange natural phenomenon, defied description until we were almost upon it. Rising at least three hundred feet, in the middle of a five-mile wide channel, from a distance it had every aspect of a man-made object. What mighty forces created this rocky monolith is beyond imagination. Captain Vancouver named this strange pinnacle New Eddystone Rock, after the lighthouse on old England's east coast. All proceeded as normal till we were in what all hoped was a channel, which would return us to our anchored vessels."

Peter Wright paused in his narrative, in his mind he had returned to the Bhem Canal. For a moment, he sat with eyes closed recalling painful memories.

"I have often thought in hindsight on the events that occurred in this tranquil and beautiful waterway. We had always managed to maintain a good relationship with the natives. It really did not deteriorate at all, until we came in contact with the Indians of the north. These people inhabited the area above the islands named by Captain Etches after his vessel, the *Queen Charlotte*." The native tribes here were of a group named the Tlingit.

"It was here in this place that we near came to the end of our voyage, well at least those of us on this small boat expedition. Up to this time we had never experienced any bad feelings or hostility with the Indians."

Both men sat quietly, the younger in mind, far away on the coast of the Pacific Northwest of America.

"I still wonder what happened to bring on such a dastardly attack. To my knowledge, we did nothing to annoy the people of the area. I overheard Captain Vancouver. He also was confused and felt perhaps we had carried out some injustice on these natives, but on reflection and enquiry, all was perfectly in order, as it had been at every occasion in past meetings with the natives. Of course, they had a considerable acquaintance with other civilized people. All these northern tribes were armed with muskets, besides their natural armaments of spears, and knives.

I have already mentioned the number of vessels on this coast, traders from Europe and America. I fear some of the traders had carried out unfair practices. You know the people of Owhyhee complain bitterly of first class material being traded for inferior goods, especially in firearms. The base metal of which some weapons were constructed would explode on firing. I could well imagine a similar problem in these waters.

Perhaps a spirit of revenge gripped them, perhaps our reticence and good will encouraged them to obtain some redress for wrongs perpetrated on them. I suppose the tranquil relations we had enjoyed over the past three years had given all of us a false sense of security. Had the conditions, which came about, occurred early in our explorations, the captain would not have allowed us to be in such a precarious position. In any event, the captain directed us towards the shore to land and take observations. The launch was some distance behind us. I saw four canoes making towards that vessel; they were large and well manned. The singing, a chant in time with the paddling, seemed quite peaceable, a normal condition that had been observed numerous times before. Just prior to landing to take our observations, a small canoe came alongside our boat. It contained two people. They received the usual gifts. As we landed, another canoe joined us and again the usual presents were civilly received. A period of barter occurred, where the exchange of skins, weapons and other trinkets took place for our goods of copper and cloth, all very friendly and natural."

Peter Wright paused for a moment before continuing. Again he withdrew his pouch. He extracted a generous quantity of the golden leaf, which seemed to give him greater powers of recollection and concentration.

"Pull into that small cove, over there."

Vancouver gestured towards a small bluff of land, extending outward from cliffs rising behind. I was the first man ashore, Captain Vancouver followed, and he leant on my shoulder. By now, I was far from the pale-faced, thin, religious fellow who first came to *Discovery*. Now I was a tall, strapping young man and had been lead oarsman in the yawl. Vancouver propelled himself forward in a vain attempt to alight on dry land, but to no avail. He grimaced as the icy cold water filled his shoes and he trod carefully over the slippery, water-worn stones beneath his feet.

"Mr. Harris, set up the instrument on that small bluff over there and attend me Mr. Humphries, bring the journals and charts, record my readings."

Vancouver advanced towards the instrument. With practiced eye, he read off angles towards prominent points of topography. Harris recorded the data in the journal, while Humphries quickly plotted the points on a chart, to be revised and corrected later.

Lieutenant Swain, who in 1792 had been promoted by Captain Vancouver to third Lieutenant on *Discovery*, had been left with the yawl to entertain the native visitors. Vancouver raised his head, his work interrupted by a loud, raucous shouting from the shore side; he saw how the natives, assembled about the yawl, were calling to the larger canoes that had surrounded the launch.

"Pack the equipment, quickly now, I am not comfortable in this situation, I fear we may have a problem in the making here." Captain Vancouver left the instruments.

"Come with me Wright and bring that musket." Vancouver gestured towards me. "Be quick about it you men."

I quickly picked up the musket and followed Vancouver down towards the yawl drawn upon the stony shore. Lieutenant Swain immediately assailed the Captain.

"Captain, these people are not to be trusted, already they have tried to steal from us. I suggest we get away from here as quickly as possible."

"You men, get our equipment on board, quickly now, pull away from shore as soon as all are aboard. Humphries, give me the charts."

The seamen heaved the vessel into deep water, clambering aboard as best they could.

The boat slipped out towards the centre of the cove. The five men who had been instrumental in pushing the vessel into deeper water, made all haste into the boat to seize the oars, except Donald McNeil, a Scott, who now clung to the side of the yawl, being dragged along in the frigid water.

"Pull him in, pull him in," both Humphries and Vancouver grasped the seaman's coat and unceremoniously dragged the sailor over the side, bedraggled and wet.

The native canoes, now five in number, paddled alongside the yawl, using every opportunity to grasp hold of the sides of our vessel, oars, or whatever part was presented. Those in the canoes still a little way off laughed at our endeavours to retrieve Seaman McNeil. One native, physically well built, was dressed in a cuirass of slats of wood, twined together to form a breastplate reminiscent of the knights of old Europe. This armored man playfully threw a salmon, which hit John Turner, a Lincolnshire man on the side of the head, an act that again brought yells of glee from the canoes.

"Take care forward. Look to that canoe, across our bow, the canoe with the hideous woman in the bow."

Canoes were all around the yawl, some four or five in number. About ten natives, vocally encouraged by a hideous old woman at its steerage, manned the canoe, which caused the most attention. This woman, with a wrinkled, lined face, looked to be about sixty years. She was dressed in a one-piece, buckskin, sleeveless covering. A decorated, close-fitting, woven cap allowed her white hair to flow out in abandon. Her most notable feature was a large lip ornament or labret. The elliptical, polished object, inserted in an incision in her lower lip, was fully three inches in diameter. As she screamed her instructions to the paddling natives, her lip ornament flapped vertically, exposing her lower teeth, decayed and rotting in a most unwholesome manner.

"That terrible woman has tied the canoe to our bow with our lead line. Watch out, an Indian has come on board, Captain."

Spellman Swain pointed forward as a well-built, young man, wearing a breechcloth, leapt aboard the vessel to crouch on the bow. At the incursion of the native into the vessel, all eyes turned to the intruder who now donned a brilliantly painted, black, red and white, mask in the design of a wolf's head, counterpoised with human features.

"Stop him. That man there, he has stolen a musket from the canopy poles, don't let them take hold of the oars."

Swain called to Captain Vancouver, who had ventured to the bow of the vessel to remonstrate with the masked intruder. Sign language persuaded the native to leave his position. As he clambered back into his canoe, the surrounding natives, now about fifty in number, brandished their fearsome weapons. Highly decorated knives with blades of iron, double-ended fighting knives of hard wood, gripped in the middle and at least two feet long, and spears single and double, tipped with iron or quartz.

By signs it was agreed that both sides lay down their weapons, the natives complied, as did Vancouver who laid his musket between two seats.

"It appears we may have avoided a confrontation Mr. Swain, where is the cutter? Ha, they are making all haste to arrive here. That old woman is starting her tirade again."

"Captain, observe that painted and tattooed old fellow, he is just as bad, he's encouraging them. Look out, they are grasping our oars again, rowing is impossible."

The fearsome old warrior had taken hold of an oar; his companions did the same, all the while continuing his loud directions, which spurred his followers to deeds of valor. Weapons were again brandished and thrust menacingly towards the yawl. Captain Vancouver, in the bow, became the object of the fury of the natives. They aggressively thrust their weapons towards the men at the oars, all at the instigation of the old woman, screaming encouragement in her native dialect. At the same time Spellman Swain in the stern, found himself in a similar position, facing the warriors encouraged and spurred on by the vociferous old man.

"That fellow, there at the muskets; he is taking my fowling piece, stop him. Look to those Indians. You men, watch out for the spears, Wright look behind you."

I turned at the warning from Captain Vancouver, not three feet away a native no older than me lunged forward with a spear. The fearsome barbed weapon was particularly effective in the confined area of turmoil.

"Jesus, my bloody arm." With no time to evade the thrust, it caught me in the upper arm, penetrating deep into my right bicep.

Richard Henley, a tough Dubliner, managed to reach round to grasp the spear as the native attempted to inflict further punishment on me. He pushed back on the shaft of the spear causing the fellow to loose his footing and he fell back into the canoe.

Vancouver called out another warning as another native managed to board. The fearsome warrior grabbed a weapon from its position on the rods holding the canopy. This canopy was a contraption devised to help keep some of the continually rainy weather from the occupants in the after part of the vessel. The Captain again retraced his steps to the stern. Suddenly spears were thrust forward towards the nearest sailor. Natives descended into the vessel grasping at any object within their reach, throwing it back into the canoe from whence they came. The noise of the ensuing confrontation, the cries, calls and warnings became deafening as the natives bellowed, ever more venturesome. Loud were the shouts of the sailors as they desperately attempted to retrieve articles being pilfered from around them. A cry of pain, accompanied by an oath, came from the bow.

"The bastard stabbed me; oh e's done it again."

A tall, heavyset warrior, who had taken a fowling piece from the canopy, pointed the weapon directly at the chest of Captain Vancouver. Being not more that three feet from his target a deadly result was inevitable. The weapon did not fire. Immediately he discarded the gun, resorting to a spear. I had an unloaded musket, which I had retrieved from the canopy in an attempt to find a more secure place for it. I swung the weapon, catching the native on the side of the head and knocking him into the water. Quickly he was retrieved back into the canoe with the aid of some of his companions.

"All is undone for a peaceable result. Mr. Swain, we must save our lives now. Fire on them. Fire."

Vancouver gave the order as he struggled to release the barbed spear hanging from the lining of his jacket and shirt under his left arm.

The crash of muskets and pistols discharging came loud and sudden over the violent scene. The result was instantaneous. Natives were seen to fall as shots found their mark, the man who had taken the weapon and cartridge case from the canopy screamed as a ball pierced his chest. He toppled into the water, to disappear immediately, carried down by the weight of the weapon and case slung over his shoulder. It was impossible to ascertain the casualties on both sides in the heat of the moment.

"Look, they jump into the water, cease firing, cease firing. Is any man hit?

"Captain, Rod Bretton and George Bridgeman are hurt. Bretton got it in the chest and leg, Bridgeman in the thigh. Peter Wright, 'e's been stabbed in the arm but 'e's all right, the others, they're pretty bad, Sir."

The natives in the small canoes leapt into the water at the commencement of firing. Those in the larger canoes scrambled overboard to raise the opposite side, putting it between themselves and danger. The natives were now in full retreat towards the pebbly beach that had so recently been the site of our observations. The cutter had now joined us and pulled alongside.

"Dr. Menzies, look to the injured, come across from the cutter."

"Captain, we have lost a considerable amount, our weapons have been depleted."

"Reload, but hold fire. They retreat; they are able to paddle sideways towards the shore. What has been lost?"

"Well Captain, it looks like three muskets, your fowling piece, as well as cartridge boxes for all weapons. Captain, I thought you were dead when that fellow snapped his musket at point blank range, thank God it did not fire."

"Yes, a close escape, he got a good whack though did he not Peter Wright? My thanks to you young fellow."

The two vessels now lashed together some half-mile from shore to take care of the wounded and to begin restoring our boat back to its normal condition.

"Bretton, I saw you stop the theft of the wall piece at the bow when you received your wounds. Make these men as comfortable as possible. What do you say doctor, how serious are they?"

"They will recover Captain. I feel we are fortunate to get off so lightly."

"Let us press on. With the wounded to care for, we will not contemplate any vengeance on these treacherous people. Wright, with your wounded arm can you row?"

"Yes, sir, I believe I will be able."

"Good man. We are some 140 miles from *Discovery* and *Chatham*; our supplies are at a minimum. Mr. Puget, Mr. Swain get us under way and let us return to our companions."

The two boats were unlashed and in unison, the men at the oars began to pull the vessels away from the scene of their near-fatal encounter. As the boats drew away to the south, the sound of lamentation and wailing came clearly across the water from the forest where the natives had gained refuge.

All was now returned to a semblance of normality. Captain Vancouver sat in the stern of the yawl beside Peter Puget.

"Mr. Puget, I feel that a good deal of the responsibility for this attack rests squarely on my shoulders. Those poor misguided natives, how many were we forced to wound, or worse still take their lives. In addition, three of our own wounded. I should never have let my guard down in such a manner. I put you all in jeopardy. If the cutter had not been so close as to arrive on the scene, we would all have ended our days in this canal.

"Yes, sir, I agree wholeheartedly, the cutter saved the day for us."

"Will you be so good as to record on paper my feelings on this matter?"

Vancouver began to put together an outline of his concerns. He spoke of the attitude of the Europeans, who were, in increasing numbers, making their way to these new lands with trade as their only purpose, he spoke of poor quality goods being traded for the magnificent skins and pelts, so valuable and available.

"Write this verbatim Mr. Puget."

"I am extremely compelled to state here. Many of the traders from the civilized world have not only pursued a line of conduct diametrically opposite to the true principals of justice in their commercial dealings, but have fomented discords, and stirred up contentions between the different tribes in order to increase demand for these destructive engines. They have been likewise eager to instruct the natives in the use of European arms of all descriptions. They have shown by their own example, that they consider gain as the only object of pursuit; and whether this be acquired by fair and honourable means, or otherwise. So long as the advantage is secured, the manner how it is obtained seems to have been, with too many of them, but a very secondary consideration. Yes, that should put the concerns in perspective, Mr. Puget, make grammatical changes as you see fit, but keep the general thrust of my words."

Vancouver continued to remark on his fault at letting himself become complacent with the years of tranquil association with the natives of this new land.

"I feel no honour in the slaughter of these innocents, but our lives were in the balance I had to order as I did."

I was seated next to Richard Henley at the oars nearest the stern of the yawl. I listened to the conversation between Captain Vancouver and his lieutenant.

"What do you say to that, Petee, me boyo?" Henley whispered out of the corner of his mouth.

"I think our captain has a gentle nature."

"Just don't get on the wrong side of him, mate, or you'll see how gentle he can be."

Reflecting on the encounter past, it seemed incongruous how, in such a beautiful and tranquil place the base mind of man would spur all to such deeds of violence and cruelty. To commemorate this incident, Captain Vancouver named the cove where we had set down to take our observations *"Traitor's Cove,"* and the point where we managed to overcome our adversity *"Escape Point."* It seemed without reason or rhyme that the miles rowed around this Revillagigedo Island should end in near disaster for us and sadness and grief for the natives. Suffice to say that I was glad to be alive.

"What an arduous adventure! Did you all recover from your wounds?"

"Yes, my wounded companions, who were in a much more serious state than I, received every treatment and consideration. In no time, we were back at our usual duties."

"Peter, you are a very fortunate man to be alive."

"The number of natives hit is uncertain, Puget said eight or ten, Baker reported six or seven, but he was not present, John Sherriff says twelve, no real estimate of the wounded at all. The close proximity of the assault made it difficult to defend oneself. All the officers had little confidence in the swivels, mainly through lack of use and this is also true of some of our muskets, it was only the fire from the cutter that saved us. We were all sad at heart that we were forced to resort to violence against these children of nature."

"Well my friend, I would say in answer that it was a case of your life or theirs. From what you recount, you had no alternative but to wreck havoc on an ungrateful people."

"I imagine you are right, but to take the life of another has always been against the Christian principals on which I have been raised. As the years wore on I found myself becoming more like my shipmates, I now used the vocabulary of the Navy and colourful language of the seamen who were my companions. I thought back to the time I was wounded and reflect on the oath I had used. For a young man who had contemplated the church, I now found myself swearing and at times of distress, using blasphemy.

We returned to *Discovery* and *Chatham* at seven, on the morning of August 7th, 1793. Supplies were completely exhausted, the final days sustenance consisted of one half pint of peas per man per day. We had been confined to the boats for twenty three days and had covered 700 geographical miles."

25

Henry Tires of Wedded Bliss and Jane Becomes Independently Wealthy

The sky was lowering and windy, the smell of salt hung heavy on the air as the turbulence of the North Sea spread a damp haze over the town of Kings Lynn. Black clouds raced across a leaden sky, an icy wind howled and cried its ominous message of winter to come. It stripped the boughs of leaves, which excitedly pursued one after the other, each desperate to find a place of rest for the coming winter.

Across the square, drawn up before the Dukes Head Inn, the horses of the Sun Coach to London, restlessly tossed their heads and stamped their feet with impatience, as they awaited their passengers. On the opposite side of the square, three coaches drew up before a building still showing the final stages of construction. The fine address facing across the quadrangle of the ancient town of Kings Lynn fully reflected the rise to prominence of Sir Neville Brown. The Tuesday Market Place, bustling and crowded, echoed loud with the raucous calls of vendors plying their wares, people from the countryside selling and trading produce and animals. Performers, musicians, and vendors all vied with each other for the attention of the townsfolk.

For a thousand years, Kings Lynn had been a mainstay of commerce and history. Placed at the entrance to the River Ouse, with its access to the Wash, the North Sea, and the Channel, with the principal ports of Europe close at hand, it was little wonder that men of commerce and finance made the place theirs. The merchants of this town were the source of its wealth. They were the urban lords and as such needed the services of the lawyers, notary-publics and men of letters. Neville Brown had rendered considerable assistance to a most prominent Whig Member of Parliament, service which had precluded this unnamed person falling from grace and being charged in a matter not of his doing. This had resulted in a remarkable increase in Neville Brown's influence in local affairs and an eventual elevation to the peerage. Now as a lawyer and family friend, Sir Neville Brown welcomed a sad assembly into the plain, somewhat dour room he used as an office in his Kings Lynn home. Apart from the high windows and three rows of chairs, there was nothing to distinguish it in any way except a large portrait obviously painted some years past, which depicted a stern man, dressed severely, in a style of another time. Only a wrinkling at the corner of the eyes gave an indication of some distant relationship to Neville Brown. A plaque, low on the gold ornate frame informed those who showed some interest that Sir John Turner lived between the years 1632-1712, but the relationship the owner of this dour countenance had to Neville Brown could only be imagined.

The assembled group was unusual and diverse, only alike in the black, which signified a melancholy visit by the angel of death. Captain West provided the only splash of colour, his red uniform jacket standing out from all the others. A black armband marked his deference to the loss of his mother and father-in-law. Jane West was dressed simply and elegantly in a high-necked dress of black taffeta, a crisp silk with a fine rib. Her mother's favourite cameo brooch at her throat, black gloves and a simple black bonnet completed her ensemble. The others, retainers, servants and tenants dressed in their best attire, grouped together near the door, waiting for directions to their proper place in this assembly.

"Captain and Mrs. West, would you please sit here at my right hand, family members please take the foremost seats and all others sit or stand at the rear according to your station."

Those in service remained standing until Sir Neville, Captain and Mrs. West took their seats. The retainers then arranged themselves in an order, which seemed to occur naturally. The housekeeper and footman were in the front, groom and stable man next, tenants and workers standing behind.

"We are here today to read the last will and testament of Edward Sawtell. It is especially depressing that we are again assembled; it was so short a time ago that our dear friend and benefactor Margaret Sawtell departed her earthly life and now Edward has joined her in a heavenly reunion. My dear Captain and Mrs. West, I will now put before you the last will and testament of Edward Sawtell."

Neville Brown adjusted the spectacles set low on his rather bulbous nose and continued.

"The document is perfectly straightforward; such was your father's insistence on good bookkeeping and simplicity; with this in mind I will dispense with formalities. Mrs. Jane West, as the only daughter and heir, I have the melancholy pleasure to inform you that your father has bequeathed to you all monies, investments and annuities accumulated over his lifetime. He has also seen fit to leave to your stewardship all the property, land and appurtenances, as well as the tenanted dwellings, 25 in all. For your enjoyment, the family home, Medhurst, is to be yours, with the stipulation that it is not to be sold or disposed of, but left to whatever children the union between yourself and Captain West brings forth. Your father has also seen fit, and generously, I might add, set aside a sum of money, 3000 pounds, to be disposed of as follows. Edward Straw, butler-footman and Mrs. Straw, housekeeper, Edward Sawtell recognizes your devoted service with the sum of five hundred pounds each, the stipulation that you both be retained in this service for the rest of your life. To John Burke groom and stable man, the sum of 200 hundred pounds, his son and assistant Tom Burke, 100 pounds. Each tenant is to receive the residue of the money divided equally between all. I believe this is in the amount of 60 pounds for each family."

Captain West, as the details of the will were spelt out, began to show his displeasure, first a scowl, then a reddening of his features, then for all to hear, "This is preposterous. I have never heard of such a thing, it is giving money to people already paid in full and tenants with the best of conditions and homes. Next we will be asking the workers how we should run the estate and when we should spend our money. Preposterous I say."

"Henry, my father was always a generous man. I will honour his wishes in every way."

Neville Brown glanced at Captain West whose face had almost attained the colour of his uniform jacket.

"I think that covers the terms of the will concerning the tenants and workers. There are a few bequests to the relatives, namely his sister who is not present today and his brother not in attendance. This amount is in the order of £20,000. I will ask you, Mrs. West and you, Captain, to remain with me awhile; there are some details to discuss."

All rose, the simply clad working people elated at the news of their windfall. All paid deference to Jane Sawtell. She graciously received their condolences as they filed out of the room. Henry West stood staring out of the window towards the square, having nothing to do with the proceedings and in no uncertain manner displaying his anger at what he considered a waste of money. When the room emptied, Neville Brown continued, "My dear Jane, I have no doubt that you are quite exhausted by the turn of events that have come to you. I am sure you will be happy to get all these legalities away and done with."

"Yes, Sir Neville, you are very correct in that. I must thank you for the services you have performed over the last year or so. I will be delighted to be relieved from the melancholy times, which have befallen me; the loss of my dear parents so close to each other will never be forgotten or understood. Only the will of God can account for such somber and distressing events. I find relief in the thought that my dear parents are together in His holy embrace."

"Amen to that my dear, but back to the business at hand, I do not have the complete figures assembled as yet, but I will tell you that you are now a very wealthy young lady. At first glance, just a cursory figure, mind you, prepared by the auditors in London, it seems your holdings are worth approximately 1,000,000 pounds. This of course includes that left you by your mother, but it does not include Medhurst and the Medhurst property, which is still being assessed and is separate from all else. A very tidy sum if I may say so. You, my dear will also have the benefit of considerable income from investments and holdings, which should be as near as I can ascertain £30,000 a year."

Henry West, still smarting at the thought of money wasted on workers, suddenly found him self at full attention.

"I beg your pardon. Could you repeat that? Did I hear correctly?"

"Ah, Captain, you are with us again. I was just saying that your wife has inherited a considerable sum and is now a lady of substantial means."

"The amount man, the amount. That's what I want to hear, the amount."

"Why, a tad short of 1,000,000 pounds."

Henry West perceptibly staggered at the impact of these words. His normally ruddy features paled, he mouthed the words ...One million pounds.... sitting down heavily on a chair, which fortunately happened to be behind him.

Jane, for her part, said nothing. She covered her mouth with her gloved hand and for a moment appeared speechless. Finally with a studied calmness she spoke.

"It seems Henry, you have married an heiress and I would quickly dismiss the lot to have my dear father and mother back with me again. I miss them so."

Pearly tears made their gentle way from misty eyes as Jane searched for a handkerchief.

Discovery

"Come now Jane dear, you must be strong; you are the mistress of Medhurst and owner of a considerable fortune. You have a husband that loves you by your side. A smile my dear, come now. Henry attend your sad wife, tears do not become her."

Henry West sat by the window, in a stunned stupor. A thousand thoughts raced through his head. For the first time in his life, he was at a loss for words.

"Of course, Jane my dear, what can I say to ease your grief? I know only time heals a wounded heart and I will do all in my power to expedite this recovery. Have we completed this day's business Sir Neville, for I would take a sad grieving wife back to the home she knows best?"

"Not quite. I will continue. Your father has seen fit to place your inheritance under the control of the Chancery Court. This is a system simply called equity. It does not nullify the marriage settlement, which will continue. There are no restrictions at all placed on your management of the estate left to you. It is complete and separate from all else. You are the mistress of your estate and nothing can take it from you."

For a moment, Henry West stood speechless. Twice he attempted to speak until finally he virtually spat out his displeasure at this turn of events.

"This is preposterous. All that is Mrs. West's belongs to me as head of the house. I won't hear a word of this nonsense."

Completely taken back, he continued to protest bitterly. Jane sat silently as she listened to a vindictive tirade pouring from her husband, most of which berated her father for his complete dismissal of his son-in-law and the norms of British society

"My dear Captain, I can only acquaint you of the law as it stands. All belongs to Jane and she can do with it as she pleases, within the law of course, which protects her interests. Her dear father is looking after her welfare even from the tomb."

Henry West was silent. The florid hue of his face and the veins pumping in his throat confirmed the conflict rampant in his mind.

"I cannot allow this to stand. I will do all in my power to change this situation to a more normal state of affairs between a wife and her master. I am the head of my house. I will not have it. I will not have it."

"Well, Captain, I am sure you have no reason for concern. Your dear wife, I am sure, will consider you in every way and surely between you, a satisfactory arrangement can be made but there is nothing that can be done to change things as they are. I think that will conclude all that is necessary here today. In a little while, I will be in touch with final assessments and papers for your signature and at that time, I would discuss the future and your wishes. Jane dear, I offer any assistance I can and I am sure Captain, together you may come to an equitable arrangement."

The journey back to Medhurst was silent for Captain and Mrs. West. Each was occupied with private thoughts. For Jane, so much had happened over the last months, too much for her to contention. She sat silently in the opposite corner to Henry. She felt a plethora of emotions, but uppermost in her mind was disappointment, sadness and shock at the tirade vented by the husband she thought made of sterner stuff. She felt joy at her financial situation and gratitude at a father who had made it easy for her to handle her newfound wealth. She had no idea of how to carry out her new situation; much less, what was required to carry on her father's dealings. She had looked to Henry for support but now she was not so sure. They sat together but apart in the coach, each with their own feelings.

The mind of Henry West had already begun to plan strategies and procedures to access the fortune almost within his grasp. Henry slowly got it into his mind that he was married to more money than he had ever envisioned. His thoughts began to attain some order. One million pounds. Unbelievable. In addition, that is not all; he seemed to recollect mention of £30,000 a year, spending money. A thousand ideas pursued each other in the recesses of his intellect. It was too soon. He knew that he must be calm. A confusion of thoughts raced about in his mind, his wife and her money were his, despite the words of that stupid old lawyer. He remembered the arguments between his strong-willed mother and his equally determined father on her place in society. Frederick March would have some ideas on how to handle the situation, but for now, he would be the sympathetic husband and devoted lover.

Jane sat silently, contemplating her future, but the most telling reaction was the feeling of remoteness from her husband. She had been shocked at the feelings mouthed by Henry and she was disappointed that he did not consider her anything but his property. She knew the norms of society and the position of subservience for any wife, but she had thought theirs was a special relationship. She had been brought up in the loving, understanding association between her mother and father and she always thought Henry and her would have a similar situation. The seeds of dissension and mistrust had been sown today. Jane for the first time saw Henry, as she had not previously known him.

Discovery

Three months had passed since the death of Edward Sawtell. Westgate House had been vacated and Jane and Henry now lived in stylish Medhurst. Gwen Pratt had taken her special place with Edward and Mrs. Straw, the groom John Burke and his son Tom. Henry West filled the part of a husband well; he managed to display a fine degree of attention to Jane. Of course, the fact that she had become a woman of means made his lot so much easier to bear. He found his military half pay well supplemented by the fortune Jane had inherited. Frederick March advised him of his rights as husband, but he was confused by the special legalities of the will and found they could not be altered.

"When you married, your wife forfeited everything to you. You are in fact one and the one is you, my friend. The very being or even legal existence of the woman is suspended during marriage. Jane legally is at the will and disposition of you, old boy. Get in there assert your self, it's yours for the taking."

Henry for his part did not assert his legal rights. Jane was generous in every way. She denied him nothing and to get at the money he would have to deal with that shrewd old fellow Sir Neville Brown.

Moments of friction would occur when Jane questioned a sum of money, usually a gambling debt. Henry with the aplomb gained through years of deceit allayed the questions of his wife; she would always pay the bills from what seemed an inexhaustible financial supply. Her fortune was managed by a company of accountants selected years before by her father, under the stewardship of Neville Brown. Arrangements remained as they had always been. The acquisition of wealth had changed Jane; she seemed completely confident and very adult in her new life as a lady of means. She accepted the deference of the townsfolk with whom she came in contact graciously and with the style only wealthy disregard for money can bring.

Their love life carried on as before. Both were of a sensual nature and one complemented the other. Jane broached the subject of children repeatedly; despite constant love making no sign of a pregnancy had as yet become evident. This of course was completely to Henry's liking and it never entered his head that he might be infertile. He usually dismissed the subject with, "Well me dear, it is not for want of trying, perhaps you cannot have children." or "It has nothing to do with me, perhaps you are barren." If Henry had thought more deeply on the matter, his many dalliances, which had not resulted in issue, surely told the story. For now, he found Jane an exciting and adventurous partner in the boudoir.

Henry West completed his conquest of Gwen Pratt. Gwen conveniently ignored the fact her master and the husband of her mistress was bedding her and put it out of her mind. Sometimes Henry would appear in her room in the early hours of the morning, at other times a liaison would be arranged in a glen in the wood, which extended to the east towards Norwich. Henry enjoyed the thrill of the deception, he found Gwen equally as adventurous as he did. Gwen for her part used Henry. She knew her situation and used her sex to gain favours for herself and her family. A pig or a side of beef, a basket of vegetables or a sack of flour would be delivered secretly to her father's house.

The relationship between Jane and Gwen carried on as before. Gwen was more relaxed and Jane found her completely satisfactory as a personal maid and companion. Jane had made it a project of sorts to educate Gwen; she found her a willing and quick student. Gwen's accent had softened; she walked with new dignity. Jane had no inkling of the relationship between Henry and Gwen. While there were many things that she would like to change in her husband, she had no complaints about the quantity and quality of their lovemaking.

Nevertheless, Henry continued to gamble, and Jane was regularly dismayed by the complete lack of explanation for his absence from Medhurst for weeks at a time. Sometimes he would return in fine humour; at other times, his mood was foul. At these moments, she would ignore him until he recovered his usually ebullient style. She paid his debts, but in her heart of hearts, she realized that he was not the upstanding character presented to her in the early days of their relationship. She was completely without any knowledge of his extramarital activities.

They fell into a relatively comfortable situation and Jane found she enjoyed the times when she was alone with Gwen as her only company. It was during these absences that Gwen, who had become a willing pupil, received her lessons. All had fallen into a habitual way of life but great forces were at work, which would soon alter their lives forever.

"Henry. Yesterday I overheard talk which distressed me when I attended my dressmaker. Lady Halkett was there. She was quite vociferous on a subject of which I know nothing. Can you tell me what it is all about?"

Jane and Henry sat together in the drawing room. Henry warmed his brandy, cupping his snifter in his hands, while Jane toyed with her Madeira.

"What, pray tell is troubling you, me love? What has that obnoxious Halkett woman been saying to you?"

"She tells me that there is more and serious trouble in France. She spoke

Discovery

of a reign of terror and that all churches have been closed. Lady Halkett said, at this very moment there is anarchy in the streets of Paris and it will most surely spread to England. She said, as people of polite society, we will all be slaughtered in our beds."

"Pay no heed to that prattling woman, me dear. Methinks she would do better to pay attention to that sniveling son of hers. He will surely come to a nasty end if he continues to cheat at cards … at least so I am told. It is nothing, and we will soon see these revolting French peasants in their proper place."

"Henry, Lady Halkett said that her husband, Lord Edward, has been recalled to his regiment, she said that war with France is inevitable. She also said that the Channel fleet is going on full alert. I must tell you I am worried."

"No need to worry, it will all blow over. Believe me, it will amount to nothing."

"Well I hope you are right my dear, you most certainly know a lot more about things political than I do." Jane deferred to her husband. She busied herself with an arrangement of flowers, the first blooms of the new spring. Gwen appeared at the door.

"Sir and Madam, there is a military gentleman to see Captain West, I have shown him into the parlour. Lieutenant Forsyth."

"Forsyth. Old 'Boxy' by Jove, haven't seen him since I went on half pay. I'll see what he wants."

In due course Henry returned. His face displayed an unusual pallor. He stood at the door in deep thought. Finally he spoke.

"Jane, I am recalled to service. Those Frog revolutionaries are killing everyone again. Bless me, even the army has joined the rebels, they have raised a conscripted army and are making inroads into the Low Countries. They are killing indiscriminately. England has a role in these revolutionary wars. They are cutting off the heads of everyone. They have even invented a monstrous machine for just this purpose. We must take the lead in the defense of smaller countries against this French Republic."

"What is to become of us, do you think we are in danger?"

"No, no, me dear, not at all. I have to present myself at Canterbury a week from today. It seems I will be at Dover or thereabouts training and arranging defenses. Boxy said the French have already made inroads into Holland. It seems we have a potential war on our hands, but nothing has been declared as yet."

Jane's eyes filled with tears, the thought of war distressed her. While she was used to his long absences and the tension apparent at the reading of the will had subsided, the thought of her Henry going to war and in danger sent tremors of distress though her.

"I shall have to leave immediately; there is so much to do."

"But Henry, you have a full week before you are required."

"No Jane, I shall leave in the morning. It is extremely important that I spend some time in London, I must have new uniforms, and His Grace the Duke of Cambridge is most particular about the dress of his officers. Of course, my hair will have to be attended, his grace is especially hard on an officer whose hair is not properly arranged and powdered, why I have seen him threaten to arrest a fellow for insufficient powder. Rowland is the best coiffeur in London, in St. James Street. I will stay at the Thatched House Tavern next door but one to his establishment. Where is Edward? He must pack for me."

Henry West became more excited at the prospect of removing himself from Medhurst. Over the past few months, he had begun to tire of his existence as the country gentleman and dutiful husband. The thought of getting back to his old life style thrilled him.

"Jane, I shall need a considerable sum to keep my end up. I shall need lodging at a fashionable hostelry. I will need furniture and weapons of course and at least three horses. I will require a groom and a manservant, why I don't think I will get away with less than one thousand pounds a year, perhaps more."

"That is a considerable amount, is all that necessary? I would have thought that barracks would be the best place for an officer. There he would be near his men."

"Come Jane that would never do. It is most important that I be near my fellow officers and be seen at all the correct functions. Of course, I may have the opportunity of buying a better rank and this can be accomplished only by moving in the proper circles. I heard from old Boxy that Major Sir John Fetherstone is retiring. I am sure I can get his commission for about 2000 guineas. Anyway, if I stay in barracks I am obliged to pay into the mess, besides paying for each meal, breakfast is two shillings and five pence and dinner at least two shillings and ten pence then there is wine and...and Madeira. No, no, no it is much better for me to stay privately."

Jane continued to inquire as to the unexpected cost of this recall to duty. To Henry, her interrogation came as a surprise. He did not like it and in his mind, he made a final decision: despite their compatibility in bed, he would not stand for a situation that made him a beggar in his own household. Once and for all, he would put this woman in her place.

"I must protest at this interrogation of my military life. I will not stand for it. I demand that changes be made. I will have complete say in the financial situation; I will have money without having to beg for it from my wife."

The argument continued for most of the day in varying degrees of intensity. Henry berated Jane for being miserly with money and she attacked him on his extravagance. The matter dragged to a conclusion with Jane relenting and finally deferring to Henry's demands.

"Henry! This is the first time we have had such a disagreement and over money, I have never begrudged you anything. You are going to leave for who knows what dangerous pursuits. I cannot let us part in anger. You will have the money you need, send me the accounts and I will take care of them."

"Jane that is better. You know I must be away, duty calls. Now I must pack, so much to do and so little time to do it."

Henry West left for London early the next morning. Jane did not wake to see him depart and he made no attempt to arouse her. He did embrace and kiss Gwen in the early darkness of the lower hall.

When Jane awoke and found him gone, she felt completely washed out and distressed. There was no letter, not even a short note, nothing. Her husband had left her again, without a word or any sign of endearment. As she lay in her bed, she thought long about her situation. Her marriage was not all she had expected. It was obvious Henry could not get away quickly enough. She had been quite content to live the life, which was expected as the wife of an officer. She had ceased to ask for introductions to his family. Henry's noble family had never become a part of their lives. She had always understood there would be times when she would be alone. Now he was gone again. What was she to do with herself? Jane felt a change was taking place within her. She found herself wishing she was not married and she rapidly tired of being locked away in the country. At barely nineteen years of age, her future promised nothing but loneliness and boredom. It did not take long for a plan to formulate itself in her mind. Three days after Henry had left, Jane called to Gwen.

"Gwen we are going to London. Come sit with me, I will not stay here in the country for another minute. What do you say to that? You and I, my dear companion, we are off to London."

26

Return to Hawaii, Alaska and Glaciers

To those English sailors on board *Discovery* and *Chatham*, world-shattering events completely escaped their notice. King Louis XIV of France and his Queen Marie Antoinette had been deprived of their heads and a Republic had come into being. Hundreds of French citizens had been executed using a new engine of destruction, the guillotine, and a war between France and Austria was in progress. A reign of terror had been established, which saw a revolutionary tribunal send political prisoners and aristocrats to their death. A campaign of de-Christianization had begun, with all churches closed and clergy persecuted and hounded often to their death. Seventeen Ninety-Four had seen the most momentous developments in Europe and great naval battles. Britain's Navy had repeatedly decimated the might of France and Spain. France, after a reign of terror, which suppressed civil war at home, raised a conscript army successful in all theatres entered and a brilliant young general, Napoleon Bonaparte cane to power. He had risen from obscurity to lead the forces of la Belle France to victory after victory. These momentous occurrences in Europe had no obvious effect whatsoever here in North America or the Hawaiian Islands. Many of the problems of the world of Europe would be well resolved before word of them ever reached Captain Vancouver and his men.

Peter Wright continued his narrative. Again, he was back on *Discovery*, this time, he returned to the tropical paradise of Hawaii. The turmoil and dissension gripping Europe meant absolutely nothing to him or his companions aboard *Discovery*. The vessels approached the Hawaiian Islands for the third time. On February 12, *Discovery* and *Chatham* finally sighted the eastern most point of the island of Hawaii, through the early morning haze.

Discovery heeled over; the course changed to make a heading towards land, laying some five leagues away. Captain Vancouver was about to have meetings with the most powerful chief in these islands, King Kamehameha.

"Peter! Look'ee there, there it is again. "

Peter Wright and John McAlpine, high in the rigging, saw the towering snow-capped mountain rising from the mist, seeming to float in the sky with no connection to the ocean below.

"Yes, I see it Mac me lad. It looks like a cloud on the horizon, aye."

"I wonder what we will be into this time round? "

"I don't know, but I do know that I would rather be here than in the cold of the country we have just left."

"Look 'ere' e comes. The bleedin' chief, he's flying a British pennant!"

Kamehameha had received a British ensign from Captain Vancouver the previous year and showed some considerable pride when informed that only naval vessels of war were permitted to fly such a mark of distinction. The English colours also distinguished his house, which was barely visible in the gap between the coconut palms lining the shore.

"He's a big'un, that boy."

John McAlpine continued to comment on the arrival of the chief. The wind blew powerfully from the north. The boats, which had accessed the bay at Hilo, returned when it became obvious there was no anchorage. Safety in the exposed bay was out of the question in the present conditions.

"Yes he certainly is a big man; he must be close to seven feet if he is an inch."

Kamehameha was an imposing figure. He was heavily built, a natural trait of the Polynesian race. His stature was made even more impressive by the helmet that graced his handsome head. In shape, it resembled the ancient helmet of Ajax or Hercules, covered with red and yellow feathers. Draped across his broad shoulders was a ceremonial cloak of similar construction, again reflecting the sacred colours of the Gods. Kamehameha stood in the stern of the vessel, firmly grasping and leaning on a great, carved war club. The canoe was propelled by forty warriors, fearsome in gourd helmets, which gave them the appearance of Praetorians, that ancient band dedicated to the protection of the Roman emperor, all the while chanting a melodious, not unpleasant chorus.

From their vantage point, the conversation between Vancouver and Kamehameha was easily audible, if not understood. The Captain was making every effort to persuade the chief to accompany him to a more advantageous anchorage. The chief, in no uncertain terms, declined the invitation. A taboo associated with the New Year religious ceremony prevented him leaving the island. Eventually King Kamehameha relented and decided to accompany *Discovery*. His half-brother was appointed to represent him with the priests at the morai, the great rocky fort-like construction serving as a religious edifice and home to the Gods of Hawaii. His half brother, Kalaimamahu, would remain as his representative and guard his treasures, mainly arms and ammunition.

"McAlpine and Wright, get down here."

The penetrating voice of Humphry Evans rang strident from below.

"You men have been long enough at that, get down here. Dr. Menzies wants you Wright, and the carpenters want you McAlpine. Jump to it now."

"Wot do they want now? Never leave a man in peace for long, do they?"

I parted from my companion and found Dr. Menzies. He informed me that there would be numerous opportunities to be ashore to collect specimens; I should immediately prepare our usual facilities and ready equipment for such a welcome event.

Discovery, *Chatham* and the store ship *Daedalus* eventually anchored in the sheltered Bay of Karakakooa. A short distance away the American brig, *"Lady Washington,"* commanded by John Kendrick, rode peacefully at anchor. Kendrick was the most prolific trader of firearms. *Discovery* and *Chatham* were presented with all necessary refreshment to complete their stores. The usual inoffensive trading materials offered still seemed to excite these beautiful people far beyond the worth of exchange. On the other hand, Kendrick received his supplies using firearms as currency. It was clear that the presence of the distinguished Kamehameha and the obvious influence of Captain Vancouver had an impact on the actions of the people.

The work of replenishment continued almost night and day. Not only did we have to load the refreshments from shore; in addition, the daunting task of unloading cattle, brought from Saint Francisco caused the usual problems. The basis of a cattle and sheep industry had been established here. These latest animals consisted of a young bull, two fine cows, two bull calves and five rams, with five ewe sheep. The final heavy work was to transfer supplies from *Daedalus* into *Discovery* and *Chatham*. It was here we would part company with our dauntless supply ship for the last time. *Daedalus* left us on February 8th, bound for Port Jackson. With her went the Honourable Thomas Pitt, who had tried the patience of the Captain once too often and who I had come to regard as more a friend than an officer. Also leaving us on *HMS Daedalus* were Thomas Clarke and Augustus Boyd Grant. These men were making their way back to England via the fledgling colony at Port Jackson.

"Wright. Attend me, please."

I was busy arranging pots for the expected influx of botanical specimens, when Dr. Menzies demanded my presence.

"I am planning an assault on the mountain near the middle of the island. You will be my assistant and servant on this expedition. Mr. Swain will be with us, as well as some others. I will expect you to arrange for the transport of specimens and other flora and fauna, which may be forthcoming, back to *Discovery*. There will be numerous native servants assigned to accompany us, so I will expect to see all specimens returned in fine condition."

"Yes, sir, I will take care of it."

You cannot imagine the joy I felt at this information. Here I would be on a shore excursion of some days.

The work continued in preparation for the intended shore expedition. Boats were readied; I had loaded the necessary means to return whatever we might find of floral interest. To our surprise, another large canoe came from the direction of *Chatham*. Kamehameha came aboard. With great ceremony, he presented an ornate, feathered cloak to Captain Vancouver. He made it quite plain that it was to be delivered to King *Georgie* in England, as a gift from one king to another. Our Captain received the gift with all possible ceremony. At this time so far from home, Captain Vancouver gave little thought as to the consequences this gift would have on his future.

Our journey would be to climb Mauna Loa, an enormous mountain, ascertained to be 13,634 feet and well snow-covered, even here in these tropical climes so close to the equator.

Our group proceeded from a point at the southern tip of the island and numbered about one hundred people. With a chief named Roohea in charge of the porters and servants, we followed a circuitous route, which severely tried the patience of Dr. Menzies. Our party attracted considerable attention; the inhabitants of the area followed us, more out of curiosity than any other motive. It was not until we passed above the snow line that the crowd began to thin. I must say these Hawaiians displayed a definite dislike of cold and snow, very quickly deserting us for the lower levels and warmer climate, which gave them most comfort.

At first glance, the mountain does not have a severe aspect; it appears more of an enormous hill. It is completely deceptive in nature, and it was not long before the matter from which this giant monolith was constructed began to take its toll. The ground was lava, dark brown to black in colour and terribly sharp. By the time we had reached the snow line, Mr. Howell's shoes were so cut up he was forced to retreat down the mountain.

The next to succumb to the rigors of the adventure was Mr. Heddington, who fell ill at about eleven thousand feet. I know not what caused his sudden malady; perhaps it was the altitude, for we were not a long way from the summit when he began to suffer stomach cramps and nausea. He was assisted from the mountain by four of the natives, who it seemed were delighted to have an excuse to get away from the cold. Finally, the summit was attained. I felt some degree of satisfaction and honour being with the party that made the final assent to the top. Dr. Menzies, Lieutenant Baker and Mr. McKenzie, with me as servant stood on the summit. Our view from here was magnificent, a vast panorama, encompassing the whole of the island. We were able to look down on the clouds funneling around the monolithic mass. We could see the rain deluging the east side of the island; we observed how the bulk of the mountain directed the clouds away to the north and south. *Discovery*, *Chatham* and *Daedalus* appeared no more than specks on a shining sea below.

Dr. Menzies was completely disappointed in our botanical pursuits. We saw many unusual plants and shrubs, but with few in flower or seed, it was impossible to establish or name the species. I must say that the work I had put into pots and soil in expectation of a fine harvest of specimens was to no avail, a few cuttings and no seeds at all being our reward.

Dr. Menzies was certain that we were the first to climb to the summit of Mauna Loa. The natives were reluctant to venture above the snow line and he was positive no other European had been where we had been. On our return, the cool reception accorded us by the Captain spoke volumes as to his feelings; we had been away 25 days, much longer than anticipated. The journey for me, at least, had been a welcome change from the rigors of service aboard a British naval vessel, but in many ways, I was glad to return to the ship and fall back into my usual routine.

"I will tell you my dear Sir Neville, that the rest of our stay here in these blessed, beautiful islands was without incident, at least anything to which I was privy. The work was hard for the remainder of our stay, constant loading of supplies and repairs to the vessels. The ships were showing the effects of the past three years. With another season in the far north of the continent, followed by a long and arduous voyage back home to England, it became a debate both above and below decks as to whether there would be enough life left in our equipment to see us home. I knew the officers were worried as to the sea-worthiness of the vessels. To return to England, would be, by itself alone, an arduous venture.

During the time I was not employed by Dr. Menzies, I was ashore with the carpenters. Captain Vancouver had ordered the building of a schooner for King Kamehameha to be named *Britannia*. It was to be the first man-of-war for this royal personage and built for his protection. The vessel was finally in such a state that Vancouver decided the Hawaiians could complete the work without our assistance. The last act was the secession of the island to Great Britain. The boat building party returned to *Discovery* to find the dignitaries of the island assembled aboard, the Hawaiians chiefs making speeches of obvious feeling and importance. The officers, in what remained of their best uniforms, paid close attention, until finally all seemed finished. Smiles and embraces were exchanged, the words, *Tanata no Owhyhee* and *Tanata no Britannee,* were heard from all native mouths. Mr. Puget and other officers went ashore, displaying the union flag and taking possession of the island in the name of King George. A salute was fired from *Discovery* and *Chatham* to complete the ceremony. Hawaii was now a British possession. I wondered how this would affect the lives of the population and the future of these magnificent islands. All business being completed here, *Discovery* and *Chatham* departed the Hawaiian Islands on March 15th 1794.

"Gawd, its bloody cold. Me fingers are going to fall off."

Unlike previous years, when we had made a course to the west, now *Discovery* and *Chatham* made a passage directly north.

Four or five days out of Hawaii the temperature fell dramatically, now it was below freezing during the day for the first time since we had left England so many years past. Daily the quantity of birds about the vessels increased. Shearwaters, albatross and petrels, along with puffins gave those who seemed to know the impression that land was not far distant. Finally, the gale, which had sped us on our way, settled, and our vessels were subject to frost and snow. This was a new experience for most of us, although several of the older hands had served in the North Sea and in the Saint Lawrence River. To a man, all agreed, never had they experienced cold such as now assaulted us.

The frost and snow was sometimes accompanied by sleet. Stinging icy pellets which cut and reddened exposed skin.

"Land ho, off the larboard bow."

The call came from the frozen men in the rigging. Complaints, loud and raucous, came from them as they battled with ice-clad lines and pulleys, which had become balls of ice and needed to be broken out before they could perform their function.

"That's enough of the complaints, you men up there. Just get on with your work."

"Sir, we need something to break the ice and the lines are like wire, can't do much with them."

"All right, I hear you. You there, Wright, get two hammers from stores and into the rigging with you. Help those men get the gear working. Jump to it now."

Through the mist, sleet and snow, the land appeared, dreary and treeless. Higher land was completely covered with snow, obviously of considerable depth and quantity. As the vessels progressed north, more land came in sight; soon island masses were in evidence at every quarter. In a becalmed situation, a canoe containing a man and a girl appeared from one of the islands. These people came aboard without hesitation. They were dressed in the fur skins of animals and in appearance seemed to have a flatter countenance than the natives of the lands previously investigated by us. They stayed some time and reported the presence of a Russian settlement not far from our position. Suddenly, as if from the depths of some fearful ghostly place, the weather changed from icy calm to a howling freezing, gale. Our visitors were forced to cut short their stay; they were last seen paddling towards an island about two miles distant in choppy, white-capped water.

Captain Vancouver was no stranger to this icy part of the world. He had served as midshipman with Captain Cook during the voyage of 1780. He was determined to investigate the area called Cook's River. The subsequent exploration established this indeed was not a river but an inlet. Vancouver renamed it accordingly, Cook's Inlet.

Again, the small boats were launched, with expedition after expedition being sent out in the most dreadful of conditions. Vast areas were charted in the most hazardous, extreme circumstances. Already some of the men were frostbitten. With this foremost in his mind, Captain Vancouver determined to find a haven that would satisfy their needs until the mercury rose above freezing. In this wild and stark coastline, the voyage progressed from anchorage to anchorage, but no port suitable for a stay of any length was found.

The vessels were visited by groups of native people. These people displayed a degree of kindness and gentility not common to the civilized society of Europe. They were honest and polite, not one item was found to be missing at any time. Mostly they stayed on board overnight and often the deck would be crowded with visiting natives. Our next guests were a group of Russian settlers, about ten in all, who arrived in a whaleboat propelled by fourteen natives. Our complete ignorance of the Russian language made this visit very awkward and unproductive. All aboard were relieved when our Russian visitors took the advantage of a break in the ice to leave us. The most dangerous time occurred at the change of tide. Great masses of ice swept out to sea only on the returning tide to thunder back into the narrow channels, grinding and swirling in the tidal races.

The enormous tides of this country constantly caused the *Discovery and Chatham* to be spun and swirled at random. At one moment all would be serene and calm, when suddenly on approaching a narrow passage, the speed would increase as the tidal race with its attendant whirlpools, swept the vessels sideways into frightening turbulence. At any time, disaster was not far removed. Only the expert directions of the Captain and officers kept us from a fate that defies contemplation. The small boat expeditions were constantly at the mercy of the elements, many times needing all the strength and determination of the crews to extricate themselves from enormous seas, gale force winds, ice and snow.

The two men left the inn. Sir Neville took his younger companion's arm; they began to stroll towards the stream running diagonally across the common.

"Well it is good to get out into this crisp autumn weather; I trust you are warm enough my friend."

"Oh yes Peter, I am very comfortable. I feel we need this break. Do you realize we have been at this narrative for almost two days now?"

"Yes. I am aware and embarrassed at my persistence in inflicting all this on you."

"My young friend I am fascinated by your tale and I wait to hear you continue. You talk of the ice and snow of this Alaska. How did you keep warm?"

"Fires were burnt continuously below decks, our clothing was wool, which seems to maintain a heat even though wet. The coldest part of the body, at least for me, were my hands, chilblains were a constant problem. Wool mittens were there for our use, but it was impossible to carry out most of our work especially in the rigging. They were not worn and usually tucked into the belt until the job was complete. By that time of course hands were frozen. It was out of the question to follow the usual seaman's practice of being shoeless. Rowing was another matter, this kept one warm and hand coverings could be worn, although the constant rain or snow kept all perpetually wet."

The two men paralleled the creek, which meandered behind the inn. The sun was warm in the shelter of the trees, but in any open area, the breeze foretold of the summer past and winter to come.

"The officers and men suffered the same distress during our expeditions. There were no privileges for any, all were wet, and all ate the same food. This was normal for the whole voyage. The officers had wine at most meals, but the ordinary seaman would not touch it. Wine is an unfamiliar substance to most seamen, salt pork, biscuits and grog that was it. Most had to be threatened with the lash before they would eat their greens, although it was obvious that the dreadful scurvy was the result of a poor diet."

"Well you seem to have come out of it all in fine health."

"Yes, I can say that despite all the deprivations, I have become a different and better person certainly not the callow youth of so few years ago. I became a sailor. I will most likely continue with it in some form or other. It seems my father has left me well provided for and I know that there is a fortune to be made in the north of Western America. Perhaps a trading vessel or an investment in this field will be my future."

"An excellent thought my boy."

"Yes there is a fortune to be made in the right season. I remember times of great pleasure, of beauty beyond compare; a beauty both gentle and fearsome; of walls of ice hundreds of feet in height, of glaciers grinding and roaring in anger. I think the most terrifying time as well as the closest I came to the end of my life has to be in the Cross Sound, that dreadful Icy Strait first seen and named by Captain Cook."

Peter Wright returned to his tale and again he relived the beauties and terrors of the Pacific Northwest.

The sun hung low in the southwestern sky. The freezing weather of May, June and July had given away to a more pleasant climate. It was still cold, a bone-chilling cold, especially during the night and early morning watches. Although the latitude had only varied four degrees from the ice and rocky dangers of Cook's Inlet and Prince William Sound, the present temperatures did not have the numbing effect that had assailed the vessels on the early days of this, the final season in northwest America. The great snowstorms, the freezing rain, the rigging transformed into icy, steel-like cables; the sails, frozen stiff and board like, which ripped fingernails completely away, never to grow again, had given way to a more temperate clime. The last days had been gentle and mild, as *Discovery* and *Chatham* slowly plied southward, along the rugged coast of Alaska.

A short distance in from the coast, a vast range of mountains gleamed icy and white. These monoliths appeared to approach the sea at the turn of every mile and to encompass the verdant growth, which assailed their slopes. With Cape Fairweather abeam some three miles, the mountainous range reached the sea, there to be washed by mighty Pacific swells, hurling themselves to destruction at the edge of this cold, frigid land. The aspect from the sea saw the coastal plain lose its wooded cover. It now appeared composed of a solid frozen mass, which shone and sparkled in the late afternoon sun. Great glaciers stretched like a highway into the distance, to become lost between the might of the mountains named by Captain Cook, Mount Fairweather, along with its companion peaks. Reports from the masthead lookout suggested the shores were covered with derelict wood. The reports told of streams rushing and tumbling into estuaries, which resembled rivers and could conceivably allow boat access.

Because of the clemency of the weather, I had very little to do. I attended the plants, which had managed to survive in their glass compartment and I began to polish the binnacle, home of that most important implement, the ship's compass. I lingered over the work in hand and listened to a class of midshipmen discussing the problems relating to latitude and longitude.

Peter paused in his narrative as he imagined himself back on the deck of *Discovery*. He imagined he heard the words and saw again in his mind the group of young men at their daily lessons.

"Now gentlemen, what do we read? Mr. Humphries you first, if you please."

Lieutenant Mandby conversed with a group of young gentlemen midshipmen; it was the time for their morning lessons. *Discovery* rolled comfortably on the high swells as the young men grouped around their teacher. Thomas Humphries held a delicate but beautifully made sextant of gleaming brass and polished ebony. He adjusted the micro gear and brought down a pale green shade before putting the eyepiece to his eye.

"You will speak the time Mr. Browne and you Mr. Ballard will record it, you others will also record it and carry out the same calculations."

Thomas Humphries trained the eyepiece on the distant, southerly sun; he slowly swung the arm across the quadrant, to bring the image down to the horizon.

"We will use the lower limb calculation. I will give you the azimuth and you will all carry out your calculation from there."

"The time." Mark," informed all that an azimuth had been observed.

John Browne closely scrutinized the chronometer, a wonderful instrument constructed by the great watchmaker Larcum Kendall. It was a fine timepiece that had seen service with Captain Cook on his second voyage in HMS Resolution and now giving *HMS Discovery* the same fine and accurate time.

"Ten hours, thirty minutes, fifteen seconds."

The assembled group applied themselves to the task of ascertaining their position. Silently they worked on their individual calculations, logarithms, sine, cosines, secants, cosecants, parallax, semi-diameter, all the young gentlemen wrestled with the mathematical problems so necessary to establish their latitude and longitude and to gain the proficiency necessary if they were to pass their exams and become officers of the Royal Navy.

"Now where are we gentlemen? Mr. Humphries please."

Humphries had calculated well, his position of latitude 58 degrees 50 minutes, longitude 222 degrees 25 minutes, placed them in the vicinity of Cape Fairweather, which appeared most conspicuous from a southerly aspect. Lieutenant Mandby chaired a discussion on their now established position; he corrected some errors, consulted charts of English, Spanish and French origin and pointed out pertinent points of interest on shore. The young men liked Mandby they were attentive to him. Four years at sea had molded them into fine, experienced seamen, ready to receive their commissions. With the voyage coming to a conclusion, all realized that exams would be required. It seemed a degree more effort was being expended by these normally boisterous midshipmen.

"Train your glass on the shore, there, Mr. Browne. I perceive an inlet, the charts show it, look to the French chart."

"Yes I see it, Mr. Mandby."

"Here it is Port des Frances, on a chart by the French Captain, la Perouse. That sad gentleman lost a great number of men there, I believe in the year 1785 or 86. A melancholy place, full of French ghosts I'll wager."

The mountains surrounding Port des Frances were steep and snow-covered; the narrow entrance to the port shrouded in mist slowly developing into heavy fog above which the lofty range seemed to float in space with no land contact below. Some five miles out to sea, *Discovery* made slow passage towards the south. The breeze was favourable, the sun, standing midway between the horizon and the zenith, remained in the heavens for most of twenty-four hours.

"Mr. Whitbey. Haul our wind for the night; we are not far to Cross Sound. I well remember the topography of the land, the way the unbroken shore quickly becomes strewn with rocks and debris."

"Yes Captain, the night will be short, but we will be at the whim of the tides and current now the breeze is falling."

Suddenly a call came from the lookout in the cross-trees excited and urgent, "Rocks; Rocks ahead," then even more urgent, "more rocks to starboard."

All eyes strained forward to fix the point of alarm.

"My God, Captain, rocks everywhere, look at the breaking sea. There and there."

With an unimaginable swiftness, *Discovery* was surrounded by what appeared to be low, brown, flat rocks upon which the swells became broken and agitated.

"Rock dead ahead, 50 feet," a call came almost as a scream from the bow.

"Come hard to larboard helmsman."

With the almost non-existent breeze, *Discovery* barely moved from her course, a collision with the object was inevitable. Officers and men rushed to the starboard side, all eyes peered at the sea about the vessel, and the call of the men at the lead line gave no indication of a bottom, as the crash finally occurred. A frightening grinding and tearing echoed in the falling twilight, followed by a report, which immediately relieved the tension and terror of a shipwreck.

"It's ice, Captain, icy pieces floating with the tide."

What appeared to be rock was in reality dirty ice, floating level with the surface of the water.

"Captain, its ice moving out with the tide, look there, it ends. The dirty colour is soil and gravel trapped in the icy pieces."

"Mr. Whitbey, we will try not to hit those icy patches, I will retire to my quarters for a time. I feel a colic about me. My malady has been playing up of late. Keep a good eye peeled."

"Yes Captain, I would suggest you visit Dr. Menzies, perhaps he may have a draught that will aid you. Have no worry about the deck."

"Thank you Joseph, call me at any alarm."

Captain Vancouver left the deck. A slow passage was made towards the increasingly foggy Cross Sound. Joseph Whitbey took command as the captain left the quarterdeck. The failing light was compounded by the increase of the shore fog, which minute by minute seemed to extend further out to sea. Whitbey was well aware of the dangers and the need for vigilance.

"McAlpine, take the man Wright with you, get to the bow. Keep your eyes opened. I am doubling the watch tonight."

"Aye, sir."

The barely noticeable breeze deserted *Discovery*. The sea moved and pulsated in a smooth and oily manner. The swells rolling under the vessel resembled dull thunder as they shattered themselves against the fog-shrouded coast. The call of the seamen rang clear and echoed hollow though the fog, as they noted the depth of water. A deep-sea lead line, 140 fathoms, could find no bottom.

Captain Vancouver returned to the deck. He had slept for some two hours, but the call of the men at the bow had awakened him.

"Listen to that. The surf, it is getting closer. Captain, how do you feel?"

"Yes it seems so, what time do we have Mr. Whitbey? How do I feel? Poor to middling Joseph, poor to middling."

"It's eight by the clock, sir."

A call from bow alarmed the officers, as the surf roared close from the invisible east.

"By the deep, four knots, 46 fathoms."

Almost immediately after the first bottom, a second call more alarming and urgent.

"By the deep four knots, forty fathoms."

The sound of the surf now echoed all around, loud and near, an anchor was let go and sails furled. *Discovery* swung head to the swells, anchor well fastened on a sandy, muddy bottom in relative safety, but with zero visibility.

By ten, the fog cleared to give an overall picture of their situation. *Discovery* had anchored on the eastern side of the sound between two rocks, lying about a mile apart, forming the entrance to a spacious harbour. Booming surf crashed ashore along the coast to the north. It was near noon that *HMS Chatham* arrived to anchor near *Discovery*, until a more suitable anchorage could be found.

When all was in order, a boat departed to search out a more suitable spot. The vessels were safe enough in the present conditions, but in danger in any heavier weather.

At dawn, the boats were once again lowered and were seen moving between a small opening, to disappear into whatever lay behind the rocks and trees visible just to the east. Immediately on their return *Discovery* and *Chatham* were towed to the anchorage decided upon by Mr. Whitbey. It was a north-facing cove, protected by two small islands.

"This should suit our purposes gentlemen, what is our depth and bottom?"

"We are at fourteen fathoms and the bottom is a type of clay, sir."

Discovery and *Chatham* swung easily on their anchors. The small islands provided a barrier to the ocean. The spray from the surf hung with the fog, wispy amid the tall firs.

"Good, let us investigate the sound now that we are at rest. You will join me Mr. Whitbey, you too, Mr. Mandby, bring two of your young gentlemen, let us use the launch. This will aid us in determining the best method to survey this area."

The launch and the cutter left the shelter of the bay. Within the hour, the men were heaving out into the sound. Captain Vancouver and Joseph Whitbey sat together in the stern. It soon became obvious that there would be difficulty experienced here. To the east, the whole waterway appeared blocked with ice, great moving pieces, swirling in the tidal race between the islands that formed the protection to their anchorage and the mainland some two miles distant to the north. Directly across the sound, a wall of ice hundreds of feet high cracked and thundered. Large masses, in towering columns broke off to fall and tumble into the heavy swell crashing against the glacial face, rebounding to form great waves to oppose those coming from the open Pacific Ocean.

"This will be a difficult time, Mr. Whitbey. Look! Look at the size of those icy pieces and the way they are influenced by the movement of the sea. I think we have seen enough, let us return and get the expeditions away."

On their return from the initial survey of the outer sound, preparations were soon under way in what had become a time-tested method of survey and investigation. The seamen, who had rowed the small boats so many hundreds of miles in all conditions of weather and sea, now a task considered second nature, felt an unusual excitement. Not only was this to be a particularly demanding and treacherous endeavour, but they knew the great voyage was drawing to a conclusion. Those staying on board were to be well occupied with the usual tasks of upkeep, becoming more demanding at each anchorage. Chalking of the upper decks was required, sails were in the need of constant repair, serviceable ropes in short supply and those in use were now approaching the last stages of their life. Very little chance would be available to acquire replacement equipment.

"Mr. Whitbey, you will take command of the pinnace and two cutters. I will be aboard the yawl, to carry out a complete survey of the outer sound as far as Cape Spencer and the southern shores. I feel that I can accomplish this to take my share of the task at hand. My health has improved enough to let me carry on. Our esteemed doctor Menzies will be with you. Joseph, you will select the people you need, as will I. Draw supplies for two weeks. I think by the broken nature of the country hereabouts, you may find yourselves a great distance inland."

Captain Vancouver spoke with more animation than he had exhibited over the last weeks. The tiredness and constant feeling of nausea had begun to take a toll on his normally exacting nature; but now he appeared returned to his usual ebullient self.

"Our native companions seem to be growing in number, they will bear watching. They seem strangely affable and friendly ashore, but very wary of joining us aboard. Very honest traders, we have a supply of excellent halibut, but the salmon is rather tasteless. Perhaps it is my condition, what do you say Joseph?"

"No, I think you are correct, Captain, I find the salmon tasteless, the time of the year more likely."

"Good, good, that influences my complete recovery even further. Let us get on with it."

Three small vessels under the command of Lieutenant Whitbey made their way out of the cove in the early morning. Eventually they reached the Cape named Spencer, where the boats commenced their survey in weather thick and foggy. The journey across the sound had been hard and eventful, giving an indication of trials to come. An immense quantity of ice floated free with the tides. Great monoliths of blue-white, agitated and undulating, the swell sweeping across the sound, crashed and ground each against the other, sending waves in every direction, to harass and annoy the small vessels as they were propelled into this maelstrom by the heaving, straining oarsmen.

"Bloody unpleasant, Doctor."

"Yes, sir, as you say, I think that some of these icy pieces could crush our vessels, were we to get between them. Look! Look over there, my God we would be no more if, if."

Words had failed the honourable doctor as he observed two enormous pieces of ice come together under the influence of the tidal race and a large whirlpool. The vessels rose high on a swell, the view of the sound to the east gave an appearance of unbroken continuous ice, as far as the eye could see.

"Mr. Le Mesurier, keep the cutters close to our stern, do not let your self fall behind now."

William Le Mesurier, midshipman and master's mate, urged his crew to greater efforts; the stronger-built pinnace led the way, with the two cutters following close behind.

"Push the ice away as best you can, two men use the oars for this, the others pull hard now. You all heard Mr. Whitbey, keep up and let us not separate."

Finally, the boats broke free into clear water. About two miles out, just visible through the clearing fog, was a vast cliff of ice, extending some three to four miles across between two headlands. It was obvious that the glacier barring their way filled a bay, the extent of which was beyond their ability to measure. The land, which was clear of its icy cover, exhibited vast mounds of rocky debris deposited by the receding glacier, mountainous piles of tortured and broken rocky pieces. The exposed shore showed a graduated return to life. Nothing grew near the ice, a devastated landscape of glacial till and polished rock. Life began to return in pre-ordained order. First black algae coated the longer-exposed rocks. Further out lichen, then grasses had begun to grow, an individual small tree, here and there, finally a forest struggled to come to life and take over where the glacier had previously been.

The frightening wall of ice exhibited jagged, blue-white spires, towering high onto the misty sky. Great icy caverns, dark and uninviting, gave forth a groaning and shrieking like a wounded animal, then a thunder like a cannon shot as large pieces of ice fell. The towers tilted crazily, moved forward by pressure from the mass behind, to tumble and crash into the heaving ocean swell. Vast chasms gouged deep into the face of the glacier, dark and foreboding, echoed to the roar of the surging tide. From deep within the body of the ice, a torrent of dirt-filled water roared from a tunnel to colour the ocean dirty and brown. All watched in awe as another great rumbling and loud cracking heralded a further collapse.

"There, doctor, is the source of the sounds that have so alarmed us. It is as if the whole thing wishes to push itself forward onto us."

"Look Joseph, look at that, the face is falling into the sea, it is immense and the waves created may give us concern."

The mass of ice, which had given way from the face of the glacier crashed with a roar into the water of the inlet. A giant wave foamed and churned outward towards the boats, rising high in a menacing and dangerous fashion. Jagged icy pieces were tossed into the air and danced on the muddy foaming crest of the maelstrom.

"Turn the boats, turn the boats, quickly, pull hard, pull hard; row for your lives."

The men at the oars needed no encouragement to get themselves away from the danger rushing towards them. Quite suddenly, no more than sixty yards from the pinnace and the cutters, the rushing wave eased its frightening aspect. The foaming crest gave way to a steep wall of unbroken, brown, dirty water, which rushed beneath the vessels. The pinnace and the cutters rose steeply on the wave, to surge forward with a sudden increase of speed and then fell back into the trough as the next wave passed beneath them.

"My God, I thought we were in for it then Doctor, we will have to be on our guard in this ice. It seems that the glaciers fall at any occasion. It was only the sudden deepening of the water that saved us from a situation marked with more peril than I care to imagine."

"Our men pulled us with great urgency to get us out to deeper water; they knew our lives depended on their efforts. In all my years I have never sailed with such a crew as we have with us. Shall we find a place and stop for the night? This constant rain and fog is very debilitating, I fear the ice does not lend itself to travel at night."

"Over there, those islands with the beginning of a forest, the water seems well clear of ice. Let us make our way towards them. Yes Doctor, we will find a camp for the night and hope tomorrow will be a little more to our liking."

The fog persisted although the rain had ceased. The vessels proceeded east towards a group of islands, the ice flows continued, and some of the pieces in the now clearer air were seen to be enormous. They rose and fell on the swell, grinding angrily, each against the other. The boats entered the channel between the islands; the flowing tide carried them into a perilous situation. The thought crossed my mind that if two of the icy masses were to encompass a boat from opposite sides, the vessel would be crushed beyond all help.

"These islands are smaller than I initially thought, look, I count five of some note, what is your count, Doctor?"

The vessels, well caught up in the tidal race, swept into the narrow passage between the larger of the islands. Whirlpools appeared in an instant, to tumble and toss the ice in every direction, then to vanish, only to reappear in a different place with the same perilous effect.

"Right ahead, right ahead," Dr. Menzies pointed excitedly towards a large mass that began to spin in an erratic fashion as it swept into a whirlpool not twenty yards ahead.

"I cannot pay too much attention to the size of islands, Joseph, when there is every chance that I may not see dinner tonight. This ice is most exasperating and I shall be glad to be well rid of it."

"Back the oars, back the oars, watch it now, steady,"

Lieutenant Whitbey took little notice of his companion seated beside him in the stern of the pinnace as he stood to watch the action of the ice, swirling into the whirlpool immediately ahead. The tide swept them forward; the churning mass began to close in on the vessels as the passage narrowed.

"Back the oars. Harder, back the oars."

The men pushed against the relentless tide in an almost futile attempt to slow the vessels down, before being drawn into the whirlpool.

"My God, it is impossible; we are into it I fear. If we are crushed we will need to rely on the cutters for assistance, try for the ice if we are capsized. Heave back on the oars."

The ice, rushing and swirling into the maw of the whirlpool, some twenty feet across and now only feet away, spelled out a deadly watery fate. The men eased their efforts and contemplated their destiny before them. All were well aware there was nothing to be done; all their lives were in the hands of the maker. Fear deformed the faces of some, while others, for what may have been the first time in their existence, prayed aloud to a God who had long ceased to be of relevance to their lives.

I was sure this was to be my last moment in this life and I feel confident my companions were of the same mind. It is strange how, though I pulled with all my might, as did all; I felt calmness at the thought of impending death. I knew fate had taken us in its dreadful hand and there was not one thing I could do about the outcome. Suddenly it was gone. The swirling maelstrom exploded in a surging conglomerate of spray and ice. The pinnace, carried along by the rushing tide, crashed into the still heaving, moving mass. We attempted to fend the vessel off with our oars as we scraped along the icy wall. Naval discipline gave way to any effort that would help to extricate us from our predicament. Hands, feet and oars all came into use to push away from the heaving icebergs. Finally, it was over, as the vessels broke free from the ice into clear water. With our ordeal now behind us, we watched the two cutters make an easy passage where we had almost met our end. The strait now opened wide and clear before us.

As the weather began to clear, a vista of unparalleled beauty presented itself. A waterway some eight miles across, liberally flecked with shining white icy bits in varying quantities and disposition, led away to the east. To the north, the great wall of ice, sheer and stark, stretched five miles across, contained by two headlands. Enormous glaciers filled the mountain valleys far into the distance in a northerly direction. To the south was a comparatively low landscape, well wooded, affording good possible campsites in the bays. The ice seemed contained on the north side of the strait and about the base of the great glacier, as it continually spewed massive chunks into the sea.

"Well Doctor, we can thank almighty providence that we are all still alive I think. I had the feeling that the ice would have not allowed us to pursue our venture, it seemed to block the passage completely, I felt that we may have had to abandon our investigations."

"Ah, Joseph, I am much relived that we are still alive."

The cutters drew up to the pinnace.

"We will make for that cove to the south and camp for the night. Your men are in good order Mr. le Mesurier, just a grapnel lost. It is needed, but a cheap price to pay for our salvation. Tomorrow we will have a clear passage for our investigations."

We saw this place in the year 1794. It struck me that these great glaciers were in a state of recession. What the place would have been like 100 years previously is beyond imagination. All around great piles of broken rock at the base of shining granite told of forces beyond our comprehension. What it would be like in the future is equally difficult to imagine. The trees of the country further inland were great of girth and of a prodigious height, but here all was in a state of newness and of a very small stature. I assume therefore all was recently under ice and that new land was constantly being exposed.

While we were on our journey through the icy strait, Captain Vancouver had gone on an expedition to the Cape Spencer at the entrance to Cross Sound. The Captain became ill and the voyage was cancelled. The seamen needed no encouragement to abandon the voyage. Certainly, they would be well employed repairing the vessels, but most agreeable to the men was the fact they would sleep dry tonight.

Captain Vancouver was a Navy Man and he was dedicated to the service and his duty. This was the first time in all these years at sea; he had been unable to respond. One can imagine the anguish experienced at this failure and if we could have been privy to his thoughts we would have seen in confused patterns, his parents, John and Bridget, as he last saw them so many years ago. Now he was in the North American colonies with Vashon on the *Europa*, beleaguered by the dreadful scourge of scurvy. Again, he was in the plague-ridden Caribbean. In his mind, he spoke with his sisters Mary and Sarah. Now he was with Cook, he heard and almost felt the blows, as the natives of Hawaii clubbed his captain and mentor to death. He was with his brothers in the crooked, narrow streets of Kings Lynn; Van and dear Charles, his twin in every way, how they enjoyed the company of each other. He stood impassive as the cat fell on the writhing body of a seaman he had caused to be punished. Now he saw his grandmother, Sarah, in his family home in New Conduit Street, she called to him as a dim memory from the past. Vancouver lay with his arm over his eyes, image after image flashing before him. In the darkness of the descending evening, in the cold wilderness of Alaska, George Vancouver, tired and ill, would have been forgiven as he was heard to murmur to himself, "I want to go home to my family, I have had enough and I have had enough of this infernal ocean."

27

Jane Has Secret Desires and Befriends a General

Jane and Gwen arrived in London, ever an exhausting journey in the heat of summer. How relieved they were to be aroused by the blare of a trumpet, the guard signaling their arrival and demanding the innkeeper alert his porters to receive guests. The Lynn & Wells Mail had made the ninety-eight mile journey in less than 12 hours. The coach swept down the dusty expanse of Mile End Road towards a building barely visible through the trees by a line of blue smoke rising straight into the hot azure summer sky.

"I shall be so glad to get to a bed that does not pitch and toss as this coach is apt to do."

Gwen did not answer Jane; the sudden trumpet sound had awoken her from a disturbed and fitful slumber. She stretched and yawned as Jane continued.

"Here Gwen, here is five shillings. Take care of the guard and the porters. Remember now, two and six for the guard, two shillings for the porters and sixpence for the postillion. I will speak to the host and see to our lodging."

The time approached eight in the evening as the coach rolled into the yard of the inn in a swirl of dust, activity and sound. The guard continued trumpeting, dogs barked and nipped at the feet of the horses, porters shouted to the coachman, and over all the snorting, puffing and jangling of the sweat-drenched horses.

"Over here with it, Tom. Get the coach as near to the stairs as you can. Have a thought for the poor lads who have to carry all this."

"What sort of a trip did you have? Never sighted the highway man Captain Streatcher?"

"No, he's a bad one that fellow. Been sighted twix here and Cambridge of late, but an easy ride it was, mind you the lady passengers might not think so."

The chaos of arrival gave way to order as the porters began to unload the baggage. Piece by piece, the cases and trunks were whisked away. Jane entered the inn and sought out the innkeeper, a jolly, fat man, barking orders, of which no one seemed to take the slightest notice.

"Sir, I take it I am speaking to the host of this establishment."

"That you are, madam."

"Well then ,sir, I require rooms for the night, for both myself and my companion. The best you have and next to each other."

"Well now mum, two rooms present a problem. All are taken but one. The mobilization of our military has placed a great demand on all the innkeepers here about. All are full, but I have a room. It is a large room and has a fine bed in it. It is only vacant because of the sudden posting of the previous tenant, General Lord Percy, who left us just this midday. "

"No, no, I must have two rooms. My companion is my housekeeper. It would not be proper for me to share with a servant."

"There is nothing I can do. It is the only accommodation I can offer you. How long would you be staying in our humble establishment?"

"At this time I can only say just for tonight."

"Well, madam, I cannot even provide a cot for your housekeeper. There is no other way, madam. I do have a fine table at your service; say the word and you will have a repast far better than most in these parts, then a comfortable bed for the night. What do you say?"

Jane was tired and hungry; Gwen had taken care of the payment and gratuities and now stood by her side listening to this exchange.

"Can you arrange for a bath for my housekeeper and me?"

"I most certainly can, water is always warm and ready. I have purchased a hipbath from Mr. Bleke, a London supplier, as we are constantly receiving weary travelers, some of who feel the need of soothing water after their journey. So you see you are in the lap of luxury."

Jane could not contemplate the problem any further. The thought of a good meal, a bath and a comfortable bed rode roughshod over propriety.

"Alright, we will stay; I am too tired to argue the point. What you propose is not correct, but what can I do? As you say the army has been mobilized, it is up to us to make the best of things, if only as a patriotic duty."

"Excellent. Let me show you to your room, I will arrange all that is required for your comfort. Come ladies, follow me."

Jane and Gwen were alone in a large room, still smelling of tobacco, whiskey and the unwashed sour odour of the previous inhabitant. Jane was first to use the hipbath, and then Gwen bathed and changed from her dusty, soiled attire. Both appeared relaxed and calm as they presented themselves for dinner, finding their way downstairs and through a low doorway into a medium sized room. Small paned windows lined the western wall where unoccupied chairs and tables stood randomly. Along the east wall, high-backed wooden booths, again unoccupied, filled the space. At the northern end of the room hot coals glowed in a large fireplace. Suspended on a spit, a shiny carcass of a porker, sizzled and steamed, turning slowly.

Jane and Gwen took a seat in a booth a comfortable distance from the fire. Both watched the small, brown and white turnspit dog, disinterestedly walking slowly in his wheel. The wheel squeaked monotonously as the small animal propelled it and thence the carcass before the fire. Round and round the little dog did his work. The smell of the cooking pork caused both women to realize how hungry they both were.

Randomly placed drawings and paintings, most of which dimly depicted great sea or land battles of past days, hung suspended on the dun coloured walls. Through an open door, a wall fireplace in an iron cupboard stood clearly visible and well in use.

The meal presented by the innkeeper fulfilled every need of the exhausted and famished pair in every way. Jane was agreeably surprised by the quality of the repast. First a fine dish of mock turtle soup followed by a brace of squab, fricasseed with bacon. The main course was a pigeon pie, well-spiced and moistened with butter, with a fine English jelly wine sauce served with a large plate of potatoes and peas. The sweet was a baked bread pudding. To consume everything placed before them was out of the question, but they accompanied their meal with numerous glasses of prime Madeira. In due course, the well-fed and slightly tipsy ladies retired to their room.

The heat of their room, the excellent meal, the copious quantity of Madeira and the warm bath both girls had enjoyed, soon put to rest all apprehensions as to their sleeping arrangements. Any of the timidity Jane may have felt at this was well allayed by the copious draughts of Madeira. The exhausted young women began removing most of their clothes, amid gales of laughter. Both were clad only in their peignoirs when they collapsed onto the wide, soft mattress. Their bed was an ornate, old four-poster, which had obviously been the scene of many an encounter. Sleep overtook them immediately. The room was warm and comfortable, the odour of tobacco smoke and the last inhabitant was soon ignored, and two weary, well-dined travelers almost immediately fell into a deep, sound sleep.

Discovery

In the dim light of dawn, Jane opened her eyes. For a time she had no idea of where she was. For a moment, she was back at Medhurst and as she lay in the drowsiness of half sleep, she began to plan her usual day and await Gwen to help her dress. Strange sounds, people talking, hoof-beats, the clash of pots and pans, suddenly brought her to the reality of her situation. It suddenly dawned on her where she was. Jane tried to move and sit up, but she could not, something held her.

"Oh, my goodness", she murmured the words to herself.

Jane found herself being held by Gwen and she in turn was holding Gwen. Jane stayed still, overcome by this most unusual situation. Sometime during the night, Gwen had rolled over to her and she in turn had entwined herself with Gwen. Perhaps, she thought the warmth beside her was Henry. Then she asked herself the question, who had Gwen assumed she was turning to. Jane looked at the sleeping girl, now so close. How gentle and vulnerable she appeared. Jane decided not to move for fear of awakening her. With a free hand, she brushed back a lock of dark hair from Gwen's eyes. This slight movement caused Gwen to roll even closer to Jane. The movement exposed her breast, full and round, Jane gazed at the dark aureole with its large, soft, pink nipple. She was enchanted by Gwen resting warm on her arm. She thought of the nights of passion and the way Henry would lay claim to her breast and lovingly caress it. An ache, deep and disturbing began within her. Gently she loosed her own breast from its cover, soft and pliant it fell against Gwen. Jane compared her milky skin to the creamy darker hue of her companion. She reached across with her free hand and touched Gwen. She felt the texture and softness; she let the hard pink bud slide between her fingers.

Gwen sighed audibly. She opened her eyes, "Oh! What is that is it time to wake?"

Gwen rolled away, releasing Jane from her embrace.

"Oh what a sleep; and you mum, did you sleep well?"

Jane answered, guilty at the liberty she had taken.

"Yes Gwen that I did. What is the time? I fear we have slept the sleep of the innocent, and it is such an important day. Let us hope we may find a place able to accommodate us in a more appropriate manner. I must say how grateful I am for your understanding of our situation and I hope your slumber was in no way disturbed by me."

"In no way mum, I slept like a baby in its own crib, have no fear of that." Gwen mouthed the words she knew Jane wished to hear but at Jane's first touch, she had been awake and aware. She too shared a forbidden desire, which for now would remain secret.

The day had dawned clear and warm. Jane immediately entered into the task of discovering the whereabouts of Henry. From the window, the ribbon of the Thames appeared, first here then there as it meandered through the countryside and into the city. The frightening yet exciting city of London was before her. Somewhere in this unfamiliar place, Henry West should be found and enlisted into the task of finding them accommodation. At this time in the morning, the Boar and Pit Inn bustled with the usual work required to operate an establishment at this important confluence of highways. Jane entered the room where they had dined the night before. Four military men, dashing and resplendent in their red, gold-trimmed uniforms, sat at their morning meal. Of course, being officers and gentlemen, they rose to a man when Jane and Gwen approached. Without hesitation, Jane immediately entered into conversation with them.

"Sirs, I beg your indulgence and insist you think me not forward in speaking without introduction. I am Mrs. Henry West; this is my companion Miss Pratt. We are ladies and companions traveling alone to London town. I throw myself on your good will as gentlemen and ask your assistance. I have the honour to be the wife of a person with whom you may be acquainted. Are you aware of the whereabouts of my husband, Captain Henry West?"

The military gentlemen ceased their preoccupation with the repast half-devoured on their plates. They listened to Jane, taken aback somewhat at the forwardness of this attractive young, married lady, ostensibly traveling alone. Jane did not notice it, but at the mention of Henry West, each officer glanced at the other. Finally, a man obviously senior to the others, resplendent in the uniform of the of the Royal Horse, those fine fellows who stood ready to defend the Prince Regent, spoke in a rather confused manner.

"I say, Jove, aw, Henry West you say. Gad Madam, know the fellow. Yes, know him, what."

"It seems I have been rewarded by my forwardness. Pray tell me sir, if you know his situation. Where can I find Captain West?"

"Well now aw. Gad. Yes, saw him in London just last week. Don't know where he is now. Posted somewhere, Kent I believe. Don't really know."

To a person of a more worldly nature, it was obvious that Jane had surprised these gentlemen and they knew a lot more about Henry West than they cared to disclose. The military brotherhood forbade any disclosure without permission.

Discovery

"Sirs, I beseech you. If you have any information on the whereabouts of Captain West, pray tell me. Of course if by divulging such information you should jeopardize some military secret or place at risk the well being of yourselves or Henry, you must be silent."

It had not become obvious to Jane; the officers she addressed displayed a degree of discomfort at her intrusion. It was not that they were not delighted to have such an agreeable and beautiful person converse with them, to a man they fancied themselves as devilish with the ladies. Their discomfort stemmed from another source, that of Henry West himself.

"Well now—umm—I say. Can't really tell you where he is at. Don't really know, my dear lady."

Jane knew the power of a woman over the male species. With no effort, a tear came to the deep grey of her eyes. As she fumbled for a handkerchief hidden in the fullness of her sleeve, the discomfort of the officers changed from how not to disclose the whereabouts of their fellow officer, to one of complete discomfort and pity for such a beauty.

"I say, there now. That's enough of that my dear." The senior man, tall portly and distinguished, took Jane's hand in his.

"Can't have tears now, I will see what we can discover. Your husband aye. Henry West. Didn't know the fellow was married. Poncenbury, see what you can find out about Captain West. Some of the regiments have left for Belgium. See what you can find."

"Yes, sir. I will report to you this evening."

Again, Jane did not notice the glance, which passed between Lieutenant Poncenbury and his companions.

"Now dear madam, tonight I trust I will have the information you require. Wipe the tears from those pretty eyes. This is a fine establishment rest yourself today. Take the air by the river. I know my man will have the information you wish to hear by tonight."

"How can I thank you sir? To whom do I have the pleasure of speaking?

"No need for thanks, madam, I have the honour to be Edward Fitzherbert and while you are here I would deem it a privilege if you will allow me to place you and your companion under my personal protection. Porter-Jones, you will stay with this lady and take care of her every wish."

Jane could not have entered into a more rewarding conversation. Providence had placed General Fitzherbert in her way, what better champion to help her pursue the course she had set for herself and to discover the whereabouts of Henry West.

After the officers had gone about their business and Gwen had left to attend to her toilet, Jane sat quietly and contemplated her decision to leave Medhurst. She thought on the long and dusty journey down from Norfolk. She marveled at her fortitude in speaking to a group of soldiers without prior introduction, but most of all she pondered on the new and disturbing feelings brought about by the previous night. She had experienced unexplainable sensations. Tonight she would sleep again with Gwen.

Jane searched out the host and made the necessary arrangements. Though another room had become vacant, she did not take advantage of it. Although she would not own up to it, Jane retained their present situation, as it was for reasons still unclear to her. A seed had been planted in the dark of the night and warmth of the bed she had shared with Gwen. A change was slowly beginning to occur, a change, which would have lasting and unforeseen consequences for both her and her housekeeper.

28

Port Conclusion, the Last Anchorage and the Death of Isaac Wooden

"Now my friend I will tell you of our last anchorage. You cannot imagine the feelings rampant and raging through the minds of the souls aboard our two vessels. Both officers and men knew our journey was nearing its end. We had explored every nook and cranny of this vast and unforgiving coast. Charts had been made and logs kept, which when published would render the intricate and dangerous waterways of the Pacific Northwest of America clear and a much safer place.

"Now we lay in the confines of a sheltered cove, which Captain Vancouver had named Port Conclusion."

Peter and Sir Neville made their way back towards the Pitt Inn.

"I had survived so far and I knew there would be no more small boat journeys. All that remained was the voyage down the west coast of the Americas, around the dreaded Cape Horn and then it was only a matter of a run up the Atlantic Ocean and home."

"My goodness Peter, what you are saying has no meaning for me. I have looked at charts in Kings Lynn; I only know it is a long way."

"Yes it is a long way, but when you consider the distance already traveled it seemed nothing. I think the biggest concern for all was the sad state of our vessels and equipment. Everything was worn out or about to fail. Even our clothes were threadbare. However, let me continue with my tale. Port Conclusion was a narrow indent lying virtually in an east west direction. High mountainous peaks raised themselves on both sides and the west end of the inlet still showed streaks of snow where the warmth of the summer sun had failed to penetrate. Such was the narrowness of the cove, the vessels lay bow to stern at the headwaters of the bay. The bowsprit of *Discovery* almost touched the stern of *Chatham*. Lines reached out to the shore on either side to steady the vessels. Our captain had named the strait at the eastern entrance Chatham Strait, in honour of John Pitt, second Earl of Chatham and First Lord of the Admiralty. I also felt it commemorated our consort vessel *HMS Chatham*. A violent, cold gale lashed the ships, it howled down from the snow-covered heights of the surrounding mountains to sing its mournful dirge through the rigging. This would be it the end was in sight. All Admiralty instructions had been carried out. There was no short cut to the lakes of the east and we had charted the continental shore and all its intricate waterways and indents."

Peter continued with his description and again saw himself in the wild vastness of the Pacific Northwest.

"A speedy departure from the final anchorage seemed imminent, but now the violence of a great Pacific storm kept us well and securely anchored in perfect safety. The vessels were confined until the gales blew themselves out. The anchorage, generally uninteresting and lonely, was completely bereft of native inhabitants. The native visits, which usually provided entertainment, extra food and an opportunity for trade, were non-existent in this wilderness area. The crews were kept busy. The vessels were in dire need of repairs. Carpenters were chalking the decks. Others were cutting planks and spars. The brewers were ashore making spruce beer; some were collecting the Marsh Samphire [*Salicornia herbacea*], a wild herb used as a substitute for greens. Another group fished at the entrance to the cove to take halibut, not in large quantities, but enough to share between the officers and men. Another group of officers and seamen, muffled against the cold, built a cairn on a small islet near the entrance to the bay. They laboriously cut and stacked rocks to mark their last anchorage."

The surrounding shore landscape was generally low, well covered with trees. Fir, hemlock and cedar, which came down to the edge of the sea. The trees grew smaller as they clawed and clung to the slopes of the mountains, finally to give up their efforts, until only stark rocky, snowy peaks remained to dominate the bay.

"Rain, rain, will it never stop, Tom?"

The man who spoke was hunched down in a heavy woolen coat, the collar held high about his neck by a blue piece of linen, knotted tightly at his throat. A sailor's straw hat, replaced his cocked officer's headgear, the wet and soggy brim drooped and dripped down onto his shoulders.

"Well, it must cease soon, Joseph. I know we will be glad to get underway again, home to England, why I can barely remember my mother. Still a long haul though. I have completed the charts to date, a little more to do, but the rain has found my workstation. The Captain is in a gentle temper, he told me to put it all off for the rest of the day, so here I am to join you on deck."

A work crew came alongside, wet and muddy. Three men appeared from the fo'c'sil, the task of loading aboard bundles of long green leaves and buckets of berries occupied their time. From the various openings of the vessel, wisps of smoke from cooking fires, as well as fires lit to dry and fumigate the ship, hung close to the water, held down by the incessant rain and fog. On closer inspection, the tranquil damp scene was in reality a hive of industry. Besides the shore party at the starboard side of the vessel, other boats emerged from the cloudy rain-shrouded mist of the bay. One was loaded with wood, logs cut to a length suitable for the cooking fires, another with baskets of halibut and other sea creatures. High in the rigging men called to others at the bowsprit as a jib-stay was replaced with the remains of a dwindling supply of suitable rope.

"You know the rope coils are almost exhausted, Joseph; we can't expect to receive much in the way of supplies; perhaps at Nootka from the Spaniards, but not likely."

"A mooring cable will have to be made into rope, tedious work, there are still two new coils below, I'll wager that will be the procedure. Damme Thomas, the rain, it's stopping, seems to be getting lighter by the minute."

Nightfall saw the weather improve dramatically. Clouds raced across the sky, though fog laid still and heavy in the cove. As the sun fell low in the west, splashes of blue appeared and became more frequent amid the flying fleece of red-tinged clouds. The gale became a strong breeze and as darkness descended over the vessels, it finally became calm. The glow of the lamps from the great aft cabin danced on the black still water of the cove. The sound of talk and laughter echoed clearly on the night, while above, the brilliant white stars glistened icily in the heavens. A bell sounded the change from the second dogwatch, to the first watch. By nine, the cabin lights were out and all was silent below. On deck, a stern lamp cast its warm, yellow glow over the deck and the watch. Tomorrow was the long-awaited day. England and home would be more than just a memory.

The morning of Saturday August 23rd, 1794, dawned clear and cool. An adverse wind still blew from the southeast, not with the intensity of the past five days, but still enough to make a passage difficult towards the open sea. On this morning the crew of *HMS Discovery* and *HMS Chatham* seemed to step more lively than before. They had reason, the terrible weather had cleared and they were going home, their challenge had ended.

The boats had carried in the stern anchors; the vessels rode head to the wind, as sailors swarmed into the ratlines and up to the booms, out onto the foot-ropes, to work on the slings and bunts holding the sails to the boom. On deck the challenge of getting vessels anchored bow to stern in a tight bay, out to open water, was underway and proceeding, as it should.

"Up anchor! Heave round the capstan."

The ship's master gave the order; Joseph Whitbey called his orders through a speaking trumpet. Once again, the seamen began the heavy task of breaking out the anchor. Round and round the men worked, slowly at first, to a chant, the words led by Isaac Wooden, his high, alto voice urging the men to united effort.

"Oh, don't yiz hear the old man say?"

The refrain answered Isaac at first tentatively.

"Goodbye fare-ye-well! Good bye fare-ye-well!"

Again, Isaac sang his shanty, "Oh don't yiz here the Old Man say?"

Now the men at the capstan entered into the happy thought they were going home, "Hooraw me boys, we're homeward bound!"

"Were homeward bound to Liverpool Town,"

"Where all them judies they will come down."

On and on, round and round, the sailors hauled the anchor.

"An' when we gits to Wallasey Gates,"

"Sally and Polly for their flash men do wait."

The vessel moved slowly forward on the hawser, until finally the anchor broke clear of the bottom.

"Up and Down," the cry from the bow.

"Heave and away," as the anchor broke free.

The jibs, already raised, flapped free in the breeze and the vessel began to drift slowly astern.

"Head braces and spanker out-haul," the jibs and spanker were drawn in to gather the breeze. As the bay widened, *HMS Discovery* began to turn to larboard and heel just a little as the breeze filled the fore sails and the spanker. The excitement of the vessel getting underway seemed to infect even the lowest ranked man on board, the time of waiting for the right weather was over.

The reports and commands came faster from different parts of the ship.

"Heaving in sight," as now the anchor is drawn out of the water.

"Avast heaving! Stand to the bars! Man the cat fall!"
Now the men in the rigging were to have their moment.
"Make sail." Loud and clear, the commands came from the master.
"Man the fore and main tacks, ease down the clew garnets."

As square sails fell billowing and flapping in the breeze, the deck crew received the order to haul in the sheets. Again, the sound of a shanty filled the air as the billowing sails were drawn taut. The breeze, almost full astern, propelled *Discovery* out into the strait, towards the rugged shores of Kuiu Island, some fifteen miles to the east, still barely visible in the misty haze that enveloped the shore in all directions.

"Trim sails there! Man the weather braces! Lee braces now, haul taut, brace in there! Belay the main brace."

The sails were set in their correct configuration, *Discovery* answered well, her speed increased, the vessel lifted on the first of the swells that surged in from the open sea. She was heading across the breeze into what the captain had named Chatham Strait. Not far behind, *HMS Chatham* followed the same procedure. Both vessels soon under full sail made out from Port Conclusion.

Clear into Chatham Strait, enormous Pacific swells swept in regular mountainous lines, the residue of the great storm of the last week. The ships rose to the top of one swell then to fall into the trough before the next. The standing rigging clattered against the masts, the sails thundered and cracked as the momentum of the vessel nullified the effect of the light wind, only to again fill and strain as *Discovery* raised her bow to the next, before rushing forward into another watery valley. Tack after tack across the strait in the light winds finally gave enough clearance to make for the open ocean.

By nightfall Cape Ommaney, just half a league to starboard, lie shrouded in the mist. Even at this distance, the thunder of the massive seas breaking along the coast was easily audible. A misty pawl of spray hung low over the jagged tortured coastline. The pungent smell of kelp torn and swept from the rocky foreshore impregnated the heavily laden salty air. All about, streaks and piles of spume rose and fell on the oily swells silently making their way ashore to thunder onto rocky foreshores. The vessels began to loose headway as the light breeze fell.

"Captain, this breeze is falling rapidly."

"Yes Mr. Whitbey, have the boats stand by, get them into the water, get warps at the ready. For now we are making headway, but the tide will change and if the wind drops, towing is our only option."

The headland that was Cape Ommaney received the full brunt of the monstrous green swells that rose steep and fearsome before shattering themselves in a great thunderous conglomerate of flying spume and foam. At six, the tide began to flood and simultaneously the breeze became variable to almost non-existent. The vessels wallowed as though reluctant to leave the safety of their recent haven. The sails dropped down to flap and beat tiredly against the masts. The rigging swung loose or heavily struck against the nearest object of resistance with the rhythm of the vessel's movements. Anxiously, the officers and men scanned the sky, or the surface of the sea for a trace of a breeze, which would extract them from what, was rapidly becoming a dangerous situation. The crew, well aware of the imminent threat to their well-being, instantly carried out the orders given.

All boats had been lowered. They rode uncomfortably beside the larger vessels and towing warps had already been laid out along the deck of both vessels.

"All right Mr. Whitbey, furl in the sails, get the boats away, that's all that can be done for now."

Lieutenant Whitbey needed no encouragement to carry out these orders. The swells, which were large before, were now enormous as they formed ranks to march closer to the terrible shore no more than a quarter mile to starboard. The crew swarmed into the rigging to take in the sails.

"Haul taut."

"Ease away the main tack."

"Haul up."

One by one, the sails were hauled to the boom to hang down in folds, which moved only to the violent motion of the becalmed and belaboured vessels.

"Boats away, look lively, come on now men, pull for your lives or we will lose the lot."

Slowly the boats took their warps in tow, the launch led the way, the two whalers one each side, but aft of the launch, to alleviate the chance of the oars becoming entangled. The sailors heaved on their oars and began to take a strain on the line.

"Heave," the call came from master's mate John Sykes, "Come on lads and heave. Pull us to England if we have to. Heave."

The abnormally large swells stood high and fearsome and rushed at the small boats constrained by the hawsers. There was no need for encouragement or threat of punishment to spur the men on to extraordinary efforts; all were well aware of the fate that awaited them if they failed.

At one moment, the boats would be high on the crest of a wave, level with the boom of *Discovery*'s main sail. The boats seemed to pause at the top of the watery mountains before making a sickening dive down into a green abyss, the warps cutting into the wave to bring the descent of the boats to a violent halt. Now only the top-masts of their charges were visible. *Discovery* rose high on the crest of the wave, it towered high over the boats like some sea denizen, about to devour the small prey beneath, but each time the straining boats would escape into the next watery valley.

Hour after hour, the men at the lead line called their marks in a futile attempt to find a bottom to enable an anchor to be deployed. Hour after hour the men at the oars ignored pain and exhaustion spurred on by the sure knowledge that their lives and the lives of their shipmates lay solely in their hands. Near six, the tide changed, the ebb meant little respite for those at the oars, but still no breeze to extricate them from their labours. The vessels were no nearer the rocks, although no further away and now darkness was about to descend with no sign of relief.

"Well gentlemen, we are still in good order, but for how long remains to be seen."

Captain Vancouver had not left the deck, he looked tired, his normally plump face now lined and drawn. He knew the straining seamen in the boats held their very existence in the palms of their hands. Lieutenant Baker voiced the concern already on the mind of Captain Vancouver.

"Captain, the men in the boats are almost exhausted; they cannot possibly keep this up too much longer. I suggest a change of boat crew, with the ebb tide it could be managed without our position being too much compromised."

Lieutenant Baker well knew the danger, which had befallen them these last hours. He was also well aware of the terrible and continuous effort made by the sailors. Their extraordinary efforts had kept the vessels off the rocks, still not half a mile away, but if a wind did not soon manifest itself, all would still be lost. He looked across to *Chatham* just a short distance to port. Her lamps had been lit and swung madly as the vessel rose and fell to the shrouded waves. Out of the darkness, the call of *"heave"* echoed across the agitated ocean, above the roar of the nearby surf as it broke on the jagged unforgiving rocks of Cape Ommaney, encouraging unseen effort at the oars.

"Mr. Baker, I feel a breeze. By God, I do feel a breeze."

The man who spoke had only moments before been relieved at the oars. The Honourable John Ainsley Browne, one time midshipman, now ablebodied seaman, was bone tired and exhausted. Because the number of midshipmen was far in excess of that required for the size of the vessels *Discovery* and *Chatham*, it had been the custom since the start of the voyage that midshipman carried out their duties alternating between the two ranks, midshipman and able-bodied seaman.

"Yes, sir it's a breeze, from the north-west I think."

"By heaven, he's right, I feel it myself, Mr. Baker, not much though, damme, I wish it were daylight. Mr. Whitbey, are you forward there?"

"Aye sir, I feel it, from the north-west, not much but enough I think."

The boats were called to leave off their efforts. A cheer echoed across the dark water as the breeze now settled about them. It was from a direction, which would take the vessels out from the land on a larboard tack across Christian Sound. The boats were soon beside *Discovery*. The warps that had served them so well were hauled aboard as the rowers scrambled on deck. Their work was not yet over, the tired exhausted men ran to their positions as Mr. Whitbey called the orders that would bring them to safety.

"Ready all, haul taut the main tack and sheets."

The sails, which had been loosely furled fell out into their full position, as again Mr. Whitbey called out the commands to get them off on a slow, larboard tack.

"Ready all, ease the helm down, haul over the boom."

The quartermaster Phillip Butcher gently eased down on the helm and as the spanker boom was hauled over, the stern of *Discovery* fell a little to leeward. The headsails had been let go to flap lazily in the light breeze.

"Helm's alee, raise tacks and sheets."

The officers of *Discovery* listened and watched closely as the vessel slowly began to move forward. All knew at the slightest mistake or if the light breeze should cease, disastrous consequences could still result.

"Let go the top gallant bow lines. Haul taut the main brace."

The men worked in the fashion of well-trained seamen with the added incentive of the crashing rollers booming out in the darkness with just the faintest hint of phosphorous to outline the breaking waves at the shoreline.

"Mainsail haul! Head braces, jump to it now! Main tack and sheets to the weather braces."

Slowly the yards came round and the headsails filled with the strengthening breeze. *Discovery* rose on one giant swell after another. The vessel came to life, headway became a reality.

"Brace up the main yard."

The final order secured the yard arm to its correct position from the eased off position, here it would not lock the fore yard. The vessel clasped the strengthening breeze to its bosom and plunged ahead, away from the perils of Cape Ommaney.

"Well done Mr. Whitbey. We could not afford to miss stays in that position, I would not want to have taken her around on her heel for any wager. Secure the boats, then an issue of grog for the men as they complete their tasks, well done again, to all."

"Man overboard, man overboard, Isaac, he's in the water."

The cry came from the last boat, the cutter, about to be lifted on deck.

Captain Vancouver and Lieutenant Whitbey still conversing on deck, moved quickly to the larboard side of the vessel.

"There! There he is," Vancouver pointed towards the head of Isaac Wooden as he broke the surface near the stern of the vessel, his mouth opened convulsively, desperately making every effort to draw air into his bursting lungs. In the light of the stern lamps, his face could be seen clearly, pale and unmarked. He raised a hand in what could be construed to be a farewell to his companions lining the rail. Just before he sank into the depths forever, the sea about him became tinged with his life's blood.

"Let the cutter go again, into it you men, perhaps he can be found, Mr. Whitbey all hands to the sails."

"Put the helm down! Shorten sail! About ship."

The men who had barely attained the deck now threw themselves into the task of getting the cutter out and away, in a desperate search for their shipmate. Once again, *Discovery* neared the Cape, which had so recently been the scene of near disaster. The men, who now searched for their unfortunate companion, heard the shouted commands and the bellowing and crashing of sails as the process of bringing the vessel round on her heel was accomplished. The cutter had moved out of sight to become invisible in a stygian darkness and still tremendous seas.

"What happened, Dillon?"

Walter Dillon, the quartermaster's mate who had not been able to join the cutter when it left to search for Isaac Wooden, stood before Captain Vancouver and Lieutenant Whitbey.

"E was just goin' up the side with the painter, 'e just fell backwards, sir, I saw his head hit the gunwale of the cutter, a bloody hard crack it was sir, an 'e can't swim. Poor Isaac's gone sir."

"All right Dillon, go back to your work. It is an unfortunate business Mr. Whitbey."

The cutter returned to report no sign of Isaac Wooden. The men who came aboard *Discovery* knew well the dangers of the life they led; they knew the perils. Despite the great social gulf between officers and men, each needed the other. Isaac Wooden had served in most of the boat expeditions, despite a flogging he had received for involvement with stolen goods; he was highly regarded by both the officers and men.

The boats were stowed, sails adjusted to allow *Discovery* to heel over in the strengthening breeze, which was soon to become a fresh gale. Daylight found *HMS Discovery* well out to sea, her nemesis, Cape Ommaney, and a terrible rocky fate avoided, with one of her sons, Isaac Wooden, claimed as a forfeit.

The fo'c'sil was quiet. The normally boisterous banter of the mess was absent this day. Each man saw the fate of Isaac Wooden as a portent of his own slender claim to life. The vessels had escaped destruction and the crew a dreadful destiny by a very narrow margin; before them lay the vast Pacific coast of North and South America and the dreaded Cape Horn with its gales and violent seas. If all was well at this point, the long journey back up the Atlantic to England lay before them. There was the added peril of war with France and the fact *Discovery* and *Chatham* were in no state to resist any attack, by either enemy or nature.

"Yer know that rock off the bloody place where we nearly bought it? Well, the Captain called it Wooden Rock."

"What Rock are yer talking about? The place was all rocks!"

"Peter Wright 'eard it, Menzies told him. It was the little island right off the tip of the place. Like a cone it was with a bit of grass and scrub at top."

Isaac Wooden had taken his place in the history of North America and along with the King's, admirals and members of parliament, would be remembered until the end of time.

29

Jane Searches for Henry in Vain and is Surprised by Herself.

"Gwen, I am a little relieved, I have made the acquaintance of a distinguished general of the King's army. He knows my husband and assures me he will make every effort to ascertain his whereabouts. Why, he has even directed an officer to make enquiries on my behalf. What do you say to that?"

Gwen had no idea what to say. She knew what to expect from Captain West, but now there was another set of circumstances, brought about by her mistress herself. The incident of the previous morning had surprised Gwen. As young country lass, she knew what to expect from the village lads and the older men who continually pestered her. She had always known that eventually Captain West would come after her. She expected it and used it to her advantage. He was a young, strong handsome man, this made his pursuit all the more pleasant, but the strange feeling raised within her at Jane's intimate touch, was unexpected and confusing.

"Why that is good news. I have been very frightened, this is the first time I have been further than the village green, Mum."

"I believe if the word of General Fitzherbert is to be relied upon; after all he is a gentleman. He has assured me, although he does not know him, he will do all in his power to find Henry for me. Come Gwen, let us change, take parasols, for it is quite hot outside and let us stroll on the banks of the river," Jane took Gwen by the hand and led her towards the stairs. "Perhaps we will find a fresh, cooling breeze off the water."

The day was spent in anticipation at the thought of what news would be forthcoming that night. The two young women found a cool spot under a large oak a short distance from the inn. About midday, Gwen rose and returned to the inn, where she procured a light lunch. The rest of their time was spent in conversation, reading, or occasionally napping.

The scene of tranquility, two attractive women quietly reclining by the stream, to all intents and purposes relaxed and calm, gave no indication of the excited anticipation, which coursed through their minds. Both thought of Henry. Jane needed and enjoyed the nights of passion, where she matched him in every way and now had begun to be more demanding, innovative and surprising at every turn. As for Gwen, she knew Henry would be after her again. She dreaded the situation. Henry West had caused her to lie and make deceit her way of life, but she also knew any protest on her part could mean a return to her father's house and a life of drudgery, hard work and poverty. Coursing through the minds of both women, though not at forefront of their thoughts, was the memory of the soft warmth, of each other's arms and an unknown burning desire new to each.

That evening there was no sign of General Fitzherbert or his Lieutenant, Poncenbury. In fact, the inn was quite deserted. Jane and Gwen sat in the large saloon before the fire; for though the days were warm, nights were still cold. Their evening meal long complete, Jane spoke to the innkeeper.

"Sir host, at what time do you expect the general to return?"

"Well, madam, I do not know. He is usually here by now, or at least he has been for the weeks he has stayed here, but this evening I have no idea. None of the officer gentlemen have returned tonight and I might add it is not to my benefit that they are not arrived."

"Why, sir, what difference is it to you."

"I have prepared a fine meal for them and now it is unused, meat and vegetables, all lying unused in the kitchen. Tomorrow night I will instruct cook to prepare *bubble and squeak* with *spotted dog to follow* as a dessert. You must blame him and your soldiers if tomorrow's meal is not up to the usual standard of my establishment."

"That is bye the bye, I am only interested in the news General Fitzherbert will have for me."

The hours sped on, until a large clock chimed the hour of midnight. Both Jane and Gwen, heads nodding almost in unison, fell captive to the rigors of a long day and the anticipation of what was to come.

"I am going to bed Gwen. Come let us go up to our room, there does not seem to be any hope of General Fitzherbert returning tonight. Come, let us go up."

The sound of voices and the clatter of horses and carriages roused the

Discovery

inn. It was almost dawn. The first glimmer of light had spread its rosy glow across the eastern sky, the stars paled before the advance and dawning of a new day. In the courtyard, a group of mounted men alighted from their horses. They gathered around a carriage, where General Fitzherbert addressed them. They received their instructions and dispersed into the inn.

"Poncenbury, listen to me. I will leave you to inform Mrs. West as to what we have learned on the whereabouts of her husband. Make my apologies to the dear girl and inform her I would consider it my duty to place her under my protection. I am always at her service. Be sure to give her my letter of introduction and this note, which is of a more personal nature. You know what else has to be done."

"Yes, sir. I will then see to the packing of our goods and join you post haste in Dover."

"Good man, jump to it now. Carry on driver."

The general's carriage left the inn. It was soon lost in the half-light of the early dawn.

Jane and Gwen did not stir at the noise from the courtyard. If one had been privileged to see into the darkness of the room, one would have seen two naked beauties entwined in each other's arms and one would have been forgiven for assuming they were more than mistress and servant.

"Madam, I have a communication for you on behalf of General Fitzherbert. Here is a letter confirming the fact that the general has placed you under his personal protection. As well, here is another letter. It is a personal note from the General. I have no orders to wait for a reply." Jane took the letters from the hand of Lieutenant Poncenbury.

"Oh, the dear man, to go to so much trouble on my behalf. Gwen we have news at last. Jane fluttered in her excitement. "Forgive me sir; I must thank you for your efforts. The general, I must see him."

"Have no thought of it, madam. My reward is the happiness I see on your face. I will see to my business and return later. Our regiment is directed to Dover, I must attend to my duty immediately. General Fitzherbert is, as we speak, on the way to his new lodgings." Poncenbury saluted, touching two fingers to the gleaming brass helmet adorning his otherwise quite plain, chinless face.

"Come Gwen, let us read these letters. As the Lieutenant said, this is a note to say we are under the protection of the general, signed by him and that all assistance is to be given us. However, here is some news. It seems Captain West is in London. Apparently, he is staying with Frederick March, at his

217

home in Holborn, at least up until last week. In some ways had I known what trials were involved, I think I would never have embarked on this excursion."

Jane opened the note fastened with a wax seal, which bore the coat of arms of the Fitzherbert family.

"Oh my goodness." Jane paled as she read the contents of the note

Jane read the note and again the words came from her lips, "Oh my goodness. The good general suggests I meet him in London. He has supplied me with an address and submits he would care to be more than my protector. He goes on to say how I would benefit from a liaison with him. Nevertheless, here is the most disturbing part. He intimates that Henry is an unsavoury untrustworthy fellow and I would be better rid of him."

Jane considered her situation. Since she had made her decision to leave Burnham, her rigidly, structured life had taken a turn she was at a loss to explain. The last two nights and the day of tranquility by the river had been the most confusing time in her otherwise circumscribed life. She had left Medhurst to search for a husband who, when they were together was wonderfully satisfying physically, but the lonely days and nights had been a nightmare of useless frustration.

Gwen as a companion had caused her to reconsider her circumstances. She had been delighted when Henry had returned from his alleged secret duty, but his long absences in the town and the nights when he had returned in a drunken odorous state repelled her. She had also come to see his extravagance and monetary demands in a different light. Since he had departed, constant were the bills and accounts sent to her. She had paid them all more as a duty than as a labour of love. If she was to consider the last few months, she had discovered Henry not to be the fine upstanding person who had courted her and claimed her hand in marriage. Now the letter from the General, despite his ulterior motives, tended to confirm her suspicions that Henry West was not the honourable officer who had entered her life and swept her off her feet. Now, another quite unexpected occurrence had happened and this she did not know how to manage. It was Gwen. Most of all it was Gwen, beautiful Gwen. Last night they had crossed the Rubicon. They had surrendered to desire and love. Whatever happened from now on, the die had been cast, and they had entered a relationship, which could see them condemned by society if it were to be revealed. They must be circumspect and careful, but she knew her life had changed forever.

The ladies were again on their way and headed to London.

"I will throw myself on the mercy of my dear Aunt Sarah and pray she can take care of us till we make some more permanent arrangements. Aunt Sarah will take us in I know it. She is a dear and my godmother."

Gwen was completely lost at the turn of events. As their carriage neared London proper, traffic and people became more prevalent. Jane had visited the city of London twice before and Norwich many times, she had always been glad to return to Medhurst and her own place and family. Now here, with London before her, she felt alone and vulnerable. It was no wonder that she would turn to the one person who could fill the void in her heart created by the death of her parents.

The coach made its way down High Street, through Spitalfields, past gardens of produce, meadows dotted with grazing cattle and occasional still-forested areas. Finally, their coach rattled and bounced its way to Bishopsgate and into London proper. The streets became busy with the commerce and activity of a burgeoning city. Their coach slowed as the throng intent on their own purposes continued towards the towers of London Bridge visible through the hazy, smoke-filled evening air.

Jane began to act the part of the tour guide and excitedly pointed out conspicuous objects, which had so impressed her as a young girl. As for Gwen, she peered from the carriage, first one side then the other and as Jane would excitedly point out another notable church or building, she would throw herself to the other side again.

"Look there; as we cross the bridge, there is the Tower, so old and such a monument to our history. This bridge itself, it has been here a lot longer than you and I, my dear. Look over there, Christopher Wren's wonderful new dome. St Paul's, what a marvelous construction, see how it towers above all. Jane was enjoying herself immensely. Gwen for her part was awe-struck at the sights and sounds; she was overawed by the hundreds of people, the buildings and the bustle of the city so different from the quaint quietness of the place wherein she was born.

Their coach came to a standstill, the termination of the turnpike at hand. This was the end of the line, now another vehicle should be hired to take them to Bedford Square and the residence of Lady Sarah Parkinson. Jane quickly arranged another vehicle, this time a four-wheeled chaise. With their luggage was transferred, they set off toward the very centre of London. Along Cannon Street to Ludgate Hill, down the Fleet, past Saint Clement Danes, to Bow and Endell Streets, finally to arrive at the wide concourses and newly built homes of Bloomsbury and Bedford Square. The whole area was a hive of activity. Great building projects with all its attendant industry, clogged streets already full with the bustle of a great city. Vendors and performers, each carrying on their business both legitimate and otherwise, vied one with the other to attract the attention of the bustling populace crowding the footpaths. Here the wealthy rubbed shoulders with the poor. Horses, coaches, carts, sedan chairs, street players, pickpockets, pedestrians and prostitutes, created a bedlam that assaulted the sight and hearing. For her part, Jane found it all to her liking. She relished the thought of living here in London and was confident of being accepted into the social echelon of London society. Her plans were formulated as they came to mind. They changed as each new and exciting thought entered her head.

Gwen was silent. Never before had she seen such activity or buildings of such size, so many people and so much noise, it was all beyond her comprehension, all in all, a little too much for her.

"Now Gwen, you must call Aunt Sarah My Lady and show every courtesy to her. I am sure you will be all right. She is my dear mother's sister and after the death of my uncle, she moved from the city of Bath to London, where she now resides in complete comfort. I am sure she will be delighted to accommodate us; her home is new and quite large, in keeping with her station. I have always been her favourite niece, I expect to be feted and introduced to the society in which she moves."

"But mum, what about Captain West. Shall we still find him?"

"Of course we will. Aunt Sarah shall introduce me to a suitable person who can find Henry and inform him of my whereabouts. I am sure when he hears I am in London he will come immediately."

"Mum, I cannot believe I am in London, I have never seen such goings on, the noise and people, I cannot understand them, and, and..."

"Now Gwen, my darling, I will look after you. My aunt is a woman of note and a champion of free thought. I know she is involved with a number of modern and liberal-thinking societies. I also know she is a devoted friend of Mr. John Howard, a man who does all in his power to influence and improve the lot of those unfortunates who are prisoners. She has friends in literary circles and is a confidant of Hanna Moore, a writer and activist, and her Sunday afternoon salon has become necessary for those who would try to change society to a more tolerant aspect. Therefore, her life is not one subservient to the usual womanly duties. I will be delighted to see her and in all respects I think of her as a substitute for the mother I have lost. "

"Mum, Jane, I will try to fit in. Please help me correct my shortcomings."

"Gwen my dear, you called me Jane. Oh, that is marvelous. You know I look on you as more than a friend and companion. Of course, I will help you. Come here." Jane embraced Gwen, she kissed her cheek and without either knowing why or how, their lips met. Again as in the inn just two nights previously, the same strange, deep feeling came over both young women. Gwen's kiss answered Jane's, with all its implications and with knowledge, which told them they had entered into a relationship forbidden by the church and society itself.

30

Nootka. A Native Reception and Homeward Bound

The journey from Cape Ommaney was without further incident, a pall hung over the vessels as both officers and men mourned in their own way the death of Isaac Wooden. We eventually anchored in Friendly Cove, we were in fine company and all enjoyed the companionship of fellow seamen from many parts.

As we gently sailed to our anchorage, the usual salutes were fired in honour of the Spanish, which was returned in full by our hosts. It always amazed me the enormous use of gunpowder wasted in salute firing by naval people who do not have to pay for this valuable commodity. It seemed at any excuse a salute would be fired and answered. Sometime four and five blasts would be returned in like manner. The use of our powder was so profligate that for our voyage home a supply had to be purchased from our Spanish hosts.

As I looked about, I saw numerous vessels, the most I had seen in all the years on this coast. To our right, three ships of His Catholic Majesties Armada, armed and newly painted, their names *Princessa*, *Aransasu* and *St. Carlos*, glistening gold in the setting sun. Across the cove, the *Phoenix Bark*, arrived from Bengal, weather worn and dilapidated, showed the rigors of her journey across the Pacific. To the south, the *Prince le Boo* swung gently to the light southerly breeze. We had met this vessel with her companions the *Butterworth* and *Jackal* in the north. As you remember, the commander of this squadron of trading vessels, Captain Brown, had shown us a way through rock-infested waters to a safe anchorage behind an outer island. Captain Vancouver had named this safe passage Brown Passage to honour Captain Brown. Across the cove near the shore, under heavy repair, was the American trading brig,

Washington. It was strange to see the flag of the new United States, red and white bars and circled stars standing out in the evening breeze above the careened vessel. With our added vessels, we made a fine show of naval power and commerce in this new, beautiful but forsaken land.

The weather was rainy and very unpleasant, as all set about to place our vessels in as sound an order as possible for the long voyage home to England. There was a constant coming and going of visitors. The Spanish Commandant of the fort made tradesmen, caulkers and carpenters available for our use.

"How did our English fellows get on with their Spanish counterparts? After all we have recently been at war and it seems we will be again?" Sir Neville spoke for the first time in what seemed an age. "Was there no animosity between the crews?"

"It all seemed to go rather well. Communication was a problem, but it was overcome by inventive sign language and shouting. Of course, the war in Europe was far removed from the area. The most important thought of sailors, was survival in cruel and inhospitable conditions and the all consuming desire to return to their loved ones."

"Yes. Yes of course, you are correct in this. Please continue without my untimely interruptions."

"I was working at the bow of the vessel, when Lieutenant Baker, with whom I originally had no acquaintance at all except for the reception of orders, came to me. I did not see him and he startled me.

"Wright, make your self ready to join a boat party. I believe you have earned this by your willingness and bravery on many occasions. George Raybold will take over your work. The boats are at the stern. Get along now."

I found George Raybold at the galley; he was not a happy German. In no uncertain, guttural tones, he told me what he thought of the officers of our vessels, and the British navy in general. Raybold had been flogged more than any other for constant infractions and insolence. Gladly leaving him to his venom I made my way towards the stern.

The boats drew away from *Discovery*. I was in the yawl at the bow, a position I had come to occupy in most of the voyages in the recent past. At the stern, Captain Vancouver and Dr. Menzies were accompanied by two Spanish gentlemen, Seniors Alva and Fidalgo. *Chatham*'s cutter was under the command of Lieutenant Puget; our large cutter was commanded by Lieutenant Swain. The rest of our Spanish companions were in their cutter with the luggage. We were 56 men out on an excursion towards the north.

"Where are we off to Petee you 'av any idea?"
"I know as much as you, Scarface."
"Well at least the luggage is in the Spanish boat, thank Christ."

All appeared in a happy state. The Captain smilingly conversed with his Spanish companions and even seemed especially pleasant to Dr. Menzies. The two had argued constantly over the state of the plants residing on the quarterdeck, which it was my daily charge to keep well watered and protected from the elements.

Lieutenant Baker made his way to the bow of the yawl and perched himself astride the basket which contained the anchor and line. I decided on the strength of my newfound relationship with him to enquire as to our destination.

"Sir, what is the destination of our journey if I may be so bold to ask?"

"Well, Peter Wright, we are off to a place called Tahsis. There we will be entertained by the great chief of these parts, Maquinna."

It was quite unusual to find the officers so approachable; it seemed the prospect of our imminent return to homes, from which we had for so long been absent, had changed the attitude of all to one of happiness and congeniality. All knew as soon as the ships were prepared and we received awaited orders from the Admiralty we would commence the long haul around Cape Horn

It was our lot to camp for the night at a suitable spot, in exceptionally pleasant circumstances. The next morning the boats finally made their way to the village of Maquinna at the head of the Tahsis Inlet. The great chief Maquinna and his people, long before the advent of the Europeans, had become well renowned for the construction of canoes. The fine lines, design and sea-worthiness were copied by other tribes in the region and the sale of these instruments had made Maquinna a powerful leader and one to be reckoned with.

On our arrival at the village, an old, white haired man repeatedly called in a loud voice, a word, which sounded as *Wacosh, Wacosh*. Apparently, this was a native manner of signifying the honourable intentions of the great chief towards the visitors. Our captains and officers reciprocated with gestures as one would make in a Hindu environment, hands clasped as in prayer and the same word *Wacosh*, uttered by all.

After this greeting, two elaborately dressed men escorted our group to the village and Maquinna's dwelling. Two sentries remained at the vessels, one Englishman and one Spaniard. My seamen companions and I were loaded with the gifts, which we had brought along with us. Our officers were directed to previously prepared seats on new mats at the end of Maquinna's house and we lowly men stood together at the edge of the ceremonial area.

The sound of about thirty, fine native men beating on a hollow tree trunk summoned the populace of the village to the festivities; about five hundred men, women and children who assembled around the official group answered the summons.

The great chief Maquinna stood and began a speech, the gist of which was completely lost on most of us, but my admiration for the understanding of the native dialect by the Captain, his officers and the Spaniards again amazed me. It reinforced my belief that despite the rigorous order and rules of the navy, the men who captained our vessels were for the most part, completely suited to their occupation. They were educated, hard, dedicated sailors who uphold and represent their respective countries in all parts of the world.

"Surely, after so long in these parts you had a little of the native dialect, Peter."

"Well, yes, Sir Neville, I did, but not enough to hold a sensible conversation. I could pick out words and the odd sentence. All I can say is the speech of Maquinna in effect said how delighted he was the Spanish and the English were his great friends. His people had been very civil and orderly towards their visitors. In consequence, they had amassed a fortune in the goods, which they held dear, namely blue cloth, copper and other articles of immense value. He mentioned with considerable venom, the disorderly and violent conduct of the chief Wicananish and other names I did not recognize. He then said he hoped we would enjoy the spectacle, which they would now give in our honour."

Peter Wright was silent for a moment. He recalled the scene and placing his thoughts in order continued.

"I imagine the performers were waiting and anxious for their moment in the limelight as would be any actor on any stage. The moment his speech ended, the drums recommenced. Maquinna was stalwart fellow; his face completely painted in black and red, which completely distorted his features. He wore a variously decorated and colourful war-dress, which reached to his calves. His hair was covered with the fine, delicate, white down of young sea birds and in his hand; he held a musket with fixed bayonet, a fearsome figure indeed.

Twenty men, all well-proportioned and dressed in similar fashion followed him. Though their attire was generally the same, all displayed various unique designs both on their dress and their faces and all were armed with different weapons. Muskets, pistols, swords, daggers, spears, bows and arrows, hatchets and even fishing equipment, all designed to display either their wealth or their ability to wage war. Although this was a fierce display, all showed no inclination for anything but the most peaceful pursuits and commenced a dance, which demonstrated their considerable power in leaping high into the air without the least bend to their knees.

On the completion of this frightening exhibition, the chief Maquinna rose and donned a mask, which showed great imagination in its design and performed a wild dance for our gratification. The skill of these native people in arranging sensational stage effects was beyond compare. Their ability to construct masks with moveable parts and concealed strings, which would alter the appearance at the most dramatic moment, was quite amazing. Maquinna changed his facial adornment at intervals during the performance, with each mask being more fearsome than the last. His dress, adorned with hollow shells and copper pieces produced a rhythmic sound to accompany his movements. On the completion of his display, our people cheered and clapped, much to his pleasure and gratification.

The women of the village were overall quite pleasing and very clean. Most wore a similar dress, straight along the top and sides, with a curved lower edge that made the robe lower in the middle than on the sides. This dress was constructed of the soft woven inner bark of the yellow cedar. Some women had further adorned their dress with the wool of the mountain goat and all seemed to favour earrings of animal teeth, tight anklets and bracelets of sea otter fur. To complete their wardrobe most, both men and women wore a rain cape of cedar bark matting and a conical hat with a bulbous top, resplendent with stylized designs of the creatures, which were their companions both in the forest and in the ocean. The terrible disfigurement of the lower lip was not in evidence in the village of Maquinna much to our delight.

Captain Vancouver now motioned us seamen to bring forth the bags and boxes, which we had brought with us. He motioned us to display the presents, sheets of copper, bolts of blue cloth, ear adornments, blankets, hatchets and some lesser items. All gifts were received with great alacrity by the chief and passed to his lesser chiefs according to their rank.

The offerings were received with great whoops and cheers, which resounded through the village. A second vocal and drum performance followed this exchange of gifts and a further speech by a chief with the strange name, which sounded like *Whaclasse pultz,* saw the festivities come to an end. Vancouver, Puget and Fidalgo received magnificent otter skins as a mark of respect by their native hosts.

That very afternoon it was our turn to have Maquinna and his chiefs, with their families, to our camp. Here he dined with our officers, while family members dined with us seamen. It was rather strange to see these diverse races, uniformed Europeans and fearsome natives, dining off the best silver plate, provided by Senor Quadra.

It was an excellent day and it gave all the opportunity to see first hand the depth of the society grown up on this coast. We, the seamen were given permission to stroll through the village at our leisure. The village was very large and housed perhaps 800 souls. It was strangely devoid of people. Winter was about to move downward from the frigid north and most of the populace were away hunting game before the cold wet season descended on them.

Their housing displayed a degree of expertise and ability. Some of the massive timbers raised to serve as ridgepoles were full logs of enormous girth. It was at this time I decided if by God's holy grace, I was to survive this voyage and be released again into polite society; I would make every effort to use the knowledge I had gained of this wild country to my advantage. I did not know how or when, but I determined then and there that I would enter the trading circle so evident in the number of vessels at anchor in the Friendly Cove."

"And this is what you will do Peter, your parents have left you in such a good financial position all things will be possible."

Sir Neville Brown listened with great attention as Peter described the return journey to Nootka and the completion of repairs to the vessels. Peter spoke of the wait for orders from England and of the various new accomplishments which, to his satisfaction he had acquainted himself. He spoke of his ability with the marlinspike, how he could warp in an eye with the best of them. How he worked on the machine constructed by the sailors to render the large anchor cable into smaller rope. He told of his introduction to the art of sail-making, hours of sewing sails, an exacting pastime ever under the watchful eye of the sail-maker, Roderick Betton. He worked with the caulkers and learned the art of repairing the seams of the vessel and when ordered, he would work with his friends the carpenters. He was comfortable on the highest point of the rigging in the heaviest seas and in effect, he had become a seaman.

"I tell you, Sir Neville, our stay in Nootka was extremely pleasant. By this time, I felt I had at last become part of the crew of *HMS Discovery* and I had discovered things about myself that I could never have known had I remained in England and entered the church or studied law, as had been my intention. It is strange the vessel I had been forced to sail aboard was named *Discovery*; no name could be more apt for the situation in which I found myself. It was a rewarding feeling to know where before I was considered the lowest of the low, the butt of jokes and the whipping boy of the midshipmen; I now was rated as seaman with its associated raise in stature and pay.

The officers were gentle and more approachable of late. Even the usually dour Captain Vancouver seemed to smile a little more often, this, I am sure, this was brought about by the fact our journey was almost at an end. We were going home."

The brilliant rich blue of the tropical swells contrasted dramatically with dazzling, white, foamy crests as they raced pell-mell beneath the hull of *Discovery*. A little way off, but well astern, *Chatham*, one moment high, clear and visible, then suddenly lost from sight in the deep trough of the surging ocean. The ultimate master of the watery domain was as always, the great storms of the Pacific. From far beyond the horizon these fearsome generators of terror created the mountains of water, which swept towards the vessels from the south-southwest. The bows of the ships were raised high towards the blue of the cirrus, streaked heavens and then be propelled forward in a sickening dive into the trough, only to again and again repeat the process.

A fine, fresh gale from the southeast, raised the approaching waves high and steep and sped us toward the south and Cape Horn. The sense of anticipation was obvious in the demeanour of the crew. The city of Valparaiso was behind us and we considered only the fearsome Cape Horn could affect our return to England and home. From high in the heavens, petrels and garnets swooped and dived, their cry at one moment loud and clear, the next faint and indistinct as the near gale whisked their feathery statements into the airy distance. The groan and creak of the tired vessels grew loud before the plunge into the trough, as through some internal spirit cried out to the gods of the sea for strength, enough to withstand the rigors of the voyage ahead.

The once brilliant yellow of *Discovery*'s trim had vanished except for the secret places where wind and salt had not penetrated. Her once-white sails, now a tired dirty grey, patched and forlorn, still gallantly received the wind. Clew lines, halyards, shrouds, even the stays, those lines that supported the masts, all displayed a dangerous degree of wear. Splices were many and obvious. Fraying areas had been replaced with line not any more serviceable, but a life remained in the vessel. *Discovery* was not finished yet.

Chatham, a mile to the west raised high on a swell. The extra ballast taken on at Valparaiso made little difference in her sailing ability and again, *Discovery*, of necessity shortened sail lest contact be lost between them.

"Mr. Johnstone, make a signal to *Chatham*, she must keep up damn it and this is the second time, fire a cannon. With the wind increasing we will soon loose contact, burn false fires through the night and we will see the situation on the morrow." Lieutenant Johnstone shielded his eyes as he peered through the haze towards their smaller consort now at least two miles to the north and astern of *Discovery*.

"Each mile will mean a change in the weather, by noon tomorrow the warmer waters will be well behind and we can look forward to squalls. Just look at the sky. There is wind up there, and I do not like the look of the horizon to the south. Mr. Browne, have the gunners load and fire a cannon, use gunner's mates Berry and Butters."

"Aye aye, Mr. Johnstone."

The roar of the cannon echoed loud in the late afternoon. Two large albatross, playing and frolicking in the airy currents aft of *Discovery*, veered off to fly high in the sky there to ponder the thunder of the gun. The officers on deck, their spyglasses trained on the following *Chatham* waited for some action that would signal more speed.

"There, a jib and look a stay-sail. I cannot see that making a difference, haul up the mainsail and reef the top gallants for the night, get the false fires in order, we will see what daylight will bring."

Through the night, the glare of the fires cast a strange reddish glow on the foam-flecked tops of the waves, and an even stranger light on the faces of the watch, now heavily clothed, to counteract the rapidly deteriorating and cooling weather. The 45th degree of south latitude was past. To the east, the dreadful coast of Chile, broken, dangerous and cold, awaited the smallest error in navigation to claim the lives and boats of the unwary traveler. Each morning the weather became cooler and more turbulent. *Discovery*, straining every part of her being, rose to the seas, which caused her to cry out in agony. Heavy winds tore at her sails like demons bent on her destruction. Violent lashings of sleet assaulted and reddened the leather brown, weather-beaten faces and coated the decks in an icy, treacherous sheet.

"Put the helm up Mr. Johnstone, we will wear ship and wait for Chatham."

"All hands jump to it now. Brace forward the after yards." At the call of the master, the seamen rushed to the lines to haul in the yards.

"Set the mainsail and spanker," now another group heaved away to bring these sails into line.

"The wind's abeam, brace up the head yards and haul aft the head sheets."

"There to the east Captain, I would think that land to be Diego Ramirez, so we are well out from the cape, if this snow would cease we may get an observation of the sun."

"Where is *Chatham*, can you detect her at all?"

"She is well behind now, we seem to out sail her in every hour. Mr. Sykes, what have you to say?"

Midshipman John Sykes was heavily garbed. His normally brown face, or what was visible of it from within a heavy scarf, showed a bluish tinge and a nose red and wet, a condition which caused him to sniff at the end of every sentence. He had secured his hat and muffled his lower neck and face with the scarf, which had seen him through the cold of the Pacific Northwest and Alaska and now served him well at the Horn.

"Sir, Mr. Masterman and I have resolved a position. Our latitude has been found to be 56 degrees 57 minutes using two instruments, we have advanced our reckoning, allowing for the variation of the compass at 23 degrees eastward, corrected by Arnold's chronometer, the longitude is settled at 293 degrees 39 minutes east." After the years of lessons and experience, Midshipman Sykes could speak with authority; he was no longer the silly boy who had joined the vessel so many years ago. Now he was ready to accept his position as a Lieutenant in the Royal Navy. Exams must be written and passed. Then, and only then, the naval world would be his.

"With this damn snow and poor visibility we must be absolutely sure of our position, so we will continue on to the south and you will continue observations at every opportunity, Mr. Sykes and will you do something about that damn sniffing. Report your findings as you calculate them."

Atrocious, frigidly cold, weather, alternating between violent squalls and periods of full gale force winds, tore at the beleaguered, close-reefed sails, heeling the vessel over, making every attempt to push *Discovery* down into the vast watery maw. Gales of wind blew heavy snow in horizontal sheets. It tore at the exposed hands and faces of the men on deck, until, without warning, the snow would change to blinding sleet.

Discovery ploughed on to the south, burying her bow deep into the trough of the seas, which surged over the forepeak to rush in a torrent of foam and spume towards the quarterdeck, finally to cascade back to the ocean through the scuppers. Cape Horn, with its dreadful, dangerous islets and vicious rocky headlands lay somewhere to the north and to the east behind a pall of snow and ice. South and ahead, the South Shetland Islands and Antarctica waited.

"Take in the fore-top-sail, Mr. Whitbey, we will see if we can let *Chatham* fetch up with us before we change course to round the Horn."

The call of orders were muffled by a hissing yet at the same time thunderous roar. Cascades of foam tumbled in savage fury to pound at the sides of the labouring vessel. The scream of the wind howling banshee-like through the straining rigging, the crack of the close-reefed sails, at one moment full and taut, the next limp and fallow, then in a second, again full to bursting. The sails noisily protested their agony as the gale made every effort to strip the vessel of its only method of propulsion. *Discovery*, worn by time, protested its agony, unheeded by the unrelenting chaos of furious nature.

The high, shrill sound of five blasts from the deck calling boson's mates' alerted the watch. From the fo'c'sil a bedraggled group of seamen suddenly appeared, to make a frantic dash to their positions. They judged their progress to coincide between the salty torrents sweeping across the deck and the constant threat of savage waves that could at any moment, whisk the unwary sailor to a cold and watery oblivion.

"Fore-top men aloft, furl the fore-top-sail."

The fore-top crew without hesitation sprang into the rigging to claw their way aloft. At their position they found themselves at one moment far out to larboard, over the churning sea, the next out to starboard in a dizzying arc, repeating the motion again and again. On deck the weather brace, foretop and clew line hands stood at the ready. The shrill sound of the boson piping the call, "haul and hoist", now his strident voice, D'ye hear there." Then the order, "Haul taut. Let go the lee sheet and halyards."

In spite of the atrocious weather, the actions of the crew were without error, the years of knowledge and repetition gave smoothness to the procedure. Despite the dreadful conditions, the sail slowly began to react to the expert hands at work, the yard was hauled in line with the wind, the fore-top men, barely visible high above began to wrestle the flapping sail and lash it to the yard.

"Hold fast the weather sheet there."

The ship's master, heavily muffled in greatcoat and hood, called out through his speaking horn.

"Square the yard, make secure, then below all."

Now the shrill call of *Pipe Down,* saw the men scramble gratefully from the rigging to move to the deck below and out of the weather.

"Captain, all done, we will see by morning how we fare with *Chatham*."

"We should be well clear of the Horn by the morrow, a fine passage round if the weather stays with us at this level. Come let us get below, James, let us get out of this."

Discovery answered the helm. The course was changed. The seas, which had assailed us on the starboard beam, now came up astern. They were still mountainous and charged down on the vessel as though to devour it, but now the wind seemed less as the stern of *Discovery* rose to the watery monoliths, answered their challenge and sped joyously into the Atlantic Ocean, five years since departing it, around the Cape of Good Hope.

Discovery again changed course. Strong gales and heavy squalls continued the assault, but now the compass showed a course towards the northeast, as the vastness of the Atlantic opened before us. The feelings of the officers and crew were filled with anticipation and thoughts of home and England with the dreaded Cape Horn was behind them. They went about their business with a joyous spirit and will. Their course to the northeast would take them towards the island of Saint Helena. The sails had been reefed constantly since the 19th of May, it was now the 30th.

Captain Vancouver came on deck, at the change of watch.

"We should let *Chatham* come up with us; I anticipate we will be seeing a change of conditions very soon. Damnation on *Chatham*, always so bloody slow, we should let her catch up again. Make the order to shorten sail Mr. Baker."

The shortened sail soon had *Discovery* traveling at a slower rate. Through the night, the squalls savagely tore at the hard-pressed vessel. The great seas spurred on by fierce gales, which raced around the bottom of the world, propelled *Discovery* into the Atlantic Ocean, sometimes at a dizzying speed as the vessel swept down the face of the monster waves. Slowly dawn broke, heralded by the cries of numberless sea birds, swooping and diving in the tempestuous winds. *Chatham,* now visible in the distance was one moment high atop a distant swell, the next out of sight as though devoured into the dark maw of a watery cavern.

Despite reduced sail *Discovery* continued to out-pace *Chatham*, soon she was again far behind her larger, faster consort. By dawn on the 5th of May, the gale, which had made their life so miserable, died during the night. The morn broke brilliantly clear and frigidly cold.

"Make the course due north, keep a watch for land, as we discussed last night I would like to finally put a definitive position to Isla Grande. I feel that it will be found in the position assigned to it by Captain Cook."

"Yes, Captain, it seems that we appear to have a discrepancy between the findings of four excellent men. Dr Halley is reputed to have seen it; Mr Dalrymple's chart shows it almost where we are, not to mention La Roche and Captain Cook." The weather remained tolerably clear with a visibility, which extended to a misty horizon some five miles away.

"Well, sir, the watches have been quite vigilant, I know we would see an island in these conditions, so I'm afraid that there is some discrepancy in the records of all three of our voyagers."

"I must agree with you, James, we have seen no driftwood or any other flotsam from a land mass. I feel if it is anywhere, it has to be in the position assigned to it by James Cook. We will continue on this course for the day and perhaps it will reveal itself."

"Then Captain, by tomorrow I'm afraid our worthy astronomer, Dr. Halley will prove the more correct, that Isla Grande does not exist in latitude 45 south between 312 and 315 degrees 20 minutes east longitude."

Captain Vancouver was determined to establish once and for all the existence of Isla Grande. Its supposed position had been discussed and argued over for many years. Vancouver was determined to enter this discussion.

Chatham continued to slow the journey despite efforts to shorten *Discovery*'s sails. No sooner would the vessels come together and then in a matter of hours *Chatham* would fall into her usual position far behind, eventually to be lost from sight. The wind continued to blow from the south. It was as though the Horn was making a desperate last effort to claim the vessels, which had defied its frightening onslaught.

Aboard *Discovery,* the ravages of time and wear daily became more of a concern. A topsail, thin and frayed, split from top to bottom. Topsail sheets, worn and tired parted, sails thrashed in the wind, as their restraints could no longer carry out their function. This in turn rendered even more damage on equipment already beyond repair. As the 39th degree of latitude came upon them, the weather became warmer and with the warmth, the humour of the crew adjusted itself to an even more rollicking aspect.

Captain Vancouver observed the heavens. He speculated on the weather and the state of the ocean. He knew the cold of the southern latitudes would lessen as they made their way towards the equator. The sun, hidden by heavy over-cast, revealed itself on the horizon. In yellow rays of light, which broke from clouds, black and low in the western sky, he saw crests of distant waves, one moment dark and foreboding, the next brilliant, dancing sprites beckoning to the warmth of the equator.

Over the past few days, the malady, which plagued the Captain, had returned with all its embarrassing symptoms. He saw no way to alleviate himself and return to health. At 36 years of age he felt old and in this lonely remote place, near the bottom of the world, perhaps not long for this earth. A feeling of melancholy claimed his thoughts, thoughts of his future in England and the reception surely awaiting him. He had completed his assignment in every aspect; there would be accolades of the highest order, also the arduous task of publishing his journals, some years of work at least.

Vancouver made a mental note as to how he would enforce the order received from the Lords of the Admiralty, specifying all writings, drawings, journals and charts, made by the gentlemen of both *Chatham* and *Discovery*, must be surrendered, a necessary move before the advent of Saint Helena. He looked forward to St. Helena, it would be the first British port visited in five years. Here England held control; the opportunity for contact with civil society once again, brightened his spirit, but no matter how he tried to raise his fortitude, this day his illness was at its worst.

"Well, Sir Neville, my dear friend, I felt much as the rest of the crew. I could not wait to get back to England and release from my situation. I must say I was elated by the degree of status I had attained on *Discovery*. I was no longer an idler, one of the lowest of creatures. I had not cleaned a seat of ease or pissdale for over two years. Lieutenant Baker informed me I had been rated ordinary seaman. This increased my pay to the sum of 19 shillings a month. Of course, I still paid 6d to Greenwich Hospital, 2 pence to the doctor and 6 pence to the purser for the supply of bowls, platters, cans and spoons. Our vessels had called at Valparaiso and though I was considered a crewman, I was not allowed ashore. I imagine I was still a risk as a pressed man, though by this time I could not think of a better way to return to England than by the vessel on which I found myself."

Peter Wright drew near the end of his tale. He had, in some way, by recounting the trials and tribulations of the last years released him self from the restraints and tensions which had consumed him.

"Sir Neville, my dear friend, I feel better for having had this opportunity to recount my recent life. This is the first time in many years I have spoken to anyone as an equal, without the fear of derision, reprisal or perhaps punishment. You have no idea how this has relieved tensions deep within me."

"Ah Peter, now you must look forward to the future as a wealthy man, with due deference to the unhappy demise of your dear parents. You have a life, which I feel can only benefit from these last years. A life full of opportunities awaits and you have the connections to make things occur to your infinite benefit." Neville Brown continued. "Why Sir William Boyd, from whom you were taken, in a letter just a week or so ago, confided how distressed he was at your complete disappearance. You must go to him; he will be delighted and amazed to see you."

"Yes, I will go back to London and I will reacquaint myself with the Boyd Family. Young Harry and I, what a time we had. It was his tutoring that enabled me to survive some of the slings and arrows fired at me by the men of the fo'c'sil. He introduced me to the manly art of fisticuffs, which held me in good stead against the likes of Pitt and a few others I have failed to tell you of."

"You mention Thomas Pitt with some affection. I must tell you that the old Sir Thomas died, so your erstwhile shipmate is now Thomas Pitt, Lord Camelford. He is quite a figure in London society, though I am told a thorn in the side of his family and many a government official."

"Pitt made it back to England, I'm glad to hear this news. He was a very complicated fellow and made up of the very best and the very worst of human nature. What you tell me is Pitt in every respect; always against authority, he would not bow to any one or any thing. This was the reason he was at odds with Vancouver and eventually shipped away. I wish him well."

Peter continued with his history, anxious now to complete his story.

"Now back to my tale. I will continue. England and home seemed closer by the day. I cannot begin to tell you of the thoughts constantly going through my mind, as I would imagine the minds of my companions. The years had changed me, I had grown to manhood very quickly, I had survived and soon, God willing, it would all be over. Now where was I? Yes, we had finally turned into the Atlantic and commenced on a north heading. A tragic occurrence brought home to us again, how fragile we were and how we were still at the mercy of the elements, despite the joyful feelings of heading for home and old England. There was no room for error. It was a Sunday morning, about five a.m. and still dark. Heavy, but not dangerous seas were running up astern of us, when a call roused all from their occupations."

"Ho there. Man overboard. There! There he is."

Immediately pipes sounded and all hands rushed to the deck.

"Who is it? You men help me here; get a grating over the side."

The deck became alive and active as men ran to stations aware time was of the essence if their shipmate was to be saved, especially in the semi-darkness of early dawn. The waves were black and cold, their hollows even darker and more forbidding, the only light being the vivid red prelude to a sun still below the horizon. Like hot ashes blown by the wind, specks of foam would pick up the red of the horizon before falling like embers back into the darkness of the sea. Pipes called their shrill cry and orders rang out to bring *Discovery* about on her heel.

"Haul aft the head sheets and fore sheets, get to it. Brail up the spanker."

The vessel began to turn her head into the wind with a great rattling of rigging, a shaking of sails and a creaking and groaning of timbers as the wind came onto the bow, rising and falling to the action of the northeast set of the waves. Eventually the vessel ceased all forward motion and wallowed in the swells.

"Can you see him?"

"It's too dark sir, I can hear him calling, seems to come from the south east, over there."

"Who is it?" Captain Vancouver had appeared on deck. He again asked the question.

"Who is it? I say."

"I don't know sir."

"Boatswain, who is the man?"

"It's Richard Jones, sir. He fell from the chain plates."

Discovery shuddered as waves crashed against her immobile hull. The sails protested their unnatural configuration, being back-winded, they flapped against the masts and the ships timbers creaked and groaned in disapproval.

"What to do, Captain? The poor fellow is somewhere out there. Hear that? I heard a cry again."

"Damn it all, James. The bloody cutter will not survive another launching. We will probably lose more men if we try to launch it. It will sink."

All aboard *Discovery* strained to pierce the gloom and sight their shipmate. Officers and men alike knew any search was futile in the present conditions, they also knew it could be one of them. To a man, thoughts of their companion, struggling to stay afloat in the heavy dark sea came to each sailor. They all knew he would rise on a wave to see the stern lamp of *Discovery*, a warm yellow spot in the dark distance; again, the trough of the next wave would devour him. At each upsurge of the sea all hope was further away into the lonely distance and his saving light became less bright. The constant breaking foam would devour him, repeatedly he would come gasping and spluttering to the surface, cold and shivering and soon his strength would ebb, until any effort became impossible. For one final instant he would raise to the surface, finally his strength and all hope would be gone. In his exhaustion, he would gasp for a last sustaining breath between the assaults of the cruel waves. The final sight his eyes would see in this earthly life were the icy stars burning bright in the inky heavens as he sank into the blackness of the ocean, never to be seen again, lost forever in the great vast lonely depths of the Southern Atlantic Ocean.

After this sad incident there was much criticism in the fo'c'sil directed at the Captain for not launching the cutter to attempt to rescue Richard Jones. It was here that I came to appreciate for the first time the heavy burden of command. I saw the officers agonizing over the fact that the cutter was unserviceable, and to launch it would place the lives of those in it at extreme risk. It is a vessel, which requires eight men to propel it. At the moment of this incident, it was heavy with rot and many of its seams had sprung. In the heavy conditions at the point in time, those men in the cutter would be at terrible risk of it breaking up. A decision had to be forthcoming; it is the Captain who must take this heavy responsibility. Poor Richard Jones, frightened, alone and drowned, but in my heart I felt a sense of relief that I was not asked to again take my place at the oar of a boat, which I knew to be in a state of disrepair through no fault but time and use.

31

Jane Finds London to Her liking and Learns a New Truth About Herself

Jane and Gwen were welcomed into the home of Lady Sarah Parkinson. The whole area of Bloomsbury was exciting. Building and construction went on at every turn. The home of Lady Sarah was a three story, elegantly styled building detached from the others. The area was new and expensive. Daily, another section of low, rustic, hovels formally the homes of the poorer classes of London society, were demolished to make way for the new. Great Russell and Montague Streets, showed at every turn all the signs of elegant development. The homes were three, sometimes four stories. The area was rich in parks and pleasure gardens where the wealthy populace could meander to their hearts content meet with their equals and display their elegant attire before their equally decorated counterparts.

It was still a time in London when cows and deer grazed in any treeless area and caused the dandy extreme displeasure, as with mincing step he would prance from one clean spot to the next. The upper classes made their appearance daily. It was a world of gilt coaches and rich liveries, where some, puffed up with pride and vanity refused to remove their hats or bow to anyone of lesser stature than perhaps a duke.

The open spaces also attracted the working strata of society. On a Sunday, the day of rest, the common people would frequent the parks and the upper echelons were not to be seen. No distinction was made by the footpads that used the grounds as their place of business, deftly and without favour relieving the wealthy or the poor of their purses.

The area had also begun to advance in many other ways. Theatres had sprung up all over. The plays of Shakespeare, Cibber, Goldsmith, Colman and Lillo were staged to packed houses every night. A great hall had been erected at Drury Lane. Here the best performances of farce, ballads, pantomime, tragedies and recitations, could delight on the same bill. Salons were sponsored by the aristocratic wealthy for the artistic great. The poetry of Blake, Cowper, Pope and Daniel Defoe, the music of Handel, Salomon and the great Joseph Haydn could be heard and enjoyed in the comfort of wealthy homes at private recitals.

It was little wonder Lady Sarah Parkinson, after the death of her dour and boring husband descended on London society to begin again. She commenced to make up for what she perceived as her lost years as a dutiful wife and loyal partner. An extremely attractive and wealthy matron, she had little trouble entering this aristocratic wealthy society. She became in demand at intimate evenings, where her style and witty dialogue captivated conversation and set aflutter the heart of any man who had the fortune to be her partner at dinner. Conversely she became the envy of those other women, who, while perhaps higher on the social scale, found themselves outclassed by Lady Sarah's charm and wit.

She developed an interest in the theatre and soon received invitations to all the best performances and became a shining light as a patron of the arts. In her married life, she had been a faithful and loving companion to her husband, without the slightest breath of scandal. Now, with her period of mourning over, she entered into the exciting society of London with energy, vigor and abandon, so much so that by the time Jane and Gwen descended on her establishment; four swains had passed her way; all of who left her as completely happy and contented as they found themselves.

"Darling Jane, how wonderful to have you here, of course you are most welcome. How brave of you to make the journey on your own, I'm sure I could never have done it at your age."

"But Aunt Sarah, I was not alone, I had my dear Gwen with me. She is my companion and now my dearest friend. So you see I was in good company all the time."

"Now where is that husband of yours, I have never met the man, but I think him quite remiss letting you venture off alone. I have heard there are robbers, highwaymen, all sorts of villains waiting to relieve a young lady of her valuables and heaven knows what else."

"Oh dear Auntie, I am safe and in good spirits. Gwen and I have had nothing but kindness shown to us as we traveled. As for my husband, Captain West does not know we are here, I have taken it on myself to come to London."

"Is your husband good to you, my dear?"

The question placed before her confused Jane, she did not quite know how to handle her new situation and what to disclose. How much should she tell her aunt? Should she confide completely in the person who was now her closest living relative? Then she thought what was there to tell. Everything had begun to occur at an ever-accelerating rate. Henry had receded somewhat from her mind as she wrestled with her newfound and confusing feelings and independence. She decided to keep her innermost thoughts to herself, especially concerning the relationship between her and Gwen. She would let the future dictate a propitious moment and then things should be disclosed.

"Yes, aunt. He is good to me."

As she spoke, she thought of Henry and the nights of bliss that had opened her eyes to love and passion. She had also realized Henry had a greater interest in her money and what it would gain for him, than any deep feelings for her. All they really had together was a mutual sexual ardour and her wealth. She now understood there was very little love in the true sense of the word. She missed the loving gentle relationship and the protective mantle under which she had lived with her mother and father. Henry was always absent on some military mission. She knew that since the death of her parents, her relationship with Gwen concerned her more than her husband. Together they had explored the depths of passion as only two women can. Now London and its promise of a new existence filled her mind.

Lady Sarah continued. "Then we will have him here as soon as it can be arranged. Tell me where he is and I shall send my man with the message he will be overjoyed to hear."

"Well unfortunately, dear Aunt, I do not know where he is, except he was in London this week past. He was staying with a Frederick March; a man I have met once at our wedding. He is a person of finance and property and has a London home, I know not where. He is Henry's friend and confidant. Perhaps you know of him.

"We were fortunate to become acquainted with a general of the army, Fitzherbert. He was of some small help and offered to assist in finding Henry. He had little knowledge of Henry's whereabouts but will; I am sure, do all he can to find him."

"You met Fitzherbert? Why, that lecherous old devil will do nothing unless a price is agreed. A price, my dear, a price I say. Propriety stops me from enlarging further, heed my advice and keep well clear of him. Yes, you with your gentle nature and pretty face would be a perfect catch for him. Believe me I speak from experience on this matter. If your husband has anything to do with that man, then I wonder about his honour." Lady Sarah did not elaborate further and Jane did not pursue the subject.

Sarah Parkinson was a tall, attractive woman of some 50 years. Her smile and style gave the observer the knowledge that in earlier years she would have been a beauty beyond compare. Although Jane and Gwen had descended on her without any announcement or warning, they found her dressed elegantly but simply in a delicately shaded peignoir of fine cashmere, designed in the latest fashion popular in Paris.

"Auntie you look so well and, if I may be so bold, so young. What have you done to yourself?"

"Oh my dear, when your uncle died, I decided, after a suitable time of mourning, to close the house in Bath, move to London and make a new life for myself. I am well taken care of financially. My finances are in the hands of a friend James Boyd, as are I believe, yours. I spend my time in charitable works, the theatre, art and poetry."

The two chattered away, covering subjects of mutual interest. They commiserated on family deaths. They marveled at family gossip and laughed together at tittle-tattle. Jane steered the conversation away from Henry West and they did not discuss Jane's marriage further. They talked of Jane's inheritance and Lady Sarah was aghast at the size of her fortune. Sarah told Jane of London and the world waiting her discovery. All the while Gwen sat quietly, listening to the joyful babble of two people who obviously had a great affection each for the other.

"Now my dear let me ring for Thomas and we will make arrangements for you." Lady Sarah rose and going over to the fireplace pulled on a silken cord, hanging from the ceiling.

"Ah! Thomas, please have Mrs. Pike arrange the fourth bedroom, prepare it for my niece, Mrs. West." Thomas bowed toward Jane, "And prepare the small adjoining room for Miss Gwendolyn Pratt, Mrs. West's housekeeper and companion. There is a connecting door so you will both be accessible to each other." Again, Thomas bowed, to the ladies. A deep bow to Lady Sarah, not quite as low as to Jane, more of a deep nod to Gwen.

"It is so good to have you here and you too, Miss Pratt. This must be your home as long as you wish it. I will be delighted to introduce you to society and all my friends I know you will be quite the sensation. My dear I must do something about your dress, it is so provincial, won't do for London at all and you also, Miss Pratt."

The first week in London went by so quickly, Jane found little time to think of Henry, let alone search for him. Aunt Sarah filled their days with introductions, visits to museums and places of historical interest. Evenings were a constant round of poetry readings, musicales, the theatre and Lady Sarah Parkinson's favourite relaxation, gambling at cards. Almost every evening three or four people would present themselves and in no time a game would be underway, Hazard, Loo, Whist, or some other mutually agreed upon battle of wits. Money would change hands, but never in the vast amounts, which distinguished the games at the gambling Mecca's of Almanac's, White's or Boodle's. When Jane questioned her aunt about the games and money changing hands, Aunt Sarah quickly put her mind at rest.

"Tut, tut, Jane dear, it is a little thing, it gives me great pleasure and I can afford to play with a small amount and I might say I very rarely lose. My dear, at some of the games, fortunes change hands. I believe that only last week Mr. Charles James Fox is reputed to have parted with £150,000. I believe my dear friend Lord Stavordale only last night lost £11,000. That is not for me, but I do enjoy the company and the game."

Aunt Sarah introduced Jane and Gwen to her favourite dressmaker and milliner. Together they visited these creators of fashion and enjoyed the discussions on their new wardrobe. The styles most in favour, generally of a French influence, were ordered. They chose silks, cashmere and velvet, handsome visiting dresses and ball gowns, light, fanciful and airy. At the milliner, hats of the latest style were selected, rich with feathers and other lace decorations.

Gwen was agreeably received as companion and lady in waiting to Jane. Jane did not tell her aunt of Gwen's working class background and portrayed her as a rustic Norfolk girl from a respectable family. She would accompany Jane and her aunt to all the daytime functions. Gwen was at first rarely included in the evening events if people of note were invited. She always took her meals with Jane and Lady Sarah if they dined alone. On other occasions when a lavish spread was set for some visiting ambassador or a new upcoming member of parliament, then she ate in her room or with the staff below stairs. This was mostly at her own request for she feared forgetting herself or perhaps reverting to her former Norfolk diction.

Gwen of course was no longer the rough girl who had come to Jane some two years ago. Her speech had changed and as a natural mimic, she had altered her discourse to reflect the society in which she now moved. Gwen retained the unfortunate habit of naturally reverting to her former speech the moment she became excited and on occasion caused much laughter at some pastoral statement, so foreign to the speech of polite London.

Their rooms being side by side, the connecting door usually remained open. Sometimes they would lie in their respective beds and converse well into the night. Occasionally Jane would go into Gwen's room to tell her of some exciting event or person of note just met. Each morning Gwen would lay out Jane's clothes for the day and assist her with her toilet. Evenings Gwen would help Jane dress and attend to her long, fair, golden hair. Finally, she would help Jane undress and prepare for bed, the final act of the day being to brush each other's tresses. Gwen now felt comfortable calling Jane by her first name, although she was cognizant enough of her situation to call her Mrs. West whenever notable guests were present, or the other staff were within earshot. Gwen mixed with the staff below stairs, but because of her situation and the fact that she was a personal attendant to Jane, she was never trusted as member of the working household.

It was about midnight and Gwen was attending to Jane's hair, both were ready to retire. Jane told Gwen of the party from which she had returned. She spoke of the various people she had met and in particular the persistence of a Dragoon and his efforts to coerce her into meeting him again. Jane thought aloud, "It's strange Gwen I haven't really thought of Henry since we arrived here. I feel quite guilty. I imagine the gentleman I was just telling you about, brought the fact that I am a married woman home to me."

"Yes Jane, I often think to myself how things seem to have changed for us both." Gwen continued brushing Jane's hair as she spoke. "I often wonder where Captain West is. It has been three weeks since we arrived here. Perhaps he has gone to Burnham Market and found Medway only populated by the servants, with no word of where we are at."

"Yes Gwen you are right, I imagine I must make some effort to contact Henry. I will talk to Aunt Sarah tomorrow, I'm sure she will know somebody who will be able to assist."

Jane, eyes closed held back her head as Gwen gently drew the brush through her hair.

"That is so nice, dear, so soothing. Perhaps you will let me brush yours, Gwen."

"I would like that."

Candles burned low on the dressing table casting a warm glow over the two. Jane opened her eyes; she saw their reflection in the mirror before her. She observed a beautiful woman, as dark as she was fair. She was aware of Gwen behind her, at each stroke of the brush, she experienced the soft pressure of her body as she lent forward. They looked at each other reflected in the mirror. For a moment, both stood as a tableau in the soft candlelight, two goddesses, Diana and Artemis. Jane moved first, she raised her arm to Gwen's head, she caressed her cheek and Gwen gently smoothed Jane's hair back from her face, she lent forward and they kissed deeply and passionately.

Jane made little effort to discover the whereabouts of Henry and as time went by, she thought less and less about her husband. She continued to attend the various social and public functions given by her new circle of friends. With Lady Sarah, she became a devoted follower of that great social worker John Howard and joined her aunt in the quest to bring some relief to conditions suffered by prisoners and those unfortunate souls in dirty, corrupt hospitals. She also became interested in the work of Clarkson and Sharp in their crusade against the slave trade. Because of her wealth, she was able to fund many of the day-to-day needs of these causes. She had discussed her finances with Boyd and Company and had made all the necessary arrangements for her property in Norfolk. The overseas investments, so judicially made by her father were to be retained without disturbance.

She discussed Peter Wright, and the mystifying cause of his sad disappearance. She became aware of the feeling of guilt suffered by William Boyd and his efforts to discover the whereabouts of the son of his friend. She became aware of some rather nefarious dealings made between her father and Henry and the large amounts of money, which was paid into the account of the Great West Indies Sugar Company. William Boyd, displeasure obvious in his voice, told Jane of his negative advice on this company. To date, no dividends were to be seen and there was no sign of either the company or the promised profits. To Jane's consternation she became acquainted with the fact that only last week £5000 had been entered into this account. Jane determined that no more monies would be paid to the Great West Indies Sugar Company until proper and in depth assessments be made of its solvency and she left strict instruction to this effect.

Jane was busy, popular and involved. With her change of wardrobe to the latest fashions from both London and Paris, she acquired a beauty and dignity, which left its mark on many a gentleman of means. She repulsed those who would be her suitors. She made sure her married status became common knowledge, but she thought less and less of Captain Henry West. When her full days and evenings had completed their course, when all was dark and quite in the home of Lady Sarah Parkinson, she entered a new, secret life, a life which assumed more importance as time passed. Jane and Gwen would join and in the dim silence of the night, with only the soft glow of a candle to light the way, they discovered the joy and bliss of the passion each had for the other.

32

Saint Helena, Ireland and England

"Well my friend, I have almost completed my tale. We were now nearing that British possession south in the Atlantic ocean, Saint Helena. I felt sadness at the death of Richard Jones. He was never what you would call a friend, but I knew him and he was one of us, one of the team, Such an occurrence must lay at the hand of fate. Here we were five years out and finally almost home. Up to now, we had lost only four men to the angel of death. Jones was a Welshman; he had joined the vessel from Daedalus, our store ship at Nootka. Now he was gone. There was nothing to be done. The sea does not give up those it claims as its own. I determined to be extremely careful for the remainder of our voyage."

Peter was silent for a time before he continued. Again, he took a plug of tobacco from its leather pouch. He drew on it, extracting the flavour, as though, through it, his memories became clearer.

"St Helena. If memory serves, it was on the afternoon of July 2nd land was sighted. We hove to for the night and on the morning of the next day made towards the bay. Just to the south and east of us, *Chatham* was sighted. The call of the boson stopped all work and all hands assembled on deck. Captain Vancouver was to address us.

He came to the edge of the quarterdeck so all could see and hear. He was dressed in his faded, time-worn uniform; the dress of all the officers had seen better days. He spoke clearly and with authority.

"Gentlemen and members of the crew of *Discovery*. I have here orders from the admiralty and I will now read them, pay close attention." Vancouver coughed to clear his throat and continued.

"By the Commissioners for executing the office of Lord High Admiral of Great Britain and Ireland.

I will come to the part, which concerns you. Where are we, ah yes?

Taking care, before you leave the sloop, to demand from the officers, and petty officers, the logbooks, journals, drawings etc, they may have kept, and to seal them up for our inspection; and enjoining then the whole crew, not to divulge where they have been until they shall have permission so to do: and you are to direct the lieutenant commanding the Chatham armed tender to do the same, with respect to the officers, petty officers and crew of that tender. Given under our hands the 10th of August, 1791.

Now you all hear this. These orders are signed at *Chatham* Yard by J. T. Townshend and A.Gardner.

Mr. Humphries you will put up a copy of these orders for all to see and you will get a copy to *Chatham* as soon as we are in port."

To the ordinary seamen this meant very little. Not only were most illiterate but the pressure of constant work left little time for those who did possess some education to record anything of note.

"Captain, as ship's botanist and under the direct authority of Sir Joseph Banks, I feel this order does not include me." Dr. Menzies spoke loudly and quickly before all the assembled crew and officers.

Vancouver's features reddened perceptibly, but he continued.

"Get the men back to work, boatswain; I will speak to you in my cabin doctor, at your convenience." Vancouver was evidently annoyed at this obviously direct challenge to orders and his authority by Menzies and most of all because it was made before the officers and men. He showed his displeasure as he brushed by the doctor and went below.

I was in the hold aft when Dr. Menzies entered Vancouver's cabin. I could not hear all that was said but it was quite an argument; until finally Dr. Menzies left the cabin with a parting broadside from the captain. Something to the effect that it was bloody un-officer like, for him to question the order before the other officers and to let the men see a discordant state of affairs. Almost tantamount to a mutiny and he would be facing a courts-marshal if the captain had his way. Both men were red faced and completely flustered.

As we drew near to St. Helena Bay, a large group of vessels was seen laying off the shore and heading in a northerly direction, I overheard Captain Vancouver, with his glass to his eye, his words quite distinct.

"Damme, what I would give to be in company with a convoy such as this for the voyage back to England. A fleet of East Indiamen and by the look of it some Dutch vessels but flying the flag of Britain. Perhaps we are at war. God knows we are in no shape to withstand a confrontation with any enemy vessel."

I knew we were nearly home. Hearing the outburst between the Captain and Dr. Menzies, seeing the number of large vessels in view, and in the distance other vessels at anchor and the sight of a large town, all confirmed to me that civilization was at hand. Despite the constant trials, dangers and tribulations, all aboard had worked as one unit, with no thought except survival. Now with land in sight and England soon to be close at hand, law and the machinations of bureaucratic man had already begun to make its presence felt.

After the usual salutes, the vessels anchored in the late afternoon near an East Indiaman, the *Arniston* and an American brig. It was always a mystery to me how we all retained our health. We had been 58 days at sea since leaving Valparaiso and no one was ill. The men constantly complained about the food and it was a reality the longer away from supplies the worse the food became. There was never any discrimination between decks, all officers and men ate the same. The men were completely satisfied with the allowance of grog. Grog was without doubt the saving factor for many a man. I can speak to this. The quantity was at all time sufficient and there was no complaint as to the amount doled out. Usually three pints of water, mixed with a pint of rum with lime or lemon juice added. Twice a day we all received this ration. Once when the ration was of a weak nature I was confused when some of the more verbal seamen demanded *"less nothing"* in their tot. It dawned on me they meant less water.

I believe it was the greatest compliment to the Captain that we had arrived in Saint Helena after four and a half years at sea in excellent health and in good spirits. As for me I had become one of the crew and apart from a burning desire to be revenged on the swine that had caused all this, I felt quite proud of myself for having come through relatively unscathed.

I did hear the dreaded scurvy had made its doleful appearance on *Chatham*. Being a smaller vessel the decks were constantly awash, the men lived in unvarying, humid dampness. I believe only five of *Chatham*'s complement were able to keep watch, the rest being unserviceable through the scurvy and rheumatic complaints.

About this time, I gave thanks I was not on *Chatham*. I learned she was to return to England under the command of Lieutenant Puget, by way of San Salvador with dispatches from Rear Admiral Elphinstone to Major-General Clarke. Once again, we were vessels of war and subject to all the orders and commands of those superior to us. I was becoming excited at the prospect of our imminent return to England; I do not think I could have survived the added voyage to the other side of the Atlantic.

It was also our lot to return to England a Dutch prize, which Captain Vancouver had caused to be seized as it entered Saint Helena Bay. Seventeen of our men under the command of Lieutenant Johnstone were transferred to the *Macasser* with orders to bring it back to England. Again, I was assigned to the carpenters. The work was hard and demanding, getting *Discovery* back into some sort of ship shape condition for the final leg of the homeward voyage. Eventually all was ready; we left port accompanied by the *Macasser*, in very pleasant conditions on the 16th of July, 1795.

As *Discovery* sailed north, all hands were occupied in maintenance, mending sails, repairing rigging, painting and chalking. Our old vessel began to regain some of her original appearance. We were exercised with the great guns and other weapons and again I had the opportunity to practice with my favorite, the cutlass. You must remember we were now a Royal Navy ship of war and entering an area under the threat and constant danger of attack. As you know Sir Neville, we were and still are at war with France and Holland.

We sighted before us a fleet of vessels. It was the same fleet, which had left St. Helena as we entered the bay and now we had caught them up. Eventually I ascertained we were in the company of some 25 merchant vessels under the protection of the 76 gun, *HMS Sceptre*. Here we were after all the trials and tribulations of the past years serving as a naval escort under the command of the captain of the *Sceptre*.

Our life had become easy. The weather remained good and our speed slowed to accommodate the merchantmen. Nothing happened of note except the destruction of the cutter. I suppose when I tell you I felt a great sense of loss at this mischance you may think me some species of fool, but this boat had been our home and our salvation for so many months. At this occurrence, I believe all those who had rowed and propelled this faithful vessel into every dangerous situation imaginable, felt similar feelings of sadness, now she was lost, stove in and sank. This loss occurred when one of the Dutch prizes caught fire. Our cutter, in spite of the poor condition, which precluded it being launched to rescue Richard Jones, was launched to render assistance and take off the crew. This being accomplished and the crew saved, the cutter returned to us. As was being hoisted aboard an exceptional wave crashed the cutter into the stern of *Discovery*, mortally damaging the vessel. I believe its almost rotten state was the reason it foundered. Sir Neville I cannot tell you of the sentimental nature of the seaman, for all felt they had lost a friend, though only a boat.

The call of *Land Ho* brought all to the deck. There, at about eleven in the forenoon, some five miles to starboard I saw it, land. I had no idea what land it was, but instantly the old hands knew it was the coast of Ireland.

My dear friend, I looked at the distant coastline low on the horizon with thoughts I find difficult to describe. Here I was almost home. Hour by hour the land drew closer. What was once a low dark line slowly became a distinct landmass. Now I was able to distinguish cliffs and the entrance to an estuary, I could make out houses, low and white. I could clearly see thatched roofs and smoke from warm fires burning inside. Now I easily saw the figures of people going about their business, giving no thought to our vessels, much less to the adventures and trials attendant on the lives of those confined within the creaking, leaking, constantly moving hulls.

Yes, we were in Ireland and our vessel dropped anchor in the estuary of the River Shannon.

I had thoughts of deserting the vessel here and making my way back to London, I could have accomplished this without any real problem; watches though kept were now quite lax. I must say that the fact I had served so much time and had pay due to me for this time had some bearing on my actions. The next day Captain Vancouver left the vessel, leaving it in charge of Lieutenant Baker for the final journey to England. I decided to see the full thing out, so I resisted any thoughts of desertion. In my heart, I felt a commitment to the crew, both officers and men, who had been my companions in every adventure and danger of the past five years. In a few days, the anchor was hauled and *Discovery* completed her voyage arriving in the River Thames on the 20th of October 1795.

I was lost, suddenly I had no aim or direction; I could please myself, I believe all the men had the same feeling, what to do next? Nearly six years, it is a long time and then to be suddenly dispensed with left me somewhat in a state of confusion. I was paid off at Deptford Yard. It was in itself a confusing exercise. My listing on the muster book was ordinary seaman or landsman and was rewarded with the sum of 19 shillings per month. As a wounded man, you will remember the incident I spoke of, our only bad experience with the natives; I was directed to present myself to the Governors of the Naval Chest in Chatham. Here I was to render a chit signed by Captain Vancouver, which stated the wound and how it was received. I was not entitled to a pension as a young, fit person. The Governors, in their magnanimity awarded me £20 as a lump sum payment. From this was deducted the cost of the slop clothes supplied to me, use of a blanket and hammock, purser costs and medical costs. My pay was calculated on a month of 28 days. I could not be paid until all the ships books had been audited, I was given a draw of £7 and the rest could be collected in 2 months. To add insult to injury, the admiralty kept the last six months pay, which would be credited me immediately if I volunteered to join the navy.

With the money I received I was able to make my here way to Burnham Market, to be made aware of the sad news awaiting me. Dr. Menzies, with whom I had been most associated, left the vessel without a word to me or I believe to any one else. The only officer to acknowledge my existence was Lieutenant Baker. He was in line for promotion and suggested I may feel it in my interests to consider a life at sea. He would arrange for me to sign on his next vessel. I saw Captain Vancouver as I was leaving the yard; I think he nodded in my direction.

The rest of the sailors with whom I had lived, suffered and nearly died a thousand times over, dispersed to every point of the compass, without a word to mark their passing. Those with family vanished immediately, those with no connections made for the nearest tavern, where I am sure the whole cycle of sea life would commence over again.

For me, I determined to return home to Norfolk as fast as I could under the impression my mother and father would be delighted to see me. I avoided the ever present press gangs preying on those fellows who had just come off any ship. Many a sailor often found himself straight back on another vessel and the whole process and a life at sea would be repeated again. This of course was not to be for me. The circumstance created by fate had ordained a different situation.

"What happens now my boy? You have told me a story, which has captivated me and I am sure there is much more not yet disclosed. I understand time and travels have made a man of you. I certainly cannot see you resuming your studies and after the adventurous life of the past years; I do not see you in the church in any shape or form."

"No, you are right there. I have no family here, those dear to me are gone. My father has left the estate well managed and in good hands, I will not alter or disturb things. Those who father saw fit to manage the estate will keep on in this manner; as for me, a sailor maybe but never a farmer. I will go to London to see Sir William Boyd. From the information you have given me, my father has numerous assets, to which I am not privy. I imagine he will be shocked to see me. You know I have always had the idea that someone in his establishment was instrumental in my seizure. The person who waylaid me in the alley had to know the way I was to go. Only four people knew the details of how I was to spend that fateful afternoon: Sir William, his son, my friend Harry, Black, his head accountant and I. The most obvious culprit is Black. He was never friendly, always finding fault. I ever had the feeling he resented those who had attained a higher learning or station than himself."

"Jane Sawtell is the other change in our lives, my boy. She is now Mrs. Captain Henry West. You are well aware all assumed you and Jane would marry as soon as you were of a suitable age. It was such a shock when you vanished; I know Jane was not herself for months. It seemed out of nowhere Captain West arrived, a relative, remote, but well connected, then almost immediately a wedding, not a big affair, in fact quite small. The couple moved into Westgate House, just across the green from here. After the death of Jane's mother and the deterioration in the health of her father, Westgate was closed. Jane, Henry and the housekeeper moved to Medway. Captain West left some months ago to rejoin his regiment. Jane and her housekeeper, who seem to have become attached, left for London three weeks since. I do not know the details, I have not been involved with Jane since her marriage and the reading of her father's will. All was left to her, in its entirety; she is a very wealthy woman."

"What of this Captain, what sort of fellow is he?

"Well that is a difficult thing to answer. He is a dashing chap, a handsome fellow, from the feminine perspective. It became common knowledge he was related to the family Beckingham. I think this may have influenced Edward Sawtell, he was always one to be somewhat overawed by a title. I know Jane's mother was not impressed with him and your mother and father had little time for him. I believe he snubbed them on a few occasions. Jane appeared completely smitten; I believe the wedding was hurried at the insistence of Jane herself. I was not at the wedding due to a bout of colic and gout, which confined me to my bed. All I can tell you is hearsay."

"Tell me what you have heard of this fellow, true or false are of no import."

"Well, it was rumoured Jane's father had invested heavily in a business venture with his new found son-in-law. It was well known how Henry West would carouse and gamble with the locals and many a time I believe he was seen in an inebriated state, riding over the fields towards Medhurst at all hours of the night. It was also rumoured he had liaisons with women of a notorious reputation, even after his marriage to Jane. He would vanish quite regularly, ostensibly on military business. On these disappearances, who knows what he did.

"And you say Jane was in love with him?"

"I would say yes, most definitely yes. Besotted with him would be more to the point."

Peter Wright contemplated the confidence he had heard. He silently reflected before he finally spoke.

"I suppose Jane and I would eventually have married. I never thought of her in that light. We were like brother and sister; in fact, my very own sister Kate was less dear to me than Jane, but always as a sister. She was my favourite. My one wish is that she is happy and contented." Peter's face clouded, it was obvious he was disturbed by thoughts of Jane, her life and his feelings. He could not explain and was completely at a loss to understand a feeling of anger at the thought of Jane married.

Sir Neville Brown rose.

"Well my dear friend, this has been a rewarding time for us both. For me the fact you are alive and well, is in itself reward enough, but the knowledge of the life you have led and the fact you will be maintaining the family farm, even though you may not be living here in Burnham Market makes me very happy. I know you are a man and not to be trifled with. Woe betides the fellow who sent you to sea if ever you find him."

Neville brown took his topcoat from the back of the door, and draped it across his shoulders. Peter rose and continued, "I will go to London; I must attend to things financial with James Boyd. It will take some time for me to realize the change in my circumstances and return to being my own man. Once I know the full financial position in which my father has left me, I will decide what to do with the future. Rest assured I will be back to my home and to you my dear friend."

The confidants parted. Neville Brown returned to his home in Kings Lynn. On the way he pondered on the tale told to him over the last few days, he marveled at the miraculous return of his young friend. As for Peter, London beckoned, a new life had commenced. He must get his estate in order and then make a decision on his future. If his finances were as sound as it seemed, he would formulate his ideas concerning the wealth to be taken in the Pacific Northwest of America. A new world presented itself. The future was all his.

33

Jane is Troubled and Makes Some Decisions

"Dear aunt, I must talk to you about a matter, which is becoming more pressing for me as the days pass."

Jane and Aunt Sarah were comfortably seated before a large fire. Both women basked in the warmth of its glow. The late afternoon sun, low in the western evening sky, cast a gold ambience into the dark spaces not lit by the light of the fire.

"Yes, my dear, what is it?" Lady Parkinson, dozing noisily, jumped precipitously at Jane's words, she started and answered in slurred tones. "I do believe I was asleep."

Jane was sitting quietly, a condensed version of *Pilgrim's Progress* lying open on her lap. She found reading almost impossible. Her mind, occupied on matters of which she had no experience she mused to herself on her circumstance. Of late, she had begun to worry about her situation. Henry made no effort to find her, but then neither had she attempted to find him. Now the relationship between her and Gwen Pratt had placed the need for Henry far from her mind.

"Aunt, I cannot stay here and intrude on you any longer. I should find a place of my own."

"Jane, I won't hear of it, there is no valid reason for you to leave and I would miss you dreadfully. I am so happy to have you here my dear. Do not even think of it."

Lady Sarah suddenly became wide-awake at the tone of the conversation.

"I have never had the joy of children. Jane, you have become the daughter I will never have. I know it can never be, but I would try to take the place of your mother."

"Why Aunt, of course you are. You are my mother and my companion and my friend. You are the closest family to me, you will always be dear to my heart, but I feel the need to have my own house, my own establishment."

"Oh, Jane, how selfish of me, of course I understand, eventually your husband will return and you will want to have a home ready. I am so sorry my dear. You must have your own place."

The light of the evening sun had ceased to be a factor, only the flame of the fire cast shadows about the room, which danced in tune to the flickering firelight.

"I have something to tell you, Aunt Sarah. My husband Henry is of less importance to me than he once was. I don't know how to explain it, but I do not want to be married."

Lady Sarah sat up; suddenly she was completely interested in the new trend of the conversation.

"What are you saying, my dear? Surely you do not mean that. I thought you were devoted to Captain West. I have not had the pleasure of meeting the Captain, but I am sure he is a perfect gentleman, and a military hero. What has caused this change of heart? Pray tell me my dear."

For a brief moment, Jane almost disclosed the relationship between her and Gwen. At the last second, she held her tongue. Perhaps in time she would tell her aunt of the turmoil rampant in her mind and the now nightly congress between her and Gwen.

"I cannot tell you why. But it seems my feelings have changed."

"Tell me my girl, is there another man? That must be it; you have seen someone who has taken your fancy. This is quite normal for a young wife, especially one whose husband is constantly away. I remember when I was your age I almost destroyed my place in society over a beautiful midshipman. I came to my senses, just in time. Your uncle and I had a tranquil life after that."

"No aunt, there is no other man you must believe me. I do not know what it is; I just know I do not want to be married. I cannot be a dutiful wife when I am so excited by life itself; to be subservient to a husband seems beyond me. Of course you must realize I am extremely wealthy and can financially take care of myself, but I have decided I do not love Captain West."

Jane could not bring herself to tell her aunt the real reason behind her statement. How could she broach the subject of Gwen? She went on to tell her aunt how she would see James Boyd and arrange for the purchase of a home in London. She spoke of the financial benefits of buying in London. She talked of the need to become involved in society in her own right and her need to hold her own evening salons. She spoke of the help her aunt would be able to give her and she finally threw herself into Aunt Sarah's arms, letting the tears of pent up emotion flow for the first time since the day of her marriage.

"My dear girl, there now, calm yourself, of course you must get your own household. I will be delighted to help and I know just the person. I hope you will consider this area; I do not want to be far from you. I believe Bedford Square is in the throes of building and will be a prime area in a few years. Let me make the necessary inquiries for you."

"Oh, my dear aunt, thank you for being so understanding. Of course, I will always look on you as my mother. I have seen Bedford Square, not a great distance from here, it would be perfect."

A weight seemed lifted from Jane's shoulders, she must tell Gwen of her decision. She thought of the madness of what she was doing. Moreover, what of Henry, how would she deal with him and his expected anger? This was far beyond her at this stage, so she decided to ignore it completely.

"Now Jane, tell me of your husband and what ails your relationship. You must be made aware of the many pitfalls, which will confront you, if you are considering any separation. It is a long and involved process. Surely you can work with Henry to rectify any differences between you. What would you do with your time if you were not a wife? Why I'm sure just the thought of you, waiting for his return from the trials of an arduous military life is of the greatest comfort to him."

Concern clouded the otherwise composed face of Lady Parkinson as she strove to understand the gist of the confidence imparted to her.

"Oh Aunt, Henry has never been anything but kind and good to me. The times when he has been away have been difficult and lonely especially in the quiet of Burnham Market. It has been a joy to have Gwen with me and I have made it a task to educate her. During this time she has become my companion and friend, we are no longer mistress and servant. This has been most rewarding for me, to see the progress in one so removed from our society. Why, I have come to appreciate the fact the poor have just as much ability as we have, the lack of resources and encouragement being the only impediment to their progress. Here in London I realize the isolation of the country. I enjoy the life of the city, the people, the theatre and new galleries, which seem to open daily. I feel I am not cut out to be a wife."

"My dear, I think I can understand what you say. You enjoy the delights of London and you wish to educate yourself and to assist your servant. Quite admirable, I dare say. Is it enough though, to give reason for thoughts concerning your husband. I want you to think carefully on this, let us get you a place of your own. I am sure these ideas will quickly vanish as soon as you see your warrior husband when he returns from the fields of honour."

Jane reiterated explanation after explanation why she felt unsure and confused in her married state and gave equally as many why she should live in London. The real reason she could not disclose to her aunt or to anyone else in the world. She could in fact not believe her own thoughts on the matter.

Lady Sarah did not have the slightest inkling of what had occurred between her niece and her companion from a class, lower in every way. She continued to put aside her disturbing thoughts.

"Now my dear let us talk of something, which I am sure will give you great joy. This Thursday coming in Hanover Square there is to be gala performance of a new work by Joseph Haydn; I believe it is a Sinfonia Concertino. Mr. Handel and Mr. Salamon have arranged this. All the notables of society will be there. Why I believe the Prince of Wales has signified his intention to be present. Therefore, we should go. You must be up for it."

While Jane was obsessed with her own dilemmas, Henry West was embroiled in his usual, nefarious activities. He had managed through subterfuge and connections to escape the rigors of service in Flanders against the French and Dutch. Instead, he found himself on the coast of Kent near the town of Dymchurch, on the edge of the wilderness of Romney Marsh, the destination and haunt of smugglers. It was a relatively deserted coastline, on any clear day, the thin blue line that was France, was easily observed.

Captain West had been charged with the task of combating the smugglers, those miscreants, who night after night would make their secret voyage across the Channel, their sailing packets loaded with cargoes of contraband liquor. Henry saw the potential here for making a handsome profit over and above the stipend awarded a soldier. It did not take long for him to encroach on the smuggler's domain and become their most prolific customer and controller of their destiny. As captain of the forces charged with stopping smuggling, he saw the opportunity to enhance his coffers by subterfuge. For a major financial consideration, Henry would arrange for his men to wait in hiding in an area where the contraband was not to be landed. Those smugglers, who had become the associates of Captain West, would unload miles away in complete safety. Soon Henry had complete control over the smuggled imports from North to South Foreland and from Dungeness to Hythe. Those who resisted his control found themselves dead or at best imprisoned.

Much to his annoyance Henry received a communiqu from General Fitzherbert, informing him of the fact his wife was searching for him, suggesting as a gentleman and an officer of the King, he present himself forthwith to calm and alleviate her fears for his well-being. From his quarters in the Ship Inn, a two storied building which looked out across the marshland and beach, Henry considered the request, which had every aspect of an order. He had taken rooms here as the centre of his command. It was also suitable for his nefarious purposes. Tunnels and secret passageways made it possible for easy access without being observed. The Ship Inn had been associated in one form or another with smuggling since its construction many years before.

Henry West ignored the General and his communiqu . The information that the general had left for Belgium and taken command of a force about to go into action against the Dutch and their allies convinced him that not to follow the order would have no repercussions. Jane, in effect, was far from his mind. If one had the ability to be cognizant of the workings of two minds simultaneously, one would know as Henry caroused in the Ship Inn, in company with Frederick March and the female companions they had brought from London, his wife was far from his mind. Jane, in her turn, lay awake, unable to sleep as she postulated her position, Gwen, warm beside her. Her thoughts were confused and in the early hours of the morn, as sleep eventually descended on her troubled mind, she decided to make a start and get her life in order. Her first objective would be to meet with Sir James Boyd, establish exactly the state of her finances and arrange for the purchase of a home. Jane determined she would worry about other things later.

34

Peter Returns to London. He Meets Thomas Pitt and Captain Vancouver

The door opened and a shaft of light illuminated the landing and beyond. It lit the fearsome spikes, iron rails and the heavy ornate metal gate, which protected the home of Sir James Boyd from the ever-bustling Montague Street beyond. The footman who had answered the sound of the bell saw a figure, rather disreputable, dressed in a polyglot arrangement of clothing. He was a big man of brown complexion, broad-shouldered, scarred about the eye, his face unshaven. Heavy, lank, fair hair down to his shoulders added to an unsavoury appearance.

"What do you want? There's nothing here for you." The footman, curt and to the point, held the door firmly and began to close it.

"I wish to see Sir James Boyd. I have business with him."

"Leave the premises immediately, or I will have you thrown onto the roadway."

As Peter spoke, three heavy-set retainers, fellows from below stairs, crowded behind the footman to reinforce and lend added weight to his statement.

"Inform Sir James, Peter Wright is returned and wishes to see him."

The door now opened wide. All four advanced towards Peter Wright, his retreating movement blocked by the spiked iron railing.

"Just get out where you belong and you will not be hurt. Come on now, get along with you." The heaviest man, obviously the head of the household retainers, reached forward to grasp the collar of Peter.

"Leave me go, I want no trouble, I must see Sir James. I am a lost friend. I remember you Scully, and you Burt. I am Peter Wright; I lived here almost six years ago." Peter prepared to defend himself.

"Mr. Scully, I remember the young fellow, Mr. Wright. He disappeared. All thought him dead. I think I see a resemblance." The tall, fellow who spoke, Burt Sparrow, had been the retainer assigned to care for Peter and Harry Boyd. Burt had been the one most associated with Peter all those years ago. He had been his servant during the time Peter had stayed in the Boyd household.

"Yes Burt, it is me, I am not dead and I have been to the other side of the world and am now back. Look carefully at me, I am older, I have changed, not the boy who stayed here."

"Yes, it's 'im, Mr. Scully. Hold off, it's 'im. I recognize 'im."

The tall lanky footman came forward and peered into the face of Peter Wright.

"Yes it could be 'im, I don't know though. I can't let anybody into the household."

Peter remained calm as he spoke.

"Mr. Scully you are perfectly correct to be wary of such a figure as I. I know you are doing your duty and whether you admit me now or later, I will see Sir James. I will report on your actions this night. Whenever that time may be, I shall commend you on your stewardship."

Scully began to relent and turned to the others.

"Watch him here, I will report to Sir James. Don't let him in now."

Within less than two minutes, Scully returned with the dignified, erect James Boyd, attired in a floral dressing gown, which favoured flowers of a neutral pattern and on his head a nightcap of a similar material.

"Where is this fellow? Now my man, you claim to be someone who is long dead. Let me look at you and woe betides you if you are here to render any disservice to my household."

James Boyd came close to Peter and peered at him, eyeing him from head to foot.

"Upon my soul, I see a resemblance, but the Peter I knew, the son of my good friend and colleague was a boy, barely 19 years. I see the resemblance, but the scar, the size, the clothes. Who are you?"

"Sir James, I am Peter Highfield Wright and I am returned from the other side of the world, where I was sent through no fault or desire of mine by some blackguard with nothing but my demise in mind. My mother, father and sister have departed this life and these last days I have been with my friend and benefactor Sir Neville Brown in Burnham Market recounting my adventures and history. I have learned to my sadness that I have inherited all which my deceased family owned both here in England and abroad. I need help and direction in the matter of the settlement of my affairs." Peter urgently blurted out the circumstances of his unexpected appearance and his needs.

"Bring him over into the light, here in the portico so I can see more clearly. If you are who you say you are show me some identification." The retainers grouped about Peter and shepherded him into the light.

"I have here a receipt for money held in escrow for me by the Royal Navy, in which service I have been engaged. I also have a pay off notice from that same service. Both items have my name engraved upon them." Peter took everything from his pocket and handed the papers to Sir James.

Sir James had donned a pair of small reading glasses and now peered into the face of Peter. His already pale complexion become even paler as it became clear to him, here was the young lad who had disappeared mysteriously so many years ago.

"Peter, it is you. Scully call Lady Boyd. Get Harry, I am sure he is in his apartment. The girls tell them what a miracle has happened and to come with all haste. Peter where have you been? What has happened to you? Look at you. You are a grown man. Come in my boy." Sir James Boyd grasped Peter by the arm and led him into the warmth of the foyer of the place he had been taken from so many years ago.

The reunion was joyous; the family attended, all in various degrees of shock and attire, all asking a myriad of questions at the same time. Peter and Harry Boyd embraced and where before Harry had been the older, bigger person, now Peter was the larger and more muscular in stature and had the appearance of one not to be trifled with.

It was the early hours of the morning before all settled for the night. Peter joined Harry Boyd in his apartment. Dawn light was beginning to cast its golden glow into the room before both young men fell asleep, where they sat.

Peter Wright's arrival at the home of Sir James Boyd caused an upheaval in the usually well-regimented pattern of daily life. Later the next day all was still aflutter in the household. When Peter appeared on the stairs at about midday, he was a completely different person. Gone was the scruffy character that had intruded from the past in the darkness of the previous night; gone the hairy stubble, which had adorned his darkly tanned face. With his unruly hair tied back in a tail and with a shirt and breeches loaned by Harry, he had acquired a totally new persona.

"Father, I will introduce Peter to Senor Gaballi, we must get him attired properly, he is the heir to his father's estate and as such he should be dressed appropriately."

"Yes, excellent Harry. Peter my boy; I will advance you a draft, which should tide you over until all the necessary legalities are complete. You are a very wealthy young man, this I can assure you."

The daughters of James Boyd, now attractive young teenage women, sat together on the window seat. They were mesmerized by this person who now claimed their attention, so changed from the pale-faced, thin lad who had so suddenly disappeared from their home. Peter was a wealthy man with property and money and a desirable catch for any young lady.

"Harry, I am sure you will be happy to have Peter share your quarters. Peter you must make our home your home. There is so much to discuss and so many questions; but first, a wardrobe. Harry will be your guide and mentor. Heaven knows he must be good at fashion if his spending account is any criteria. I'm sure you will enjoy that, aye Harry."

"Nothing will give me greater pleasure, Father. Come along, Peter my friend, let us see about those clothes."

For Peter, the first days in London were a non-stop whirl of shopping. The first visit was to the tailor where Mr. Gaballi did his best to convince Peter to dress in the latest fashions from France. Peter was indeed fortunate to have Harry there as advisor. Senor Gaballi did his best to influence his new customer, dazzling him with the latest and most colourful materials, laces, brocades and feathers. He displayed various wigs, which he assured Peter, all the men of substance were wearing. He brought forth hats, wide-brimmed gracefully turned, curled and feathered and of course carried in the hand for effect and never worn for fear of incommoding the foretop of the wig. Gaballi became more and more excited as he displayed hose, shoes, high-heeled and pointed, silver snuff boxes and cravats of fine Italian lace. A bewildered Peter finally called a halt to the proceedings when Gaballi produced a hand-warming muff in fine silver fox fur to carry on a cinch about the waist, for young men of fashion in the cold of winter. Harry who had been enjoying Peter's discomfort finally spoke up.

"I say old man, wear that lot and they will call you a French dog or at best a bloody fop."

"By God, Harry I would not want to be seen dead in that lot. Are you sure this fellow knows his trade? I want clothes that are well cut but plain."

"Yes, he is a fine tailor, but tends to get carried away with the fashion he has helped to establish with, the, shall we say, more delicate of our young blades. You like my wardrobe. Leave it to me I will make sure Senor Gaballi does right by you."

After much discussion and argument, Gaballi, to his dismay, followed the desires of his new customer. He toned down the colours, the flares and the flounces to a more dignified and traditional English style. Next the boot makers; here Peter ordered half a dozen pairs of boots and shoes. Next at the haberdasher, he ordered shirts, gloves, hose and all the necessary accoutrements of a young, well-placed man.

Evenings at the Boyd residence were restful and spent in retelling his experiences, enjoying the comforts of a home life and generally returning his existence to some sort of order. All the while, the girls Melissa and Edith dwelt on his every word and both were completely smitten by him. Harry, instead of being the dominant one, now looked to his bigger, stronger, more rugged companion as the leader, although each, as before, enjoyed the company of the other. Peter took little notice of the sisters, of course, he was polite and extremely gracious, but he felt nothing but the warmest of brotherly affection for them

"I say Harry; I have to go to Saville Row tomorrow. Mr. Gaballi will have my goods ready. Are you coming with me?"

"I surely am. I will tell Scully to have the carriage ready. At what o'clock were you thinking about?"

"Let us say, one. Then a visit to that coffee shop, you know the place, on Conduit Street, where you took me just two days ago. What do you say?"

"I'm up for it my friend."

It was a fine September day. The sun shone brightly with just a hint of winter to come. Peter and Harry had completed their business in Saville Row. Burt Porter, the groom had taken Harry's favourite phaeton with Peter's purchases back to the Boyd residence. The friends decided to walk to Conduit Street, where the Prince of Wales Coffee House would be full of men of the sea. The Prince of Wales had become a meeting place for those naval men on half pay and for captains and mates of merchant ships waiting for their vessels to load or unload. It was a place where matters relating to the sea were discussed, argued and sometimes brawled over well into the night.

"I like the feel of the place, Harry. You know I have an idea to purchase a vessel. It is here I feel I may find the right captain for it."

As the friends strolled along, Peter quietly voiced his thoughts and plans for the future.

He talked of ideas barely formulated. He spoke of the vastness of the

North Pacific. He told Harry of numberless fish in vast schools, of furs in grand abundance, there to be bought from the Indians for a pittance. He told of the forests and trees, huge and tall, which covered the country for thousands of miles. The lure of the Pacific Northwest of America had captured him. He realized the potential of the country and the fortune to be made. Whether he would go back himself remained to be seen, but if he did, he would return as an owner of a trading vessel, never again as a pressed man.

"I will talk to Sir James and establish my worth; I need direction in the path I have decided to follow. Ah, here we are, Conduit Street."

Peter and Harry stood in the sun on the corner of Conduit and Bond streets. They talked of Peter's ideas for his future and together they pledged to carry out a joint venture in trade and commerce.

"Good God, Harry, look over there. That lieutenant, I know him well. He was a midshipman when I last saw him."

"You mean that fellow over there, why he is Lord Camelford. You know him."

"Of course I do, I fought with him below decks, he was on *Discovery* and we became friends of a sort. I must speak with him, come along Harry."

"I say, Peter, you know Camelford." Harry incredulously looked at his friend before he continued. "He has a rather bad reputation, you know he fights duels and has killed a few fellows. Always seems to be in trouble."

"That's Pitt. He was ever on report and Vancouver flogged him and had him chained in the fo'c'sil.

The two men crossed the street and approached the tall, good-looking fellow, lounging nonchalantly against the wall in a shaft of afternoon sunlight beaming between the buildings, resplendent in the uniform of a Lieutenant of the Royal Navy.

"Good day Mr. Pitt."

"What. Do I know you, sir?"

"We are well acquainted sir, but in different circumstances than we find ourselves at this moment."

"I do know you, you're the idler, the landsman. Yes, I do know you. By God, you seem to have fallen on better circumstances. Petee that is what they called you. You were the pressed fellow. But look at you now all the rage and quite the tippy." Pitt straightened to his full height.

"Allow me to present my good friend the Honourable Harry Boyd."

"Honourable aye. Harry Boyd." Pitt, with wrinkled brow, delved into his memory. "Your father is a member for somewhere and is the financier Sir

Discovery

James Boyd, pleased to know you. Now you Peter, by your dress I see you are either an impostor or man of substance, I know you to be an upright fellow, so I must assume you have regained your place in society."

The two men equal in height and size shook hands.

"And I see you have become a lieutenant, far cry from our last meeting. Harry tells me you are now Lord Camelford. I assume I should defer to you as M'lord."

Tom Pitt laughed and clapped Peter on the back.

"Wright, you will do no such thing, I am Tom to you. You beat me fair and square in a fight and you saved my life and aided me when I was unjustly beaten. I am delighted to see you old fellow and on a more equal footing. You must acquaint me of your good fortune."

The three stood in the warmth of the sun. Peter informed Pitt of the death of his family and the inheritance that was now his. He spoke of the final months of the voyage and the rounding of Cape Horn. All the while Harry Boyd listened intently as his companions' reiterated incidents, which only Peter and Tom Pitt could appreciate. When in the course of their conversation the name of George Vancouver was brought up, Pitt would noticeably scowl and when Peter spoke of the Captain's illness, Pitt was wont to remark that the poltroon would get all that was coming to him.

"Wright, I will never forgive the man who was captain of *Discovery*. Till my last day, I will make his life a misery in any way I can."

"Well Tom, be that as it may, we must not let old grievances mar our meeting. We are both men of substance and have our lives before us. Harry and I are going into the Prince of Wales Coffee House would you care to join us. I have an idea for my future life, I would consider it an honour if you would allow me to tell you of it and hear your opinion, either for or against."

Peter realized Tom Pitt was not listening to him and appeared not to hear the invitation. Tom stared into the distance towards Bond Street. The street was deserted with the exception of two figures strolling leisurely in the shade, on the other side of the road towards them.

"Devil take me, there's the damn swine now." Pitt spoke aloud. His normally tanned face paled, his jaw clenched and veins stood out on his forehead.

As the pair drew to the entrance to the Coffee House, Pitt, without a word rushed across the road, brandishing his cane, shouting at the top of his voice.

"There you are, you scurvy swine. You ill-used me too many times and you refuse to meet me on the field of honour. Now it is my turn."

Pitt rushed at the men, one tall and the other short and quite portly. The taller dressed in a manner that displayed a person of class, the other attired in the undress uniform of a Captain of the Royal Navy. Both stopped short at the verbal onslaught issued at the top of their assailant's voice.

Peter and Harry who had not noticed the two strolling men, the object of Pitt's wrath, stood aghast at the strange turn of events. Shouting at the top of his voice, Pitt aimed blows with his cane, directed at the stout Captain.

"I demand satisfaction and if you won't meet me honourably, I will thrash you within an inch of your life, you swine. Take that and that." Pitt swung his cane and proceeded to assault the person of the naval man before him, who warded off the blows as best he could with his raised arm.

"By God Harry, it's Captain Vancouver. Come, let's do something, Pitt will kill him."

By the time they reached the fracas on the other side of the street, Pitt had begun to receive blows from the cane held by the taller of the two men, which did not deter him as he again attacked Captain Vancouver. Peter and Harry ran onto the scene and attempted to pull away the Captain's companion who had dropped his cane. Harry grasped Pitt by the throat, even as Pitt continued to rain blows at Captain Vancouver, all the while shouting epithets and obscenities, which echoed about the narrow confines of the street.

"Cease this, Tom. Come along man, think of your career, think of your position in society and cease this attack."

Peter and Harry clasped Pitt by the arms and began to drag him away; twice he broke free to renew his assault. Finally, Peter extracted the cane from his hand; between them, they managed to manhandle the furious Tom Pitt across to the other side of the road.

Pitt shouted a final challenge.

"I swear to you, every time I see you I will thrash you. Do you hear me?" He stood trembling with agitation and distress between Peter and Harry who in turn tried to calm him. Eventually he returned to some semblance of propriety.

"Well, Petee you have helped me again, you stopped me killing the fellow. You know how I suffered at his hands; he will not give me satisfaction and continues to hide behind the coat tails of naval law and my uncle Lord Grenville. However, I will have him. I swear I will. I must go. Come see me at my home, both of you. Camelford House. Oxford Street."

Pitt turned abruptly and strode away towards Bond Street without looking back. Peter and Harry looked across towards the two who had been the object of Pitt's wrath. A group had formed before the Prince of Wales Coffee House, mostly naval men, with a few street urchins who had danced about the combatants in gleeful joy. Peter and Harry re-crossed the road and approached Captain Vancouver and his companion. Captain Vancouver, pale of face, leant against the wall of the coffee house. It was obvious he was not a well man and appeared affected by the violence of the encounter.

The taller man spoke, "Thank you gentlemen for your intervention. Pitt is a lunatic. I am Charles Vancouver and this is my brother, Captain George Vancouver. I am sure I speak for my brother; I believe proceedings would have been much nastier had you not intervened. We are indebted to you gentlemen. To whom have I the honour of speaking?"

"I am Mr. Peter Wright and allow me to introduce the Honourable Harry Boyd. It was chance alone that placed us in a position to be of assistance to you. Lord Camelford has always had a violent streak in his make up and I fear his mind and manners failed him completely on this day."

At the sound of the name Wright, Captain Vancouver looked intently at both men; he stared at Peter and finally spoke in a voice agitated and tremulous from his recent confrontation.

"I know you, sir." Captain Vancouver wrinkled his brow in thought and peered into the face of Peter Wright. "I have met you before sir, but where?"

"Captain it was our duty to help an officer of the King in need. I trust you will not be in any way inconvenienced by this unfortunate outburst, sir. Tom has always been of a wild nature and ever has spoken without forethought."

As Peter addressed Captain Vancouver, it suddenly became obvious he had recognized him. His peered at Peter with a quizzical look, a faint smile, just for an instant crossed his otherwise dour countenance.

"Now I know you, sir. I thank you for your assistance. Come Charles; let us be on our way, we must not keep Lord Grenville waiting. Good evening gentlemen and again my thanks to you, Mr. Peter Wright."

The two men left and went on their way. This was the last time Peter Wright would see Captain Vancouver, the man who had played such a part in his life. Although nothing was said, Peter knew Vancouver was well aware of whom he was and the circumstances under which they had been involved

35

Jane Makes Some Decisions and Arranges Her Future

Jane awoke on the morning of October 25th 1795 with the feeling that all was well. She had considered her future and had decided to change the whole thrust of her life. The success she had had with Gwen, who could now read and write and who spoke with an accent far removed from her Norfolk upbringing, except when she became excited, was, she considered, a feather in her cap. She had taken a surly, uneducated, country girl and made her an agreeable companion. The fact that they had entered into their special relationship so far removed from that which was considered normal by polite society also was a factor in her considerations. She knew this was the happiest she had been since the death of her father and mother. She knew she did not want or need her husband. Each day Gwen was becoming more and more important to her.

Since Jane had come to London, she realized this was the age of innovation, the populace of this city was increasing and becoming more affluent, a middle class of society daily grew all across England. It occurred to her there must be hundreds of young ladies of this new class, who could use her talents as a teacher. She would establish the London School for Young Ladies. Here, girls whose parents had risen in their society without the benefit of a complete education would be able to learn deportment, reading, writing and some social graces. In all parts of the country, factories were blossoming into existence and people began to possess money. This was a new class, a *"nouveau riche,"* not of the aristocratic ruling class, but of tradesman and entrepreneurs who had seized the opportunity to innovate and commence new methods of production. Surely, it would be advantageous for a young woman to have a better education, both in respect to positions in service and to attract a more affluent suitor. Jane thought long and deeply on her future and finally she decided not to consider herself married to Henry.

Some weeks after she had arrived and settled into her new life, Aunt Sarah had taken her to a lecture by the noted reformer and author, Mr. Daniel Defoe. This captivating man had outlined in a few short words the unequal plight of women and the surrender of very life and freedom brought about by the vows of marriage. He spoke of the cruelty perpetrated on wives and the fact most men of substance had a mistress. He spoke of truths not readily mentioned in polite society, how under law a woman became the chattel of the husband. Although there were moves to liberalize the marriage laws, all was still weighted in favour of the husband. This was brought home to her when she accompanied her aunt to visit the grave of her late husband. Jane was incensed by the inscriptions on many of the gravestones, which spoke of the surviving wife as the relic of the departed husband. The only lawful way out of a marriage was death. Jane gave thanks to her father for his foresight in settling the estate in such a way that it could never be used except by her. If there was a way for legal release from her situation, she knew she had the money to accomplish it.

Jane formulated a plan in her mind. First, she would see Sir James Boyd. She would establish exactly how much money she would be able to outlay per year. She was sure he would assist in the purchase of a suitable place in London where she could live and commence her school. Perhaps he would have some idea as to how she could be released from her marriage. Yes, she determined that would be the plan.

"Gwen my dear, today I am going to visit Sir James Boyd. You recall our discussion of the other night. Well, I am going ahead with it. What do you say to that?"

"I don't know what to say, are you sure?" Gwen sat beside Jane on the edge of the bed.

"Yes dear Gwen, I am going to change my life and if you will allow it, yours. I want you to come with me. I will do it even if you feel it is not what you want, but I need you with me, not as a servant, but as my companion and friend. I am offering you my love and a future. Just think, together we will help others to better themselves and unlock the potential latent within us all."

Jane took Gwen by the hand and continued.

"Think about it. Together we can do something of importance. I cannot think of any better way to spend my time and money."

"But dear Jane, what about Captain West? He is your husband and he could return at any time. What will he say about it all?"

"I don't care what Captain West says or does. I am going to lead my own life with you and be damned to all the rest. Now let me wash and dress. I am to be with Sir James Boyd at 11 in the forenoon."

Jane arrived at the financial establishment of Sir James Boyd precisely on time; the obsequious Mr. Black immediately escorted her into the presence of Sir James.

After the necessary pleasantries and the condolences offered on the death of Edward Sawtell, Jane and Sir James began to discuss the matters that had brought her into his presence.

She sat amazed as she learned of vast holdings in foreign parts. She was informed of property here in London itself, investments in the West Indies and holdings in Norfolk, all of which made her a very, very wealthy woman and all held under the law, which retained it all for her. There was no impediment to her buying a suitable house and Sir James happened to know of a fine dwelling, recently built on Oxford Street. With his help, he was sure the seller would come down in price. She told him of her plans to commence a school for lower class women. While Sir James was most interested in the financial side of the matter, he displayed no great interest at all in the cause, which she now espoused and in fact did all he could to dissuade her.

"My dear young lady, I think it is most commendable what you propose, but I believe it a waste of money and time. The lower classes do not have the ability to learn more than is necessary for their sustenance. A complete waste of time and the money your father spent a lifetime accumulating. But against my better judgment I will assist you if this is what you want to do."

"Yes, I am sure Sir James. I have made this decision. I also need to include in some way my companion Miss Gwen Pratt in all my undertakings relating to my proposed school. I trust you will assist me realize all my plans. I do this for my own sake and if it is a success it will be to the memory of my father and mother."

As Jane spoke, James Boyd saw a startling resemblance to her mother, Margaret. He had known her as a girl when she was the same age as Jane; he had loved Jane's mother from afar in those early young days. Of course, he would help her.

"Now to one other matter which needs attention. From time to time, your husband, Captain West, has drawn a sum of money from an account set up by your father to cover the costs of an investment in the West Indies. I must state here, I advised against this venture. My associates in Havana have heard of this company and have assured me it does exist in Havana, but in what form or state of solvency is completely unknown. It seems a sign adorns a building in a lower part of the city and from which no business appears to be carried on. The last amount drawn has exhausted this fund. The question is do you wish to re-establish the fund and let it continue?"

"This is the first I have heard of such a thing. There was no mention of it in my father's will. Henry has been drawing from it. How long? How much?

"Jane was quite distressed that Henry had been in possession of funds all the while he had been drawing on her for the settlement of his debts. "Tell me about it."

"The most recent draw, which has exhausted the account, was in the amount of £3000, quite a considerable sum. Over the last four years, the special account was exhausted by the amount of £15500. I informed your father of the financial situation of Captain West and his estrangement from his family. This had occurred long before your marriage. I advised against any business involvement with him or his friend Frederick March."

Jane paled at this disclosure. Finally, the absence of family connections had become clear. It was obvious Henry had lied as to his relationship with his family. It was a moment before she regained her composure and spoke.

"Frederick March, I have not seen him since our marriage, what has he to do with this?"

"It is a well known fact in society that your husband, long before your marriage, had broken with his family. He squandered his inheritance in gambling and licentiousness. Frederick March has a reputation as a rake, gambler and womanizer; it is well known in fashionable circles of London. He would join with Henry West in dubious business dealings. The fellow is a slaver and quite ruthless when crossed. His vessels are notorious in the various ports at which I have dealings."

Jane sat silent and grim, as these facts were imparted.

"You were not aware of any of this? You must know it is with great sorrow I disclose it to you at this time."

"Tell me, Sir James, hold nothing from me. Do you know where my husband is?"

"I believe he has attained the rank of Colonel. It is my understanding he bought a commission from a retiring officer and is engaged in the pursuit of smugglers on the coast. I do not know for sure, but I believe the money last requested by him went to the purchase of his commission, not to the struggling

West Indies investment, which has ostensibly consumed so much of your father's and now your fortune."

Sir James ceased his disclosure and he was troubled. How much should he divulge? He could see she was distressed and surprised. He saw a tear begin its journey down her cheek.

"There will be no more. If you are asking me to renew the account, which my father saw fit to open, close it. I must inform you Sir James; I have decided not to continue with my marriage to Captain West. Other circumstances have unfolded, which I find more to my liking than my previous life with Henry. Henry was always kind to me and never beat me. However, his long absences, drunkenness and complete disregard for monetary prudence have rendered my life lonely and pointless. I will be married to him no more.

Sir James called for the obsequious Mr. Black and arranged for the immediate preparation of the necessary paperwork to carry out the afternoon's business.

"Then I will say no more. When next I receive a request for money from the West Indies Sugar account I will have great delight in refusing it."

Sir James rose and began to rearrange papers.

Jane signed first this, then that. Seven times in all, she affixed her signature; the final business was to nullify the account set up by her father for the West Indies Sugar Company. Sir James kept his fears to himself, although he was worried at the probable reaction of Henry West and Frederick March. He knew them to be despicable and untrustworthy characters.

36

Peter Wright and Jane Sawtell

Peter Wright arrived at the financial house of Sir James Boyd, near to noon. On entering the establishment, he noticed nothing at all had changed, except perhaps the faces seated at the high tables poring over ledgers and journals. He saw himself as he had been, mirrored in the pale faced, hunched, weak fellows. They barely dared to lift their heads under the watchful eye of the black clad figure of the chief clerk, Mr. Black. He sat in his elevated position at the end of the long, stuffy room. Black immediately scurried forward, bowing and fawning to Peter. He did not recognize the heavy-set young man as the person he had helped consign to a press gang and Peter did not enlighten him. Black informed Peter that Sir James was engaged, he would, however, be free shortly should he would care to wait. Some five minutes passed before the door opened to Sir James's inner sanctum. The tall stately man directed Jane Sawtell into the foyer where Peter Wright sat perusing a gazette from the pile assembled for the use of waiting clients.

Peter raised his head and instantly recognized Jane. For a moment, she looked at him vacantly scrutinizing his face as she would any stranger. As she drew near Peter rose and bowed. It was then a cry escaped her lips, "Peter, oh my God. Peter Wright, oh heavens."

She staggered for a moment and then swooned, falling to the floor in a faint.

The financial house of Boyd was thrown into turmoil at this unexpected event. The men were useless spectators at such an unexpected female occurence. All had different ideas as to how to revive her. Some began to fan her vigorously with sheets of paper and another had a cup of water from which he splashed droplets on her face. Those not engaged in assistance hovered in the background giving ineffectual advice and showing just how little they knew of feminine distress. It was at this time it became noticeable that Black kept his distance, for he now knew the identity of Peter Wright.

"Jane! Come now Jane, how do you feel now? Jane reclined in an armchair brought from the office of Sir James.

"Oh, Peter, is it really you Peter? I thought it was a ghost, an apparition. I could not believe my eyes."

"Yes, Jane, it is me. Come, drink, it is brandy and a little water."

The colour had returned to Jane's cheeks and she sat upright.

"Oh, Peter, you were dead, what has happened to you, you have changed, you are a man. I must know all. We gave up all hope you were alive. I wept for months."

"Come Jane and Peter; let us return to my room. There you can hear a recount of some history and recover yourself." Sir James led the way as Peter assisted Jane to return to the privacy of the inner office.

For the next hour, Peter and Jane spoke quietly together. They recounted their thoughts, experiences and history one to the other. They spoke of their families and consoled each other on the sad deaths of both their parents. Despite their melancholy at the loss of family, they were still able to marvel at the good fortune this sad occurrence had engendered. It was late in their conversation when Peter told Jane of the circumstances of his disappearance and the name, which had been indelibly imprinted on his mind from the very time he had been taken

"I know Frederick March. Peter I know the fellow. Only today I have today learned some distressing facts about this man and my husband, Captain now Colonel West."

"You know of March. Tell me I must know. I have waited years for revenge on this fellow or somebody. I know what happened to me was no accident of fate. The fellow who hit me most definitely lay in waiting. I believe there was a conspiracy to get me out of England, for what reason I do not have any idea, but again it seems, the hand of fate has played another card and brought us together this day."

Sir James Boyd sat quietly, listening to the young people rekindle a lost friendship. Now he spoke up.

"I have little or no comprehension of the business dealings of Frederick March, but they are reputedly suspect. There are rumours afoot in the circles with knowledge of these things that Henry West and Frederick March are involved in a conspiracy to defraud His Majesty, by being in league with smugglers, and in fact are smuggling themselves. I have heard how Colonel West ruthlessly arrests any smuggler who will not surrender the major part of his consignment to him, while the vessels of March have unfettered access to the coast which is under the command of Colonel West."

Peter listened intently to this information.

"In my years at sea I have had many hours to contemplate the circumstances that saw me waylaid and to all intents and purposes sent to my death. I could not understand the reason for it at all. I was waylaid by a fellow waiting for me, a person who had knowledge of where I would be, the words I will remember until the end of my life confirm this. The only question I have is why. With a person and a name to pursue, I will find Frederick March and face him. Sir James, do you have any idea where I can find the fellow?"

"No ,Peter, I do not."

The three sat and discussed their mutual associations. Pete postulated how a person with inner knowledge would have had to be involved. He broached a subject, much to the distress Sir James Boyd. He proposed Black as the most likely suspect in the matter.

"No, no, Peter. Black has been with me since I first took over the company on the death of my father. He has been a tower of strength and a fine steward all these years."

Peter continued, determined to have his suspicions investigated.

"Let me say this, I do know this fact. There were only four persons privy to my actions that fateful day. You, sir, Harry and of course, myself. The only other is the man who drew my directions and saw me on my way. I can suspect no other. No, it has to be Black. If I may suggest, perhaps some sort of investigation or whatever it is you financiers do to check the state of the accounts handled by Black, there may be some trace of the name March, which would make a connection. For my part, I will go to the home of Tom Pitt, Lord Camelford. If any one will know March and whatever he is about it will be Tom, he will surely assist me. The reason I was taken and put to sea completely escapes me. But I will find out so help me."

The afternoon seemed to pass with unusual speed. For hours, Jane and Peter reminisced and renewed the past joy each felt in the other's company. Scully arrived at five that evening to convey Sir James to his home. By that time, old relationships had been re-established. "Peter, you will join me for the journey home and Jane, allow me to deposit you at Lady Parkinson's residence. I believe it has been a most rewarding time, two long-parted friends have been reunited, matters discussed which would be of mutual satisfaction to all and I have serious circumstance to ponder in view of the suspicions aroused. Come let us get underway."

The coach made its way through the darkening streets of London, the air heavy and sulphurous, thick with the smoke of innumerable fires and the odour of open sewers and refuse. Throngs of people, those inheritors of the night had begun to congregate in their usual places. Occasionally a ragged fellow would run breathlessly beside the coach, cap in hand, "Yer got a copper ta spare."

From the deepening blackness came cries, obscene and raucous, which told of groups already heady from the ravages of overindulgence. A shaft of light from an opened doorway for a brief moment revealed a face almost as an evil apparition from Hades, a parody of what was once an attractive woman, her pock-marked cheeks sunken and made hideous with patches of rouge. The curses she called displayed teeth blackened and rotted, devoured by mercury, the dubious cure for the sexual diseases endemic to those areas of lower London. A little way on in another doorway, a soft glow illuminated and revealed young and beautiful girls, not yet more than sixteen years, still with the bloom of youth and health, fan in hand, presenting nubile bodies to the passing concourse in quest of money.

Seated beside Jane, Peter pondered on his life at sea with all its trials and hardship, but in no way near to the degradation, he saw here in the streets of London. As the coach progressed on its journey, it drew towards the new built areas and the homes of the more affluent. At each turn a different strata was presented, vagrant women and their children, haunting the shadows, supplicant and desperate, their pleas for alms being ignored.

Now the carriage moved out of the old city and into fashionable Soho, with its shops and tradesmen, their guild signs bright and colourful. Stationers and booksellers operated under the sign of the Bible, goldsmiths and bankers under the sign of the grasshopper. The Golden Boot of the shoemaker and the Indian Queen of the linen drapers all vied with the Civet Cat of the perfumers, the Hand and Shears of the tailor and Maiden's head of the mercers. Finally, they arrived at St James Square with its surrounding areas of elegant and wealthy homes. Sir James deposited Jane at Aunt Sarah's in Montague Street. Here in a tender moment Jane and Peter vowed never to let time again rob them of the companionship lost these many years.

Peter dispatched a note to Tom Pitt requesting a meeting. He knew the reputation of Pitt. If any information was available relating to Frederick March, Pitt would be aware of it, or at least know of someone who could discover it. The evening meal had well passed. Harry Boyd and Peter lounged comfortably before a fire in their apartment when a messenger arrived with a note scribbled on stationery displaying the family coat of arms of Lord Camelford. The note was short and concise, to the effect Thomas Pitt was leaving London two days hence for Boconnoc, his Cornish family home and he would be glad to meet with Peter Wright Esq. at the Prince of Wales Coffee House at 3:00 p.m. the next day.

Peter had become a devotee of the coffee house. Each had its own clientele and had become known to those of a particular occupation. Some became the resorts of learned scholars noted for their wit, others for dandies and politicians, while others became the resort of newsmongers or men of law. These houses were a place to meet the learned fellows of the Royal Society. Sir Isaac Newton and Edmund Halley were often to be heard expounding on their latest scientific discoveries at the Grecian in Devereau Court. Whig politicians frequented the St. James and the Tories would only be seen in the Cocoa-Tree near Pall Mall. Colonel Henry West, the nemesis of Peter Wright, was well known in the gambling establishment of White's in St James and was a frequenter of Kings in Covent Garden, said to be the resort for all gentlemen to whom beds were unknown. The Prince of Wales in Conduit Street was for men of the sea. It was to this establishment Peter Wright made his way.

As usual at this time in the afternoon, the Prince of Wales was crowded with its usual colourful clientele. Naval officers of all ranks in their distinctive uniforms, those on half pay or the retired, sporting various undress uniforms, captains of trading vessels, merchants, traders and a sprinkling of others not of a seagoing nature.

He made his way with difficulty through the noisy throng all heavily engaged in loud conversation seemingly related to deeds of valour at sea, or perhaps narrow escapes from certain death in nautical encounters. More mundanely, the value of a cargo or the price of a vessel would be beaten down by a smartly worded phrase. The place was heavy with smoke and those that did not puff on their long clay pipes were wholly engaged in the new art of taking perfumed snuff with all the resultant noisy effects.

Peter discovered and recognized a shabbily dressed Tom Pitt, quite out of character for one of his station and wealth. He sat in a box reading the latest copy of the Flying Post.

"Tom, I must thank you for meeting me at such short notice. I trust all is well with you." Peter spoke as he slid into the seat opposite.

"Ah! Wright. Yes, all is extremely well with me." Tom Pitt answered with an unusual degree of amiability. He continued, "I believe Peter Wright I am in love and I would recommend it to you with all my heart. I am off to Cornwell to see Lady Hester Stanhope. She is an angel, possessed of the loftiest principals and has the best of influence on my life. Here she is the most beautiful of women." Pitt drew a miniature from his pocket. Peter lent forward to examine the object in the light of the candle on the table.

"My goodness, I say, she is beautiful Tom."

Before Peter could continue, a person, uninvited, threw himself down heavily on the seat beside him. He was dressed in the most eccentric fashion and in a speech almost unintelligible, loudly called to the waiter for a pint of ale and a candle placed in the next box. He then, without a word, drew the candleholder from Tom Pitt over to himself and began to peruse a pocket book, rudely ignoring the pair into whose company he had intruded.

The waiter filled the order. Immediately the intruder left, moving into the next box.

"Those idiots! The popular name for these fellows is Bond Street Loungers. I take it you have had no experience of them. They dress outlandishly and speak with the most tired diction; they pretend sleep is but a syllable away. However, most of all they are uncouth before the gracious and do everything to be obnoxious. I hate them with a passion." Pitt motioned to the waiter and mimicking the speech of the intruder asked for a set of candlesnuffers. "I must put this fellow in his place."

Pitt rose with snuffers in hand. Going to the next box and without the slightest ceremony snuffed out the candles by which the garish fellow sat reading his pocket book. Without a word, Pitt returned to his seat with Peter.

The fellow, completely surprised by this action, leapt to his feet and demanded of the nearest waiter, "Who is that fellow who dares to insult me? What is his name? I will demand satisfaction."

The lounger, red-faced with obvious distemper and anger, quite forgot his slovenly speech and for a moment raged against what he perceived as an insult. The waiter with apparent relish provided the fellow with the information he demanded.

"That, sir, is Lord Camelford."

Peter, who was facing the miscreant and had a splendid view of the fellow. He observed the sudden change of appearance at the mention of Pitt's name. Instantly he modified his tone. From a look of studied nonchalance and contempt for all about him, to a pallid, fear-stricken shell of his former self, he quickly paid his bill and rushed to the safety of Conduit Street. Thomas Pitt, Lord Camelford had established a reputation as a duelist and as a prizefighter; he was well known in London Town and was not to be trifled with. Peter knew here was the man to assist him in his quest.

"Now, tell me the urgent matter you wish to acquaint me on?" Pitt laid his paper on the table and became attentive as Peter began to speak.

"It is a matter of great import to me. It concerns the reason for my being pressed and the subsequent voyage on board *HMS Discovery*. I am now sure it was not by accident I found myself on board ship. Things have been revealed concerning this event and the name of one person, the name last remembered by me and consequently imprinted on my mind. This person, I believe, holds the answer to why I was so cruelly waylaid."

"So what do you want from me?"

"A name has come to my attention, in fact two names." Peter decided he may as well include the husband of Jane Sawtell and continued, "The first is the name that has been with me since the evening of my incarceration. Does the name Frederick March have any meaning for you?"

"Frederick March, you say. You have disclosed a name steeped in infamy. I do not know the fellow, but those who have had dealings with him come away the poorer, both in the state of their finances and in their spiritual well-being. He is a wealthy man and maintains that wealth through the activity of his slave vessels. These vessels trade between Africa and the West Indies. They are renowned for the violence and cruelty of their captains and crew. Poor unfortunate devils taken from their home and family are traded. They are lucky to survive the ocean voyage. He is a gambler, known as a cheat and will relieve unsuspecting and gullible fools of their wealth at the slightest provocation, which is then wasted on debauchery of every kind."

Peter listened intently as Tom continued.

"Now you mentioned a second name."

"Yes, the second name is Captain, now I believe Colonel Henry West."

"I have heard he is a companion of March and a fellow gambler. That pair are ever involved in any nefarious deed, which will gain them the capital to continue a life of gaming and licentiousness. They have been banned from the Kit-Cat Club for cheating at cards, as well from Wisbourne's and most of the houses in Drury Lane."

Peter was confused. He did not know the names bandied about by Pitt.

"What is Wisbourne's and houses in Drury Lane and the Kit Kat Club? What are these places?"

"I forgot you are unschooled in the flesh pots of London. Although you are a man, you are still an untried boy where London is concerned.

Wisbourne's is a brothel, the best in London, run by Mother Whybourn. You should try it sometime. Drury Lane is the home of many of the lesser houses and the Kit-Cat Club is the most exclusive gaming club in all of England. Your friends have worn out their welcome in London society."

"All this does not explain why I should be taken and sent to sea."

"I will enquire further. If at all possible, I will return here with what information I can glean. If not, a messenger will bring a note with whatever I can discover. Tomorrow I will be away to Cornwell to place myself before Lady Hester, as a candidate for her hand in marriage. Be here at 10 this very night"

Pitt rose suddenly, shook Peter by the hand and strode out of the Prince of Wales Coffee House.

It was already late when Pitt left. There seemed no sense in leaving only to return in a couple of hours. He dined lightly and the time passed swiftly. He engaged in conversation with men of the sea, men who had made this establishment their place of relaxation. Peter took this opportunity to sound out the possibility of purchasing a vessel and the most advantageous method of attaining a good captain and crew. The fellows to whom he spoke would not have passed the time of day with him just a short time ago. He marveled at the change in attitude brought about by fashionable clothes and the appearance of money. It was well after 10 before Pitt finally returned and threw himself into the empty seat across from Peter.

"Waiter, bring me a pint of porter and something to eat." Pitt appeared tired as he continued. "I have some news for you."

"I cannot thank you enough Tom, whatever you can disclose will place me in your debt forever."

"Have no mind of that. The fellows whose names you gave me, Frederick March and Henry West, they have been compatriots for years. As I mentioned earlier they have a reputation as rogues of the lowest order, preying on those of a superior class. I was correct when I said before that March maintains vessels, which transport poor unfortunate devils, plucked from their homes and family, sold as slaves and sent from Africa to the West Indies. His vessels are the vilest hellholes imaginable. West Is repudiated by his family and at one time was but a hairsbreadth from prison. It is here where you come into the picture. He escaped debtor's prison by marriage. He married the daughter of a wealthy Norfolk family. A distant cousin, I am informed. A generous settlement and I believe some dubious business dealings have kept him in financial comfort these last five years."

"I don't understand. How am I involved?"

"West was under the impression you and the young lady, to whom he was distantly related and he had set his sights to marry, were betrothed. My informant tells me, because of your youth and religious leanings he could not challenge you to a duel, so he had you pressed and the person best suited to arrange this was Frederick March. You were rendered unconscious. Then taken on a channel cutter to *Discovery* as it lay off Start Point. The owner of this cutter was also Frederick March. It was assumed you would not survive the voyage."

Peter sat speechless. All became obvious. The years he had endured now became clear. He had been removed by March to smooth the way for Henry West to marry Jane Sawtell. He found it difficult to understand the thinking behind it all. Peter was speechless. West had married her to gain financially and thereby escape debtor's prison.

"I am told Colonel West, as he is now ranked, has become commander of excise men on the coast south of the Thames estuary. He is, in conjunction with March, holding those who would smuggle goods from France to ransom. He will turn a blind eye to those who will pay him; all others are taken. March's vessels have access free and clear; all profits pertaining are divided equally between them. I have it on excellent authority he is being closely watched and will be soon taken into custody."

"How did you acquire this information? What is your source? I find it hard to swallow that any man could take advantage of one as sweet and gentle as Jane. We have been as brother and sister and still the same feeling prevails between us; although I see her now as I have never before. She is beautiful and in fact quite ravishing in a way I had not considered. I find it hard to believe an officer of the crown could stoop so low. West has desecrated her trust in the vilest manner. Tell me, what is the source of this information, is it reliable?"

"Lord Grenville, Foreign Secretary of England, my guardian and I hope, brother-in-law to be. He still has a regard for me despite the turmoil I seem to attract. Let me warn you Peter Wright, these are dangerous men. They will stop at nothing to have their way. I am informed smuggling in the area under the command of West continues unabated, despite the fact bodies of murdered known men are constantly found, and those who do not fall in with the plans of these rogues are taken. They languish in prison as we speak. West, March and their cohorts in high places share the profits of their actions. It will all fall about them quite soon."

"Where can I find these two?"

"Take my advice; leave it to the authorities, who as we speak are making their way to apprehend these fellows. Already a Member of Parliament who is involved has fallen. It is but a matter of hours before the whole affair comes crashing about their heads."

"I feel cheated. For all the years spent at sea one thought kept my sanity intact. I lived to be revenged on March. Now they are to be taken, which cuts me out."

Tom Pitt rose. He shook Peter by the hand.

"I must be off now, take care Peter Wright. Live your life as it is now. Forget the past. If these fellows were not about to come to their just deserts, I would help you in your quest. My blood fires at such an obvious fraud and ungentlemanly action against a youth and a young gentle girl. I will see you again; wish me luck with Lady Hester. She is a woman after my own heart."

With these words, Thomas Pitt was away.

For a time Peter sat deep in thought. It was not the actions of March and West that occupied his mind, but thoughts relating to Jane. It seemed he no longer saw her as a sister. He began to experience feelings new and strange. At almost 26 years, Peter, for the first time experienced the dizziness of first love and he did not recognize it.

Peter rose and made his way out into the cool foggy night. The cold air after the heat of the Prince of Wales and the liquor consumed had a staggering effect on him. He wavered for a moment, his mind confused and in turmoil. He brushed away the beggars and the women of the night. The feel of a hand groping into his pocket caused him to lash out, sending the pickpocket flying headlong to the pavement. By the time, he reached the Boyd residence his head had cleared.

He had decided on his future. Now he would purchase a suitable trading vessel; he was wealthy and could easily arrange it. Sir James had shown interest when he had first broached the subject. He would make use of his time at sea, he would use his newfound knowledge of the North American coast to trade and do business in that vast untouched wilderness. First he would look to Frederick March and Henry West if only to calm his feelings of anger and outrage at their treatment of Jane and himself. As he walked the feeling that disturbed him most and set his heart aflutter, was a desire to see Jane and be with her.

37
Henry West's Life has Ended

Lady Sarah Parkinson left the residence on Montague Street quite early, leaving Jane and Gwen to their own devices. It was raining gently and constantly, the first showers of the winter to come fell quietly. It saturated the countryside and those whose business took them outside. In this more affluent area, it was not uncommon to see that new invention, the umbrella, carried by gentlemen making their way towards the city. Of course, no woman of class would dream of venturing out onto the muddy streets of London on a day such as this.

Jane and Gwen sat together near the fire. Jane continued to school Gwen and today they had been reading from one of the many morning newspapers and gazettes and periodicals, which seemed to increase daily in the modern London. Lady Sarah subscribed to a considerable number of these publications. It had become an every day part of Gwen's study regime that they read, understand and discuss topics of general interest. Lady Sarah, who had become quite interested in the education of Gwen, felt any person with an interest in charitable work and good government should keep abreast of all events occurring, both in parliament and across the land.

Gwen could now read and understand all the articles and publications placed before her. Jane had spent countless hours instructing Gwen in the English language and the Rules of Syntax and she had trained her in deportment and style. Jane discussed her plans to commence a school for young women. Gwen was entranced by the whole idea and the fact she too would be involved in the scheme. The relationship between them had progressed over the recent months. Both understood their situation. An appearance of propriety must to be maintained. Though they slept together and loved each other, polite society demanded that they must appear no more than mistress and companion. Aunt Sarah suspected a liaison of some type existed between the two, but she said nothing. She enjoyed the company of her young ladies and determined not to interfere in any way with their lives.

"Madam, there is a person who wishes to see you. I have left him at the door. He will not give a name. He insists he must speak with you immediately. I hesitate to admit him. His appearance leaves much to be desired, but he does appear to be a gentleman."

"Thank you Griffiths, I will come immediately."

"Who would this be Gwen? I was not expecting anyone. I'll see who it is and then we can continue with our studies."

Jane went to the door accompanied by Griffiths; at first, she did not recognize her husband. She saw an almost disreputable figure leaning tiredly against the portico sheltered from the rain.

"You wish to see me, sir."

The figure at the doorway started perceptibly and turned suddenly to face Jane

"My God. Henry. It is you. What has happened?"

The man who stood before Jane had no resemblance to the Henry West of old. Gone was the splendid uniform. The elegantly powdered and pomaded hair was replaced by limp wet strands, which hung about his lined face. His boots were caked with mud and his civilian clothes wet, stained and torn. As he stood, stooped in near exhaustion, he deposited a pool of water on the tiles of the entranceway.

"Henry, what has happened to you?" Jane was aghast at the appearance of her husband.

"Thank you Griffiths, I know this man, I will be all right now."

"I am on his Majesty's business. I have been in dangerous situations since I last saw you, my dear." At Jane's appearance Henry raised himself up to his full height. Again, he presented the bearing of a military man.

"I am engaged on a mission, my whereabouts must not be known, my dear. I must have money to continue my work. How much do you have in the house?"

For a moment, Jane was speechless. She was filled with confusion. Her selfless gentle nature demanded that she to take him in her arms and soothe his obvious distress. She was torn between the duties of a wife to her husband and the knowledge she now had regarding Henry and his activities. These feelings saw her torn between duty and loyalty, as opposed to that which was in the best interest of her new life.

Henry came to her as they moved into the salon. He took her in his arms and attempted to kiss her. Jane turned her head away from his embrace.

"Henry, please stop. Stop it."

"Come my dear, it has been so long. I have missed you and longed for your touch. We have so much time to make up. My nights have been lonely and long, but now I am returned to take my rightful place as head of my household."

Jane broke away from him and moved to a place where a table stood between her and her husband.

"Henry, please, you must not carry on with your lies any longer. I am completely aware of what you have been doing. I know all about your reason for marrying me. I also know you were instrumental in sending one who was no threat to you at all to sea, thereby putting his very life in danger and making his every day a misery. I cannot forgive you for that. He is back now, no longer the boy but a man, tall and strong, ready to wreck vengeance on those who heaped such an injustice upon him. I would not want to be in your shoes if he ever catches up with you. How could you be so devious Henry? What infuriates me most of all is the way you treated my father. I also know you have been continuing to use the finances set aside for a company, which I believe does not even exist."

Henry staggered at her words, completely taken back by the strength of Jane's remarks. He had never considered it of great importance what she knew or thought. He knew eventually he would be uncovered, but always assumed it a matter of small Import His greatest shock was the fact Peter Wright had survived. He realized he should have taken the advice of Frederick Marsh and killed the fellow.

"Madam, I am your husband and as such you will bow to my wishes. I am head of my household."

Jane did not stop; she took no notice of him and continued as though he had not uttered a word.

"You have financed your deeds by the good will of my father. Hear me Henry, it is all finished now, I have stopped any financial dealings with the sugar plantation, the account is closed and dissolved. It is all over Henry. I know of the criminal acts you have engaged in over the last months. I know it all."

Henry stood, mouth agape, speechless as Jane continued.

"As for being head of your household, hear this. You are head of your household but not of mine. Measures have been taken, which has placed all I have out of the reach of any that would take advantage of me. Your household is all that is yours."

The words and sentiments coming from this youthful beauty staggered Henry. He did not recognize the young girl he had so deceitfully married and used.

"Tell me the truth, you have been discovered by the authorities, haven't you?"

Henry thought for a moment; he understood the predicament in which he found himself. He contemplated bluffing it out, but on reflection and faced with the strength Jane exhibited, he decided to throw himself on her mercy and the good nature he knew her to possess.

"I am in desperate trouble Jane. I am undone. There is no one else to turn to. I need help. As my wife you are bound to assist me. It is your duty to me."

For the first time in his life, Henry was unsure of himself. His normal bravado had deserted him and he hesitated to continue. The reality of his desperation was not lost on the astute young lady standing before him.

"I have not been truthful to you. I have never been fully truthful to you. I must leave England immediately. I do not know how to explain to you all that has befallen me. Suffice to say I need your assistance. I must leave for a few weeks; my business dealings demand it. I have resigned my commission and I...."

As before, Jane cut him short.

"Stop it, Henry. I know everything. Now is the time for us to be truthful for the last time.

I am fully aware of the smuggling, the gambling and the women. I know your family had cast you away before you ever married me. Tell me the truth."

Henry could see there would be no sympathy for him if he continued in his present manner.

"All right Jane, I will tell you everything. Perhaps you can find it in your heart to forgive me. If I do not get away and am caught, I will more than likely be executed for crimes against the Crown. I throw myself on your mercy. What we have been to each other must count for something. There is nothing I can say or do to make up for what I have done. I have been caught pilfering the King's excise. I did not for one moment realize I was being watched." Henry hung his head.

"They came in the early hours of the morning, my own uncle and a group of soldiers. They took me from my bed. While they were searching the place, I managed to strike my guard and made my escape through a secret, hidden passageway into Romney Marsh. As I came into the marsh, I heard the shouts and the call for my capture. I had killed the fellow who was my guard and am now wanted for murder as well as treason. I must escape the country or I am a dead man." Henry slumped into a chair, head buried in his hands. "I am so tired Jane, I must sleep."

Jane stood silently staring at her husband, completely at a loss to know how to handle the situation. Her mind was in turmoil and speech would not come. What was she to do? Looking at this pathetic person who bore little or no resemblance to her husband of old, natural pity, which had always been one of her most charming traits, began to assert itself in her mind. She closed the door.

"This is the home of my aunt Lady Sarah Parkinson. There are servants and retainers here, all of whom would question your appearance, must less your presence. Henry, how could you?"

Henry West raised his head, with bloodshot, tired eyes he stared at Jane. He was at his end and he finally realized he could expect little from her. As he observed her beauty and style, he saw the loss of a prize, which had been his for the taking. He knew and understood love for one other than himself. This woman, his child wife was lost forever, a treasure never to be regained.

"Henry I will help you. Let me look out into the hall. I believe the servants are in the lower apartments. Come along with me." Jane hurried Henry upstairs to her room. "Wait here, I will get some clean clothes and return in a moment. Jane returned in a few minutes with clothing and a bottle of brandy.

"Here are some clean clothes. They should fit; they belonged to my uncle who is now deceased. Come now Henry, a shave and I will do your hair. Give me your boots and I will clean them and here, I think you need a brandy to bolster your spirits. Rest here in my bed"

Henry slept deeply for some hours until Jane woke him.

"Come Henry you must be away." Jane shook her husband awake. "It is time for you to go."

He roused from the deepest of slumbers. For a moment he did not know where he was but then it all came flooding back.

"Jane there is nothing I can say to justify my actions." Henry saw a new Jane and realized his only chance was to throw himself on her mercy and good nature. "I have not been truthful with you, but now all must come out. I did marry you for money, but believe me I came to love you."

"Come now Henry, how could you love me and at the same time behave so poorly to my family and deceive me so dreadfully?"

"Jane, with you I came the nearest I ever could to loving one person. I could not stand the constriction and the boredom of a place like Burnham; I found it necessary to do the things I did to keep myself sane in that country atmosphere, but those wonderful nights with you. I will never forget them as long as I live. Yes Henry, you educated me in the ways of love and I too loved you, I still do. You were the first and only man in my life. Come now dress yourself, let me see the Henry of old."

Henry shaved and dressed, and with Jane's help he again displayed a little of the swagger of the past.

"Tell me what plans have you made. There is absolutely nothing I can do. I cannot place this household in jeopardy, so you must go. Here is all I can lay my hands on at this time, £200. Take it Henry."

"Jane, what can I say? This money will get me to France and from there I will make my way to Lisbon. I will go to Devon; there is a packet there, which will take me across the Channel. My military experience can be of use in the East. There are countries, which crave the expertise of the British Army, and I have a contact who assures me I will be welcomed in the army of a particular Moroccan potentate. Tell me my dear, did you really love me?"

"Yes Henry I did and I imagine I still do. The days when you were away were like an eternity for me. The loneliness, the longing, it was more than I could stand. Now all that is at an end. You have been a fool and destroyed yourself, along with our love and life together. You must go Henry; take my love with you and try to survive. Come now I will take you out by the rear entrance into the laneway; it leads to old London; here you will be more hidden. Tell me one thing. Frederick March, is he involved in your present plans?"

"Yes. We are partners in all that has passed."

"And are you going to meet him. Will he aid you in escaping the country?"

"Yes Jane he is my only friend and the one man I can trust implicitly. He will be waiting for me in the fishing village of Plymstock. I tell you this with the knowledge it will go no further. There I will board one of Frederick's packets and make my way to France."

Henry rose, he drew Jane to him and they kissed. For a moment Jane felt all the old excitement and desire, she knew Henry felt the same. She began to kiss him again drawing him to her. Suddenly she stopped; her inner voice had alerted her. Like her mother, Jane possessed an attribute, which had served the female side of her family through the generations past. It was indisputable and stronger than reality; hers was the understanding of what was best for her. It precluded all her feelings, it told her what to do. She instinctively knew the part Henry West had played on the stage of her life was ended.

"Come with me Henry, be on your way and God bless you. Our life together is over."

Two weeks passed before Jane heard the news of the death of Henry West. Sir Thomas Purcell of the Home Office dined at the home of Lady Sarah Parkinson. In the course of the evening, Sir Thomas voiced his concern at the vast amount of revenue lost to smugglers on the East Coast. He mentioned how in the course of his duties, he had informed the Earl Marshal of England, His Grace the Duke of Norfolk of the fact a Colonel Henry West had been shot and killed. He told of the warrant issued for crimes against the state and murder. How on the south road, just a mile from the fishing village of Plymstock, acting on information received, authorities had waited near an inlet just north of the town, where smugglers frequently unloaded contraband from the continent. West was apprehended hiding in the low gorse, which clung tenuously to life on the cliffs of the windswept coastline. He died resisting arrest while waiting for a craft to take him to France; a vessel, which never appeared.

Jane heard this news and it was with amazing self-control that she constrained herself and gave no outward appearance of the turmoil deep within her breast.

38

Peter Experiences Feelings of Doubt and Jane Discloses Her Secret

"A letter. By messenger, it's for you, Peter."

"Who is it from, Harry?"

"Don't know old boy. There is a crest in wax on the seal so it must be important. I can make out "ter ardua libert." I was never any good at Latin, Peter. What does it mean?"

"I'm a bit rusty at this sort of thing, haven't used it in years; something about thrice, steep and liberty. I think."

Peter Wright lounged before the fire and felt good about things. He had been accepted into the Boyd household. He was considered family and if the truth were known, Sir James Boyd was delighted to see the return of Peter. He considered him a calming influence on his son Harry. Sir James knew Harry liked Peter and now Peter, who had matured well beyond his years, displayed a degree of style, which had already begun to influence the Honourable Harry Boyd. Peter caught the letter thrown towards him.

"It's from our friend Camelford. Tom Pitt has sent us an invitation. Seems we are invited to a boxing match tomorrow night. Wimbledon Common, a match between the fighting Jew, Elias Bitten and Tom "Paddington" Jones. What do you think Harry? Shall we go? And here is some news; he tells me there will be a gentleman, for want of a better word, in attendance that will be of interest to me. If I still wish to meet the bounder who had me dispatched to sea, he will be there with his master Frederick March."

Of late, he had begun to relax under the gentle influence of the Boyd household and to quell the ghosts of his past. Now, suddenly, these specters returned in full force to haunt him.

In his mind, he again saw the tall heavily set man and the lions head cane suspended, just before it crashed down on his temple. He recollected the words, which had plagued him all these years. Now the opportunity had been placed into his hands to be redressed for the wrongs done to him. How to handle this unexpected state of affairs? While he seethed inside at the recollection of his past, he also had some new misgivings. His youthful upbringing had steered him along the gentle paths of love and forgiveness, the last six years until the present had been one of survival, trial and tribulation. Now he was a wealthy man with new aims and ideas. He was about to set himself on a new tack, which would be his future life. Did he need requital on the fellow who had hit him and Frederick March, who had arranged it?

He knew of the death of Henry West. Jane had told him of the last meeting with her now deceased husband. He also was well aware March had been involved in the deceit and treachery, which had sent West to his death.

Peter took little notice of Harry chattering away, excited at the thought of attending such a famous boxing event in the company of Lord Camelford.

Peter sat quietly, showing little of the turmoil within. Should he continue to pursue his revenge or should he forget about the wrongs done? Perhaps he would just let these fellows know they were discovered and leave it at that.

"Oh I say what a good show. We are invited as Pitt's guests. Marvelous. Just marvelous. What do you think Peter. We will go of course. I will bet on Paddington, of course I will, he will beat that Fighting Jew any day. Oh I cannot wait, when is the day? Peter, you're not taking any notice at all of what I am saying, aren't you in the least bit excited?"

For the first time since childhood, Peter felt the need to confide in someone. He needed help to place his thoughts in some kind of context. He considered the ramifications of a confrontation with these fellows. He searched his mind, was he up to the task; did he need to do anything? Now the moment for redress was almost at hand he felt feelings of fear.

His last years were behind him. Now he was faced with a decision. One voice told him to walk away and take pleasure in his life. He should enjoy his newfound wealth and stature. The question, must he face two men, one a ruthless renegade making a considerable living preying on the unsuspecting and the other a villain who had had no hesitation dispatching him to his fate. Harry was brave and relentless in normal circumstance, but he would not be much use in a brawl where life itself could be the prize, nor could he help Peter with his private thoughts. It was he alone, who must direct his future actions. For now, he needed an ear to hear his uncertainty. He must turn to someone. Sir Neville Brown was out of the question. Time did not allow a journey to Kings Lynn. There was only one other he could rely on here in London. Jane would hear him, the only other who would listen, not as an acquaintance but as a friend and confidant. His decision was immediate; he knew she would know what course he should take. He would go to her and lay all his fears and uncertainty before her. Yes, that is what he would do. Peter also had another problem. It was a strange and unnerving ache deep in his heart; it was a longing and a sickness he could not explain. Had he been a more experienced fellow he would have recognized it immediately as the first stages of love.

Peter Wright walked to the home of Lady Parkinson. As he strolled through the streets, he took no notice of the hustle and bustle or the throngs milling about him. The hurly-burly of every day life in the London of the late 18th century completely escaped his notice. The hour was early especially for a gentleman of means. The sun made its watery way into the morning sky, it was not cold nor was it warm.

Although a relatively short distance separated the Boyd residence on Shaftesbury Avenue from Lady Parkinson's residence on Montague Street, Peter found himself meandering through the lanes and roads of working class London. Here muffled figures left grimy residences to pursue the day's work. Now he was in Cheapside and Fleet Street, here trades of all description were followed by poorly paid working men and women. The usual multitude of signs displayed and touted the handicraft being carried on in the dim recesses of the old and grimy buildings. All along these streets the industry and manufacturing might of London was supremely evident. Peter deep in thought did not notice the trade signs; nor did he not notice the people about him, vendors calling their wares, beggars pestering, sundry workers both male and female going to their place of drudgery. Even at this early hour, the roads were thronged with carts loaded with goods of every description. Sedan chairs, transporting those of a higher station jostled with pedestrian traffic. Weavers, cabinet-makers, tradesmen, were busy and occupied in the business of survival in this new London, the economic centre of the world.

Now he approached Drury Lane, where memories of his early days in a new city environment flooded back. He digressed to look at the place where he had been waylaid so many years before. The erection of buildings, which had been in progress around Alwych, was now complete and he could not find the lane where he had been so cruelly treated. He walked about the area. Where he thought it should be, a new building stood in the way, there was no dark lane-way to the Temple from Essex Street.

Peter found his way to Covent Garden. This had changed little since he last made his way down its busy streets. The playhouses were still there, even at this early hour the brothels, and gambling houses appeared busy. At every turn, some degenerate staggered out of a doorway after a night of obvious debauchery, to shield his eyes from the morning sun. Prostitutes both male and female accosted him at every turn and the fruit and vegetable mongers called out their best buys to already willing shoppers.

He crossed busy Holborn Street and made his way towards Bloomsbury Square, he passed St George's Church. Here in earlier days he had attended service with the Boyd family. Strange he thought how he had not entered a church since that time. As he walked out of Bury Street, He noticed the beginning of the construction of the newly proposed British Museum; new buildings overwhelmed the area, which before had been the dilapidated dwellings of the poorer workers of London.

For a moment, he hesitated before the elegant residence of Lady Parkinson. He was not sure what he wanted to say to Jane, he knew the fear he felt at confronting the men who had had such a bearing on his life. All he needed was some reassurance. Jane was the closest to family in London and now this feeling of anticipation and longing, which intensified by the mere mention of her name. Peter grasped the ring hanging from the shining brass jaws of a lion. He heard the chime deep in the recesses of the house.

Peter expected a butler or some other male retainer to answer the door. The door opened and he was surprised to see an exceptionally elegant, young, dark-haired woman.

"Good morning, madam. Is this the residence of Lady Sarah Parkinson and the home of Mrs. Jane West?" Peter was completely taken aback by the most unusual sight of a woman, elegant and obviously of class, opening the door and for a moment he was unsure if his memory had not served him well.

"Yes, sir, indeed it is. Whom shall I say is calling?"

"My name is Peter Wright and I am here to call on Mrs. West."

"If you will come into the library sir, I will inform Mrs. West of your presence."

Peter watched the young woman leave the room. Her dress was simple, a morning gown. A type of peignoir in fine cashmere, opened in a V shape to the waist revealing a corset tied with ribbons and belted with a jeweled buckle above her shapely hips. The change in the pattern of fabric did not mean much to Peter, but one more schooled in the mysteries of women's fashion would immediately have known her dress was of the latest Parisian cut. Her abundant, black, wavy hair severely arranged in a compact neat style, displayed a fashionable hand well beyond his experience.

Peter had no experience of any concourse between the sexes. Perhaps the trauma of the past six years had left him bereft of normal affectionate feelings for any other than those nearest him. He felt great affection for Neville Brown, the only remaining connection to his youth and deceased family, apart from Jane. It was with some trepidation, Peter found himself completely taken by the manner and style of Gwen Pratt as she left the room to inform Jane of his presence.

He looked about the room and was sure the young lady had called it the library. For one of a literary bent, it was obvious a lot more was carried on here than the quiet pursuits of reading and contemplation. There were shelves of books on two walls, which gave the room its only claim as a place of study. At one end stood a spinet, lid closed and strewn with music, papers and well-thumbed books. Beside each chair, a small table was piled high with incomplete work of a feminine nature, knitting, crochet and frames with half-completed petit-point. Everything about the room spoke of a retreat reserved purely for ladies, a place where they could be themselves and take their leisure. All was silent in the house as Peter stood browsing through a book of coloured prints depicting scenes of rural happiness in a picturesque sylvan setting. He was not aware of Jane's approach. Suddenly she was behind him.

"Peter my dear, how wonderful to see you and so early. I will get cook to prepare some breakfast and we can have it together. I am delighted to see you." Jane did not wait for an answer; she immediately pulled a bell cord beside the fireplace. In a few moments, a grey haired woman appeared and Jane issued her request for breakfast.

"Would you please prepare breakfast for three, we will take it in the small dining room. Thank you dear. Yes, Gwen will join us. Now Peter, what a surprise to see you; come let us sit."

Jane selected what was obviously her chair out of the three in the room. Peter remained standing. At the appearance of Jane, Peter felt all the tremors and fluttering of a lovesick youth.

"Jane you should not have gone to the trouble of breakfast. I must speak with you on a matter serious to me and in a way just as important a concern to you.

Jane saw Peter was troubled. His normally clean-shaven face displayed the dark shadow of one that had seen fit not to attend to his morning toilet.

She liked what she saw and if Peter had some inner secret knowledge relating to the ways of women, he would have known that the same fluttering of heart that assailed him, also assailed the beauty seated before him.

"Jane I don't know where to begin. Tom Pitt has given me the opportunity to confront the swine who sent me away. What should I do? I need your advice."

Jane understood immediately, this was not a social call.

"Peter, come sit near me." Jane gestured towards the chair beside her. "What do you mean? Are you going to challenge these two?

"I must tell you I am frightened. These are vicious people and I wonder if I am up to the task. To face and accuse them, I don't think I want to do it, but in my mind I feel I must."

Peter told Jane the history relating to his association with Tom Pitt. He explained how he had asked Pitt, through his connections in high places to seek out March and now he had the opportunity to settle the score with those who had changed both their lives. He unburdened himself, pouring forth the uncertainty of his future, his sadness at the death of his parents, his anger at the circumstances that had prevented him being of comfort to them in their last moments. He told her of the structure and discipline he had experienced in the navy. He told her of his initial confusion at the attitude of his fellow sailors who accepted punishment as long as it was just and fair, but later how he came to realize there was no assistance for them. The slightest mistake would render them castaways in a most desolate savage country, without hope of aid or succor. He confessed his fear of the two men who he must now face. He told her of his hopes for the future and his plan to purchase a suitable vessel and enter into merchant trading along the coast of the Pacific Northwest.

"Jane you have never seen such a wonderful country. Beautiful beyond compare, rich in every resource known to man, with gentle inhabitants, children of nature living in complete harmony with their surroundings. I feel there is opportunity here for the taking, but first I must put my past behind me. We have both lost our youth and our families; in this, our life has been strangely conjoined. We both have fallen prey to the same villains. You, dear Jane, are the closest person to me in the world. I look on you as my dearest and closest friend. What should I do?"

"Peter, how destiny plays its tricks on us all, I think I understand your feelings. I cannot sanction anything that will place you in harm's way. My husband is dead, whether his enemies are brought to justice or to punishment is of little concern to me. All that came to Henry he brought on himself. I do fear for you and I would say to you, do not go and look for these people, forget the wrongs done to you, that is my advice and I hope you will take it with all my love and affection."

"Jane, please excuse my intrusion. Mrs. Scully has prepared breakfast and it is served in the small dining room." Gwen spoke from the door surprising both Jane and Peter, but especially Peter by her familiarity.

"Oh thank you, Gwen dear, we will be along presently. Come Peter let us eat and then we can continue our discussion, I must introduce you to one who has become as dear to me as life itself. Come along."

Jane rose and led Peter towards a room off the main hallway, large and furnished in severe style, dark heavy beams, heavy tapestries, paneled wainscoting and a long Queen Anne table with twelve chairs. It was a distinguished room, which for want of a better name had become known as the small dining room. A long dark sideboard stood on the west wall facing the small paned windows, which looked out to a well-tended garden at the rear of the house. The sideboard, Elizabethan in design and obviously quite old, appeared to stagger beneath its burden of silver tureens, dishes of all sizes, cutlery, bowls of fruit and flowers. Two large candelabra were thick with yellow bee's wax flowing down to cover a silver pedestal in swirling mounds.

"Peter, I want you to meet my dearest companion. Gwen is the most precious person and is dear to me above all others."

The three sat together at the long table. Jane informed Peter of the circumstances of their relationship and her tutelage of Gwen over the years, although she did not enlarge on the deep feelings of love and desire now consummated between them. Peter marveled at the idea of their proposed school for young women, he could see the determination both the women had for this project. He encouraged them in every way to carry out their convictions. He told them of his plans and when he mentioned the thought of a merchant vessel, Jane excitedly suggested they might become partners of a sort. She suggested because of her vast fortune, she would invest financially, with the idea being implicit that it would be as a silent partner. Peter thought for a moment on this and then excitedly agreed. Considering the relationship, they had had over the years, the mutual financial advisors both shared and the strange state of affairs, both thought it provident to engage in a common venture.

"Jane, I know we spoke briefly of this, but I must approach another and more troublesome pressing matter."

Discovery

Gwen who had been taking in all the excitement generated by these two made a move to leave.

"I will leave you to discuss your private matters."

"No Gwen, please stay. Peter I hold nothing secret from my dear Gwen; we share in everything and are devoted to each other. I must tell you, that without dear Gwen I would never have been able to cope with these last years. We are more to each other than mistress and servant. We are partners in life and are complete confidants each to the other. So please, continue Peter my dear." Jane had moved beside Gwen and had taken her hand.

Peter looked at the two seated across from him. He noted the glance, which passed between them. He saw a soft knowing smile and he was confused. He was not sure of what they spoke, or more to the point of what remained unspoken. Peter had grown to a fine stalwart man, but where the opposite sex was concerned, he was a complete neophyte. His adventurous years at sea had made him resilient in most conditions. In the company of the two beautiful women in which he now found himself, he was all at sea again, lost in a situation the likes of which he had never experienced.

"Let us talk more of your ideas and the vessel which we partners will be purchasing."

"Jane, there is nothing yet to tell. All I have done is talk to acquaintances in the Prince of Wales Coffee House, an establishment frequented by men of the sea. It is my desire to employ only those who can assure me of their complete trustworthiness and regard for their fellow men whoever they may be. I would like in some way to redress the wrongs done to simple native people by unscrupulous traders, who take fine goods for less than quality merchandise."

"My dear Peter, that is a fine sentiment and I am wholly behind you in your aim. Since Gwen and I have come to London, through the auspices of my Aunt Sarah, I have met people who are distressed by the state of our society and the plight of prisoners and workers here in our own country. The excellent Mr. William Wilberforce speaks well on this matter. Another cause dear to my heart is the despicable practice by some of our fellow countrymen of taking people, both men and women, of the Negro race and selling them as slaves. It is my understanding these people are subjected to the most foul treatment and conditions in our erstwhile colonies of America."

Peter listened intently as Jane continued, warming to her subject.

"There are people here in our own lands that make their fortune from this horrible practice. I have become familiar with a group, those who have devoted all their resources and time to eradicating this blot on our society."

"Why Jane and you Gwen, I am amazed at the scope of your activities. I am very impressed you should be involved in such a cause. It is one I would support wholly."

Jane continued to speak of her friendship with certain people and groups who are doing great things to abolish this scourge. Jane rose and went to a cabinet, she returned to Peter handing him a medallion.

"Look at this; it was produced by Mr. Wedgewood."

Peter took the item and saw a medallion with the legend, *Am I not a man and a brother?* This sentiment embossed clearly above a chained blackamoor slave.

"I know the man Frederick March is a slave trader. He needs to be shown the error of his ways and brought to the realization all men and women must be equal in every way. If you are inclined Peter, you could be the instrument of this man's redemption."

"My dear Jane, from my experience of this fellow and my past life at sea, I fear our friend March and mankind in general are not ready to lead a life of a more gentle nature. I fear the violence I have witnessed, both to others and myself, is pandemic in our land. Even the children of nature in the northwest have learned to keep slaves and carry on war with their brothers without any assistance or instruction from us of European extraction. I do not know if I am made of the right stuff to be a crusader." Peter thought for some moments before continuing, "I will go to this encounter as arranged by Lord Camelford. Heaven only knows what will be the outcome of it. So, dear Jane and Gwen, wish me luck for I am sure I will need it."

Peter rose and began to make his way to the foyer. Gwen said goodbye to Peter. She curtseyed graciously before him. Jane accompanied Peter, leaning on his arm as they walked. They congratulated themselves on their proposed business arrangements and the success of their merchant vessel partnership. Jane was sorry she could not be of more help in imbuing Peter with the courage he needed to redress his wrongs. Both agreed they would contact Sir William Boyd and make the initial necessary financial arrangements to embark on their mutual venture.

Peter was completely confused as to the relationship between Jane and Gwen. He sensed, without words being spoken theirs was a deeper companionship than anything he had ever experienced. As they approached the foyer of the Parkinson home, Peter almost questioned Jane. He noticed how they held hands at every opportunity; he observed furtive touches between them, but most of all it was the deep and knowing glances. Peter held his tongue, for in reality he did not have the worldly experience to know what to ask. Jane clasped him to her and she lifted her face to receive his kiss.

Peter left the home of Lady Parkinson. The sun was high but the weather cool. His conversation with Jane had helped him make up his mind to pursue Frederick March and his henchman. He thought on the glances, which had passed between Jane and Gwen. He was also confused by the kiss, which Jane had unreservedly bestowed on him. As he walked in the afternoon sun, he reflected with some excitement on their parting. Was it only his imagination abetted by the fires of youth? However, while he had kissed Jane, as a brother should, he was sure he had detected a velvet tip and the full pressure of her beautiful body pressed close against his. At this time, other deeper considerations filled his mind and he determined to put this distraction from his thoughts and summon all his courage to face his enemies and put his demons to rest.

It was after the Boyd household had retired for the night that Peter, in a sleepless and agitated state, repeatedly thought he felt Jane's velvet kiss. It was almost dawn before he fell into a disturbed slumber.

39

Peter Meets His Nemesis and a Duel is Conjoined

"Come along, Peter. I say old chap, how long will you take to be ready? I am sure my sisters would take less time to dress than you would. If I didn't know better I would swear you don't want to go."

"Well, Harry, I doubt your dear sisters would rush to prepare for the place we are off to this night."

"Well, of course you're right. But if they had a liking for the manly art of the Marquis of Queensbury, I'm sure they would be sitting waiting at least two hours ago as I have been."

Peter Wright and Harry Boyd bantered back and forth. Peter joined in the usual repartee, which had become part of their daily manner. Despite the banter and laughter, with Peter it was all a front. He knew society demanded he challenge his enemies and within he battled with his conscience, his upbringing screamed against violence and retribution, but the hour was at hand, he could no longer avoid his destiny, whatever it may be.

"All right, Harry, I'll be ready in a moment. I must shave."

Peter had tried to discuss his fears with Harry. Harry was born with a silver spoon in his mouth. He had attended the best of colleges and would eventually take over his father's business. Harry had a gentle nature and despite his privileged upbringing was sensitive and sympathetic to all, but he could never understand the depth of Peter's indecision.

"You are aware of the reputation of Pitt, aren't you Harry? You know he has earned some eminence as a duelist and fighter. He can be quite difficult to his friends and terrifying to his enemies. I know you have met him in the most serene time in his life. He is a man in love; I know he procures the excitement he craves by promoting and partaking in boxing matches. I can assure you since he has been associated with Lady Hester Stanhope he has been a complete saint. I shudder to think what will happen if they ever have a falling out."

"Yes I have heard of the duels he has fought, as well a few of his adversaries that did not show. My father insists I should cultivate a friendship with Lord Camelford for the influence he can bring to bear on my future, but he also suggests I should keep him at arm's length."

Harry sat on the edge of the table while Peter completed his toilet.

"Good advice, I should say. Tom has a generous nature, but God forbid you ever fall out with him. He is a wild fellow and I think he will eventually meet with disaster, and it will be most likely of his own making. There, I think that does it." Peter wiped his face with a towel and donned his shirt. "Come along Harry; let us get on our way."

The bout was to be held near the home of the notorious politician John Horne Took. His residence bordered on Wimbledon Common. Took had been supported by Lord Camelford when denied a seat in the House because of his near-conviction for high treason some years previously. Took and Camelford had remained friends ever since.

"This place we are going? My father would be most upset with me if he knew what we were doing. He does not in any way condone prize fighting and if he knew it was to be held on the property of John Took he would be furious."

"I must confess Harry; I know nothing of this person, what is it about him that so distresses your father?"

The two set off on their way. They rode side by side filling in the time with conversation. Harry informed Peter on parliament and contentious issues. He spoke of the support of John Took for the American colonists in their struggle for independence. He told Peter the details of how Took had been charged with high treason and acquitted. He explained the support of Took for the French Revolution and other contentious matters of the time.

"I understand he is something of a demagogue, but all believe he is a genuine lover of liberty, a scholar and I am told he has great personal charm. I hope it will be our lot to meet the fellow."

The journey was completely uneventful. They followed the King's Road and rested their horses before the rise of Putney Hill. By the time they arrived at the home of Took a huge crowd, more like an unruly mob, had assembled on the open heath.

"I say Peter, how exciting. I do not think I have ever seen such a mob. Nothing like the bouts we attended in London, aye. That fellow hanging up there has the best view I venture."

Harry gestured towards a gibbet. The grisly skeletal remains of the notorious highwayman Jerry Abershaw, hung as a reminder of the price of crime. For six years his bones, now sparsely covered by the remains of his tattered clothing had swayed in the breeze. Two hollow, vacuous eyeless holes stared disinterestedly from his clean picked skull, long sparse strands of still attached hair moved spectrally in the breeze, as he dispassionately surveyed the raucous crowd.

"Yes, I dare say. I am sure I would not want to change places with him though. Now all we have to do is find Camelford."

The field was awash with people from every walk of life. The sea of humanity milling about a roped area boasted every degree of pervert, libertine, miscreant and scallywag known to the season.

"It strikes me Harry that anything that looks like fighting is delicious to an Englishman. Put your purse in a safe place Harry or you will not have it more than five minutes. I venture to think there are many here who will one day be elevated to the heights attained by our underfed friend up there, or at best shipped to the netherworld of Port Jackson."

Harry and Peter made their way through the pickpockets, the dice games, hagglers, jugglers and sellers of bread and liquor. They glanced at balladeers and actors; they brushed off the dregs of society as sly hands found their way to private places in vain attempts to relieve them of their cash. The air seethed and pulsated to the strains of fiddles, hurdy-gurdies and singers. Over all, the call of bookmakers vied with the cheers of those closest to the arena. A preliminary contestant spat out a few teeth as his opponent stood over him, eager to continue the contest and inflict further punishment on his bloody fallen adversary.

"I see Camelford! There he is Peter, on top of that carriage over there."

Harry was beside himself with eagerness. The London fights were of no comparison to what transpired before him, it was beyond his wildest fantasies.

"Come along Peter, let's go over to Tom and tell him we're here. By God, it is so exciting. I wonder how long before Paddington and the Jew meet each other. Come along Peter; stop dragging back, old boy."

Despite his anxiety at the outcome of the afternoon, Peter was completely taken by the scene about him. Like the younger Harry, he too was mesmerized by the excitement and vigour of the moment. He saw many an unsuspecting gentleman relieved of his purse; he was completely taken by the people, the rich with their elegant dress and the poor in their shabby attire, co-mingled in mutual distrust, all with the same drive to see a brutal conflict between two brutal men.

Peter had no knowledge of the whereabouts of Frederick March and his man. March was completely unknown to him, though he found himself looking into the eyes of those who milled about, searching for the fellow responsible for his scars. He had decided to let the cards fall where they may. He would confront March as soon as he found him and give him a dressing down if that was all it took and if the scene resulted in a more violent outcome well that too would be up to the Gods. The unbridled, primitive atmosphere, the noise and tempo of the scene seemed to give him the degree of courage and resolve he found hard to muster in the company of his gentle London friends. He found himself fascinated by and entering into the spirit of the untamed, raw barbarity about him.

"Here Peter have a swig of this." Harry had also entered into the spirit of the moment. He had purchased a bottle from a vendor. "I don't know what it is. The fellow said it was rum from the West Indies. It tastes awful but it has a fine kick to it."

Peter took the bottle and downed a draught.

"Ah that's rum. I will tell you some fine tales about this wonderful stuff if I survive whatever is in the cards for me today."

The thought of dealing with March and company did not seem to hold the same fears, which had plagued him in gentle society. Peter was, in fact, completely taken up and thrilled by the whole scene. He felt the influence of the drink, which had provided him the courage to become a sailor. Of late, he had begun to detect a yearning for the life he had so recently left. He found the daily rounds of the coffee shops and the constant preoccupation with society beginning to wear thin. He longed for the adventure of his past years. As the crowd milled about him, the calls, shouts and cheers of the motley rabble, the smells and sounds of the performers, all influenced him, at that moment. He determined to pursue life in whatever form it came, with all its trials and joys.

Lord Camelford was standing on top of a coach, surrounded by an odd collection of elegantly dressed gentry and broken-nosed, swollen-faced practitioners of the manly art of self-defense. Over recent years, Pitt had become a renowned sponsor of boxing events and patron of promising young fighters. He was considered a first class man in the ring himself.

"Me Lord, sir. Here is my man, Knolly Butt. He is the best man in these parts. You could test him out yourself, sir." Another repeated a shouted invitation

"Lord Camelford, Toady Mac here, my men will take on any other, they have no regard for size and will give a fine account if you will but try them, sir." Still another, "My man has had no expense spared on him My Lord; raw eggs for the wind, raw beef for strength and to make him savage. This fellow will thrash either of Toady's fellows."

Camelford saw Peter and Harry mingling with the wild crowd; he leapt down from the top of the coach and pushed his way towards them, shoving away the pestering, shouting throng about him.

"You're here Peter, and you have Harry Boyd with you. Your man is near the centre over there." Pitt gestured in the general direction of the ring. "And he has his lackey with him."

"Tom, it is good to see you." Peter took the proffered hand, "But how will I know my man when I see him? I remember the face of the fellow who blasted my head, but I have never laid eyes on March."

"Come with me and I will point them out. I must enter the ring and announce the contestants." Pitt moved towards the site of the challenge, a square enclosure where posts were been driven into the grass and ropes strung about them. Here the crowd was at its thickest. Pitt ducked beneath the ropes and joined in conversation with those, already attendant in the square.

"There are your men, Wright. Those two near that corner, the fellow in the Jean de Bry coat and striped waistcoat. I have fulfilled my end, now it is up to you." Pitt gestured towards the opposite corner and immediately became engaged in the business of the bout.

Peter looked across the throng of shouting, excited people. He finally made out the figure indicated by Camelford. He saw a tall rakish fellow of dark complexion. His attire displayed the height of fashion, with padded shoulders, low-backed collar and tight waist and the tilt of his hat rendering him an easy man to spot. He used a quizzing glass disdainfully and affectedly to view those near him. His demeanour and manner set him aside from the motley crowd about him. Peter observed March, he was as expected. It was the fellow standing near March who occupied all Peters' attention. He was a tall, heavy-set, middle-aged man without any of the affectation of his companion. His dress was of the serviceable nature, which one would expect in trade.

As Peter watched March and his companion, the elder man had become engaged in a heated conversation with an equally stalwart fellow. Quite suddenly, he lashed out with his cane and struck his opposite number a hard blow to the side of the head. The recipient fell to the ground to be trampled

Discovery

on and ignored by the almost riotous crowd. It was not the savage action that struck Peter, it was the cane with the silver lion's head, the same implement that had rendered him unconscious all those years ago and used with the same ferocious abandon.

Cheers were raised and the call of *"here comes Paddington,"* the cries were taken up by the crowd to end in the chant of *"Paddington, Paddington, Paddington."* From another direction the cry, *"Bitton, Bitton, Bitton,"* was joined by the supporters of the Fighting Jew. The cheers, the call of wagers, the chants of supporters and the haze of dust raised by the milling crowd coupled with smoke from the cooking fires created a surreal scene of movement and sound. The spectacle of the two fighters accompanied by their seconds and bottle holders was lost on Peter Wright. He had found the fellow, the face, which had filled his dreams for so many years stood not fifty feet away.

"There he is Harry, there's the man who pressed me; there is the bastard who nearly killed me." Peter did not wait for any answer from Harry Boyd. He set off to force his way through the throng.

Lord Camelford now called for silence and announced the fighters, who were standing quietly, still clad in their greatcoats. Camelford's voice was lost to those not at the ringside. Peter heard nothing except the rushing of blood in his ears; perhaps it was the liquor that spurred him on. In his struggle to move to the other side of the arena, he was assailed both verbally and physically by the writhing mass of humanity, who made every effort to protect their hard-earned place closest to the contestants.

The Fighting Jew and Paddington Jones came at each other and exchanged their first blows. Peter saw none of the thrusts and parries as the two danced about each other. He did not see Bitten hit Jones flush on the beak, further spreading an already flat nose, nor did he see Jones catch Bitten flush in the mouth with a resulting flow of blood down and across his dancing frame. He did not hear the cheers at each blow or the groans of anguish from supporters whose man seemed to be on the losing side.

"You sir, are the bastard who struck me and near cost me my life." Peter was finally face to face with the man whose countenance had bedeviled and consumed his thoughts.

"I don't know you, get away from me." The man pushed Peter, thrust close by the surging crowd.

"I demand satisfaction sir, my second the Honourable Harry Boyd here beside me will call on you." Peter looked back to indicate Harry Boyd, but

Harry was nowhere to be seen.

Harry, caught by the frenzy of the crowd at the commencement of the bout struggled to regain Peter's side. He was firmly sandwiched between two overweight men, the ropes and the crowd behind. He struggled to no avail to extricate himself from the confining, pressing grasp of those about him.

"Get away from me if you know what's good for you. I don't know you."

Peter heard the words as he saw Harry's predicament and turned to face his man. All he saw was the lion's head glistening high above him. The crowd miraculously pushed back to create a space at the onset of the confrontation. Peter grasped the arm swinging the cane at his head and plucked it from his adversary. For a moment, the pair stood face to face, Peter holding the cane by its slender end.

It was obvious by his demeanour that this man had no fear of Peter much less any consequences brought about by his actions.

"Ill fix you right now. Get away from me."

Peter's adversary was a solid man whose face bespoke years of conflict and complete disregard for his fellow creatures. He had consigned hundreds of honest sailors to a terrible life at sea and his years on the slave vessels of Frederick March had left him with no regard for life. Here was a different and new situation. He found himself confronted by a man as well built, but much younger and stronger. He noticed Peter's tattooed hands and saw the scars on his face. For the first time he felt a tinge of concern.

Peter saw the fellow reach inside his coat and observed the steely glint of a pistol withdrawn from within. Instinctively, he swung with all his might, bringing the silver head down on the shoulder of his assailant. The crack of his breaking clavicle was clear and sharp above the cries of the crowd. At the same instant, the report of the fellow's pistol came loud and unmistakable, but the constraints of the man's coat caused him to fire down into his own groin. He dropped to the ground instantly, a sickly paleness sweeping across his face. He screamed in agony as he writhed in the dirt and mud of the crowd-trampled sward and quickly passed into unconsciousness. Peter stared in shock at the man lying still at his feet. Blood spreading across the grass confirmed the terrible wound, which would claim his life's vital fluid and his very existence.

The sound of the shot brought the fight to a complete stop. The contestants and the crowd centered their attention on the drama, which had taken precedence over all other matters. Peter stood quietly, the silver-headed cane still clasped firmly in his hand. He was shocked at the outcome. Frederick March, the unfortunate man's companion, bent to one knee and looked up.

"This man is dead and you have killed him, sir."

Lord Camelford intervened immediately.

"I witnessed this man shoot himself with his own pistol after attacking Mr. Peter Wright. See he still has his weapon in his grasp. I want all to bear witness to this occurrence."

Immediately a chorus of assents as to the incident came from those near by.

"Lord Stanhope here, my lord, I saw it all."

"I saw it all, sir. Mr. Tufton here, as witness, sir."

"I too sir. It was the man lying on the ground who fired the shot. John Oxford as witness, sir."

Camelford stood between Frederick March and Peter Wright. Around them, the crowd voiced their opinions, giving raucous advice and calling for the blood of anybody and everybody. Their entertainment had been interrupted and they demanded recompense.

March stood tall and straight and spoke in a quiet and deadly manner.

"Lord Camelford, I saw this fellow strike Harris with a cane and then I saw the man fall to the ground, dead. I see a murderer standing before me."

"I am not a murderer, the man shot himself. I would have challenged him, but he underhandedly tried to strike me with his cane and I have already had a taste of him and his cane." Peter brandished the weapon in his hand. 'The same swine now lying dead on the ground dealt me the scar about my eye."

"Lord Camelford, sir. Would you introduce me to this man, I cannot let the death of my associate go unanswered.

"Mr. Frederick March. Mr. Peter Wright." Camelford formally introduced the two.

"Here is my card sir; my seconds will call on your associate. That is if you have any."

Peter had no familiarity with the niceties of a society where formality must be observed even when the outcome could mean the injury or death of both parties.

"Harry do you have a card, will you act as my second?" Peter spoke to Harry who had finally extricated himself from his fleshy prison and now stood open-mouthed beside Peter.

"Why yes, yes I have." With trembling hand, he passed a card to March. "What do I do now?"

March snatched the proffered card and turned on his heel. He followed the body of his friend Harris, now being carried away from the arena by a couple of bystanders, coerced into service by March with the toss of a coin.

"Well young Harry, the seconds appointed by Mr. March will call on you and it is your duty to arrange a field of honour and act for your friend Mr. Wright." Camelford clasped Harry about the shoulder. "Don't worry Harry; I will explain it all to you. The one who has cause for worry is Peter Wright. Come on now lads, the side show is over, let the boxing match resume."

Immediately the match recommenced, the protagonists began to spar and dance, throwing punches each at the other. The crowd again began their roars of approval or dissension. Bitten and Jones pummeled each other unmercifully. The space where the altercation had occurred re-filled with bellowing screaming fans. The red stains, which marked the fatal spot, were soon trampled underfoot; within minutes, the fact a person had surrendered his life in the mud and dirt was completely obliterated.

"Peter, you killed the fellow. I can't believe it, you killed him."

"Harry, I did not kill him, he killed himself. For God's sake, pull yourself together, Harry."

"Now you have to fight a duel with this March fellow. In addition, I am your second. My father will be furious when he hears of this. I can hear him now, a duel, how could you be so stupid as to get involved in a thing like this? He will say, think of the family name and what your mother will say, it will kill her. Oh my goodness Peter, from now on my life will be a misery."

"Harry, do not worry about it. I am the one who has been challenged; I'm the one in trouble."

"Mother will have a heart attack when she hears it. And my father, oh my father, he can be quite a martinet when he has been roused. I know he will make my life a misery. I have never seen anything like it. You killed him."

"For God's sake, shut up Harry and let me think."

Peter had been listening to Harry's prattle all the way from Wimbledon Common to London. He felt relieved he had not been the sole reason for the death of the man he now knew as Harris. It was a case of pure self-defense. The unfortunate fellow really had shot himself; it would have been him shot at close range if he had not defended himself with the cane. Peter had no apprehensions on the score of recrimination in law; the witnesses were all of note and friends of Camelford. Peter marveled at the strange twist of fate, which had now set him on another course. It was not going as he had imagined. As the mounted pair trotted along the Kings Road towards London, Peter's thoughts slowly came into focus. He decided another visit to Lord Camelford was in order, who else to advise him on the matter but the most notable and deadly of duelists in all Britain.

"Well Harry it seems to be well arranged. The second representing March is Mr. Collins, he seems to know his business."

"Yes, which is more than I can say for your second, old boy."

"I think you did very well, Harry. Tom schooled you well in the niceties of polite arrangements. For a chap as devious as March, Collins seems a remarkably good sort of chap. I wonder what their relationship is. So it is set for the village of Kensington two days hence."

"Peter you seem so relaxed about the whole affair. How can you not be worried? This fellow will try to kill you."

"I will tell you, my friend, I am concerned. I intend to do my best not to be hit, but if that is the will of God then so be it. I think of the past years at sea, the almost charmed existence, which has been my lot. My very life seems to be directed by a higher authority. If I can come out of this in a whole condition then I will have put all my demons to flight and my life will, I believe, commence from that point in time."

"Well I wish you would not do it, Peter. Walk away from it all. No one will think the worse of you. March has a terrible reputation; he is not welcome in polite society. Even among those in his business, he is noted as a hard and unforgiving man."

"No, I will go ahead with it for myself, it was him that arranged for Harris to press me into naval service and I also have Jane to think of. The wrong done to her and her family should be redressed. No, I will meet him at the appointed time."

"If you are adamant in this, I have a present for you. It is a gift I would rather not give."

Harry reached into a drawer in the bureau, which stood near the door. He withdrew a rectangular polished box, resplendent with brass fittings.

"This is for you, my dear friend. If you are determined to proceed with this folly, as the challenged party yours is the choice of weapons. I determined you must have the best in England and I purchased them just this morning."

Peter took and opened the box. The weapons were cold and deadly lying on a bed of luminous dark velvet. Their polished, hard octagonal barrels rested gracefully on highly decorated bone handles. A brass plate with the name Tatham and Egg signified their maker and quality. Peter placed the weapons on the table and went to Harry, sadly standing with his head bowed as though deep in thought.

"Harry, my friend, what can I say?" Peter clasped Harry by the hand. Harry did not look up; he did not want his friend to see his face, much less the tears, which had filled his eyes.

"You know that the law of the land forbids dueling. It has already been well published that an event is to take place. I know the Bow Street Runners and any Jack-o-Lantern will be making every effort to stop this happening and to be honest Peter, I hope they do. I would rather you go to prison than lie dead on the grass of some cold field."

Peter did not sleep. He rose from a fitful rest well before dawn. He could hear the sound of Harry's snoring, reverberating rhythmically from his room across the hall. The rest of the house was quite as usual at this early hour. It seemed no knowledge of what had transpired had reached the ears of the Boyd family. Peter was sure Sir James was well aware of it, but never a word was uttered. Peter knelt beside his bed and tried to pray, he found he could not summon the words, which had come to him so easily when his thoughts were of a life in the church. He realized how long it had been since he had called on almighty God for solace and strength. He rose and attended his toilet. Peter smiled to himself as he considered the correct dress for such an occasion. In reality, it mattered little, when it was considered he might not live more than another few hours. He threw on his great coat, placed a scarf about his neck and drew on his gloves.

Harry had risen, and donned his clothes without attending to his toilet and he appeared drawn and quiet. Both men met on the stairs with barely a nod. They made their way to the stable where a carriage and driver waited. They quietly left the house and set off on the most fateful of excursions.

The journey to Kensington was carried out in complete silence. The men sat facing each other, lost in their own reveries. It was extremely cold. The horses blew clouds of steam into the heavy frosty air as they hauled the chaise to its vicious destination. They stopped at the home of Doctor Halsey, surgeon and physician, family doctor and friend of the Boyd family. He was ready and waiting. It was 4:00 a.m. when the lonely vehicle made its way down a deserted Oxford Street. It was lost from sight through a forested area only to reappear and finally come to a halt a short way from a large Inn of Elizabethan design. Trees, divested of leaves by the caprice of nature, partly concealed the building. In the grey gloom of an early autumn morn, the smoke from distinctive round chimney clusters hung like a shroud over the steep pitched roof.

Discovery

From a vehicle, already stationary in the shelter of the trees, three figures came forward. March's second, Mr. Collins introduced William Bent, surgeon and Thomas Landry, who had agreed to act as in a supervisory capacity.

"I believe we have been followed by 'Runners,' so I suggest this business be got about with all haste." As he spoke, Thomas Landry led the way through the trees behind the hedge and into a copse bordering a flowing stream. The carriages were left in the care of the grooms.

A tall, silent, figure stood by the edge of the stream wrapped in a great coat against the chill of the early morn. To the east, the sky had already lightened considerably and the day grew colder with the advent of the sun. The frost-clad grass crackled underfoot as the group assembled.

"Mr. March, Mr. Wright, I would beseech you both to call a halt to this thing." Thomas Landry, a tall, narrow-faced man addressed Peter Wright and Frederick March. "Surely this does not have to happen. I ask you both go back to London and resume your normal lives. Come now gentlemen, what do you say?"

"It was never my intention to fight a duel with Mr. March, it was the man Harris with whom I had an altercation. I still bear the scar of our first meeting. I believe Harris acted under the direction of Frederick March who in turn acted for the deceased Colonel West. I am perfectly willing to desist if Mr. March will do the same."

Peter seized on the opportunity to escape from the situation in which he found himself and spoke directly to Frederick March.

March raised his head. Staring straight ahead, looking at no one and everyone, his glance cold and merciless as he spoke.

"Get on with it. This fellow is nothing to me. I look on him as unfinished business."

"Then that is it. Seconds, will you join me to pace it out?"

Harry and Mr. Collins joined Thomas Landry. They measured twelve paces in either direction from the stump of an oak.

Frederick March beckoned to his second and the two conferred for a moment. Collins, white-faced stood before Landry.

"My principal protests at the distance of twelve paces and requests eight be the stretch."

"Never! I will not participate in such a travesty. Twelve will be the distance. I am sure none of those present are here to witness annihilation. We are here to see the courage and honour of the protagonists is fair and not murder."

The paces were measured and marked. Mr. Landry took his position, a white handkerchief in his hand. March and Peter divested themselves of their greatcoats.

"God ,Peter, don't do it, what is the point? Let us just get in our carriage and be away from this vile place." Harry spoke in low tones as he took Peter's coat in shaking hands.

"Harry Boyd, you're a good man and a fine friend. I cannot walk away from this. It must happen. It is fate. Give me your hand, I have made arrangements and left letters, which have been forwarded, to Sir Neville Brown. He will be in touch." The two shook hands.

"Keep clear, gentlemen. On my signal." Landry raised his handkerchief; the two white-shirted men stood back to back, both men holding the deadly pistols, lethal and lustrous, glistening in the cold dawn light and pointing straight down towards the icy ground.

The handkerchief dropped.

With measured pace the two commenced their virulent walk called by Mr. Collins.

The crack of the first shot startled a covey of partridges; nosily they flew close to the ground in a desperate attempt to escape the disturbance of their slumber. Frederick March had fired first.

At first glance, it appeared Peter had not been hit. Both men stood facing each other. Frederick March, his arm outstretched stood swathed in the issue of pungent, acrid smoke from his pistol. Peter Wright staggered for a moment then slowly raised his weapon. As he did so, an effulgent red stain appeared on the white of his shirt below his left shoulder. It quickly suffused his sleeve. He swayed as he took aim. He fired.

Peter fell, face down to the icy turf. Before he lost complete consciousness, he marveled at the dark stain spreading about him. As a black void enveloped him, he did not comprehend the frozen grass beside his cheek, now red and wet, was stained with his own blood.

40

Peter is Recovered and is Released From His Demons

In the stygian darkness and deathly silence of unconsciousness, peace reigns supreme, unbroken even by whispers, the troubled cease from concern and rest in serenity. The jailer and the prisoner, the great and the low repose together and the slave is free, but now the peaceful darkness perceives a murmur, a sound ever increasing. An echoing roar becomes a word; a word becomes a sentence. In tones, turbulent, garbled and slow Peter Wright regains the awareness that he is still alive.

For over a week Peter had lain at death's door. The ball fired by Frederick March had struck him in the left shoulder. On impact, it had shattered into fragments, which embedded randomly in the area of the scapular, chipping various bones. Unhappily, it had not passed through him in one piece. The major problems were the fragments, infection and the operation required to remove the offending pieces.

"He tried to speak, I heard him. What is it, dear Peter. Thank heavens you are back with us at last." Jane Sawtell leant close to hear his words; he spoke in a hushed raspy tone. "What was it you tried to say, my dear?"

Peter again spoke this time a little clearer, but still barely understandable.

"Oh my goodness Gwen and Harry, he asked is he in heaven. No Peter, not in heaven, you are here with those that love you and who are overcome with joy that you speak to them."

"What was that?" He asked where is he and how long has it been?"

Gwen sat on the other side of the bed she leant close, "He asked where Harry is?"

"I'm here Peter; please don't tire yourself with speech. You are back in the land of the living. There will be plenty of time to talk. It has been almost two weeks

"Yes Peter, now you must recover, here let me adjust your pillows. Your fever has subsided at last. In the morning I'm sure you will feel much better."

Jane fussed about puffing pillows, smoothing sheets and wiping the brow of the gaunt, pale figure. Gwen placed a glass of water to his lips, which he sipped with obvious relish. All the while Harry stood at the foot of the bed arms folded, sagely looking on as the ladies fluttered about and administered to their charge.

Sleep again claimed Peter. This time it was not the fevered sleep of the tormented, but the deep sleep of one on the way to recovery

With the passing of three days, Peter's health had improved to such an extent that he was able to sit in an armchair by the side of the bed. His wound, which had been made more extensive by the efforts of the doctor to extract foreign bodies and chipped bone, had begun to heal. He was now able to take nourishment and colour had returned to his otherwise pallid features. Although speaking was still painful and difficult, each day saw a dramatic improvement.

Lady Sarah Parkinson did all she could to make Peter feel comfortable and at home. Jane had prevailed on her aunt; she must bring the wounded Peter Wright to Montague Street. She had insisted it was the only way she could look after her dearest friend.

"Harry my friend, what happened after I was shot? I feel well enough to hear it all now. What happened to March, did I hit him? How did you get me here? I want to hear it all."

"If you are sure you are up to it I will tell you the whole story until the present. The dear ladies who have ministered to you throughout are downstairs resting. They have been wonderful. I am sure without them you would not have survived." Harry drew up a chair and sat facing Peter. Peter's arm hung in a sling, heavy bandages about his upper body constricted his motion and at each movement, a grimace of pain would pass across his features.

"When you fell to the ground on that cold, somber morning I thought you were dead. As you fell, you fired your weapon. I don't know if it was a reflex action brought about by being hit or if you did it by design."

"Harry I know as I fell I had every intention of shooting March. Did I hit him?"

"No my friend you missed him by a mile. As soon as he fired and saw you hit he turned on his heel and made away with out the slightest interest in your well-being. I have never met such a cold-hearted fellow in all my years. I asked him to help us get you to the carriage. His words were cold and without any pity. I will remember his words till the day I die, *this man means nothing to me, he was meant to die when he was sent to sea and he has only received what was always his.'* He turned and was gone." That is the last time I saw him and he has not at any time enquired after your welfare, as would a gentleman. Harry rose from his chair; he went to a corner, glass-fronted cabinet and extracted a bottle from within. "I'm up for a brandy, how about you old boy? I do not think it would hurt. When I see the foul-smelling concoctions forced into you over the last while, a brandy must surely be the lesser evil.

"What happened after March departed?"

"Landry went to the coach, the driver made an attempt to bring it somehow through the trees so we could get you into it. I must say March's second was very helpful and furious at the bad form shown by his principal and the fact that he was even associated with such an unfeeling bounder. The coach left the road to be completely concealed by the trees. It was fortunate for us, for that is when we heard a commotion further along the London Road. I heard shouting and shots fired eventually all was quiet. A few days later, I discovered the reason for the disturbance. Apparently, March had been followed from London; it seems he was a man wanted by the authorities for crimes against the Crown. His pursuers had lost him in the fog and dark. As he was returning towards the city, he virtually ran into them and they apprehended him. I've heard little more."

As the men spoke, Jane and Gwen entered the room and took a seat on an ottoman beneath the window.

"Ah, here are the ladies. I hope you are both rested. Our friend Peter is well on the way to a full recovery. I am recounting the situation in which we now find ourselves."

"What are you doing, Peter? What is it you are drinking? Is it what I think it is?

"Come now Jane, Peter has had the most awful concoctions poured into him over the last weeks."

"My dear Jane, it was only the daily ration of rum that enabled me to survive my years at sea, so I see no reason why a tot or so at this time can do too much harm."

Harry continued.

"Of course the fact that a duel was to take place was common knowledge. We are all aware of the law where dueling is concerned. The incident at Wimbledon Common did not escape attention; the resulting challenge and March's involvement was brought to the notice of the Chancellor, Tom Pitt's uncle, Lord Grenville. There was never a doubt regarding what had occurred at Wimbledon. As far as you were concerned it was a case of self-defense."

Harry began to relate the circumstances, which had come to pass while Peter lay in his unconscious state.

"From what I understand, Colonel West had been discovered for his smuggling activities. The complete involvement of March in his affairs was also brought to light. Over the years, he was clever enough to keep in the background, out of the eye of the authorities. Of course, he was well known as a slave trader, but his smuggling ventures only came to the notice of the government just before the death of Henry West. March had informed on his friend when he saw the game was up. March never at any time intended to assist West to escape to the continent. It was assassins in the employ of March that did him in. Henry West met his end on a wild coastal road in Cornwall.

"I would imagine that when West was discovered for the villain he was, March decided to finish with him before he could implicate him in the business in which they were jointly involved. It seems so much poetic justice that March himself was taken only by being so callous towards you. Had he waited and assisted us he most likely would not have been arrested. He was incarcerated in Newgate to await trial for smuggling and embezzlement. It was unfortunate he was not taken earlier, it would have precluded your meeting with him, with the almost disastrous results to your person."

The four friends sat quietly. They mused over the strange twists inflicted by fate to alter the lives of those it touches. They pondered the years that had passed and the friendship, which had developed between them. Harry spoke first.

"So what now?"

"A good question, what is for us all?" Peter Wright reflected on the last six years, he thought of the way in which all their lives had changed. "For me, as soon as I have recovered I will obtain a place of my own. I will pursue the opportunities I know to exist in the land of the Pacific Northwest. I will buy vessels; employ captains and crews to trade between China, America and England. However, I tell you this, with recollections colored by past experience, I will insist the commanders of my vessels be honorable men and maintain a respect for their crews and treat them as human beings and God's creatures. Join me Harry and you Jane and Gwen in this venture, we are in an age of discovery, almost in a new century. Let us grasp it with all our might. What do you say?"

Epilogue

Peter Wright followed his dream. He eventually became the owner of a fleet of six vessels, which, over the years, were blessed with amazing good fortune. His ships became the prime instrument in a major trading company operating with enormous success between the Far East and the lands of California, New Norfolk and Alaska. Harry Boyd, later Sir Harry Boyd and Peter Wright remained firm friends until Harry died of an unknown complaint at the age of 51.

Peter married Jane Sawtell. They remained childless, but completely devoted to each other for all their married years. Jane died in 1825 during a minor outbreak of smallpox. She left a devastated and lonely Peter, who devoted himself to his business dealings and the London School for Underprivileged Ladies, which his wife and her dearest companion and friend, Gwen Pratt, had so earnestly established and enjoyed all their lives.

Frederick March was taken from Newgate Goal. At Old Bailey, he was sentenced to the term of his natural life in the penal colony of Port Jackson, Australia. He was transported to the antipodes on board the vessel *HMS Destiny*

Harry Boyd married Gwen Pratt, much to the displeasure of his father, who considered her to be in a class below his only son. It was only on the birth of his grandson that Sir James Boyd relented and accepted Gwen as a full member of the family. On the death of his father, Harry inherited the title, as well as a seat in the House of Lords, along with all the privileges pertaining to his knighthood. Lady Gwen and Jane remained devoted to each other until Jane's death. Gwen surrendered at 91 years to the ravages of old age.

Gwen and Jane, after their respective marriages, never continued their intimate relationship, but they remained the closest and dearest of friends. They never told their husbands of the love each had for the other.

Printed in the United States
26459LVS00002B/1-9